I0594066

THE SERPENT'S
BRIDGE

THE SERPENT SERIES

SZ ESTAVILLO

OLIVERHEBERBOOKS

All rights reserved.

No part of this publication may be sold, copied, distributed, reproduced or transmitted in any form or by any means, mechanical or digital, including photocopying and recording or by any information storage and retrieval system without the prior written permission of both the publisher, Oliver Heber Books and the author, S.Z. Estavillo, except in the case of brief quotations embodied in critical articles and reviews.

PUBLISHER'S NOTE: This is a work of fiction. Names, characters, places, and incidents either are the product of the author's imagination or are used fictitiously. Any resemblance to actual persons, living or dead, business establishments, events, or locales is entirely coincidental.

The Serpent's Bridge Copyright 2024 © S.Z. Estavillo

Cover design by Kim Killion

Published by Oliver-Heber Books

0 9 8 7 6 5 4 3 2 1

ACKNOWLEDGMENTS

To my husband, my greatest fan and steadfast supporter—thank you for everything you do, from watching the kids to being my pillar throughout the years.

A special thanks to Tanya Anne Crosby at Oliver-Heber for your unwavering support, and to the incredible Kimberly Cates, an editor like no other, for championing my work and greenlighting my series. Also, a heartfelt shout-out to Giovanni Jacobs, who told me, "I do not see how this book series will not get published!" Thank you, Gio, for calling it and believing in me when I was down. Sometimes, we need true friends to lift us up.

This book is a voice for the underrepresented and the marginalized—for the immigrants who come to this country seeking a better life, yet are too often left unheard. Through these pages, I hope they feel seen. As someone whose Korean mother immigrated here from Korea, I deeply understand and value these experiences. You matter. Your stories are important. Through my writing, I strive to ensure your voices are heard.

I am immensely grateful for the opportunity to share my stories with the world.

ONE
THE DETECTIVE

DENSE FOG CURLED off the Santa Monica coast like a living thing—thick, cold, uninviting. It accosted her senses, dissolving visibility. She had managed to block out every other sound since the chase began a little over a mile back, but the crunching asphalt ahead still pierced the silence. Detective Anaya Nazario zeroed in on those faint footsteps—a beacon in the void.

Second wind kicking in, she surged after the perp. He wasn't getting away.

Not a single person on the Gang and Narcotics unit had been able to catch Connor Morris, aka *Speed*. In fact, they lagged half a mile or more behind. Her out-of-shape partner, Detective Wilson, trailed to the rear like a slug. She had transferred from Gang and Narco to Homicide over a decade ago to get away from the Connor Morris types.

In Connor Morris, she saw the deterioration of the neighborhoods: the teenagers hooked on drugs, the result of more lives lost to ODs and shootings. Too many young women—almost all addicts—selling their bodies for another hit. In Connor Morris, Nazario also saw her father, who lost the fight working undercover trying to take down a drug ring.

She had yet to brave the sealed crime scene from Daddy's cold case.

In the man she chased, she saw the homeless, exacerbated mental illnesses, and the proliferation of wasted talent. Through Connor Morris, hopelessness was injected into the veins of countless lives, forever chemically changed.

Daddy, I'm getting him: she spoke to her father's spirit as she dashed through the Santa Monica mob.

The popular oceanfront city bustled with activity. Crowds of SoCal beach lovers slathered in suntan lotion and impervious to the cool, overcast day pranced in barely-there bathing suits, mindlessly moseying along the sidewalks, blaring music from their smartphones. Too many folks on bicycles took their sweet time. A tall, gangly man on a red beach cruiser with oversized tires dropped the beer in his hand and yelped, finally aware of the foot chase. The cruiser swerved, avoiding a collision, as Morris nearly slammed into the man.

Nazario's thighs trembled with each long, demanding stride. Nostrils flared, taking the air in short bursts to avoid burning out too quickly. She dug her fingernails into her palms. Morris was a three-time UFC champion who had turned to taking—then selling—drugs after an injury he suffered in the ring left him with fractured vertebrae. While it was easier to run with her automatic on the inside of her ankle, she regretted being unable to reach it.

A group of teenagers stood in the way, staring at their cell phone screens.

"Move! Move! Move!" Nazario screamed. "LAPD! Outta the way, people!"

Morris smashed into them. Cellphones and bodies crashed to the ground.

She continued to holler, "Outta the way! Outta the way!"

An elderly woman and her poodle absently plodded into her path.

Nazario shouted for her to step aside, and the lady let go of the leash. Her long legs hurtled the dog as the old lady cried out for her pooch. Morris crashed into a man selling spiced Mexican fruit bowls and managed to dodge the upturned stand. Nazario wove through the onslaught of foot traffic. Her long, dark brown hair was pulled back in a sleek ponytail that whipped in the wind. Parents hugged their kids close and scattered while some nosy bystanders stood on the sidelines recording the action on their smartphones.

As she sprinted, Daddy's gold wedding band thumped against her chest, keeping time. It dangled from a thin gold chain around her neck that she never took off. Bouncing off her damp shirt, each thud echoed his heartbeat. Despite his untimely death, she had never stopped speaking to him. For every impossible task, her father was with her in spirit. So were the memories that replayed over and over in her mind.

Almost got him, Daddy.

Nazario's arms pumped in a blur as she picked up tempo, teeth clenched. Her long legs moved faster, taking over the chase, adrenaline coursing through her veins, pushing her body at a pace she didn't think was possible. She made one final push, grunting, commanding her body to keep going. She was closing in, so close she could taste his sweat.

Nazario slowed to a pause—he was somewhere in the fog.

Where are you, you son of a bitch?

Spinning around, she scanned, eyes straining for clarity through the ashen clouds. Anxiety swelled in her chest as doubt crept in. Her legs burned, and a dull ache in her joints reminded her that while she was in decent shape, age was getting the best of her. She walked with caution. Out in the open, she was both exposed and enveloped in the Santa Monica coast fog.

She gulped, hearing her pulse pounding in her ear.

Thump-thump. Thump-thump. Thump-thump. Thump-thump.

He could be anywhere. Her fists instinctively tightened at her sides.

Suddenly, Connor Morris emerged beneath a foggy veil.

A flying side-kick hit Nazario's left temple before she could block it, sending her careening, the back of her head clubbing hard against the ground. A wave of darkness threatened to engulf her. Her hands gripped the pavement. Rocks on the asphalt dug into her palms as she scrambled to her feet.

On her way up, the bastard tried to knee her in the face. She evaded with a sharp move to the side. She locked eyes on Morris and, in one full swing, delivered a jumping spin kick to his jaw that knocked him to the ground. The drug dealer hurtled through the air and crashed into a trashcan, scattering garbage all around. He gasped as the wind left his lungs.

Nazario bridged the space between them, cursing the fact that her Smith & Wesson 5906 pistol was still strapped to the inside of her ankle, out of reach. No, she'd never had to draw her weapon and kill anyone. She prided herself in taking down perps without the use of her gun or even a taser. But as her lungs struggled for air after the power run, she knew that it'd been a big mistake not having her weapon closer to hand.

Nazario eyed the bulge at her ankle and then looked back up at Morris.

"We've got things in common." Morris wiped blood from his mouth, then said, "We like doing things the old-school way—no guns."

"You and I got nothing in common," Nazario growled, despite knowing the decades of dedicated training they shared. Morris didn't give her time to reach for her weapon. He was back on his feet, delivering a back fist punch to her face, but she locked onto one hand and pulled him toward the ground. Down for a second, Morris arched his back, legs folded beneath him. He leaned on his heels and performed a no-hands kick-up to jolt himself back on his soles.

Damn, he was fast.

Where are you, Wilson?

Nazario tried to deliver one final blow, but Morris kicked her knee. Pain surged up her leg and coursed through her body.

Nazario swayed, fumbling to her feet.

Limping and balancing on her left leg, she mustered a standing kick with her right, which landed a crunching blow to his nose, tossing him to the ground. But Morris staggered to his feet once again, blood rushing down his nose. She had to admit the bastard refused to go down without a fight. He swayed, stubbornly upright, as she thrust her foot against his face hard enough for him to swallow gravel from the bottom of her boot with a chaser of blood.

Morris hit the asphalt face-first.

Nazario grunted, elevating her body beyond the pain of her wounded knee. She straddled Morris, now prone. Blood seeped from her own nose and dripped on the drug dealer's hair. She balanced on his back, hooked his left arm behind his back, and managed to cuff his left wrist. He bucked wildly, sending Nazario flying. She landed a couple of feet away.

"Why doncha run?" Nazario gritted out, each breath sending a knife-like pain through her ribs.

"Run?" Morris coughed up blood. "Not from a fight. Think I'll just kill you instead."

Despite the wind being knocked from her, she moved swiftly to avoid being in the vulnerable prone position. But it was too late. Morris pinned her on her back. His fingers gripped her neck, squeezing her carotid artery.

"You can join your dead narc-ass dad," he taunted.

"Fuck...you," Nazario choked out with her last breath and strength she could muster, earning her a tighter squeeze around her neck.

She couldn't breathe.

If she wasn't injured, she could easily perform a reversal and be back on her feet. But her knee throbbed. She nearly blacked out, but just before she was lost, her body reminded her that oxygen was required to remain alive. It snapped her back into reality, though his jeering recharged lost energy—and jolted her back into the fight.

Nazario kicked between his legs. Morris grunted in pain and lost his grip, allowing her to throw a front strike to his face. He recovered quicker than any man she'd ever sparred with in her decades of martial arts training. She attempted to lock her good leg around him to flip him off, but he regained control. Doubling down and still on top of her, he launched a fist that connected with her jaw.

Morris and Nazario exchanged more blows with equal strength and skill.

Nazario was relieved to see her partner, Detective Isaac Wilson, stagger closer along with members of the Gang and Narco unit she'd blown past earlier. Nazario and Wilson had happened to be closer to the drug dealer's location and got to him first. She spotted her best friend, Captain Augusta "Gus" Humphrey of Gang and Narco, calling out from a distance.

Wilson drew his weapon and shot. But Morris ducked at just the right angle, avoiding a bullet to his back.

Either Connor Morris was one lucky SOB, or her partner had gone rusty.

"Hold your fire!" screamed Gus as she broke past Wilson, whose paunchy frame panted for air. "I got 'im."

Still struggling beneath him, Nazario punched his rib cage. He heaved all his weight onto her knee, landing more punishment. Ligaments snapped like twigs. She fought back the scream, threatening to claw its way out of her throat. Finally, a slug to the center of his chest made the SOB reel back. Nazario rolled out from beneath him, gasping desperately for air. Morris tried to run, but Gus twined her arms around him, and they stumbled to the ground.

Nazario glanced at her best friend, noticing the sweat trickling off Gus's eyebrow-less forehead. Rivulets of moisture soaked the black bandana covering her bald scalp. Vertigo spun Nazario's world. Her vision alternated between blurred and focused as air returned.

Gus grunted out his Miranda rights, coupled with a colorful choice of swear words, as she got up from the ground and hoisted Morris to his feet. She took the loose handcuff dangling on his left arm that Nazario had already cuffed and hooked it behind his back, securing his right arm to his left.

Nazario inhaled long and hard. A shaky hand wiped blood from her nose.

"He got my knee," Nazario moaned.

Gus kneeled and examined her knee. She barely touched her thumb to Nazario's kneecap, and it moved like a loose tooth ready to be yanked out. Nazario pulled her shirt up and bit a mouthful to muffle a scream.

Gus barked into her radio, "Echo-Charlie One. Code-Three assistance. Foot pursuit. Suspect in custody. Officer down— severe knee trauma. Requesting Code 3 RA and additional units to Santa Monica Pier, underneath Pacific Park. We're west of the Pier. We've got Morris!"

Static noise, and then the operator's voice cracked through. "10-4, Echo-Charlie One. All available units, Code Three to Santa Monica Pier. Head west of the pier. Rescue ambulance is en route."

"Doncha dare stand on it. You got no ligaments attached to

that kneecap," Gus warned Nazario. "Stay your ass down, or you'll make it worse."

Stubborn, the detective attempted to get to her feet, but her knee bent in a way it shouldn't and landed her back on the ground. She collapsed, writhing and groaning in pain. Her eyes refocused on the pink ribbon pendant on Gus's collar. They'd been expecting one of the lieutenants on Gang and Narco to be part of this chase, but not the captain, who was supposed to be on leave recovering from breast cancer.

"Gus, what'n the hell," Nazario grunted, "thought you were OFD?"

"When am I ever off fucking duty," Gus said. "Putting in some *nover*-time."

Nover-time—unpaid overtime, which was cop-lingo for what Gus was doing to herself. Many cops, Nazario included, frequently worked outside of allotted duty hours. She wanted to shake some sense into her friend of many years, going back to their years in grad school at George Washington University. Like Nazario, Gus rarely took any time off, not even when she was ordered to.

Nazario's mind refocused on the blinding pain now piercing the numbing effect of adrenaline. She breathed through it as the strident sounds of approaching police cars screamed toward them, and within seconds, a half-dozen squad cars pulled up.

"Hang on, Nazario," Wilson urged, "the ambulance is running behind. Traffic is terrible. They're five minutes away."

Blue and red lights broke through the ashen atmosphere. It wasn't until Morris was taken away and locked in the back of one of the squad cars that Nazario squeezed her eyes shut.

Curling onto her side, she clutched her injured leg. "Gawd...I need a drink."

Her AA sponsor was quick to chime in. "Whatcha need is a

hospital," Gus told her. "Think about Sammy. Think about them girls we teach how to defend themselves each and every week for moments like this. They'd be proud of you."

"And he busted my kneecap," Nazario grunted through the pain, though her mind did drift to Samantha Friedrich, who'd been abducted when she was sixteen and victimized in the most brutal ways. She was eighteen when Gus and her Gang and Narco team found her. She'd inspired them to start the self-defense class. Gus was right. They had taught their girls how to fight back.

So how come Nazario felt like she'd lost this one?

"Hang tight. I think I see the ambulance. Besides," Wilson reminded gently, "you're supposed to be attending Sanctuary Baptist on Wednesday nights."

Perhaps her partner was trying to keep her mind off the pain, though it wasn't working.

To hell with AA. Her body burned with the strongest urge for a bottle of red Zinfandel.

"Keep an eye on her, Wilson. Don't let her bend that knee," Gus sized up the gash on Nazario's head. "Surprised the asshole didn't also knock her out."

"Will do, Captain." Wilson's voice faded from Nazario's ears. Her eyelids were lead shutters, drawing slowly to a close. Wilson patted her cheeks several times.

"Stay with me, Nazario. C'mon...we need you conscious. You hit your head pretty bad, it's bleeding...think you've got a concussion."

Her mind sank back to a rainy November evening, her father in his formal class-A uniform, breast decorated with medals right over the place where the bullet struck him. Family, friends, and the entire LA Police Department clustered around his coffin-like black crows perched silently on a wire. He was the highest-ranking Puerto Rican narcotics officer and the best undercover narcotics agent on the force. Nobody could replace him, not even Anaya Nazario herself.

I got him, Daddy. I got the son of a bitch.

Body going limp, everything turned black.

TWO
THE PASTOR'S WIFE

THE 105 WEST parallel to Compton was smooth, but the 405 North was congested into one long, red snake. Millie Ann Goodwin sighed and brushed a hand over the tan trench skirt that wrapped subtly around her thick hips and ended just below her knees.

The dress was perfect for her curvy figure, the sales associate at Dressbarn Women's Apparel had told her, with conservative sensibilities and yet year-round simplicity that never went out of style. As God's representative, Millie never wore her clothes skin-tight. Her gel nails were nude—*not beige*—a safe color to match anything in her closet. No one knew colors the way she did.

Millie smoothed her champagne—*not off-white*—silk blouse. Her fingers tugged on wrinkles that formed while sitting in Los Angeles traffic for too long. She never ventured down to Santa Monica unless Stan was asked to participate in a pro-immigrant protest. Oh, the work she must do for the Lord.

Was there an accident? There must be.

Behind her, a red truck managed to maneuver to the left

lane before the right turn signal blinked so it could squeeze in front of her. To get one car length ahead? Millie gripped the steering wheel as she read a faded bumper sticker.

Support Legal Immigration.

He was one of those types. Was he going to the rally, too? Millie hammered her fist on the steering wheel several times and then left it there extra-long for good measure.

Beeeeeeep!

An arm sprung out of the driver's window; it was sinfully muscular with tanned biceps that contrasted against a sunshine yellow shirt. He waved as if to say, "Thank you for letting me cut you off."

Millie took a deep breath to collect herself. She flipped open the visor mirror; her cheeks were flushed. Her blood pressure must've been through the roof. She tapped the gas to move maybe half an inch, then, turning her attention from the road, fished into her purse for pocket tissues. Her hand clutched a small hand towel wrapped around a child's pair of shoes...

Sometimes, she almost forgot that they were in her purse, like a good luck charm that could bring her son home. Lost hope she'd been trying to hold onto. Millie's hands trembled as she unwrapped the white and blue hand towel until the old baby-blue suede moccasins sat in the palms of her hands. Weathered but still intact, they remained just as she preserved them.

Her fingers trembled as they grazed the soft leather. She closed her eyes, bringing the shoes to her nose in search of the scent from her son's little feet. She took in a deep breath, and everything returned. The morning, she saw those two lines that told her she was pregnant. The moments she felt him move and kick inside her. Screaming in agony when she pushed him out of her body. Holding him in her arms, his limbs moving wildly and uncoordinated, his face scarlet from a lung-filled scream. He was so small and so delicate. She was afraid she'd break him, her Gideon, her little warrior.

He was now in a mental hospital in his own cage.

She wanted to believe that she was not a wretched, failed mother.

I did fail you, Gideon, and I'm sorry. Mommy is sorry.

Millie inhaled and exhaled, practicing her breathwork.

Traffic was at a dead stop, so she seized the opportunity to rewrap Gideon's baby shoes in the towel like they were made out of fine China and placed them back into her purse. She was a mile from her exit, but it sure felt like the end of the earth. Millie inspected her bob, freshly cut to frame her face and colored to cover those nasty fifty-year-old grays.

Millie didn't feel or look fifty.

Where did all the time go? It sped by. How long had it been since she'd seen her baby? Ten, twelve years? Had it been that long? Her eyes grew wet again.

C'mon, Millie, pull yourself together.

She turned up the radio, and a local news report pulled her thoughts away from her son and the sensitive immigration rally led by Stan, her husband, pastor of Compton's Sanctuary Baptist Church. It was one of the few churches safe for Mexican immigrants, and as a result, nearly all of its members were undocumented.

"Most of the exits and roads heading toward Santa Monica Pier have been blocked off due to an active crime scene," the radio host reported. "The 405 northbound is gridlocked for several miles. If you're thinking of heading to Santa Monica, consider taking side streets or avoid the Pier altogether."

Like everyone else stuck in the same traffic, Millie grabbed her cell phone. Her fingertips danced as she logged into her and Stan's joint email account. Her palms were damp with expectation.

She scrolled. Checked the spam folder. Searched. Nothing.

She sighed in defeat and dropped her phone into her purse. Stan believed God commanded that husband and wife should have no secrets. For transparency, they shared the same laptop at home and email. She always erased the search history and deleted any email to or from Dr. Marcel Bennett. Some topics were best left unmentioned.

Beep! Beep! Beeeep!

Millie jumped as another motorist yelled at her to pay attention to the road. She motioned her apology. Traffic started to let up, and she finally made her exit just as a wailing ambulance rushed past. It looked to be coming from the direction of the Santa Monica Pier. A squad car led at the front, and three more patrol cars flanked at the rear, sandwiching the ambulance protectively. She whispered a brief prayer for the person injured and reached for her phone.

Millie sent a quick text to Stan:

5 min away - bad traffic. Something with police at Pier.

A few seconds later, the phone chimed Stan's reply.

Drive safe. Park at school.

———

Santa Monica College wasn't as packed as Millie had imagined. When the rallies were held in Downtown Los Angeles, it was next to impossible to find parking. So, Stan organized the current immigration rally with the dean at Santa Monica College, who'd readily agreed. However, parking at the college was more accessible, which meant more attendees. Clusters of curious students and a small number of faculty stood among a majority Hispanic crowd.

A scattering of signs read, "Better Immigration Reform," held up mostly by Mexican immigrants and Mexican-American

THE SERPENT'S BRIDGE   15

supporters. An even larger collage of non-Hispanic ethnicities—white, black, Middle Eastern, and Asian—joined in solidarity along with faculty. They shouted, "Let's End Brown Fear!"

Millie felt a sense of pride that so many cultures had come together to demand their collective voices be heard. All of them, and not just the Mexican community, were affected by a regressive culture that still discriminated. It was a radicalized fear against minorities from all regions worldwide trying to come to America for a better life.

Millie continued to scan the crowd. Her husband waved at her from the stage.

"#Closethecamps" signs mingled with "All immigrants welcomed" carried by the attending Jewish community. The former hashtag was made popular in 2019 by Jewish supporters who argued against the inhumanity of caging immigrants, taking it a step further to draw comparisons to the Holocaust. They protested outside of the Metropolitan Detention Center in downtown LA when there was a rise in family separation and deportation, another protest Stan had advanced knowledge of and made sure he didn't miss.

Millie noted that this rally was a lot less contentious than the one in 2019.

"I am a mother. I am a Mexican, and I am a DACA recipient," a young immigrant stated into the microphone. She bounced lightly on her toes to keep her infant child, strapped in a sling to her front, from crying.

A chant began: *"Immigration reform now! Immigration reform now!"*

The young mother continued. "This is *not* a Republican or a Democrat issue. Lack of immigration reform has been going on for decades. It's not about who's our sitting president and there's not one administration to blame. We all work hard to live here in this country—to be in this country. How hard is it to create an inclusive immigration reform that works for everyone, includes everyone? Immigration reform is necessary to reduce the red tape and help us realize our dreams of citizenship."

"Thank you," Stan said to the woman as she stepped aside.

Stan looked more like a professor with the square, black-framed glasses Millie had convinced him to wear today. She was pleased he also wore his simple khaki pants and white dress shirt instead of his first choice. His navy-blue business suit would've been a bit too dressy.

Stan put a gentle hand on the young woman's shoulders and then brushed the back of his fingers against her baby's cheeks. The baby squealed and smiled. Millie's hand wandered into her purse with a mind of its own. She clutched the towel that contained Gideon's baby shoes, and her eyes watered.

"At least fifteen immigrants have died this year alone at the border, and the real number is probably higher," Stan announced.

Stan's neck and cheeks flushed pink. "How many more immigrants need to *die* before someone realizes that it's a problem?" His voice began to rise the way it did when an unexpected sermon happened upon him. "God is calling us to do more. Out of love, we must come together, stand united, and open our doors, not shut them." Stan paused and then shouted. *"We must do more!"*

The crowd erupted with whistles and shouts.

"If you're in the Compton area, our church, Sanctuary Baptist, will not close our doors to the Dreamers. Our congregation is mostly made up of Mexican immigrants, and frankly, I don't believe God would have it any other way. Can I hear an amen?"

"Amen!"

"We will not close our doors to those that are hungry. Every Monday, you can rest assured that our pantry, which has collected generous canned goods and food donations, will be there for you. Every Wednesday night, our doors are open to members of Alcoholics Anonymous. Stop on by if you're in need. We welcome you. We welcome all. To enter His kingdom. Don't need to be a U.S. citizen. You just need to believe."

"The U.S. isn't a church, Pastor Goodwin," a familiar voice boomed from the back of the crowd. Millie spun around and seethed at the bald man standing there. Intimidating, tall, and well-built, Eric Myers was an agent of the U.S. Immigration and Customs Enforcement and a regular attendee of Sanctuary Baptist Sunday services.

Millie gritted her teeth as the annoying argument she'd had with Stan echoed in her head. Her fists clenched at her sides. Oh, she and Stan had plenty of disagreements about Eric Myers.

"You should kick him outta the church. He has no business being there," Millie had ordered her husband.

"He's just doing his job. I can't tell him to not obey the law that he swore to follow," Stan had countered. "Just like we can't condemn those that break laws. Such as most of our undocumented members."

"He's ICE, Stan. He's undoing everything we stand for. He's sitting in the pew on Sundays just to find people to arrest. I dunno, something's not right about that man."

"What am I supposed to say, Millie Ann? You're not allowed in our church 'cause we don't like what you do for a living? We disagree with your moral conviction because it's not ours?"

"YES!"

Her husband, who "only took orders from God," refused to listen to her. Millie's mind returned to the rally. Flanked by police officers stationed at the back, a safety measure required by the school, Eric continued, undisturbed by the shouts of anger erupting around him. That was when Millie noticed a little Hispanic boy holding Eric's hand.

"We're running a country, and to be in the United States, *legally*, requires following the law and taking the necessary steps to do so."

Eric tucked the boy closer to him, and he wrapped his arms around his waist.

"Nicky's mother and father came into this country from Mexico *legally* with work visas. They worked hard, built a small, thriving business, and got their citizenship. They had Nicky, who's a naturalized citizen. And then, a year ago, an undocumented with a criminal record broke into their home, robbed, and killed them. Nicky was hiding in the closet, and he saw the entire thing. He's ten years old and now without a mother or a father," Eric said, his voice rising with passion as Nicky hugged Eric's legs. "I'm all for immigration reform. I think we need it. But let's not dismiss that law breakers—*criminals*—took his family away from him."

"And how common is that?" cried out a protestor from the crowd. "That's not representative of the majority of immigrants that are here."

An odd lull made Stan pause, and the vein that ran up the middle of his forehead when he got especially stirred by "worldly folk" protruded. The corners of his lip twitched into a teetering smile.

"Thank you for sharing." Stan's voice quivered the way it did when he was trying to control his anger. "We'll keep Nicky in prayer."

"Go home!" someone else shouted.

"It's because of you people that boy is without a family! Make our peeps do crazy shit when they desperate!" another one hollered, blaming Eric Myers for circumstances they knew nothing about. It was easy to make the ICE agent the scapegoat.

"We don't want ICE here!" screamed another protestor.

"Fuck ICE!" one said, and a chant ensued. They repeated the phrase over and over.

Unfazed by their words, Myers flashed Millie a wry grin, catching her off guard.

"Well, I think if Christ were standing next to me, he'd support *legal immigration*."

Millie's eyes grew wide, recognizing that saying. Then, for confirmation, she noticed that sunshine yellow shirt and those tanned bulging biceps. The saying that spewed from his lips was the bumper sticker on the back of his truck.

Stan looked like he had been slapped. He stood there, shaking from the loss of control over the situation and losing his composure. Millie watched her husband, mouth in a tight line, blinking rapidly, fists closing and opening, closing and opening as though he was warring with his human nature and duty to be above it all, God's representative.

The crowd exploded into an angry roar of name-calling and swear words.

The school's dean got up to announce the rally would end early.

Millie narrowed her eyes at Eric. Unlike Stan, she wasn't afraid of her sinning side.

"You shouldn't be exploiting that poor boy's private story!" Millie shrieked before she could stop herself. Stan called her name, trying to settle her down, but she ignored him.

"He begged me to share, Mrs. Goodwin," Eric replied, the words laced with sadness. His brown eyes pierced hers with something she hadn't expected: fatherly tenderness that Stan had never shown Gideon. The therapist in her wondered why he couldn't be loving to their son, but then, Stan claimed he had never got along with his mother. It damaged boys to have a contentious relationship with the first and most important woman in their life.

Could have Stan's absent mother-son bond affected his ability to parent, impacting their son's mental health? The only thing Millie knew for certain was that, at sixteen, Stan went to live with a deeply religious Mexican family—long-time workers at his father's ranch—after his father became ill and died.

Millie never learned what the illness was exactly, but his decline had been gradual. She recalled trying to unearth more about the mother-in-law Millie had never met.

"Why didn't you live with your mother?" Millie had asked her husband, unable to understand the unusual living arrangements kept secret and out of the court system. It wasn't official, but his mother sounded like she'd all but given up her parental rights.

"You don't know my mother," Stan replied, then urged, "and you know how I feel about the subject. Don't wanna talk about it no more."

There were two subjects Stan couldn't discuss: Gideon and his mother.

"Told you it wasn't gonna be easy. You okay, buddy?" Eric's voice pulled her from her thoughts as the ICE agent reassured Nicky.

Nicky hugged Eric's thick neck and finally spoke, loud enough for Millie to hear.

"Thank you," Nicky said shakily. "Thank you for telling them about my parents."

Eric kissed the boy on the forehead. Millie gulped down a knot in her throat as Nicky's watery eyes glanced up, then looked away. He hid his face in the crook of Eric's neck. Millie watched them walk toward the parking lot, unable to stop herself. Just before they disappeared, the ICE agent turned and paused briefly. Eric's mouth opened and then clamped shut. A small smile brushed his lips, exposing a dimple on his cheek. His brown eyes met hers, and they shared a strange but honest moment before he was finally gone.

Suddenly, Eric Myers was no longer the bastard she'd thought him to be.

The man she'd been hating actually had a heart.

THREE
THE WITNESS

ESPERANZA FLORES AWOKE to the smell of coffee, scrambled eggs, and chorizo. Her calloused hands rubbed her aching back. The pain had been a constant companion since the birth of her son, Alejandro, who was twelve years old but going on thirty. Being raised by a single mother, her independent son had been forced to grow up and mature too quickly.

The dull, never-ending ache surged up her spine. The king-sized bed the Goodwins had donated was worn, and the absence of a box spring made sleeping even more uncomfortable. But it was Alex's cooking—he took after his father in the kitchen—that made waking up on Saturday mornings a little easier.

The Goodwins insisted on a spotless home. Esperanza would wash Mrs. Goodwin's windows today until there wasn't a smudge of dirt. She wasn't a weak woman. If perfectionism was what was required of her, then so be it.

The alternatives? No money. No job. Deportation and child protective services taking Alex away. She knew where that led: a child without love or guidance. No, her son wouldn't be another statistic, another Mexican hoodlum gang-banging his way to prison or the grave.

"Morning, Mama," Alex said, stirring the eggs and chorizo in the pan without looking-up from the book he was reading.

Esperanza knew her son was special beyond his 4.0 in school. Her little *niño* had advanced and skipped several grades. His teachers helped enroll Alex in the National Association for Gifted Children.

"Mrs. Flores, Alex has an IQ of one hundred and sixty," exclaimed his teacher.

Esperanza still didn't understand such tests. However, one thing was for certain: her son was not just some number. It didn't matter if they said he had the "potential for genius."

He was still a boy, still twelve years old.

Alex paused his reading and served her the eggs and chorizo. Esperanza scanned the title of Alex's book. She never knew what subject or type of book he'd read. Rarely was it fiction. His most recent reading preference had been more complex topical subjects.

Fundamentals of Physics: Mechanics, Relativity, and Thermodynamics. Esperanza read the title to herself several times and shook her head.

"Why're you reading this?" Esperanza shuffled into the kitchen and sat on the wooden chair that moaned from age. Living in a small two-bedroom apartment in East LA, all the furniture was handed down. A one-bedroom would've been cheaper, but her bright child needed space—his own room, his own privacy. So, she worked two jobs, sometimes more, just to make it work.

The morning sunlight shone through the bars on the kitchen window, creating a gleam on the plate before her. Steam rose from the food as she whispered a quick prayer, grateful for one more meal.

"Your school's making you read it?" She inhaled the rich

smell of eggs and chopped pork wafting in the air, filling their small apartment.

"No." Alex shrugged, turning to face the microwave as it dinged. "How many times do I have to remind you—gonna be a doctor, Mama? That means I have to work hard now. I wanna find a cure for cancer and help people live. So, they don't have to suffer the way Papa did."

"I know you've told me. Of course, I remember. I just thought you'd wanna read...I dunno, something more fun, *mijo.* Like *fiction?*" she said.

As an immigrant living at the poverty level and a single mother, yes, she wanted him to live up to his dream of becoming a doctor. But something about Alex's advancement made her uneasy. Her only child was growing up too quickly, and it worried her.

How could she let her son skip his childhood this way?

He removed the warm milk from the microwave, poured it into the coffee cup, added sweetener, and then the coffee. Alex plopped down the mug next to her dish.

"What am I missing out on? I don't do *fiction—*"

"And why not? You won't know you like it if you don't try, Alejandro." Esperanza brushed her fingers through Alex's hair.

"Stop," he complained, like some college boy who'd come home to visit his mother during spring break. "I hate it when you do that. I've got gel in it."

"Such a big boy." Esperanza took her last bite of the scrambled eggs peppered with the spicy sausage into her mouth while Alex waited patiently. She handed her plate over to him and watched Alex walk the dish to the sink. "My big helper."

"After the Goodwins, if we have time, can we go to the Santa Monica Pier?"

Alex didn't wait for the answer. He grabbed her cell phone and typed away. "Never mind, it's blocked off. They're calling it a crime scene, even though they arrested the guy already. So stupid."

He read the headline aloud. "Will be re-opened for public use on Monday."

"Why don't we go to the library and pick out a fun fiction book."

"Wizards? Fake worlds? Really? It's ridiculous. It's not real," Alex scoffed, "and it bores me. It's not a challenge. Science, on the other hand, is a challenge, and it *is* fun."

Esperanza sighed to herself. Alex seemed to get older every day. He was reading a physics book for recreation, for crying out loud. As it was, he was speeding his way through childhood because Alex didn't want to do "kid things."

Her son should have a childhood, a normal childhood.

"Thank you for breakfast, *mijo*."

Esperanza chose not to speak Spanish to Alex when he was younger, not out of shame for their culture, not for fear of deportation. Since being in the United States, she'd toiled with language, often fluctuating between an anxious wave of struggling to understand and often being misunderstood. After Hector's death, she'd never felt more alone, more lost, more scared.

She didn't want Alex to ever feel those same insecurities.

She wanted his English to be perfect.

She wanted her son to be understood.

American.

She couldn't remember her own dreams, not since Hector died. In many ways, it was a reflection of what her life had become. Her only dream, her only hope, was sitting right next to her. Twelve-year-old Alex was a U.S. citizen with a promising future she never had for herself.

———

Esperanza's mind was dizzy with the chemical smell of window cleaner. Sweat glistened along her sore neck and made the back of her shirt stick to her skin. She wiped her hand across her brow. The atmosphere felt too stagnant, making her beg for a breeze.

"Almost done, Mrs. Goodwin." Esperanza sprayed the window twice more, even though she'd already cleaned it.

Putting a hand on Esperanza's shoulder, Mrs. Goodwin comforted her.

"It's clean, dear—as clean as it's gonna get. You've stayed an extra hour, and I feel terrible for it."

Although she was alone tonight in her home, Mrs. Goodwin was dressed as though she was ready for a business meeting, donning a dress skirt and blouse. Esperanza had never seen the pastor's wife wear the same outfit twice.

"You haven't taken a break. The pastor's out visiting a member at the hospital. I'm solo tonight. Why don't the two of you have dinner with me?"

"It's getting dark," Esperanza said hesitantly, glancing at her son. She wished she had extended family or support here, so she didn't have to haul Alex around. That was the price she paid coming here for a better life: leaving behind those she loved and having to hustle to make do with what she had.

"Of course," Mrs. Goodwin trotted to her purse, dug out cash, and handed it to her. "You sure you don't wanna stay for supper?"

"Sure we do," Alex said.

Esperanza coughed, glaring at her son.

"Thank you anyway," Esperanza gave her employer a slight bow in appreciation.

"Mama, we can stay for dinner, can't we?" Alex insisted.

"We've got dinner at home," Esperanza bit out. "I said it's getting dark, and we have to walk home."

"I'll drive you," Mrs. Goodwin insisted in an almost pleading way. Esperanza could see in her eyes that Mrs. Goodwin was a lonely woman, and it made Esperanza feel sorry for her. But she couldn't stay. All she wanted to do was get home and crawl into bed.

"It's okay. We can take the bus," Esperanza said, too prideful to take up the offer.

"Very well," Mrs. Goodwin flashed a sad smile. "Here's a little extra for your troubles. Get Alex a little something. Such a sweet boy." The pastor's wife's eyes began to tear up. She blinked them away, but there was grief inside them.

"No," Esperanza blurted more forcefully than she'd anticipated, staring at the cash. Her voice softened as she repeated, "No, thank you."

But Mrs. Goodwin handed her an extra thirty dollars. "You earned it."

The pity in Mrs. Goodwin's kind eyes was more than she could bear.

———

Esperanza didn't like walking at night in East Los Angeles, where rent was affordable, but the streets could be unsafe. Most nights, her neighborhood didn't deserve its reputation.

Tonight, she and Alex turned down their usual shortcut home. *La gente* in the barrios—nosy neighbors, really—whispered on about how she shouldn't walk under The Serpent's Bridge, that too many people had been killed. Named for its python-like body climbing up and down, a design inspired by Thailand's Chao Phraya River Memorial and Museum in Nakorn-Sawan, this bridge was cursed with evil that tempted the sinner to turn to their dark side.

But Esperanza didn't believe in luck or in silly superstitions.

As they approached the passage of broken asphalt bordered by graffiti-marked walls, something morbid churned in her stomach.

"Stay close, *mijo*," she said, stricken with déjà vu despite having walked down this alley toward home many times. Somehow, tonight felt different.

A thin layer of fog diffused several feet in front of them, making visibility difficult, yet the sound of footsteps made her stop in place. Grunts followed—then stumbling footsteps over gravel—a scuffle.

She put a finger to her lips. "*Shhh,*" she commanded silently.

Two figures were in the distance, wrestling. Silhouettes danced against the graffiti-tagged walls beneath the bridge.

A cry pierced the night, "*¡Ayúdame!*"

The voice was gasping for breath.

In the absence of streetlamps, the light of the moon guided them.

Alex instinctively clutched closer to her.

He whispered, "Hey, did you hear that?"

Esperanza covered his mouth with her hand.

She and Alex crouched against the bridge's cold concrete. Regretting taking the shortcut locals never dared cross, she swore she'd never again risk her son's safety—if she could only get them through this night alive. A familiar foreboding alerted her. Esperanza gripped Alex's arm and pulled him close. Loose dirt and gravel ground obnoxiously beneath her worn sneakers. She froze, petrified of exposing their presence.

The sound of the victim's pleas drew them in. "*¡No! ¡Por favor, nooo!*"

Alex's face held child-like curiosity above fear. She could barely catch her breath and heard her son's breathing, short and staccato. Alex followed her cadence as they took a single step toward the bridge, then another, and another.

The voice screeched now. *"Ayuda..."*

They made it to the side of The Serpent's Bridge, cowering against the side pillar while darkness enveloped them. Shaking, Esperanza inched her nose around the left wall of the bridge so she could peek into the clearing. Inquisitive, Alex attempted to look. She put a hand over his eyes and whispered a silent prayer to God, begging for their lives to be spared.

The two figures continued the death dance. Esperanza could make out little except that the man in control wore black gloves. His hands tightened around the victim's throat.

Choking sounds escaped.

The dark figure moved with slow deliberation, following the body to the ground and its final resting place. Kneeling over the body, the man in black completed his death grip. One last gurgle bubbled out, the voice deep enough to indicate the victim was indeed a man. His body went limp. Esperanza wanted to scream but instead clutched Alex more tightly.

The body on the ground shuddered and went still.

The killer turned cautiously as if sensing that he was being watched. He looked around. She determined he was wearing black clothing, a long trench coat, black gloves, and a baseball cap. Esperanza, hand still resting on Alex's mouth, edged under the bridge: one step, two steps, three. Backs against the wall, they squatted toward the ground without making a sound, thankful for the twilight and lampless street that kept them hidden. All she could feel was Alex's rapid breath through his flared nose.

The killer loomed over the lifeless body.

Her heart pummeled erratically in her chest.

The killer must have been able to hear their frantic breathing, Esperanza thought. Yet, as suddenly as the scene unfolded, the perpetrator, shrouded in darkness, turned and was swallowed up by the night.

She should have never come this way.

They stayed crouched against the wall, arms tight around one another.

"Think he's gone?" Alex finally broke the silence.

Slowly, they emerged from their hiding place. They tiptoed toward the body. The man, Hispanic and maybe in his forties, was dead. He resembled her late husband, Hector.

"We need...we need to call the police..." Esperanza's lips trembled. "We have to call the police. My God, we can't just leave him here."

"No, Mama," Alex hissed, "you do, and you'll never see me again. They'll deport you."

"Leaving a dead man, it's wrong," Esperanza gasped, her calloused hands covering her mouth. "Maybe we call and we... and we don't leave our names?"

Esperanza quivered in dread. Alex tugged at her hand with urgency.

"We don't have time, Mama. We need to leave! What if he comes back?"

Esperanza wept into her tired hands.

"Mama, we have to go!"

The sound of crunching asphalt sent a jolt through them both.

"He's coming back. *We need to run!*"

Alex clasped his mother's hand and pulled her.

They ran and didn't stop until they were home—somewhere in East Los Angeles, where their lives had been normal until now. She couldn't call the police because if she did, she'd be gone, and Alex would never see her again.

They lay in bed, holding each other.
The dead man must be their secret.
They would never speak of this again.

FOUR
THE DETECTIVE

HEAVY EYES SURVEYED her surroundings as the room fluctuated in and out of focus. Nazario remembered a familiar male voice soothing her in the dreary charcoal of unconsciousness. Her wishful thinking knew who the man was, but she dared not say his name. Now awake, she was unsure if it was real or a lucid dream.

Groggy, she adjusted her arms as her eyes followed the tubing to the IV attached to her veins. Her face felt bloated and inflamed. She rubbed her jaw and tried to open her mouth but could barely complete the task without incredible pain as she relived every strike from Morris' skilled hands. Nazario's right eye strained to open wider. Without looking in a mirror, she was acutely aware of its black bruise forming—if not already blossoming—on her face.

Standing at the foot of her bed was Captain Augusta Humphrey, without the bandana that frequently adorned her hairless scalp. The once-thinning patches of hair were skin-smooth now, her perfectly arched auburn brows now equally bald. Gus's tenacious fighting spirit glinted in her golden hazel eyes. They were the color of the fading sun, contrasting brightly against the margins of dark circles underneath. It was the distinct strength in her smile that filled Nazario with warmth.

The captain was beautiful and perfect in this moment. She rubbed her bald head and asked in a child's voice, "Wanna feel?"

Nazario flinched, trying to exercise her jaw; she could barely open and close it.

"Thought you didn't need another round. What happened to reconstruction?"

Gus's eyes broke away to her shifting feet, then raised again, her gaze moist.

Nazario swore to herself and sighed. "Double mastectomy?"

Gus made a downward motion with flat palms and said, "All gone."

"Damn you, Gus, what the hell're you doing here? You should be resting. I should be visiting you. When was this? You should've called. You should be OFD?"

"I brought you and Wilson on to work on those homicides that Morris was responsible for, remember? You were slammed. Course they want me off fucking duty, but screw all that. No breaks for me, and to hell with light duty. Ain't no way they're making me Office Bitch."

She extended a hand, and Gus moved to her bedside to clasp it.

Nazario's voice cracked, "I would've made the time to be there for you."

Gus took Nazario's hand and ran it over her scalp. "That's baby-butt smooth."

Nazario's lips curved into a wobbly smile and then admitted, "I think I officially lost my first fight." She looked down at her wrapped knee and full leg brace. She could still feel hands around her throat, the air draining from her lungs. "I got too cocky, and it caught up with me. Should've drawn my weapon."

Gus squeezed her hand for support, reminding Nazario that her friend knew all too well what almost dying was like. During a sting operation, Gus had hesitated when a sixteen-year-old Mexican boy began shooting. The hesitation nearly cost Gus her life. She'd been shot three times and survived. If Nazario had drawn her weapon on Morris, she wouldn't have been in this situation. She'd underestimated Morris' martial arts skills and overestimated her own.

Nazario stared at her trembling hands, torn between a bruised ego and the urge to thank Gus for getting there right on time. If Morris had had a little more time, she would've been dead right now.

Gus leaned in and put a stable hand on her shoulder.

Her best friend always had firm and steady hands.

Hands that, in one touch, spoke of trust and reassurance.

"Trying to run at top speed—and aim—ain't so easy. Don't second-guess yourself. No one's dead, and you got the perp."

"He's got one hell of a strike. Best skilled motherfucker I've ever fought," she said, the words sounding muffled as Nazario did her best not to overwork her jaw. "I should've seen his moves coming. Shouldn't have let him take me down to the ground. My gun was strapped to my ankle. I couldn't reach it, and the fog was so thick—"

She was making excuses and felt stupid. Nazario asked Gus for a mirror, and her best friend didn't hesitate. Gus didn't coddle or try to persuade her not to look. The captain was the type that didn't hide from battle scars but faced them head-on. Like she had with cancer. Nazario lifted the mirror and studied her swollen face. Stitches ran against her left jawline.

Twelve? Fifteen, maybe?

Lip was busted, and right eye—as suspected—was partly shut and already turning magenta.

Her mind spun, replaying her moves and his, like a coach rethinking a lost game.

"Hey, it happens to the best of us." Gus put her bald head against Nazario's and whispered reassurance. "Don't go down self-misery road, Detective. It's a dead end."

Nazario looked into her amber eyes and nodded.

Gus's phone buzzed. "Guess who just texted to see how you're doing?" She looked down at the phone and laughed as she handed it to Nazario. "Sammy got the girls together; they all wanted to make sure you're alive and breathing."

The image on the captain's phone was of four young women huddled together. They squeezed behind the lens, waving and blowing kisses at her. The impromptu selfie tickled her soul, causing a rumble of laughter to escape from her aching chest. The guffaw alone made her ribs and back throb, causing her to wince.

"We miss you!" the text read. Her eyes pooled.

"Can you believe it's been three years since I found Sammy kidnapped by those skinheads, and we started our little all-women self-defense group?" Gus reminisced.

"Renegade survivors come from all walks of life," Nazario said. "I hadn't expected we'd end up helping so many victims of violence. Avery's the only one that I've never been able to figure out. She's real private, that one."

"Speaking of—Avery asked me if you could have coffee with her. Said she wanted to talk to you about something important."

"I can barely open my mouth to breathe, let alone chit-chat over Starbucks brew-of-the-day." Face on fire with raw bruises, Nazario shifted uncomfortably in bed. "But I'll be there Saturday, and doncha tell me no."

"I'm not fixing to change your stubborn mind." Gus shoved her iPhone in her pocket and then nodded at Chief Trevor Johnson at the doorway.

The chief walked in and put a large ebony hand on Gus's back.

"Captain, thanks for looking out for my detective." Chief Johnson, Daddy's former partner, was one of the first Black cops to rise through the ranks to captain and commanding officer of Robbery-Homicide—before ascending to the top post.

Gus gave him a smug smile. "She was mine first."

"Not trying to throw shade atcha, but I don't miss my Narco days." Nazario winked at Gus. "But I do miss you."

"And I'd prefer to avoid DBs." Gus laughed, patting Chief's shoulder as she left. The hospital bed was like laying on a brick slab. She adjusted, then said, "I work better with the dead than the living."

"Don't blame you. Homicide suits you, Nazario."

"See you and the girls Saturday," the words roughly scraped out of her parched throat.

Gus shot back over her shoulder, "I'll hold your limp ass to it!"

Chief took a seat next to her hospital bed and waited until Gus left.

Nazario gave Chief Johnson a weary smile.

"He gotcha good." Chief Johnson eyed Nazario's disabled limb, constricted from ankle to upper thigh. "Just talked to the Doc. Jaw's fine. It ain't broken. Knee's another story. Torn ACL. Torn meniscus. You won't be doing any of those Jet Li moves for at least two months."

She sighed, looked up at the ceiling, and confessed, "Never been in a leg brace."

Chief continued, injecting positivity where he could, as her boss tended to do. "The Feds said Morris had a larger operation than we thought. I think we got all of them. An operation in the millions. Talking lots of dough. Special Agent Blake Huxley, apparently the FBI's golden boy, was just here. Guess he wanted to send his regards with a personal visit."

Nazario cleared her throat. *Blake Huxley.* Of course, it was him.

Recalibrating her attention to yet two more people waiting at her doorway, she forced old memories away. Her partner, Detective Wilson, along with a Hispanic doctor, entered the room. Already overwhelmed by the number of visitors she'd had and despite their best intentions, Nazario wished she could process what had happened—*alone.*

As a homicide detective, she knew privacy was the last thing she'd receive.

The orthopedic surgeon introduced himself, then asked an idiotic question, "How're you feeling, Detective Nazario?" He glanced down at his clipboard. "I saw that you guys were catching up and didn't want to intrude. Now a good time to chat?"

Understanding how interrogations work, Nazario naturally skipped the stupid question and answered the second, "No better time, Doc."

"Would've broughtcha flowers," Wilson said with a wink, "but you're not the type."

Nazario threw up her middle finger, sending Johnson into a fit of laughter.

Chief rose from the hospital chair. "Well, you heard it from Captain Humphrey. The Narcotic and Gang Unit wanted me to pass along their thanks. I know you guys were brought on to work those murders. Narco couldn't have caught Morris without you. Take a few days if you need it, Nazario." He wagged a finger. "I mean it."

"I'm not taking time off." Nazario ignored the doctor's disapproving look.

"You should," the doctor began in a matter-of-fact tone, "and if you refuse, it won't be so easy. You can't agitate those stitches on your face, and under no circumstances can you be on that leg. We'll be sending you home with this."

The doctor pointed to a black box on the ground. It was an ice machine that required adding equal parts of water and ice. The machine was attached to long rubber tubes that sent cold liquid to a wrap that encircled the knee.

"Ice it as much as possible. Keep it elevated. No weight on it. No bending it."

"Great, really great." Reality hit her. No more running, training on punching bags, or going after perps without drawing her weapon. It was her worst nightmare come to life.

Wilson's phone rang. It could only mean one thing. Nazario and Wilson exchanged a glance. "What're we looking at?" Wilson raised his brows. "Where? Okay, got it." Wilson took out a small notebook and scribbled. He looked at his watch, "Be there in a half-hour. No one touches anything, alrighty?"

"DB?" Nazario turned to Wilson.

"Yep, dead body, unfortunately, and under that Serpent's Bridge. Like the sixteenth in its history." Wilson shivered. "Kinda gives me the heebie-jeebies. Damn historians voted against the county. My vote was with the city to knock it the fuck down."

"C'mon, you don't buy into that cursed bologna, do you?" She didn't wait for an answer from her partner, already knowing what it would be. "Am I free to leave, Doc?"

Wilson nodded. He carried a separate cell phone dedicated to murder cases, and only a handful of cops knew the number.

"We have no reason to keep you," the orthopedic surgeon said, explaining that it would take ninety days for the apparatus to come off.

"Cool. Can y'all get the hell outta the room so I can put my clothes on?"

"Broughtcha your shorts since I got the spare key to your apartment. Doc said it'd be easier for you." Wilson furrowed his brows. "Y'know, partner, I can head to the scene. You should go home and relax."

Nazario laughed, shaking her head.

"No!" Chief barked at Nazario. "Doncha even think about it."

She jabbed her finger toward the door. "Out. So, I can take this stupid hospital gown off."

The doctor looked to her boss, who wore a concerned, paternal expression because no one was changing her mind. They exited the room, leaving her to fumble with her clothes. Hobbling on one leg and getting dressed in a full leg cast proved much harder than it looked. However, Nazario refused to call the nurse.

One thought ran through her head again—*three months of this shit.*

———

Yellow crime tape flapped in the August breeze, but it wasn't the only thing blocking either side of the bridge. Thick, pewter layers of fog smothered the entire area for miles, daring humans to pass through.

Wilson ducked under the tape and lifted it for her. Nazario grunted into a low squat, forcing her left knee to take the brunt of her weight. The full leg brace on her right leg made even the simplest tasks awkward. East LA was two dozen miles from the coast, yet the fog hung thick and played tricks on the officers as they stumbled about the crime scene, trying not to disturb what shouldn't be disturbed.

A young officer approached, ignoring Wilson as he extended an eager hand to Nazario.

"Detective Nazario, you uh..." he stalled, eyes flickering between her face and leg.

"Look like shit? Well..." Nazario read his name badge. "Officer Gomez, I've already been told. You can say I've been better."

"What I...meant to say is, I followed your father's career. Detective Lucas Nazario was my idol. As a Puerto Rican, you know he's the reason why I joined," the young officer gushed. He and his ginger-haired partner both looked like they were still in high school. Under different circumstances, she'd have let the chit-chat with Gomez go on. But with a DB buried under the fog, she'd have to cut it short.

"Appreciate it," Nazario said. "So, the two of you new to SID? What're we looking at?"

The Scientific Investigations Division, the Los Angeles Police Department's version of CSI, could be territorial. Their primary focus was to collect crime scene evidence. Since Nazario had a reputation, not to mention a graduate degree focused on crime scene investigations, SID often gave her more leeway.

"Yes, ma'am. Training under Yang and Whittier. They're busy on another case and couldn't step out. As evidence techs, we were told to take pictures. Glad we had the flash. Can't see *nada*." Gomez fidgeted with the flashlight, twirling it between fingers like a baton. "There's no identifiable cause of death, no gunshots or knife wounds like we usually see out here."

She hobbled toward the body and asked over her shoulder, "Wallet?"

Nervous, Gomez combed a hand through his hair and said, "Oh, right."

Nazario extended her right hand, her left balancing against the crutch.

The kid was green. Real green. She watched embarrassment spread across his face.

Officer Gomez handed Nazario a bagged black leather wallet. It looked to be a decade old, weathered and falling apart. Wilson sauntered over and pointed his flashlight at it while Nazario dug it out.

"Yago Rios, thirty-five, lives in Mexico Central," Gomez said, earning a steely look from Nazario. The muscle in her angular jaw flexed, causing searing pain near the stitches on her face. Gomez corrected himself, "East LA, sorry."

Nazario inspected the ID. Wilson adjusted the light closer, and they exchanged a look. The young officer, his red hair a vivid splash of color under the shadowy expanse of The Serpent's Bridge, joined Gomez. He planted his hands on his hips like he was ready to be grown up.

"Notice anything? About the ID?" Nazario asked. Gomez and Redhead looked at each other. Both SID trainees seemed stumped, like it was some pop quiz.

"It's not expired?" Gomez offered.

"It's fake," Nazario schooled him. "Yago will do for now. Reality is, we've got an unidentified. No papers."

Yago's face was frozen with a look of fear in his eyes, his lips a light shade of blue. Nazario scanned downward, trying to find a trace of something, anything on the body. Then she saw it.

"Light," she called and grabbed the Mag light from Wilson. Tucked away, she could see faint red marks covered by thick black hair. "COD—strangulation."

Searching, she illuminated the ground, making her way toward a dark corner of the bridge where the SID newbies likely hadn't trampled.

"Redhead, mind taking pics?" Nazario ordered Gomez's partner, pointing at the far end of the bridge. The ginger officer followed Nazario's gaze like a dutiful trainee.

There was a set of small muddy footprints next to ones a bit larger, maybe a woman's size seven if she had to guess, because the smaller ones belonged to a child. Nazario lifted her gaze to catch the trainees looking like a couple of trapped idiots on their first day on the job. Near the muddy footprints, something caught her eye.

Is it trash or evidence?

She walked closer to the scrap of paper on the ground.

Donned in the latex gloves she'd put on in the car, Nazario removed a plastic Ziploc bag from her pocket. Wilson came to her side and shone the light on a piece of textbook paper. He picked it up and dropped it in her gloved palm.

Fundamentals of Physics

The piece of paper and the footprints were the only things she saw that stood out among the fog and stale crime scene. Something twisted in her gut, as it always did when she was onto something. There wasn't anything else around. Nothing but a ripped piece of a physics book—and judging by its condition, it hadn't been there for very long. It didn't look worn by external weather conditions. Her gut said their only evidence wasn't just another random piece of litter.

At a distance, the coroner van was now visible, and it was perfect timing, as her iPhone calendar dinged for tomorrow: *Mrs. Goodwin Pastoral Counseling.* While not religious, Nazario was mandated to see a therapist and attend AA for her drinking, per Chief Johnson. As the coroner and his assistant approached, she reached for the Gabapentin she always carried for her anxiety attacks and popped a pill. Nazario wanted a drink. Craved it after a shit day. Determined not to relapse or lose her job, she'd make tomorrow's counseling session—no excuses.

FIVE
THE PASTOR'S WIFE

MILLIE THOUGHT Detective Nazario looked like she'd seen better days: her right eye was blackened and nearly swollen shut, stitches decorating her left jawline. Detective Nazario wiped her hands on her jeans going on three times, and Millie knew what this meant. Her left knee bobbed manically up and down as she chewed her bottom lip.

For the first forty-five minutes, Millie managed to get the detective talking about everyday stuff to warm her up, and it actually worked. After all, Detective Nazario was one of her most difficult clients. She didn't say much, yet Millie knew that the detective had a lot to get off her chest—more so than some of her other clients who droned on, and she couldn't shut them up.

Millie picked up a rubber stress ball she kept handy on her desk and handed it to Nazario.

Nazario wordlessly took the yellow sphere and, as neither spoke, repeatedly squeezed.

After two long minutes of silence, Millie asked her most stubborn client, "Wanna talk about what's really on your mind?"

She hoped to get to the root as to why Nazario was here in the first place.

"Almost didn't come," said the detective, the words mumbled from her fat lip. Her eyes were cast down, watching her own hands squeeze and release the ball. "I'm...really struggling tonight. You know I wouldn't be here if I wasn't mandated to come. I take my anxiety meds for the same reason. Kinda wanna keep my job. Now I need another doctor for my knee and the stupid crutch to help me walk."

"I know it's hard for you to be receptive to help, but you showed up today," Millie said gingerly. "You get all that on duty?" She gestured to the injuries.

Nazario nodded. "You know, I've never been without the use of my legs. I've never been laid up like this. I got cocky. Could've taken him down, hell, killed him had I drawn my weapon."

"But that's not how you do things, Detective. It's not your style. You chose to fight. You took him down, didn't you?"

"Almost cost me my life." Nazario tightened her grip on the ball. "So many things could've gone wrong."

"All those things that could've gone wrong didn't—though, did they?" Millie gave her a reassuring smile. "Your knee, it'll heal. You did your job without killing anyone. In talking to you for more than two years now, I'm certain of one thing: you're very brave, and you always do your best. Were you thinking of your father again?"

Rather than answer the question, she said, "I should've drawn my weapon." The frustrated detective raked her hands through her oily hair. "I should've drawn my *fucking* weapon."

"But you didn't. And it's okay that you didn't," Millie paused and repeated the question she already knew the answer to. "Now...were you thinking about your dad again?"

Nazario lifted her eyes to meet hers. "Daddy's all I kept

thinking about, and then I wanted to numb it all away. I've had a long day, and you have no idea just how bad I wanna drink right now."

"I know you do, but sometimes it helps—" Millie paused a beat before continuing, "—to talk about the trigger. Can you explain how it happened? How you...almost died?"

"He got my knee pretty good, and I...I couldn't get him off me. Not at first." The detective tightened her hold on the malleable hand therapy tool until it looked ready to pop.

"And what did that feel like? Inside. Not being able to get him off you?"

"Had no control. I felt...t-trapped. I had my damn gun strapped to my ankle. I...couldn't reach it," her voice cracked. "His hands were around my throat. Because of my knee, I was pinned. I threw some strikes. I tried...but there was this moment where I couldn't...I just couldn't breathe."

"That was a very traumatic experience for you," Millie said, swallowing a knot in her throat, thinking of her son and the accident. Gideon couldn't breathe either.

Her fingers contracted around the ball once more. With raw honesty, Nazario said, "Scared the shit outta me."

"Can you take a deep breath right now? Take five deep breaths. I'll do it with you."

Millie showed her, and the detective followed. They took each long breath together.

She looked at the time. They'd gone five minutes over. It was the first time the detective had stayed for an entire session. And the most she'd ever spoken.

Likely sensing the time as well, Nazario looked down at her watch and hobbled up.

Millie helped her with the crutch, and Nazario put a hand on Millie's.

"Thank you," Nazario said, looking into Millie's eyes. "Seriously."

"Will you be going to the AA meeting tomorrow?" Millie asked. "Can you call Gus or Wilson? They are your sponsor and partner respectively, after all. Only if it gets too bad tonight, that is?"

"I'll be fine." Nazario avoided her eyes now. "And I'll be at the meeting tomorrow."

Millie knew not to spoil this meeting with scripture or prayer, as it often turned off the non-church types. With some clients, good old-fashioned listening was the best medicine. This undoubtedly kept Detective Anaya Nazario coming back, and Millie planned to keep it that way.

———

As she walked outside toward the food pantry, Millie thought about Detective Nazario and prayed she'd stay sober tonight. The food pantry was still open—which was unusual. It ordinarily closed at 7:30 p.m., but it was 8 p.m. What caught her off guard as she joined Stan was the harried donator with a giant container rushing through the door.

It was a philanthropist she didn't expect.

"Glad I'm not too late," Eric said, coming in with a generously sized box. Millie looked out the window and noticed Nicky waiting for his guardian on his bike out front. She tried not to stare at Eric's biceps but found herself doing so. Eric caught her in the act, and instead of looking away in shame, she looked right at him.

Yes, sir, I was looking, Millie thought.

"Mighty generous," Millie croaked, absently twirling a lock of hair. "Thank you."

"Anything to help the community, Pastor Millie. By the way

—no offense to you, Pastor Stan—but I think you should let your wife preach a couple of Sundays," he said. Millie raised a brow, surprised that the ICE agent recalled that Stan wasn't the only one who was qualified.

While Stan led most Sundays, Millie was an ordained pastoral counselor helping with everything from marital problems, financial, mental health, and even the complicated types like Detective Nazario. That's how she met Stan—in seminary school. The thought of her college years aged her. She was so young then. How long had they been married? Twenty-five years already? Millie sighed. While going down memory lane, she'd somehow ended up ogling Eric's broad chest.

His smile brightened as he caught her for a second time and gave her a wink.

Stan changed the subject. "I do apologize that the crowd got a little heated."

"Don't faze me none. I get my line of work isn't all that popular. So, no need to apologize for the First Amendment." Eric gave Stan a tired smile, one that showed off his dimpled cheeks.

Millie flushed, fanning her face. Her hot flashes were acting up.

"Just came by to drop off some canned goods. Thought the pantry might need a donation," Eric continued. "Oh, and Nicky wanted to know if he could ride bikes with Alex sometime. I was thinking when Esperanza's at the church during the AA meeting tomorrow. I mean, I don't attend—never been a booze man. Got an extra bike for Alex I can throw in the back of my truck. Give Alex something to do while his mom cleans. Will you ask Esperanza when she comes by? They're best of friends, and it would mean so much to Nicky. Been complaining he hasn't gotten to spend time with Alex."

He plunked the box down on a wooden table at the center of the room.

"I don't see why not," Stan said.

"Of course. I bet the boys would enjoy a ride together," Millie said.

Their deacon and longest attendee shuffled in with her two little girls in tow.

"Eric," the deacon spat out tersely, "didn't expect to see you here."

Eric tilted his head at the senior member. "I was just leaving."

Millie watched the large man walk off with Nicky at his side, riding his bike.

"Good evening, Deacon, I see you brought the girls," Stan smiled.

"I didn't just come here for milk, although we can use some. With two mouths, I'm already out," the deacon said, tired. "I was at the rally. Pastor Goodwin, we, the Mexican community, appreciate you putting it together. But I come here, and I speak for many concerned members. We don't understand. Why is Eric Myers still attending our church? He has the nerve to hide behind that Nicky boy."

Millie lifted a thin brow at her husband, curious to see if he'd react. Stan's mannered expression ordinarily adjusted like a chameleon changing its skin to blend with its environment, but this time his façade unexpectedly dropped. His child-like eyes turned beady and insectile, blinking at a frantic speed. The vein at the center of his forehead announced itself like a crooked branch, extending into his thinning hairline. His head made a slight twitch, and his hands expanded and contracted as if the sinner and the saint were in the boxing ring. She'd only ever seen him behave this way once before—after that awful accident. The day Gideon almost drowned, and police officers came asking a battery of questions.

The horrific accident had blindsided her—then came the accusations of parental neglect, turning her world into a maelstrom of sheer humiliation. She wondered now if her husband would allow himself anything other than disciplined responsiveness for once. For a moment, she prayed that he'd get angry. That he'd let himself get defensive and react the way anyone outside the church would. But the pastor had isolated himself, and yet only Millie could see the slightest clamp and release of his fists against his sides. The way his face looked sour and pinched.

Stan breathed noisily through his nose—deep and long. Such a turn-off.

Silence settled over the pantry and expanded for a beat.

The wind whipped against the thin polypropylene plastic walls of the large storage shed they'd converted into a food pantry in the yard behind the church. The shed squealed noisily, accosted by a dusk breeze. The deacon's two little girls kept quiet, mirroring the adults, understanding that an important conversation was taking place.

Breaking the silence, Stan's voice scratched out, temperate and low.

"There's darkness in us all, Deacon. We're not here to judge, but to serve." His lips parted into a broad grin. Too wide. And for the moment, it flushed color across his cheeks. "But you're right on time. Pantry ain't closed yet. We're open to *everyone*."

Millie rolled her eyes and spun away from her husband, causing her skirt to *swoosh* about her. She smiled brightly at the girls who had been standing so patiently next to Mama. They were too sweet. She handed them each two lollipops.

"One for now and one for after supper." Millie winked at

them. She always wondered what it would be like if she had had a girl. All she'd ever known was Gideon, her little boy. She had always hated it when her mother kept sweets from her and did that fear-mongering thing she'd do, warning her that all her teeth would fall out.

Well, Mother, I've got all my teeth.

The girls giggled, unwrapping their candy. Millie smiled warmly at their mom. "I hope it's okay with you?"

Millie waltzed to the fridge, took out a gallon of milk, and handed it to one of their longest, most faithful church members. The deacon had been attending since before she had her girls and before her divorce.

"Oh...thank you," she said, putting her hands together prayer-like before taking the milk from Millie. "Girls, what do you say?"

"Thank you!" they said at once.

"See you on Sunday?" Stan asked.

"Thank you for the milk, but I think, Pastor Goodwin, we'll be looking for a new church. I have two young daughters—U.S. citizens who rely on their mother, who isn't one. I can't attend a church where *un minuto* I'm worshiping God and then the next, being deported by some *gringo* pretending to come to church to pray," she said. "Go ahead, keep that ICE agent as a member, but we're not coming back. Find another deacon to replace me. *Buenas noches.*"

Millie's shoulders collapsed. "You've been with us since we started. Please—"

The deacon paused, turned around, and hugged Millie in a fierce embrace. "No, *Señora* Goodwin, this is something I can't reconsider. Not when it comes to my life and many others like me who might be deported because of that man. I'm sorry, but I can't lose my girls. They need me."

Her daughters skipped ahead. Millie watched them disappear behind the rusty front gate, eroded by weather and age. It slammed behind them, making her jump. Arguing with her husband over Eric Myers had never worked. Millie lifted her chin and considered an alternative method of persuasion.

It would just take a little feminine touch.

———

Millie brushed her hands down her newly purchased champagne silk nightgown that ended mid-thigh. It was the shortest gown she now owned. The fabric felt smooth against her flesh. What was especially eye-catching was the deep, plunging neckline that showed off her full breasts. As they said, honey was better than vinegar, and Millie was prepared to use her God-given curves to entice her husband to reconsider his decisions.

Half an hour passed. Then, an hour. Millie nodded off just as the door opened; she jolted awake, and Stan shuffled in without looking at her. He headed for the bathroom garbed in a dark jacket and boots he rarely wore. Then the shower came to life. She looked at the time. It was almost eleven. Stan went to bed at ten every night. Since the encounter with the deacon, her husband had withdrawn. He parted ways shortly after and headed to a late men's Bible study.

Earlier that day, Millie had taken the opportunity to head to the mall to shop for her first lingerie and got there just before they closed.

"It's our most...modest nighty," the college-aged clerk had said, smacking her chewing gum. "I wouldn't call this lingerie. If ya really wanna wow Hubby, I got just the thing—"

"Oh, sweetheart." Millie laughed, fanning her face, suddenly feeling like this girl's grandmother getting one of them hot flashes. Hormonal changes would do that to you. Her chest and breasts were slick with sweat. Her cheeks felt like they were on fire. Were they trying to kill her with heat or what?

She blamed it on hormonal imbalance and not a naughty purchase at a sex shop.

Millie continued, wishing the AC was working. "You don't know my husband; this is...ahem...risqué. Trust me when I say this. With a neckline like this and as short as it is, this'll do the trick."

"We've got shorter ones," the clerk challenged with a devious smile.

I want to seduce my husband, not give the poor fool a heart attack, Millie thought. The shower turned off, and Millie adjusted her large, weighty breasts that disobeyed, flopping lazily to either side. What gravity and age did to a woman's body! She made her "girls" behave, fluffing them so that they looked like a baby's butt poking out of her plunging v-cleavage.

Stan shuffled into the bedroom dressed in old cotton shorts and a t-shirt. He took off his glasses and plunked them on the nightstand. Millie straightened up her spine so that her breasts were jutting forward. *Fifty is the new forty,* she thought, twirling a golden strand of hair nervously around her finger.

Her husband glanced at her the same way he looked at the car when it needed a wash, but it was one of those things that he could do another day. Stan's shielded eyes never traveled below her neckline. He clicked off the light on the nightstand and laid down flat on his back.

"I thought we could..." *Talk about Eric Myers and what happened at the rally,* she thought. But, said instead, "...do something a little unscheduled?"

She put a hand on his shoulder—ran her fingers down his chest. Millie curled her body and pressed her breasts against him, but Stan stiffened and turned to his side.

"Bible study ran late. There were members in need of

prayer," Stan explained. "Stick with the schedule, Millie Ann. I'm not up for impromptu right now. I'm real tired."

"I put a lot of effort—"

"I appreciate the gesture, honey," Stan yawned. "But you're bustin' outta that thing. It don't even fit'cha right. Did you get the right size? It looks like, like—"

"Like what? Oh, go on and spit it out."

"Never mind." He drew the covers tighter like they'd protect him from his "needy" wife.

Millie was livid.

"It's not right how you handled the deacon today. I'm all mixed up over that Eric Myers," she said, smoothing out her nighty. "I think he's that Nicky boy's legal guardian. What do we do if more members leave, Stan?"

"So that's what this is about?" Stan adjusted his pillow. "If they leave, let 'em leave. That was kind of him to drop off canned goods today. He's watching after that poor orphaned boy. I told you he's a good soul. Don't care what his job is. Now, we got an early morning, and tomorrow night's the AA meeting."

"I know what tomorrow is." Millie felt shame and outrage twist inside.

"Goodnight, Millie Ann," he said dismissively. "What you're trying to do might help some of your clients, but we're not twenty and in college."

For a second, Millie stared at the back of her husband's head, wishing all kinds of evil things. Frustration filled her, expanding her lungs. A wave of heat crawled under her skin, as a burning sensation caused her skin to slicken with fresh sweat.

Hot and bothered, and she couldn't even say it was from her husband's rejection or sexual sterility. Hot flashes and night sweats—*not sex*—were her big night.

She stomped to the closet.

Welcome to turning fifty.
Welcome to married life with Stan.

Millie wrapped herself in her robe, shoved her cell phone in her pocket, and headed to the bathroom. She was furious. Still, she closed the door softly—didn't want to cause a ruckus. Didn't want to wake Stan. Once in the bathroom, she fumbled for her phone in the pocket of her robe and quickly checked her email.

It had been three days. Anxiety filled her as she saw Dr. Bennett's unread email.

How she longed to hear her son's voice again. Her whole body ached from the loss of him. Ever since that near drowning when he was a boy, things had never been the same.

Re: Checking In
Dear Mrs. Goodwin,

Thank you for checking in again; however, things have remained the same. As I've explained to you before, Gideon is not a minor. Due to doctor and patient confidentiality, I must honor his wishes for all medical records and therapy to be kept private. He still remains mute and has been unresponsive to sign language. He communicates through writing only.

At the moment, he's informed me in writing that he wishes not to speak with you or your husband. I understand your concerns as a mother and a parent, but Gideon is an adult now and entitled to make his own decisions. I'm sorry. I wish I had better news. Should anything change, I can assure you that you'll be informed immediately.

Sincerely,
Marcel Bennett, M.D.

Still mute and unresponsive to even sign language? Her sweet Gideon, now a disabled soul and not by a genetic mutation but ruined by his dysfunctional, zealot parents. With a heavy heart, Millie deleted the email and cleared the browser search history. Straightening before the mirror, she wiped her wet eyes.

"Okay, Stan." Millie slipped off the silk nightie. "Have it your way."

The nightie, soft like butter, glided off her curves. The silk sent an exquisite sensation that overcame her. She felt...sexy. No, she wouldn't be returning it.

Another cold shower, she thought, *another night of self-pleasure.*

She always told clients: If Hubby refused to care for your needs—do the job yourself.

SIX

THE WITNESS

SITTING IN THE BUS, Esperanza watched the homeless tents and the dilapidated grunge of some of the most run-down parts of Los Angeles pass from her seat on the LA Metro. No one was following them. She knew this. They were not in danger, yet her body seemed hyper-alert. They would never have witnessed a murder if she'd only said yes to the pastor's wife—let her drive them home.

Instead, she was too filled with pride, and it had cost them dearly.

¡Ay, Dios mío! How stupid could she be? What was she thinking?

If she hadn't gone to Serpent's Bridge, she wouldn't be so jumpy, having to look over her shoulder. How long would it take before this country felt like her own?

Esperanza bit her lip. She could get a fake license so she could feel a little safer by driving Alex and not have to take the bus. But Hector had done that. Look at how he ended up—deported. ICE and law enforcement had become stricter. She had her *Instituto Nacional Electoral* (INE) Mexican identification card with her at all times. It was hard enough staying in hiding; it would be worse to take on a false or stolen ID, but she decided to bring it up with Alex anyway.

"I hear you can get a driver's license now without papers," she began, watching the city pass her by. "They don't really check at the DMV. Maybe I try?"

"Forget about it. It can be a felony charge for an undocumented," her twelve-year-old explained, then whispered, "This is about that dead guy, isn't it? Wouldya stop thinking about him?"

"How am I supposed to forget?" she hissed, crossing her arms.

Her unscathed Americanized child returned to reading his physics book, ignoring her, having snapped back from seeing a murdered man faster than a rubber band. Was this an American thing? Or was it Alex's analytical mind that made him able to dismiss it? Because teachers took a liking to him and thanks to scholarships, Alex attended one of the best private schools in Palos Verdes, which ranked near the top nationally.

Palos Verdes was in the South Bay, where wealth was the predominant race. There was no in-between to Esperanza. Either you lived in Boyle Heights, or you could afford to live in Palos Verdes. Maybe there was a middle class, but she couldn't see it through the dirty bus window. She wanted to shield her son from questionable strangers, thugs, the slumped over homeless, and the disgruntled working class forced to take one of the worst public transportation systems in the U.S.

Exhausted from lack of sleep and the nightmares that kept her awake all night, she yawned, watching Alex read. He'd progressed much further into his physics book, and it amazed her that her son was so resilient, as though the events the night prior didn't faze him at all. Just the day before, he'd begun reading and was now already somewhere in the middle. She peeked at the book this morning, curious. The language seemed complex, and the subject matter itself was so foreign and challenging.

She *could not* see the appeal.

Esperanza adjusted on the plastic bus seat, lower back aching as always after a long day at the Goodwins' house. She needed a new bed, one that was comfortable, one with a box spring and memory foam. But the money she received from cleaning had to go toward rent. Esperanza sat up and looked around the bus, gulping a nervous breath. She hated this feeling of guilt. That she let a killer walk away. Wouldn't she and her son be safer today if she'd just come clean to the cops? Called them yesterday? Would they have protected her or deported her?

Everything had changed since last night. She closed her eyes, dizzy with fatigue.

Her mind recalled events in short, vivid bursts as the nightmares jolted her awake and into an early morning panic. Gasping the way that dead man had. Clutching at her throat. The clock read 3:14 a.m. Awake. Like a crazy woman, she scrubbed her kitchen floors along with every inch of their two-bedroom apartment. It was simple, keeping tidy with one couch, a medium-sized television in the living room, two small bedrooms, and the old dining room table—still sturdy, despite having bought it used at the Salvation Army.

They didn't have a landline, even though she really wanted one.

"No, Mama," Alex had chided, "trust me, no one has a landline unless you're seventy and retired or a couple of dinosaurs like the Goodwins."

Mrs. Goodwin had helped her pick out a pay-as-you-go phone. "You need a cell phone so people can reach you," the pastor's wife said.

Sure enough, it was her day off, yet her phone chimed at six this morning with a text message requesting that she come and clean before the AA meeting. Esperanza reminded herself that she should be grateful that Mrs. Goodwin wanted her to clean for extra pay. The pastor's wife invented chores for her to do. Sometimes out of loneliness. Other times, because she knew Esperanza could use the money.

"Mama, can I ride that extra bike Nicky's got?" Alex looked up from his book.

Nicolas often asked to play with Alex. It was fine during daylight hours, but Compton was dangerous at night, and the neighborhood was unsafe. It also didn't help that an ICE agent was Nicky's guardian.

"No," Esperanza refused, "too much craziness has happened. It's dark out in that parking lot, and the streets aren't safe. You will not be running around at night, *mijo*. It's danger-ous. Cars, they come and go, and who knows what can happen to you."

"I get it, you're worried about that Eric Myers guy." Alex pouted in disappointment.

Esperanza's voice softened, "Are you...are you okay today? I mean, after—"

"For the hundredth time," Alex whispered, rolling his eyes, "he didn't see us. You've been paranoid ever since. It would've been a whole lot worse if we'd called the cops."

Esperanza hugged her arms across her chest.

"I'll never do that again," she swore, "never just leave a dead man and run."

"Let's hope there isn't a next time," Alex said, resuming his reading.

Hector, oh Hector, I wish you were here with us.

She watched the soot of Los Angeles slums pass by her window, and a wave of depression began to weigh on her soul. She glanced up at her son again, reading his physics book, and reminded herself that she was doing this for him. It was all for him, and the sacrifice was worth it.

She was here for a better life and not to regret decisions that already led to consequences.

They shouldn't have walked through The Serpent's Bridge.

Esperanza recalled being pregnant with Alex and staying with a sixty-five-year-old, semi-retired, Mexican-American *doula*. The doula kept the knowledge of her immigration status a secret. Because of all of his chemo rounds for his stage four colon cancer, Hector lived separately near the hospital in a small studio with a U.S. citizen who worked at the auto body shop with him.

Esperanza could hear her own piercing scream ripping out of her all over again, and not from the pain from labor. The most agonizing thing was that once her husband was abruptly deported, the chemo treatments stopped. Hector's cancer finally ate up every bit of recovery—and then, at last, killed him. She was perpetually afraid of deportation.

But what terrified her more was one unanswered question: Who killed the dead man?

SEVEN
THE DETECTIVE

NAZARIO WORE an LA Dodgers baseball cap, her hair tucked in a low braid that fell to the middle of her back. She leaned into the lone crutch wedged under her left armpit and slowly hobbled into the room.

The regulars were seated in a circle. Nazario nodded, diverting direct eye contact. Leaning the crutch toward the ground, she let it drop, and it landed with a light thud on the hardwood floors. The kid was the first to greet her, as he always did every meeting. He was a young Cuban with a provisional tic disorder that mostly revealed itself as rapid blinking and sometimes uncontrollable facial spasms.

"Slipped on something wet, or what?" the kid asked, blinking as if using Morse Code.

Nazario folded her arms across her chest. "Something like that."

The kid always talked to Nazario, but the rest, not so much.

Meanwhile, the AA group leader was a first-generation Puerto Rican from New York and twenty-five years sober from alcohol and heroin. What impressed Nazario was that the man went from homeless to getting clean and taking night classes at a community college. He was also the first in his family to go to college, earning an associate degree, and later transferred to NYU, where he earned a bachelor's in business and then his MBA.

"If I can do it, I know you can do it," he always said.

Twenty-five years clean seemed like several lifetimes. Shit, she passed up four liquor stores on her way into Compton and a Trader Joe's, where she often found the best variety of good and inexpensive wines. She couldn't go twenty-five minutes without salivating for a drink, let alone twenty-five-freaking-years without a single sip.

"How's everyone doing tonight?" the group leader asked, providing his usual aged and sensitive smile. It was a small group of regulars—and maybe that was what kept Nazario coming back. That, and the fact that if she didn't, she'd be off the force.

The small church was built in 1928 with a classic A-framed roof. Brand new white paint was freshly touched up once a year, and old-fashioned stained-glass windows gleamed. In spite of the outward appearance, there was something ominous about the church. Inside, the house of worship contained original parts that exuded an antique yet eerie vibe. Its hand-carved pews looked like they bore the weight of a century of lost souls. The ninety-year-old wooden floors were always polished and moaned from bearing the load of every sinner's foot that had tread on its steadfast planks.

A fresh scrubbing with Pine-Sol scented the room and somehow made the circle of alcoholics tolerable. It had been hard for her to find an AA meeting where her presence didn't make half the members leave.

Since Nazario arrived ten minutes late, she'd skipped the literature reading.

The group leader said his name, accompanied by the standard admission that he was an alcoholic, and in turn, everyone said hello. He explained that they'd be sharing on the topic of anger instead of going over one of the twelve steps and then began with his share. Nazario listened as the man complained about being micromanaged at work but concluded with the generic "turning it over to God" bit that always annoyed her.

Nazario didn't like to admit to powerlessness, but that was why she chronically relapsed.

A familiar attendee decided to go next. He was a former director of marketing at Canon who had showed up at a client meeting reeking of booze. Summarily, he was fired, yet was lucky his wife didn't leave him.

As a detective, in ten seconds, she'd memorized his clothes and persona. The former executive's regular uniform of Madewell slacks and button-up shirt demonstrated to her that he was a creature of habit and too comfortable in today's yuppy corporate version of business-casual to wear anything else.

Crossing his legs, he introduced himself, admitted to his alcoholism, and then explained how the commute from Beverly Hills left him stuck in infuriating traffic. That he was still sober was an "effing miracle." The executive who hated to use swear words had been attending Sanctuary Baptist as long as Nazario and for similar reasons.

"Where I live, it's all money and posturing," he continued, steepling his fingers. "People are more real here, which is why this is my home group. Real life. Real people with this real disease. The constant obsession for a drink. To numb it all away. Thanks for letting me share."

Yes, Nazario agreed. *Numb it all away.*

The nervous, youngest attendee shared next. After his intro, he said, "Thirty-two days off *lean*." He blinked at Nazario. His nervous tick became more rapid as he reminded the group what *lean* was. "Lean's—uh—cough syrup with codeine."

Everyone turned to Nazario like she was going to arrest him for once possessing the illegal substance also known as 'purple drank,' 'syrup,' and 'sizzurp.' Developed in the 1960s in Houston, it was now widely used mostly by youth and in the hip-hop scene. In all her years working for the LAPD, she'd only heard of one major bust for the sweet, purplish drink.

The kid needed to relax. Nazario exhaled, folding her arms across her chest. She couldn't arrest someone for an illegal substance they no longer had in their possession. Even if he had a stash, she'd look the other way.

She was a homicide detective with a dead, unidentified immigrant on her hands. Everything else seemed elementary in comparison, not worth the pursuit, and endless paperwork and resources, especially in a group where anonymity and trust were paramount. Badge or not, there was a code she abided by: keep her mouth shut when need be.

She got it, though. When it came to cops, everyone got paranoid...*everyone*.

"I'm pissed about a few things." His blinks were so rapid they were dizzying. "Like, ever since I got tested, and the results came back with fatty liver disease, my mom flipped, nagging me about how I'm twenty and I need a job."

He scratched at his shoulder like a dog with fleas and continued, "So, I go on a job interview at that Best Buy down the street, and the dude was looking at me all funny 'cause I get nervous, you know, and I blink a lot. God, that interview was so *humiliating*. I've had these nervous tics all my life, you know, like, I can't control it."

The kid buried his head in his hands and rocked back and forth.

The group waited out a patient beat before Vivi, a memorable in-your-face brunette, took her turn. She was newer to the group and the most suspicious of Nazario, who had made her name stick in her head like super glue.

"Not to crosstalk, but better your liver than mine. I can't do that nasty-ass purple drunk...drank, whatever you call that shit. I'm all about vodka and cocaine, baby," Vivi said. "I'm definitely pissed."

Blow and Stoli. A signature mix that aged her fast. The beauty was dulled now, but Nazario could see what it used to be. Gaunt and tall, she ran her hand through greasy chestnut hair.

Nazario, as well as the others, waited in non-judgmental silence.

Vivi folded and unfolded her spaghetti arms.

"You know what, I don't feel comfortable spilling my shit in front of a damn cop."

Chairs screeched as bodies fidgeted in knowing adjustment.

No one but the nervous kid made eye contact with Nazario.

The group leader addressed everyone, explaining, "There is no crosstalk in our groups, but as lead, let me remind everyone that Detective Nazario is welcome here, whether she works at McDonald's or for the LAPD. We leave our professions at the door. And by the way, she's not the first cop to attend AA. We all have one big thing in common: our disease."

Vivi exhaled loudly.

"Fine. I got into an argument with my boyfriend in front of my five-year-old daughter. Nosy neighbor called Child Protective Services, and now Caylee's in a group home or one of them foster homes. My baby. She's gone over some stupid ass argument. Hell, I can't even remember what it was about. They're calling it 'child endangerment' or some shit. Now I've gotta get a lawyer I can't afford."

Breaking the crosstalk AA rules, Nazario raised her hand.

"Lemme try and help. I need your full name, daughter's name, and the case number if you got it."

Vivi glared at her wide-eyed, mouth open.

"You...you seriously gonna help?" she asked. "Caylee's all I got."

The woman scurried to take a pen from her purse, jotted down the necessary information, and then handed it over to Nazario.

"Are you willing to take anger management and parenting classes for a full calendar year? That's what'll take, and it won't be easy. CPS's looking to bust you. Once you're in their system and on their radar, forget about it. Gotta prior, right?" Nazario asked, then clarified, "Previous record?"

"I know whatcha meant!" She scrunched up her face, insulted. Some of the attendees nodded. Most folks involved in the criminal system knew what a prior was, but Nazario wanted to be sure. "DUI and an assault charge," Vivi said.

"Where do you live?"

"Torrance. They're crazy strict," she said, seething. "Don't get in trouble in the South Bay; the cops got nothing better to do out there, and the courts are the worst."

The weight of the long night heaved itself onto Nazario's body.

Despite being in a meeting, she was tired and craving a drink.

"Make some calls, try to reduce it to a lesser charge," Nazario told the mother. "But you gotta keep under the radar. I won't be able to do this again."

"Can't even thank you right." Vivi buried her face in her hands, sobbing.

The quietest member, a sixty-year-old retired prison guard who always carried tissues for the "criers," handed the mother a few from her stash. The meek prison guard tucked her long brown legs against her chest and let her ankle-length turquoise sundress cascade to the ground as she began her share. She had stage three liver failure and was hanging on with the help of medication.

"I might be dying, and I can't cry. Got the tissues in case I do—in case it hits me one day. I've spent thirty years working in prisons with the hardest criminals you can imagine. Murderers, rapists, drug dealers, pedophiles, white-collar. Everything." A moment passed, and then she repeated herself. "Might be dying, and I should be crying, should be angry, but nothing comes out."

The prison guard looked up to meet Nazario's eyes, and in that moment, they connected beyond their addiction. Anyone working in any degree of law enforcement could empathize.

"At least I'm not drinking. At least I'm here. That's all I got," the former guard said softly. "Thanks for listening, and I'm very grateful for this group. I really am."

Nazario was left. She didn't have to share. Still, the group waited. So did the memories.

After a beat, Nazario began, "Anger..." The word stalled in her throat.

For a brief moment, she was standing again before the body under The Serpent's Bridge. Her mind transported away from the AA meeting at the rustic church and back to the scene she couldn't escape. There was a lingering superstition in the streets about that creepy bridge, like something bad would happen to you if you crossed under it. That eerie fantastical lore intensified beyond mere rumor and was made all the more real now with someone dead—again.

The unknown deceased was staring, wide-eyed in horror, brown eyes dark, fixed dilated pupils, the mark of death. Then Nazario noticed with more clarity, as if her mind exposed more detail—bit by bit. The man's palms were up and spread horizontal, which was unique. The arms had been maneuvered, positioned.

Nazario recalled the thick, calloused palms that told more about where the man had been and how he lived his life. The fog obscured the body of a lone man dead beneath a bridge like her dad had been, the corpse sharing that same olive skin and dark hair. Daddy had been murdered under a freeway underpass, leaving her and Mama behind.

Did this man have a family?

Did he have a child or a wife?

Who would he be leaving behind?

Would the department even care?

Unidentified, would his life matter?

In her mind's eye, the sooty fog thickened until she could no longer see where she was going; her pulse sprinted. The body was consumed by a blanket of condensation.

She could see the thick, ebony head of hair. Daddy had beautiful hair most men would kill for. He had a groomed beard that scratched her face when he nuzzled and kissed her cheeks. She'd caught those tired, hazel eyes, pooled with pride when she was five and won her first Taekwondo tournament. Searching the bleachers, her eyes didn't have to scan far. Daddy was there, waving with a beaming smile spread unabashedly across his face.

"This is one win of many to come, *mija*. I am so very proud of you." Nazario remembered Daddy hugging her tight against him. His beard tickled her face as she jumped into his open arms, a protective space that no one could penetrate. She felt safe lying against the thick bullet-proof vest he wore under his shirt. He never took it off until he went undercover.

"He was undercover, deep in, and he was alone." She'd never forget Johnson's voice cracking with guilt before he broke down in tears and said, "I'm...I'm so sorry."

While her would-be-boss shed tears, Nazario had been more like the retired prison guard—unable to cry. She stiffened her spine, draped her arms around her inconsolable mother, and stared into the void, vowing to find the killer, vowing to take back what was ripped from her soul. She recalled being totally zoned out, fueled by the kind of rage that craved revenge.

She continued fighting and had always figured she'd find the bastards and cry later.

Taking down the Connor Morris types was now a small victory—temporary anesthesia.

"You good, Detective?" the group leader's voice broke through the haze of memories. She dragged air into her lungs, her mind snapping back to the present. She was no longer under The Serpent's Bridge, no longer facing a dead body.

"Sorry," Nazario shut her eyes for a moment, rubbing her temples, feeling the sweat form on the palms of her hands.

Oh, Daddy, I miss you so much.

Her share came out soft and low.

"I'm very angry," Nazario's voice broke like it hadn't before. "Haven't talked to my mom since my father died. Dunno why—just never got close relationship to her. She begged me not to become a cop. I wasn't the daughter she always wanted. Too tomboy for her, too rough around the edges...like her husband." Nazario adjusted her crutch, looking absently at her shoes. "His senseless death makes me angry. But no one cares about...you know what," she blinked moisture from her eyes and swallowed the knot in her throat, "forget it."

A dead cop, she thought.

It was the price that came with the badge and the hollow reality she lived with daily.

An old-fashioned clock chimed on the wall, returning her focus. Feeling vulnerable and worn, Nazario got up, put her weight on her left leg, and grabbed her crutch under the chair.

She made wide strides out the door, working in unison with her crutch, which suddenly operated as if it had always been a part of her. In the hallway, she heard the group finish with the Serenity Prayer and thought about how much she hated it.

Serenity was bullshit. Impossible.

Nazario hobbled down the darkened corridor. At the far end, a large barnwood cross with three steel nails in the center hung there. It had seen a hundred years of sinners, rumored to be older than the church. Outside, she hurried to her car. Usually, there was visibility near a building, light coming from somewhere. But at Sanctuary Baptist, there were buildings and trees blocking light. She could hear the AA members noisily shuffling out of the church behind her as she retrieved her iPhone from her rear jeans pocket and turned on flashlight mode. Cursing under her breath as she made her way through the parking lot, she wondered why there were no streetlights.

The ancient church needed more than a few upgrades.

Nazario fumbled for her keys, accidentally dropping her phone in the process. The light shut off, and she was alone in the pitch black. Nazario had never been afraid of the dark, not even as a child. But the old place of worship loomed in the twilight, filling her with a foreign nervous fear as a sense of foreboding washed over her.

Car keys rattled in her hands. She gripped them until they dug into her palms.

As if on cue, a car engine roared to life, the taillight dispelling the darkness. Cursing under her breath, Nazario reached for her phone and unlocked her car as the driver threw it into reverse. Screeching brakes cut the dark silence, followed by a *thump*.

"Oh my God!" someone shrieked as another attendee shone their phone behind what Nazario thought was the kid's truck. A body sprawled across the pavement. She was not supposed to apply any weight to her right leg, but Nazario limped toward the scene as fast as she could, ignoring the pain pulsing through her injured knee.

Nazario stumbled against a mangled bike frame, but it was the limp body of a boy that forced her breath to sprint as fresh panic filled her body with adrenaline. He must have been flung at least five feet from the impact.

"Call 9-1-1!" Nazario screamed, keeping her right leg straight and to the side. She squatted, kneeling with her left on the gravel, unable to bend her right knee. She checked and found neither pulse nor breath.

The kid got out of his vehicle, rattled. He began to repeat, "I didn't see him, I didn't see him, I didn't see him."

"I've called 9-1-1. They're on their way," the former Canon executive cried.

Nazario began administering CPR. Her hands trembled as they pumped the boy's chest.

"C'mon, c'mon..." She paused to breathe into the boy's mouth before continuing to pump his chest, alternating between the two techniques.

"*Nicky...Nicolas*," A large man screamed, rushing toward the boy.

"Grab him!" Nazario ordered, looking up briefly, sweat trickling from her forehead and down her neck. Biceps and triceps burned with every chest compression. Nazario glanced down at her watch. Five minutes had flown by. The group leader went to the hysterical man who looked to be Nicky's guardian. She'd seen the two of them at the church.

"I'm an immigration customs enforcement officer," Nicky's guardian shouted, "and I'm his guardian."

"Well, she's a cop, so it's best to give her room to work and stay back," the group leader said, but the struggling man was so strong that it took several AA members to hold him.

Shocked voices turned mute as the world around turned black.

Nazario's vision tunneled with determination.

It was just her and Nicky.

She didn't know how long it had been, but as the minutes ticked away, sweat crawled down her forehead, sticking her shirt to her chest. Nazario's arms burned, and her left knee throbbed from the bite of gravel digging into her flesh. She finally glanced at her watch and was stunned that it had already been more than forty minutes. Her freshly sutured knee protested—personal physical pain dissolved as the boy's blood collected on her fingers. Splatter from the open gash of his cracked skull sprinkled the front of Nicky's faded Batman t-shirt. Her vision blurred with tears.

Nazario pumped Nicky's chest, desperate to save him no matter how long it took.

"Please...please..." Nazario begged. "Goddamn it...breathe. Breathe."

Nazario clutched her fists tight, pounding compressions on his chest. But the boy was fading out of her grasp, and she knew it was too late.

Please, Daddy, please...not another innocent life, not another death.

She begged her father as if, somehow, he could help from the other side.

Nicky was at last gone; his life force extinguished before her eyes.

EIGHT
THE PASTOR'S WIFE

THE TALL BLONDE WORE AN A-LINE, honey-colored cotton dress that made her golden skin glow, and the dark brown belt around her waist accentuated her figure. The V-neck in the front dipped just enough to not overpower the simplicity of her look, the way her glossy nude nails matched her glossy lips.

Millie couldn't help but gasp at the mid-twenties woman wearing the perfect dress.

"Oh my, is that Prada?" Millie asked, fingering the pearls she wore with her one-piece grey pencil dress. *Not Prada*.

The young woman nodded quietly and stood at Millie's doorway, clutching her Prada skin-colored purse, which matched the dress, nails, lips—oh, and those opened-toed wedged shoes that were just darling!

"First time seeing you around here," Millie said, trying not to think about dress shopping, which had become a slight addiction. "Come on in, dear. Have a seat. Let's start with your name."

The woman seated herself in front of Millie's desk.

"Avery." She tucked a strand of hair behind her ear and bit her lower lip.

"No offense, but it looks like you could afford a fancy psychologist in Beverly Hills. What brings you in, honey?"

"I can't stay long," Avery said. "I saw that...that Detective Anaya Nazario sees you?"

"Did she recommend me?"

"No, I...saw her leave here the other day. I've been...I've been trying to talk to her. But she's always busy."

Avery wrung her hands nervously together—something Nazario did, too. Millie gave the young beauty the same yellow stress ball. Avery took it and thanked her quietly.

"Nazario's my client, but you know I can't involve myself in your private matters. I certainly can't disclose what she and I discuss. There's a confidentiality agreement I must adhere to." Millie hesitated before continuing, "I've gotta ask...have you been following the detective?"

Avery abruptly rose to her feet, her face flushed like a ripe plum.

"I'm sorry," she said, sitting the stress ball back on Millie's desk. She hugged her purse to her chest. "It was a mistake. I shouldn't have come."

"Hold on...um...Avery, right?" Millie stood. "Didn't mean to scare you off. Look, something is obviously on your mind. What does this have to do with Nazario?"

Avery dug into her purse and put on trendy oversized sunglasses.

The fashionista dithered for a beat before probing, "I've got a bit of a mystery I think I might've figured out, but I'm not sure what to do about it."

"I know Nazario's a detective. But I don't believe she's a PI for hire."

"It's nothing like that...what if," she paused and bit her lower lip, "what if I know something but I'm not sure...I dunno if I could prove it or share it, or what will happen if I say something?"

"We've all got secrets," Millie said, her mind drifting—unbidden—to Eric Myers, though she had no reason to think of him now. The kind of arms that looked strong, commanding, safe. "Secrets feel bigger than they are until they come to light. But all things eventually come into the light, and sometimes, no matter how bad it hurts, how scary—"

"What if it's big?" The girl's voice was shivering now. "What if it's really, r-really big?"

"Lugging it around is a much bigger burden." Millie's eyes misted. "But you'll be guided by your heart, and you'll know what to do with, well, with all of it. Whatever you're carrying around."

The woman pulled out her wallet and tried to pay, but Millie put her hand out in objection.

Avery paused for a beat, dropped her wallet into her purse, and nodded. "Thank you."

Millie watched her disappear out the door. She locked up the office and decided to check on the AA meeting. Her mind still in a fog, Avery's voice whispered to her. She wondered if she should contact Detective Nazario but decided if Avery had a secret, it had to be hers to share.

She turned down the long corridor to the meeting room and didn't hear the usual post-AA meeting chatter. The walls made their usual crackling sound as her high heels click-clacked down the dark hall.

Is that a siren? Where is everyone?

She grabbed her phone to shine the light in the hallway.

A text came in from Esperanza, *"Running late, be there soon."*

"Be safe," Millie responded, feeling bad now that she'd made her come all this way.

Millie, you should've offered to pick Esperanza up!

She scurried down the hall, vowing to get the electrician to fix the lights *again*. Ordinarily, the sounds of ambulances and police cars in the neighborhood were normal, but this time, they were closer, much closer. She lifted her phone into the void, letting it lead her down the lightless halls and outside, where she froze. Her phone dropped to the asphalt, like the bag of groceries she had in her arms the day Gideon had nearly drowned.

A boy was on the ground. It was Nicky. She knew it was him by that black hoodie he always wore and that bright green bike, its bent frame the only color in the night. Detective Nazario was heaving on his chest. Pools of sweat dripped off her forehead, down her glistening neck. Eric Myers broke from the AA members trying to hold him back. The detective moved over and allowed Eric to continue CPR, but it was no use. He cried out Nicky's name, scrambling to find a pulse.

The ambulance pulled up.

The EMTs ran toward the boy and shoved Nazario and Eric aside.

Millie's lips trembled, tears wetting her cheeks. "Gideon, oh...Gideon," she whispered to herself, seeing his wet hair, still in his little Superman swim trunks, his face blue from lack of oxygen. Her husband was to the side, drenched from head to toe, as the paramedics worked.

Pounding and breathing.

Pounding and breathing.

Pounding and breathing.

It went on for an eternity.

Even now, looking back, she could still feel her whole life crumbling, as if she knew deep down that nothing would be the same again. Eric's scream echoed her own all those years ago as he collapsed to his knees.

The EMTs grimly searched for a pulse.

Millie was that mother all over again, and all she could see was her son's face.

All she could see was Gideon.

NINE
THE WITNESS

BLUE and red lights from the police car illuminated the cold night. Just as an ambulance, with its sirens turned off, quietly passed by. How odd, Esperanza thought. Shouldn't their sirens be turned on? It was the silence that clenched her guts. She gripped her son's hand, her stomach twisting into knots.

A lone police car was parked in the dim church parking lot, amplifying the terror in her.

"*¡Ay, Dios mio!*" Dread filled her.

This wasn't good.

This was very bad.

Please, dear God, not someone else.

"Why's the ambulance leaving so soon? I bet one of them boozers had some sort of relapse," Alex said dryly.

"*¡Cállate!*" she scolded her son.

A woman stood hunched over her full-leg brace, eyes raw, voice trembling as she spoke with two uniformed police officers. The tall man beside them stood silent, grief twisting his face. She'd seen both of them. It was Eric Myers and that woman detective...what was her name?

"It's that cop chick, Nazario. Don't know her first name but that's what everyone at the church calls her," Alex said, "and that ICE guy who watched over Nicky. That's why he's here. It has to be. Nicky wanted to go biking."

Alex was right, it was Detective Nazario. She went to the AA meetings, and that Mr. Myers was the only gringo at every Sunday service.

"Alejandro, as I always say," Esperanza began with her typical lecture, "it's not our business."

Nazario, Myers, and two uniformed cops turned their heads toward an approaching white van. Esperanza squinted her eyes and read the black lettering on the back. A gasp escaped just as Alex's voice rose to a panic as he asked, "What's the coroner doing here?"

Headlights from the squad car dispelled the darkness at last. Eric began to cry as the coroner's van parked and two men exited. His baritone voice sounded animalistic and raw. It was an ugly cry that shattered the night with anguish and echoed through Esperanza's body. That lady detective talked briefly to one of the coroner personnel and then turned to Eric, saying something that looked like words of sympathy.

Looking defeated, Nazario clopped across the lightless parking lot and climbed into her vehicle. Esperanza doubted she should be driving around with a full leg brace on.

Esperanza saw the face as they zipped up the body bag. A shaky hand covered her mouth.

Esperanza rushed to cover Alex's eyes as she had under The Serpent's Bridge.

Too late. Alex broke away, sending his physics book crashing to the ground.

"*Alejandro,*" she yelled, picking up the thick book, helplessly following Alex as he ran, screaming his friend's name into the night.

"Alex," Esperanza called out again, "get away from there!"

Breathless, Esperanza trailed behind, jogging to catch up to her son.

"*NICKY,*" Alex cried, trying to shove his way next to Nicky, reaching out for the body bag. Uniformed cops put their arms out to stop him. Nazario poked her head out of her car window and watched Alex and the coroners as the child dissolved into tears the way any kid his age would, regardless of his IQ. And even from where Esperanza stood, Nazario's glassy eyes told of someone on the verge of her own breaking point.

The two staff members from the coroner's office climbed into their van, and the boy, little Nicky, was gone. The night was dead silent. No lights. No sirens. Just a police cruiser crawling behind the coroner's van, dark and deliberate. As it drove past, it filled her with foreboding.

She'd witnessed two deaths since that night at The Serpent's Bridge and couldn't help wondering: What if the dying had just begun?

TEN

THE DETECTIVE

DETECTIVE ANAYA NAZARIO limped into the bar without an ounce of hesitancy or remorse, glad to have at least found a jacket in her car that helped cover Nicky's bloodstains on her shirt and jeans. She slumped down onto the barstool.

She waved to the bartender. He leaned in and asked her what she wanted to drink.

"Red wine," she mumbled, "your house is okay and make it a long pour."

The bartender sifted through his wine supply, then turned to her with a bottle. "That bad of a day, eh?"

"You've got no idea."

"Ever try Vanwell Winery?" He nodded to the television above the bar. Some reporter was covering a charity event, mid-interview with the self-made millionairess of the winery. "California wine and one of the best."

Nazario hadn't met Madison Vanwell but was quite familiar with the Vanwell Zinfandel. In fact, Nazario had often stolen the bottles of donated wine from the LAPD charity storage unit that kept odds and ends like donated clothes, toys, and even alcohol that only a certain population would take. Alcoholics like Nazario could never let good wine go untasted, sitting around collecting dust.

She looked back up to the television screen to see Madison Vanwell. The vintner was seventy, though she appeared more like fifty, with shiny silver hair and skin so smooth it seemed airbrushed. While most dreaded aging, the wine entrepreneur made it look like the best stage in life, better than being young and stupid.

"My late husband William fell ill and passed away thirty years ago," Madison began, "but all throughout his life, he had a real passion for helping the needy. He regularly donated to food banks that would help impoverished areas. I am proud to continue his legacy by donating five hundred thousand dollars to the Los Angeles Regional Food Bank, which will be dispersing the funds to every local food bank in Los Angeles County."

"First time seeing Vanwell. She's gorgeous," Nazario said, "and generous."

"Isn't she, though?" the bartender agreed, turning the bottle so she could read the label. It was one of her favorite local wines.

"That the Vanwell Zin or the Cab?" Nazario asked the bartender as they watched the charity event crowd applaud the very generous Ms. Vanwell.

"Zin," the bartender said, sliding her a full glass. It had been three long months since she'd had a drink. Tonight, she caught a bad case of the "fuck-its" and had no intention of calling her sponsor quite yet.

Nazario kept her head low, thankful she was in a baseball cap. For a moment, she closed her eyes and was pounding on Nicky's chest again, exhaling into his mouth as his life slipped away.

She hunched over her drink, protecting it like her anonymity, staring into the glass, brooding over what had taken place just an hour ago. A young boy was dead, and she couldn't save him. The desperate sound of Nicky's friend running after the coroner's van. Eric Myers, crying like she'd never seen a man break. Too vivid. Too raw. It replayed in her head like a bad infomercial she couldn't seem to turn off. She took a generous gulp of her wine, returned it to the mahogany bar, and lost herself again in the red abyss staring back at her. The taste of zinfandel warmed her throat. The sweet and bitter juice of the fermented grapes swam through her vulnerable veins.

She should be home, icing her knee, doing anything but drinking.

Nazario pinched the bridge of her nose as the pounding migraine came on. Unable to stop seeing the little boy with the unzipped black hoodie and bloodied Batman shirt underneath. Unable to shut out that man's animal-like wail. It wrenched her gut. Her fingers curled around the wine glass, freshly dried blood still under her nails.

Why had she been there to witness such a senseless, freak accident?

Why did it have to be a little boy?

All she wanted was to escape the pain and have herself a bottle or two.

Daddy, the marrow of her life, even in death, would be disappointed in her, frustrated that she let a substance control her because he always believed in her, believed she had it in her to practice self-control. Nazario took another large drink, feeling the tepid liquid coat her throat, the pleasant buzz already working on an empty stomach. For a moment, she could see both bodies under The Serpent's Bridge: one of Nicky's smaller frame and the other merely a silhouette of a man. Yago Rios, with his dark-haired and rich, tanned olive skin like Daddy's, was swallowed up like a helpless rat in the relentless grip of a snake.

The local news switched from talk of donations to traffic complaints, droning from the TV mounted above the bar. It temporarily kept her company in the same way the wine paralyzed the disquiet that rumbled inside her. Neither Nicky Sanchez nor Yago Rios' deaths would make it on air. If it were someone famous or perhaps someone other than a person of color, it would've hit the news within minutes of the incident occurring. She'd seen it before, hundreds of times.

"There was a protest in downtown LA over new state legislation limiting qualified vehicles for the California clean-air decals," the reporter droned. "Qualifications target income levels as well. Some commuters that rely on the carpool lane are furious that they'll now be stuck in traffic."

The carpool lane was more important than a couple of dead Mexicans—welcome to Los Angeles. The warm buzz of wine enticed her. Her phone pinged from one of her social apps. She rarely used any of them and had been ignoring an alert. It was Gus. Her rainbow-framed profile picture showed the top of her smooth, bald head.

Caption: *At least I don't have to worry about frizz.*

Gus had always complained that genetics and humidity were mortal enemies of her gorgeous curls. Nazario smiled at Gus, who never took herself too seriously. There were old photos of her shoulder-length auburn tight curls, like loose wires going every which way. An aged picture of them in grad school, Nazario in the middle, Gus kissing her cheek on one side, Blake Huxley on the other.

Gus just tagged both Huxley and Nazario; the time stamp was yesterday.

C'mon Gus, what're you up to?

Did Gus tag her to get her to look at Huxley's profile? Make her remember the man that "you let get away," as Gus put it.

She had forgotten about this picture. It was the latest

activity on her best friend's page as a "memory" dating twelve years ago. Wow, time had flown by. Gus and Nazario were different in many ways. Gus was the long-term commitment type—Nazario, just the opposite. She still wondered why Gus and her girlfriend of many years broke up. They were the perfect couple. But there were some things that Gus preferred not to discuss, which Nazario respected. In fact, the two rarely chatted about their dating lives.

Curious, Nazario tapped Huxley's tagged name and waited until his profile populated on her phone. The wireless connection was spotty at the bar, but the wine dissolved inhibitions. Without fail, every time she got drunk, she'd self-destruct and enjoy torturing herself. Fucking Zuckerberg had sabotaged the healing process for all future breakups and divorces around the world.

What're you doing, Nazario? Number one rule: stay off your ex's social!

She should have listened to her inner voice but didn't.

Blake Huxley's profile was of him kissing his wife on the lips.

She swiped through his pictures, quickly skipping the ones she'd already seen. A recent picture of him now juxtaposed with a photo of the Huxley she knew. He'd aged well. In grad school, he'd sported hair just past his shoulders. It worked well with his surfing and pot-smoking persona. But it was that gregarious smile slicked across his mischievous lips that never changed. She ran her fingers over today's Huxley, who stood shirtless next to his surfboard.

Blake Huxley came from impressive genetics and made building muscle mass appear elementary. The Huxley men were big boys. She recalled the surprise "meet my family" lunch. While his mother was tall, slender, and looked like a swan, his father and two brothers had physiques similar to

Blake's, as if they lived in the gym. But the truth was, while he'd always been athletic and disciplined, staying fit didn't take much effort. Huxley stretched out to six feet, four inches.

Her lips trembled. She gulped more wine.

His arms once held her, and it was as though nothing could harm her. She'd felt at peace for once since her father had passed. And the way he'd touch her face, like her hard exterior, was a mask. Did he touch his wife the same way? Kiss her as deeply?

Did he...she stopped herself.

Jesus, Nazario, stop it!

After so many years, she should've moved on, let him go. On some of her worst days, like this one, she reflected, her mind returned to him. She should've forgiven herself for walking away, for screwing it all up like she always did. There were hundreds of pictures of Huxley and his little wifey. She had to be a travel agent or some shit because the two had seemingly vacationed in every country around the world.

Cursing Zuckerberg again, Nazario logged off and waved the bartender down. Lifting her empty glass, he nodded. "Another, please," she directed, "long pour. Fill it to the top."

He grabbed a bottle in response. "Still the Vanwell Zin?"

"Sure."

The bartender poured an even fuller glass. She'd have to tip him well.

She took a sip. The tangy warmth soothed her throat.

A distracting woman laughing a little too hard a couple of barstools away—snatched her attention. Although sitting, she was taller than Nazario's five feet, eight inches. The fair-haired gazelle must be six feet or more. A model? Nazario had wished on occasion that she'd received her mom's golden hair and blue eyes, but she'd taken after Daddy's brown eyes, dark wavy hair, and olive skin.

Nazario watched the woman from under the brim of her baseball cap. Pink nails matched her strapless, form-fitting cocktail dress that was short enough to expose long, moisturized legs. Her hand ran up her date's thigh. She tilted her head and kissed...*him*.

Nazario nearly dropped her wine.

His conservative haircut was the first thing she noticed. What used to be luscious chestnut surfer-beach waves that reached to his shoulders, locks he'd been known for through college and graduate school before entering the academy, were now tamed short of his collar. Despite his father being French, with dark hair and eyes, Blake Huxley took after his Scandinavian mother—chestnut hair, pale complexion, and ice-blue eyes, so lacking in pigmentation, they looked translucent.

His eyes shot open as if Huxley had sensed someone watching him.

Mouth still on his date, he seized Nazario with his gaze.

In grad school, he was just Blake, and she was just Anaya.

Now they were facing each other again after so many years.

Time stalled as color drained from his face.

Blake Huxley pulled away from the woman like his conscience had awoken.

Whoever the woman was, it wasn't Huxley's wife. If he was cheating, it was none of Nazario's business. Though, the federal agent looked like he'd seen a ghost. The muscles in his angular jaw twitched with the gritting of his teeth. His intense eyes pried open her soul, shooting a cool wave through her that made her shiver.

The woman stroked his face, shoulders, chest.

Nazario clenched her fists and tore her eyes away from him, underestimating the difficulty in seeing her past mistakes resurrected before her. Why did she pick a bar near the FBI headquarters? *Damn it.* Hardly breathing, she stared down at the wine glass. To leave, she'd have to pass them. Elbows on the bar, both hands clutched each side of her baseball cap.

It was too much of a coincidence that he was here.

Did she want to run into Blake Huxley?

Did she subconsciously choose this bar out of all bars?

She felt Huxley's eyes on her and couldn't get out of there fast enough.

The woman droned on, complaining about being denied the clean air decals after purchasing her new hybrid. At least she paid attention to the news, Nazario thought. The ache in her head could not withstand much more of the woman's torturous chatter. Nazario couldn't even relapse in peace.

Shut up already. Everyone in the bar can hear you. Jesus H. Christ.

Nazario ignored how her grumbles sounded like a jealous and overworked alcoholic detective. *I'm not jealous. Why would I be jealous? It was my idea to walk away.*

Nazario waved the bartender over. "Another top-off." Like it would fix anything.

The bartender filled the glass again, so full that she found herself noisily slurping until the level was safely below the rim, then said, "Fuck it." She grabbed the glass, kicked it back, and began guzzling the wine like she was playing a losing match of beer pong.

She flagged the bartender down yet again, who, on cue, about-faced with a freshly uncorked bottle of the Vanwell's award-winning red zinfandel and gave her another large refill like an ER nurse injecting morphine into the veins of a patient in severe physical agony. How many glasses had she had? Three long pours or the entire bottle? It hadn't been very long, but Nazario didn't need that much time. When it came to getting drunk, she was *the* reigning queen.

Many people weren't as good at denial and slamming down

drinks meant for sipping, but Nazario was pretty damn good at both. Huxley leaned against the bar with his hands folded before him. Was that so she could see he wasn't wearing his wedding ring? He feigned as though he'd been listening, nodding absently, but his eyes were fixed on her. He glanced at her wine glass and then scanned her face. The buzz was hitting her pretty good and dissolving filters, like the obvious misery she couldn't hide.

The heartache was mirrored in his eyes—a silent apology she hadn't asked for. The indisputable longing, coupled with years of history, was evident in his gaze, and she wondered if he could see it in hers. The one thing that perhaps they had left in common. The one thing that she'd been unable to numb no matter how blacked-out drunk she'd tried to get.

Regret.

Heavy regret sank her deeper and deeper into a sea of emotion she'd kept segregated from the rest of her life. Feelings had always come second to logic and reason. Nazario had mastered the art of cold detachment, like a weary doctor who'd become desensitized by decades of seeing the dying and the sick. With Huxley, it was as though he could nuke every thick, stubborn wall—dismantle her defenses, leaving her soft. Emotionally disarmed.

The bartender returned with her card and a pen.

She gave him a thirty percent tip, chugged the rest of her wine, and grabbed her crutch resting against the bar. Limping toward the exit, she refused to look anywhere but straight ahead, given that her buzz was nowhere near strong enough. In a couple of short steps, Nazario was right next to them, awkwardly blocked by one long leg hogging up the aisle, trapping her from moving forward.

"Excuse me," Nazario said, but the woman talked away. "I said, excuse me."

"Oh." She giggled. "Sorry."

Blondie whipped her hair back and turned to face her. She was young, Gen-Z, and the traditional blue-eyed stunner. Why wouldn't she be? She moved her leg, leaning closer to Huxley.

Nazario murmured, "Thanks."

Avoiding Huxley's burning gaze, she leaned against her crutch and limped steadily out the door. She could smell the rare Los Angeles rain drizzling outside as the night whipped at her face, the mist kissing her cheeks. She was shaking and not because of the weather.

"Anaya...hang on." Huxley strode toward her.

The rain dampened his shirt, making it cling to his barrel chest.

"Leave me be, so I can irresponsibly drive home," she said, "after I've drunk, who in the hell knows how much...a bottle?"

"I...wasn't stopping you for that. But I can get you an Uber—"

They stood for a moment, the rain falling on them.

Nazario broke the silence. Her words came out softer than expected. "She's gorgeous."

"It's not like that." He said, brushing damp hair away from his forehead.

"Don't think your wife would think that, but it's none of my business."

"Divorced six months ago...I've totally neglected my social accounts."

"Can start by updating your profile picture," she said. "Heard you came by the hospital."

"Wanted to see how you were." He reached out—placed a wet hand against her face. She flinched as if struck by fire. Eyes closed, steam curled off her wet flesh. Her body burned despite the cold.

She opened her eyes.

He leaned in even closer and whispered her first name.

"What're you doing, Huxley?"

She wanted to back away from him but was cornered against her car.

"Can we talk?"

"Isn't that what we've been doing for the last few minutes?"

"I mean a real talk. Later on? When you have time?"

"Later, as in after your date? Look, Huxley, there's *nothing* really to talk about. Don't ditch this one on my account. She likes you, I can tell, and other than her incessant blabbering, she's...she's almost perfect."

Rain drizzled off her baseball cap, keeping her face partly dry.

She continued, "I'm not gonna be the reason why your date goes south. I hadn't intended to run into you after all these years —total buzzkill. And I appreciate the hospital visit, but I'm fine. I'm a big girl."

"Wait a second..." Huxley's voice sounded urgent, his eyes both apologetic and worried—as if he'd waited all these years to finally speak to her again, only for the moment to be slipping away. "...don't go."

"It's rude to keep her waiting."

"Hang on...can I just talk to you? Gimme five minutes?"

"Please don't," she begged. He reached for her hand, but she batted it away. "In a single week, I've had my ACL and meniscus torn, knee surgery, a murder under The Serpent's Bridge, and about an hour ago, a boy got hit by a car."

Nazario pulled open her jacket.

Huxley absorbed the sight of her blood-soaked shirt with wide, concerned eyes.

"Nicky was his name...gave him CPR for over forty minutes. Died in my arms. Found out the kid's parents were murdered during a home robbery. He was a poor Mexican orphan no one cared about—now he's a dead Mexican orphan that no one cares about. And then you and your girlfriend top off my shitty night." She bit her lip until she drew blood, until the emotions that threatened to spill from her eyes returned to the vault buried somewhere inside. "This has gotta be one of the worst nights of my life, so if you don't mind, I'd like to stop by Trader Joe's before they close so that I can grab a bottle of cheap red and get properly drunk at home...*alone.*"

She drew away from him, dousing their heat.

"Can we *not* leave it like this?" Huxley asked.

Nazario pressed her lips into a thin smile. "Nice seeing you again, Special Agent Huxley...you look good."

She tossed her crutch in the back seat and drove off, leaving her past standing in the rain.

———

Feeling numb but not quite numb enough, she zipped up her jacket to cover her bloody shirt and found her favorite bottle of red Zinfandel five minutes before Trader Joe's closed. She limped, soaking wet, into her apartment, grabbed a wine glass from the kitchen, and slumped onto the couch. Nazario uncorked the zinfandel with the cheap opener conveniently on her keychain and poured herself a large glass.

She thought about the girls.

She promised to be there Saturday.

She thought about Gus.

Double mastectomy, and she wasn't there, buried in work as always.

Damn it. Alcoholic. Workaholic.

She stared down at her phone, hesitating over the number, afraid to call, afraid to ask for help. Nazario took another gulp of wine and made the call.

Gus answered on the first ring. "You're not okay, are you?"

"Gus..."

"Been drinking?" the captain asked, her voice competed with wind noise and the radio. It sounded like the captain was driving.

"I dunno if I should be alone right now," Nazario admitted to her best friend.

"Where are you, Nazario? Bar? Home? C'mon, gimme your location."

Her voice slurred. "Home."

"On my way."

It took Gus less than fifteen minutes to arrive, most likely due to hauling ass.

"Where'd you go for a drink, Detective?" Gus asked as she entered.

"How'd you get here so fast?" Then it hit Nazario. "He called you, didn't he?"

"People are worried about you," Gus clarified, "that's all."

"Only person Huxley should worry about is his damn self." She took a swig. "I don't need him trying to save me."

In quiet anger, Nazario looked down at the half-empty glass now in her clutched hands. Gus didn't dare pry it loose but took away the bottle from the middle of the coffee table instead and walked it to the kitchen sink.

"You went to that bar near FBI headquarters, didn't you?" Gus emptied what little was left down the drain and tossed the empty bottle in the trash. "Were you really expecting to not run into him?"

"Didn't expect his date." Nazario closed her eyes and pinched the bridge of her nose.

"Shouldn't have tagged you on Facebook." Gus walked back and slumped down on the couch next to Nazario. "This isn't about the special agent...okay, maybe *a little*."

Her skin began to turn hot as her pulse quickened, heart whamming viciously in her chest, and then the tightening began, that wretched squeeze that pressed against her lungs, collapsing the air. Her blood pressure rose as a panic attack took over, warring with buried emotions trying to dig their way out.

She forced back tears, turning sadness into rage.

"Don't give a damn if he's divorced or who he's banging now," Nazario said, throwing her wine glass against the wall.

Shards of glass and zinfandel sprayed across the room.

Gus didn't flinch.

"Sure, you don't," the captain scoffed and then pivoted, tone growing serious. "Look, I heard about the boy. We all did. Wilson's upset you didn't call him. Told me about that undocumented under The Serpent's Bridge, too. You should've been OFD, resting at home. You've had a rough week. Anybody would drink after the week you had."

"You're not the off-fucking-duty type— neither am I," Nazario defended.

"And just for the record, I took two weeks after my boobs got axed. You, on the other hand, just had major knee surgery. Your limp ass can't even walk. Woman, what the hell're you doing? You shouldn't have been at The Serpent's Bridge. Ain't that place bad luck? Wilson could've filled you in on the scene. Sounds like a leadless case, anyway. You should've gone straight home after the AA meeting," her best friend lectured, giving Nazario one of those stern looks of hers. "You shouldn't have been at a bar near the FBI headquarters where you knew Huxley would be. You should've been at home icing that knee. You keep this up, and you'll drive yourself to continue to drink."

"He was...he was a sweet little boy," Nazario's trembling hands wrapped around the back of her head, words staccato. "I...couldn't...I couldn't get him to breathe. He wouldn't breathe, Gus. He wouldn't breathe."

Gus put a firm hand on her face; Nazario met those unyielding amber eyes.

"Think you can breathe life into the dead? Got news for you, Detective, you're not God," Gus pointed out directly. "Boy was hit too hard. Nothing in the goddamn world you could've done to save his life."

"I tried..." The words quivered out. "I tried..." she repeated.

Gus, "Guns," as some of her peers had called her, wrapped her muscular tattoo-sleeved arms around Nazario. Her infamous tats helped her blend with the gangs when she was deep undercover.

"You damn right. You tried. I know you did." She stroked the back of Nazario's hair and rocked her gently. "Go on and cry, Detective. I got nothing but shoulders now."

Nazario could feel the flat surface of Gus's breastless chest and a knot wedged in her throat. She hugged her dear friend, who was jesting about her battle with breast cancer at a time like this. Leave it to Gus. Nazario squeezed her tight, wishing she could be half as strong in spirit, and let out a sob that cracked her wide open, one that she'd been holding in for decades.

The tears came rushing out.

ELEVEN
THE PASTOR'S WIFE

MILLIE COLLECTED herself before the congregation, wearing a black blouse and matching loose ankle-length maxi skirt. She clenched her fingers around a travel-sized tissue baggie, taking in a shaky breath.

"We're grieving a deep loss. Nicolas Sanchez was struck by a vehicle three days ago in our parking lot after the AA meeting. It was an unfortunate and tra...tragic accident." She paused, unable to continue.

Stan put a hand on her shoulder and stepped forward.

"Eric Myers, you wanted to come up and say a few words?"

The congregation murmured as Eric eased up from his seat in the last pew at the very back. He lumbered forward, making his way toward them, his large shoulders slumped. Something about his swagger, coupled with a raw, gaping wound of grief palpable in his demeanor, caused more than a rise of pity inside her. Every night since Nicky had passed, Millie had struggled to fall asleep. Eric's guttural scream as Nicky lay dying stayed with her.

Eric adjusted the microphone for his height.

Bodies continued to shift uneasily among the congregation, most of whom were undocumented.

They'd received multiple complaints and had lost plenty of members due to Eric's attendance at the church. Millie admitted that his presence had been a liability and that even she wanted him gone. But seeing him with Nicky, that fatherly tenderness at the rally touched her soul. The boy clung to him the way Gideon used to cling to her. Some women went through stages where they had difficulty bonding. Millie was thankful never to have issues like that. Stan, on the other hand, refused to pick their son up or touch him.

The moment Gideon was born, something changed in her husband, and it changed her too. She discovered a love she hadn't known existed, which made her longing for her estranged son even more pronounced now. It made her grieve with Eric Myers like she, too, had lost her son, in many ways for good.

The mother in her even now worried over each member, as she'd memorized them all by name. She looked around, noting each face. Yago Rios' seat was vacant. He was always early and never missed a Sunday. She'd ask around and see if anyone had seen him. Did Yago quit because of Eric, too?

Eric's bass voice boomed into the mic, causing her to jump back into the present moment.

"I had the privilege of looking after Nicky when he lost his parents. His extended family in Mexico are still recovering from the loss of his parents, and now...they're devastated over the loss of their only grandson." Eric gripped the podium. "If you can donate anything...Pastor Goodwin has agreed that today's offering will go to their family. I'll be paying for the funeral."

"So, you took care of one Mexican boy—a U.S. citizen, of course—while you deport the people who really need help," a member shouted. "You're just another white face pretending to save the brown man!"

"*¡Vete!*" screamed out another member as he got up to leave. "If you don't, I will."

"C'mon now, let's settle on down." Stan took over the mic, but some of the members were too upset. A few got up to leave, including Yago Rios' employer, Isabelle Jimenez.

Millie turned to Stan and said, "You're gonna need to take over."

She jogged off the stage, Stan's voice trailed behind her.

"It's a tough time for us all. We're called to love without judgment. Now, we'll be adding porch lights in the entryway until we can get a permit to install a proper streetlight in the parking lot," Stan began, tone gentle. "We pray that peace is with Nicolas, and I pray for his family during this horrible tragedy. The donation basket is going around if anyone would like to donate to Nicolas and his family in Mexico."

Some of the remaining members wept as the basket went around. Millie snuck out the back door just as Eric made a beeline to the bathroom. She moved faster down the hall as tears came speeding out. Her makeup would be ruined! There was no way she was letting the members see her crumple.

She was the pastoral counselor and had to display control over her emotions.

Above all else, Millie was a mother, a mother who missed her son, one who would no longer talk to her.

Millie could never forget all of their arguments. One particular time, Stan had gone on a rant about their son, how Gideon was now in Jesus' hands, and as parents, they'd tried everything humanly possible to help him.

"We have to let him go, Millie Ann. It's no use trying to force our will upon him. He has to come around on his own. It serves us no purpose discussing this again and again," Stan always lectured. "I've prayed about this. Love Gideon by praying for him. We can do no more—otherwise, we're nothing but enablers. It's not that I don't wanna talk about it. It's that we've talked about this to death. Let. It. Go, Millie Ann. Pray for him and let him go—*please.*"

Millie dabbed her face with a tissue, just as a voice returned her to the present. "Mrs. Goodwin...Mrs. Goodwin?"

She straightened her back and prayed her mascara wasn't smeared. Millie swirled around to address the woman, calling for her attention.

"Yes?" Millie presented a forced smile. It was Isabelle Jimenez in her bright yellow dress. Her Bible poked out of the oversized purse hanging on her forearm. "How can I help you, Isabelle? I hope you're not upset about Eric Myers. He's grieving over Nicky's loss—"

"I didn't leave early because of him, not that I care for him," Isabelle said, striding toward her with urgency. "It's about Yago. You seen him around?"

Isabelle was a first-generation Mexican-American born and raised in California by immigrant parents. The Jimenez family were hard workers and owned a trendy, authentic Mexican restaurant called Jimenez Mexican Grill. It was located in central Los Angeles. People from all over the city came there to eat. Millie hadn't eaten there because she didn't want to disappoint Stan by breaking their meal schedule, but trusted the good reviews. Isabelle employed immigrants when she could and took them in as Sanctuary Baptist had.

"He's always on time, never late for work." Isabelle clutched her car keys. "Never once called in sick. The last time I saw him was last Friday. I'm worried, Mrs. Goodwin."

Millie's stomach turned as she bit her lower lip. "Does he have any family here?"

"I don't think so." Isabelle sighed, shaking her head. "I think he was staying somewhere in South Central."

"Do you think they found him?" Millie whispered, leaning in. "Got him deported?"

"Los Angeles is supposed to be a sanctuary city. No?" Isabelle shrugged, though a look of concern flickered in her weary eyes.

"Oh, sanctuary city or not," Millie hissed, "it doesn't matter."

Thick-soled boots pounded aged wood, calling attention to the owner.

Isabelle moved closer and, under her breath, whispered, "Here comes the Devil himself."

The restaurant owner diverted her eyes from the ICE agent, changing the subject.

"Thank you, Mrs. Goodwin. I'd love to come to the women's morning Bible study. Wednesday, yes?"

Millie played along. "That's correct. It'll be a bit early, seven in the morning."

Leaning in for a hug, Isabelle whispered in Millie's ear, "I'll call if I see him."

Isabelle left just as Eric stalked past Millie.

He was dressed in his usual flannel button-up with the sleeves rolled to his elbows. He seemed at least six feet, or taller, in those lousy boots. He looked like a lumberjack ready to wield an ax. Millie ogled the man's large, chafed hands, ones meant for shooting. Eric Myers probably went to the shooting range instead of the movies for recreation.

"Eric...hang on..." Millie called out, rushing through the front door behind him.

He stalked to his red truck, a Toyota Tacoma, and slammed the door. She went to open the passenger side, but he locked it. Millie pounded. "Eric, open up, please. I just wanna talk to you."

He reversed out of the parking lot and was gone.

She stood there astonished at the profound sense of disappointment she was left with.

"I can't let him leave like that," Millie told herself, not realizing someone had overheard.

Isabelle revved her engine, leaned out of her car, and said, "He stays at the Casa Bella Inn in Huntington Park Sundays through Wednesdays—for work, I believe. Closer to the immigration and customs federal building in downtown LA. My girlfriend works at Casa Bella. Cleans his room. He told her he lives on a farm in Ojai—too far for commuting. He's Room 326. That's what she calls him. She doesn't do names."

Millie was now confused. Had she heard Isabelle correctly? "Doesn't use names?"

"I know, it's a little strange. She's undocumented, too. Real pretty," Isabelle clarified. "She's been harassed by men—*not by Eric Myers*—but by gringos like him, so she refuses to call them by their names. You know I can't get away with such practices at my restaurant. We make our living, get more tips when we memorize their names. It makes them feel special. Returning customers aren't just a number at Jimenez Mexican Grill," Isabelle reversed her car further and, before she drove off, said, "they're *mi familia*."

Her conviction and culture left Millie in awe of the Mexican restaurant owner.

Driven by an internal need to reach out to Eric and right this wrong, she jogged back inside the church. Millie grabbed her keys and purse from her office and told Stan she was going to visit a member, which wasn't a total lie. She typed Casa Bella's address in her car's GPS and arrived at Huntington Park in twenty minutes.

She gathered her courage, looked in the rearview mirror, and told herself, "You can do this, Millie. Eric Myers needs to know not everyone in the congregation is out to get him."

Eric wasn't her favorite member. On many occasions, she'd argued with Stan, saying the ICE agent should be kicked out of the church. The change of opinion wasn't anything she expected of herself, but as a mother who watched her son almost die before her eyes, she related to Eric's loss. She related to Nicky's death in the deepest way, despite Eric Myers not being the boy's biological father.

She spotted the red Toyota Tacoma in the parking lot and climbed the stairs to the third floor until she found room 326. After a measured five-count, Millie straightened her spine, unnecessarily smoothed unseen wrinkles from her black skirt, and rapped lightly on the door.

"*Señora, por favor, no me molestes,*" Eric said. Millie understood that he was requesting to be left alone.

Instead of introducing herself right away, Millie found herself knocking louder.

"I said, not right now," his voice boomed as he opened the door. "*Luego.*"

Eric leaned against the doorframe. His large arm propped up above his head.

"What part of keeping the passenger door closed and driving off did you not understand, Mrs. Goodwin," he began rhetorically, "unless you'd like to keep me company?"

"Company?" she repeated dumbly.

His eyes raked her up and down. "I suggest you leave. 'Cause, honey, whatever broughtcha here, I can tell you right now, you're in over your head."

Insulted but determined to remain professional, she met his eyes. "Mr. Myers—"

"Call me Eric."

"And call me Millie."

"Well, *Millie*, I've had the kinda week that can drive a man to jump off the tallest bridge or slowly kill himself with a little booze and a whole lot of Vicodin," he admitted, "so pardon me, but I'm not up for house calls or in my case, a motel visit."

The soft fleshy areas under his eyes were shadowy from lack of sleep and pink.

"I'm here as pastoral counselor of Sanctuary Baptist." Millie braved her way past him.

"Well, come on in, why doncha?" He waved an arm after her.

Millie looked around. There was a king-sized bed with burgundy sheets, a tan sofa stained and worn, a small desk with one chair, a forty-inch television mounted on the wall, and a mini-fridge. She swooped her skirt under her rear and sat stiffly at the edge of the couch.

There was a box of what looked like items that belonged to Nicky. She picked up a twelve-ounce black and yellow stainless steel Batman thermos and pressed the yellow button at the top. The lid flipped open, and a built-in plastic straw popped out.

"He loved Batman," Eric said wistfully, as he sat on the chair that leaned against the computer desk with his laptop on it. Millie caught the screen saver. It was of Nicky and Eric in a selfie with their backs to the ocean.

Eric nodded toward his laptop and then said, "San Diego. He loved going to the San Diego Zoo. I got us an annual pass and an annual to Legoland, too. Sometimes, we'd stay at a hotel down there and then cross the border—visit his family at least once a month."

"I'd imagine it was easier to be personally escorted by an immigration and customs officer. Did you...find it a challenge to be accepted by Nicky's extended family?"

Eric nodded his head, and a light laugh followed. It was the first time she'd ever heard the serious man chuckle. The combination of his dimpled cheeks and light scars from acne in his youth offered an unexpected masculine appeal. He raked the stubble on his jaw with a brawny hand. She crossed her legs and fanned her face with a hand.

"Oh...you could say something like that," he said, laughter winding down. "Wasn't easy, but when his abuelo and abuela saw that I was making an effort to ensure they saw Nicky..."

"So, they appreciated the effort?"

"Nicky was an orphan." Eric gulped, then continued, "His happiness made what was left of his family in Mexico happy, too."

"Do you wanna talk about the accident?"

"Is this an official counseling session, Millie Ann?"

"Just Millie will do. Told Stan it wasn't necessary to list it on my office door, that it confuses people. Old fool. He calls me that, and, well, it drives me crazy."

"So, change the plaque and tell him to call you 'Just Millie.' Why've you been allowing your husband to call you something you hate unless deep down you hate yourself?" he countered, getting up from his chair.

Millie knew not to respond to that answer. Her years of professional pastoral counseling training taught her that she asked the questions. Rule number one: Never take the patient-reversal bait. Not that Eric was her patient.

Eric walked to the mini fridge, grabbed a couple of bottles of water, and returned to her. Her heart fluttered wildly. He handed her the water and sat down next to her on the couch. She placed the bottle on the coffee table and abruptly shot up to her feet.

"I've gotta use the restroom," she said.

"Of course," he replied with a hidden smirk. "Straight ahead to the left. It's a matchbox, but it works while I'm here during the week."

Indeed, the bathroom was a matchbox. Millie didn't have to pee; she found herself needing to remind herself to breathe. She checked her lipstick—of all things—pleased that she chose Covergirl Outlast. The blush-colored lipstick worked perfectly with her skin tone, and it was the only lipstick that did what it promised, lasting all day. She brushed strands away from her face, and then something caught her eyes. There were black gloves on the toilet lid and a black trench coat hanging on a hanger on the shower rod.

The outfit didn't look like something Eric would wear. She picked up the gloves and inspected them for a moment before returning them to their place. When she left the bathroom, a part of her hoped Eric had returned to his desk chair, but he was on the couch where she left him. If she chose the desk chair, it would be a silly move. She'd look weak and intimidated by the man everyone already despised and feared at church.

No, she thought. She wasn't about to move from her original spot. It would send the wrong message.

"Don't fancy you as the type to wear black leather gloves and a full-length trench coat."

"It's not every day that I have to bury a ten-year-old boy," he returned, making her blush.

"I'm sorry, I didn't mean—" She found herself getting personal and crossing professional boundaries. "My son Gideon's twenty-one now, and when he was about Nicky's age, he...there was a terrible accident where he almost drowned. He hasn't been the same ever since. It's not something Stan and I talk about."

"He may be a decent pastor, but I can't say I find him to be a good husband. I don't think he takes care of you. Not the way you want, and not talking about your son isn't gonna make him go away. He's still your child."

"Didn't come here for me." She pictured Gideon's baby shoes in her purse. "As a mother, Mr. Myers—*Eric*—I under-stand what you're going through. I wanted to let you know that you're not alone. If you ever need to talk, I'm offering my services. You can come by my office Monday through Friday. I have select hours on Saturdays, too."

She took out a business card and held it between her index and middle finger.

He took it, moved closer, and said, "You always pay church members a personal visit just to hand them your business card?"

She didn't move away, and he moved even closer. "I was just...I was just concerned."

Eric put a hand on the back of the couch, leaned in, and captured her mouth with his. It took her completely by surprise, freezing her body. His tongue glided into her mouth with gentle and yet urgent need. It was a lustful kiss and nothing she'd ever done before. Stan never kissed her this way. In fact, he'd never used his tongue...*anywhere.*

"I appreciate the visit, counselor," he said against her lips, then drew his mouth from hers, leaving her stunned and shaking. "I don't do office visits. Why doncha come by, and we can do a trade."

"Trade?" she said, the word wobbling out.

"Ask me anything," he said. "It'll do me some good to talk it out."

"And what will you offer in return...in this trade?" she asked.

"What you deserve," he said, running a hand up her leg, "to feel beautiful in every way."

She could feel the callouses on his large palm roughly scraping against her thighs through her black polyester skirt. Her mouth dropped open, and she grew wet for the first time since before she married Stan. It'd been decades since she felt like this, and she found herself unable to think or want anything else but more of this. Then Eric pulled his hand away and stood up.

"Better get going," he said, "wouldn't wanna worry Pastor Goodwin now, would we?"

Desire spread through Millie. A yearning for more overcame her. It took her a minute to yank herself off the couch, where she wished she lay naked. Her knees were ready to give out. She was married, she thought to herself. *Married*, she reminded herself again. Though, it didn't seem to matter—regret and shame didn't trouble her conscience.

"Thank you for telling me about Gideon and for coming by," Eric said. "I hope you'll consider my offer 'cause I'll tell you one thing: if you think I'm fixing to apologize for kissing you, you got another thing coming."

Instead of reprimanding him for his actions, she took her car keys from her purse, straightened her spine, and lifted her chin. "There's nothing to apologize for," she said—because it didn't feel wrong. "My cell number is right on my business card."

He opened the motel room's door, and she left despite wanting to stay.

In the car, she prayed. The next call—let it be Eric.

TWELVE

THE WITNESS

"IT'S NOT EVEN on the news," Alex complained. "I Googled Nicky and that man...it's like it never even happened!"

Fatigue wore on Esperanza. Every bone begged for sleep that didn't come. Alex's words swam in a void. Every time her eyes closed, a dark figure gripped her throat, looming over her as a thick web of fog coated the night. Her hands tried to reach for the fingers, squeezing against the pulse in her neck.

She woke up gasping, drenched in sweat, reaching for her throat. It felt real.

Anxious, she looked to the left, to the right. Alex was done with the physics book. He was now reading *The End of the Third Age*. Eric Myers gave Alex the *Lord of the Rings* series after Nicky's funeral. If it hadn't been for the death of one of his closest friends, Alex would be reading a biology or chemistry book instead. Over the weekend, he'd already finished reading all three of the Tolkien collection.

His teacher told her at a parent-teacher conference, "Alex is incredibly gifted. It takes him twenty seconds to read a page. That's not a twelve-year-old reading level. That's not even *adult* level. The average adult reads a page in two minutes."

Esperanza didn't need to be told this. She knew Alex was different from most children his age. Alex acted as though his speed reading and aptitude at comprehending just about any subject—faster than kids twice his age—was perfectly normal. He turned a page of his book as she surveyed her surroundings. They were on the LA Metro Blue Line heading toward Compton. The bus jostled, as the amalgamation of stuffy body odor and plastic hung in the stale, congested air.

"Did you hear what I said?" Alex's voice pierced her thoughts.

"What did you say?" She straightened against the unforgiving seat.

Alex sighed, "I said I Googled Nicky, and that man—"

"Yago Rios," Esperanza reminded her son.

"Yeah, Nicky and Yago, and they don't show up. No one reported it. It's not on the news, not even on the local stations."

Esperanza took a deep, shaky breath. She'd have preferred to talk about anything else.

"I don't know, Alex. Maybe they haven't had the time?"

"Been plenty of time," Alex crossed his arms. "They just don't wanna talk about it."

Esperanza didn't have an answer. Silent, she watched as the abandoned businesses, run-down homes, and graffiti-stained walls raced past her bus window. A Big O Tires stood vacant now, its letters removed from the side of the building. Only the outline of the name was visible, as if hope could return one day.

There was the Dollar Store she frequented for low-quality produce.

She got what she could pay for.

She got what she could afford.

East Los Angeles ghettos were depressing with their run-down, decaying businesses and unrenovated, broken-down urban streets. But she'd still rather live and raise Alex in the

United States than Mexico. She watched her son turn pages. He'd started the book when they got on the bus just an hour ago and was already nearly finished.

Esperanza would do *anything* to make sure her son had a better life.

The LA Metro Blue Line pulled up at their stop. The walk to Sanctuary Baptist made her uneasy, reliving the memory of the coroner van pulling up at the church. The night Nicky died changed how she felt about the house of worship, tainted it in an ominous way.

"I miss Nicky." Alex enfolded the J.R.R. Tolkien book to his chest. Esperanza hugged him to her and kissed the top of his head, whispering her reassurance as best as a frightened mother could. He might be intellectually advanced, a smart boy who occasionally gave her a little sass, but he was still only twelve, with twelve-year-old feelings and friends. He had wanted to go bike riding with Nicky that night. Esperanza knew she would've caved if the boys had begged her enough.

It could've been Alex who died in that parking lot. Was it pure luck or a mother's intuition that caused her to delay things and take a later bus? She was certain about one thing: she was glad her son wasn't the victim. Yes, she felt sorry that Nicky became an orphan and then died, but Esperanza would never in a million years want Alex to trade places with the dead boy, nor would she want to trade places with Nicky's dead parents.

———

"Esperanza, it's so wonderful to see you." Mrs. Goodwin smiled warmly as Esperanza stared in surprise.

The pastor's wife was humming and walking on air. There was a glow to her skin. Her hair was freshly cut into a fashionable bob complimented by impeccable makeup. She took a little extra time this morning, Esperanza thought. Her lipstick, normally a muted nude, was bright red today.

"Are those homemade tamales you've brought again?" Mrs. Goodwin asked.

"Yes," Esperanza said, eyeballing her Tupperware. "I always bring extra just in case."

"I think I'd like to try one. In fact, I'll buy them from you. We can trade." Mrs. Goodwin giggled, fanning her face. Her cheeks glowed rose-red, matching the shade of her lipstick.

"Trade?" Esperanza made sure she'd heard correctly. "You want tamales?"

"Yes, if you don't mind eating steak and potatoes, I'd love to try your tamales. I'll buy all of them from you."

Esperanza waved a hand. "No, you don't have to buy. I give them to you."

"I insist. I'm not taking no for an answer," Mrs. Goodwin said. She took out a hundred-dollar bill.

Mrs. Goodwin was never this generous.

Mrs. Goodwin had never tried her tamales.

Mrs. Goodwin had never worn red lipstick.

"Where's Mr. Goodwin? You feeling okay?"

"I'm feeling fantastic!" Mrs. Goodwin squeezed Esperanza's hands while flashing an exaggerated smile. "And I believe my husband can take care of himself. You know, he's a busy man. The Lord's work never ceases."

There was something very different about Mrs. Goodwin, Esperanza thought, as the pastor's wife thrust a Benjamin Franklin into Esperanza's hand.

Alex leaned in. "C'mon Mama, consider it a business deal where we win."

"It's not about the money," Esperanza scolded.

Alex wrangled the hundred-dollar bill out of Mrs. Goodwin's hands.

"Go for it, eat all the tamales you want, Mrs. Goodwin," Alex said, stashing the money in his mom's purse. Esperanza wanted to shove some sense into her son, but she was too distracted. In the nine years she'd worked here, Esperanza had never witnessed Mrs. Goodwin behave outside of her customary, rigid guidelines. Not to mention eating anything *not* on the scheduled menu.

She ignored Alex's jab to her ribs, code for, "Are you seeing what I'm seeing?"

Mrs. Goodwin opened the Tupperware plopped on the church's kitchen island and grabbed a tamale. The pastor's wife peeled the corn husk, lifted Esperanza's homemade tamale to her ruby-red lips, then took a healthy bite.

Millie Ann Goodwin closed her eyes in ecstasy as she chewed. The pastor's wife moaned her pleasure, gripping the kitchen island with her one freshly manicured hand, her red-painted nails gleaming. Esperanza knew her tamales were good, but she'd never seen anyone react to them like this.

Something was up with the pastor's wife.

Something inside her had changed.

THIRTEEN
THE DETECTIVE

RUNNING LATE, Nazario looked down at her watch as she entered the station the next morning, armed with an annoying hangover. Despite her pounding head, she'd managed to wake up early and keep her promise to the AA member. She'd made a few phone calls on the mother's behalf.

By seven-thirty that morning, Vivi joined Nazario and the social worker assigned to the case. They met outside the foster home, where the recovering alcoholic's five-year-old daughter was temporarily living. Nothing felt better than the sight of a sweet little curly-haired girl running toward her mom.

"Mama! Mama!" Caylee had screamed, bolting into her mother's arms. The elated woman scooped her daughter up in a fierce hug, looked at Nazario, and mouthed, "Thank you."

Clopping toward the Chief's office, Nazario smiled to herself, thinking about the happy family. Regardless of her good deed, the stupid crutch put her back in a foul mood. God, how she hated hobbling around.

Everything took twice as long.

Would you stop your whining? Nazario reprimanded

herself. *A busted leg isn't as bad as having your child taken from you and placed in CPS.*

Still in her head, Nazario framed the reunion—child and mother, whole again—as giving back to her community. Not paying attention, she walked past the men's bathroom and collided with a man who was hurriedly exiting. Nazario nearly dropped her crutch. Wobbling, she clutched hard against the tall man's neck, embarrassed as her full breasts pressed firmly against his chest.

"Sorry." Mortified, she glanced up. *Huxley.* His hand lingered at the small of her back.

"It's okay," he said in a husky tone. They hung in the moment, an arm still clutched around his neck.

"I didn't see you. I'm late for a meeting." She quickly dropped her arms. However, his grip remained firm, as if he was hesitant to release her. She took a step back, forcing his hands to unwind.

"I'm sorry that I called Gus," he confessed. "I was just worried. Wanted to make sure you got home safe. Hope you... had a better night?"

She decided not to reply to the fact that he'd called her sponsor, their mutual friend, to ensure she was okay and had someone with her. Had he counted how many glasses of wine she drank? Nazario tried to brush away the feeling of humiliation, but it commonly occurred post-relapse and didn't go away that easy either.

"I can't say I did." Nazario met his eyes again, keeping her expression as empty of emotion as possible. Attempting aloofness, she asked, "You? How'd the date go?"

"Oh, it didn't. I ended things early," Huxley said. "Plus, I had a morning meeting."

"Sorry to hear. She seemed to really like you," she said, shifting in place.

"Well, it wasn't mutual," he returned under his breath.

The kiss sure seemed mutual, Nazario thought, but said instead, "Sorry for...uh...for crashing into you." She gave him a lopsided grin and motioned to her crutch. "Still trying to learn how to use this thing."

"*Ça ne me dérangeait pas*," Huxley said in French. "*I didn't mind.*"

She flushed, hobbling past him in the direction of Chief Johnson's office.

"Anaya..." Huxley began, then corrected himself, unaccustomed to calling her by professional title. After all, the last time they saw each other was in grad school before the start of their careers. Twelve years had passed, and yet old habits remained. "I mean...Detective Nazario."

With her back to him, she paused to take a long drag of air, filling her lungs to capacity before she turned around.

"Can we grab a coffee?" He held her with an anticipatory gaze. "Saturday morning?"

"My schedule's crazy." She adjusted the crutch. "Got a women's self-defense class Gus and I co-teach Saturdays. Can't do much with the leg, but I kinda promised I'd at least stop by."

"Can we play it by ear?"

She shrugged a maybe. "I dunno, I'm really," then stalled him with, "hungover and running late for my meeting. I'm sure you'll figure out a way to find my unlisted number."

Huxley hollered as she hobbled away. "I'll be texting you."

"I'm sure you will." She waved her fingers without turning around. "But I gotta full schedule, Special Agent."

———

"Nazario," the Chief sighed, scanning her face, "you look terrible. I mean, I can see the pain all over your face. Start taking better care of yourself, or you'll drive yourself right into the ground. Won't help anyone if you burn out."

"It's been a rough couple of nights, sir," Nazario admitted, running her hand through her oily, unwashed hair. "Taking a shower is a real bitch. Didn't wash my hair 'cause it's a pain in my ass. Gotta wrap a garbage bag over my leg. Forget trying to find a comfortable sleeping position. I mean, I can't even shit comfortably. I've gotta go spread-eagle with my leg propped up on the trash can."

Chief Johnson burst into laughter, wiping his eyes. "Nice visual, Nazario. Been a while since you made me laugh; too much seriousness around here." He coughed out residual chuckles.

Nazario nodded reflectively. Wilson kicked the door open, shut it with his foot, and somehow balanced three Starbucks coffees like a pro. He handed the first cup to Chief Johnson and then read the label, giving Nazario hers.

"Café au lait. Don't worry, don't worry, I had them use whole milk. None of that almond or soymilk crap."

"Aw, shucks, you shouldn't have," Nazario said, sipping her coffee.

It was perfect, as always.

Wilson had an incredible memory when it came to food and drink—not to mention, the man was a superb cook. The running joke was that he was an undercover chef.

Wilson sat down. "What'd I miss? Oh…" He dug into the interior pocket of his blazer and handed Chief Johnson a thumb drive. Nearly hyperventilating, he sat down as if he'd run a mile, wiping the sweat from his forehead.

Chief plugged the thumb drive into the USB port and began scrolling through the digital images of the crime scene. "And you said you found something. What did you get back from forensics?"

"A torn page from the book *Fundamentals of Physics: Mechanics, Relativity, and Thermodynamics*. No fingerprints," Nazario added. "It looked freshly torn and a little out of place. I mean, under The Serpent's Bridge in the worst part of East LA? It stood out. There were sets of fresh muddy footprints; one looked to be...maybe a woman's size seven. Guessing a woman because the other set was from a child."

Chief Johnson analyzed the picture.

"An accomplice?"

Confident in her years of experience, not to mention higher education focusing on crime scene analysis, Nazario said, "Likely witnesses, judging by the child's footprint."

She'd had multiple job offers from the FBI, but Blake Huxley was FBI. At the end of the day, she'd wanted to return to Los Angeles to join the LAPD and follow in her father's footsteps.

She also wanted to run from Huxley.

Sorry, Huxley, coffee is off the table.

Chief Johnson finally got to the picture of the body.

"Yago Rios, an unidentifiable from Mexico," Nazario said. "ID's fake—died of strangulation. We haven't been able to find any known relatives. Not even sure if Yago Rios is his real name."

"Run fingerprints? Autopsy report?"

"Came back rather quick," Wilson filled in. "Straightforward. No drugs. Nothing found in his system. No defensive wounds. Died of asphyxiation."

"Fingerprints returned clean. Nothing in the criminal database either," Nazario said.

Chief Johnson leaned back in his chair, rubbing his chin.

"Unknown. Illegal. And no family." Chief threw his hands in the air. "We got nothing. A torn page in some physics book and footprints? Means absolutely nothing. We may need to file this one away. If ICE had him on their radar, he would've popped up. Case would've gone to a grand jury, subject to Penal Code 470b PC. But there's no misdemeanor or felony on record 'cause he's not in the system."

Nazario felt a wave of frustration rolling in. As much as she wanted to find Yago Rios' killer, the chief was right. They had nothing. But she couldn't give up. She couldn't let it be filed away so quickly.

"I'd like to do a little more digging before we put this one away. I get that he's some illegal, but he's still a dead human being." Nazario's nostrils flared. The words came out with more force than she anticipated.

Wilson cleared his throat and put his hands out.

Chief Johnson and Nazario both swore.

A few years ago, the department underwent sensitivity training. Since then, Chief had started collecting money every time anyone in any LAPD division used the word "illegal." Their personal rule: using the term cost each officer five dollars.

"A human cannot be illegal," the sensitivity trainer had said. "We don't go around describing other convicts by their criminal history. Using illegal to describe an undocumented Mexican immigrant is a racial slur and something the department should be cognizant of. Don't use it in public, ever. Do your best to eradicate it from your vocabulary in private."

Wilson and Nazario had made a concerted effort to collect the funds every quarter from each department, which all ended up in the chief's leather moneybag. The "kangaroo court" of donations went to Madison Vanwell's charity organizations that helped undocumented immigrants and separated families.

Chief swiveled to his locked safe behind him, opened it, and took out a bloated moneybag labeled "immigration relief fund."

"Of course, I'm not dismissing his death in any way," he said, plucking out a ten from his wallet and doubling his deposit for letting the word "illegal" slip out of his mouth when discussing Yago Rios.

"Where y'all gonna dig?" Johnson continued, stuffing the cash in the moneybag. "We've got nothing. We don't even know the man's name. The question is—why? There isn't a clear motive. He wasn't robbed. Some middle-aged man. He sure don't look like the thugs we've locked away. Don't look like a gangster. Could it be drug-related?"

"The way he was killed is not your typical drug dealer's method of snuffing someone out." Nazario took out her wallet. She handed Chief five dollars.

Today's gangsters and drug pushers still used knives, but mostly preferred guns.

"I'm gonna ask around," Nazario said, "maybe start with Sanctuary Baptist."

"Where you go for AA?" Chief furrowed his brow. Nazario's love for red wine was no secret. "And where that Nicky boy was hit? Why?"

"They're a known church in the area, not far from where the body was found. They're open to undocumented immigrants," Wilson added.

"It's not a Latino-run church. I believe the sermons are in English, run by the Goodwins, a white couple," Nazario continued. "About ninety percent of the church is Hispanic. Don't know how many without papers, but I'm thinking a decent chunk."

"Think it's too soon to speculate on anything. Drugs, hate crime, gang-related." Chief sighed. "Do what y'all gotta do. Let's hope for some discovery."

Nazario and Wilson got up. When they cleared the door, Wilson turned to her. "Call me or text me next time," he said, searching her face. "Back on the sauce?"

"Am I that obvious?"

"Haven't been partners for twelve years not to know you by now." Wilson surprised her by pulling her into a hug. Careful not to make her fall, he held her steady. After a beat too long, he said eventually, "Call me, call Gus, but call someone, m'kay?"

Nazario squeezed her eyes shut. "Should've called after I left Sanctuary Baptist."

"Gotta take better care of yourself. C'mon, we better get to the Goodwins' and ask some questions before they change their mind and shut us down." As they walked out of the building and toward his car, he asked, "Using that ice machine?"

Once in the car, she said, "Trying."

Another day without ice meant more swelling. She'd been given pain pills but refused to take them. One addiction was more than enough to handle at the moment. "Got on the fuck-it train and got drunk after the boy died."

"Heard about that. Calling Gus or calling me after the fact is *not* how it works. You're supposed to call before you drink. I would've picked you up." Wilson turned the key in the car's ignition and headed toward Sanctuary Baptist in Compton. "And here's the thing you might not know: alcohol has the same molecular structure as anesthesia in the body. Did you know that? It's different by just one molecule. See, all you're trying to do is anesthetize yourself. But here's the thing, Nazario—and you look at me. Come on, look at me."

She ground her molars and met his eyes.

Wilson continued, "Wine isn't gonna numb you for long. You're gonna have to tough out the tough stuff—*sober*. There's no way I'm fixing to let my partner, one of my best friends, die the way my father did. Not a chance in hell."

Diverting her watering eyes, Nazario shifted her gaze to the sun as it dropped out of the sky, sneaking under the mountains, flooding the deep sapphire horizon with shades of burnt orange.

"I know...I know, and I screwed up," she said.

Back to zero days sober, it was time to restart the clock.

FOURTEEN

THE PASTOR'S WIFE

"CAN I GET YOU ANYTHING? Water, lemonade, tea? I can make coffee if you'd like." Millie smiled cordially at Nazario and her partner, who'd been staring at her oatmeal cookies with disciplined restraint.

"You can have one if you like," Millie offered, "fresh out of the oven."

Nazario glanced at her partner, and he decided. "I'm gonna pass."

"This a good time to answer questions?" Nazario asked.

"Of course. I'm happy to help," she said, "in any way."

Millie swiped the bottom of her lemon-yellow pencil skirt cut just above her knee and crossed her legs. Her skirt rose, exposing more leg than she had in a long while. She wore deep-red high heels to match her lipstick and the scarf adorning her neck. She felt alive, like new juices were flowing in places she thought had long ago gone dry. Though, one look at Nazario's sober disposition stifled the endorphins that seemed to be returning her to life, reversing the years, making her skin glow. She felt ten years younger and, for once, beautiful in multiple ways.

Something was shifting, something undeniably raw.

Nazario had unreadable eyes. No wonder the detective was the best at her job.

It was a lot easier being her counselor asking questions than being the one Nazario questioned.

Millie sipped on a glass of water and left a stain of *Hot Passion* on the rim.

She fanned herself.

Millie met Nazario's steely stare and saw her son again, his wet hair, pale boyish frame, and drenched favorite Superman swim trunks. His lips were so blue. She'd thought for sure he was dead. The new flush of jittery life vacated for a moment. It was hard not to look at her client, Detective Nazario, without thinking about Nicky and how her son had almost died, too.

"Mrs. Goodwin." Nazario held a pocket-sized Kleenex.

"Huh?" Millie looked down and saw the tissue paper, not understanding until she touched her face. Was she crying? Her face was wet, her mascara wasn't waterproof, and her foundation and the setting powder would streak like muddy trails. She dabbed her face with a napkin, then took out a compact to check herself. Thankfully, her makeup looked like she'd just put it on. She closed the compact and put it back in her purse.

"Mrs. Goodwin, we'd like to talk to you about—"

Millie interrupted Nazario, "This isn't a counseling session, Detective. Go on and call me Millie. By the way, we're putting in porch lights until we can get proper zoning for a streetlight to be installed in our parking lot. The trees make it awfully dark."

"Millie, we're familiar with you and your husband's mission to open your church to undocumented immigrants," Nazario said, forcing Millie to shift in her seat under the new spotlight.

"That's right." She lifted her chin, making eye contact with Nazario.

"How well would you say you know your members?"

"A shepherd knows her flock," Millie said proudly. "I know everyone who steps in this door. Can't say I go around stalking people. I'm not that nosey neighbor. I give them their privacy. But I know each and every one of them."

"Can the pastor be available to answer some questions?" Wilson asked, steepling his fingers, though his eyes flicked toward the cookies like he was fighting the Devil. Millie removed the temptation and put the cookies away. While he might be on a diet, Nazario looked like she could use a pound or two.

"I've got the best tamales in Los Angeles in the fridge if you're hungry," Millie said, figuring the popular Mexican dish must be healthier than filling up on sugar.

Millie, you fool. They'll never leave now.

Wilson negotiated with Nazario. "Just one. Ain't no way I can turn away Mexican."

"What do I look like, your mom?" Nazario surrendered her hands in the air.

Millie turned to Nazario, "And for you?"

"Appreciate the offer," Nazario said, "but I think I'll pass."

"Knew you'd say that. You should really try one, Detective." Millie glanced anxiously at her watch, checking the time, then back up again. "They're out of this world."

Nazario watched her with those steady, poker-faced eyes, then observantly asked, "We're not keeping you from anything, are we?"

Yes. You're keeping me from sinning.

She flushed and fluffed her hair, newly highlighted with platinum streaks. Maybe the detective was amused by Millie's new and improved disposition?

Esperanza and Alex had given her similar stares.

But that Stan, he was like an old blind slug.

Oh, she almost forgot. "I believe Stan's in his study. Should be down in a bit. Don't like to bug him during prayer time."

Nazario cut in. "Yago Rios, thirty-five—"

"Yes, of course." Millie left the detectives sitting in the dining room and warmed the tamale in the microwave. Nazario was a heck of a lot friendlier as a patient than a pushy detective, Millie thought. But she put on a smile and said, "Have you seen him? He didn't make it to church, and it's odd. He never misses a Sunday. He's always one of the first to arrive and the last to leave."

The microwave dinged. She pulled on an oven mitt and opened the microwave door. She handled the plate with care, the steaming tamale wafting its invitation to Wilson's nostrils. Like in their counseling sessions, Nazario kept her cards close to the vest, though her partner was much easier to read.

Millie slid the plate in front of him. "You might wanna wait for it to cool, wouldn't want you to burn your..."

"Hot...hot...hot," Wilson impatiently unwrapped the tamale, fingers jumping from the heat searing the tips. Steam surged upward, carrying the scent of cornhusk and pork into the air.

"...fingers." Millie looked at the time again as restlessness stirred in her belly.

A member of the congregation is missing. Pull your head out of the swamp.

It was Wilson's moan of delight that triggered heat to spread inside, causing her hand to wander down her thigh until it clutched a fistful of skirt.

Fifty...eight minutes before I can get unwrapped, she reminded herself, thinking of Eric.

She bit her lower lip at the ravenous thought and glanced back up. Nazario pinned her with those hawk eyes, then smiled as if to say, "I saw that." Millie jolted her gaze away, caught in some high school wet fantasy. She fanned herself with a hand.

"Need a fork?"

Nazario answered for her partner. "That's a negative."

Wilson busted out laughing. Oh Lord, it took effort for Millie to play along, forcing out a twitchy smile. She snuck the Tupperware of tamales back into the fridge, not trying to be rude, just hoping Wilson stuck to one-and-done so she could end this interrogation and get them out of here already.

"Jimenez Mexican Grill. Ever been?" Millie knew what Wilson's answer would be.

"That place serves the best Mexican food in the city," Wilson said. "Are the tamales from there?"

"My cleaning lady made them." She'd have to tell them about Isabelle, although it felt wrong to involve other members.

"What about the restaurant?" Nazario redirected.

"Isabelle Jimenez spoke to me after service last Sunday." Her fingers fidgeted. "Now, I...I wanna make sure she doesn't get in any sort of trouble. We've worked real hard to build Sanctuary Baptist...we don't want any sort of trouble, either."

"You don't have to worry. We've got much bigger concerns than trying to chase down every worker on your payroll without papers," Nazario assured. "We're not here to interrogate you. We're here for Yago Rios—if that's even his name."

"Millie?" Stan walked down the stairs and entered the kitchen, each step creaking.

Stan adjusted his glasses and let out a cordial laugh, "Did I miss dinner? Thought I smelled something."

"You must be Stan?" Wilson mumbled in between bites. "Pastor Stan?"

"I am. I heard something about Isabelle Jimenez. Does this have something to do with Yago Rios? Have you found him?"

"Oh, we found him." Wilson swallowed the final bite, wiping his hands on a paper towel.

"Dead," Nazario finished soberly. "We're investigating his murder—anything you can share, anything you can remember will help us. Now, what's his connection with Isabelle Jimenez or her restaurant?"

Stan took off his glasses. "It...it can't be," he whispered, putting a hand over his mouth.

Millie gasped. "Isabelle, she told me he worked at the restaurant, said he's never late. That's all...she wanted to know where he was. I knew...knew something was wrong. He's never...he's never missed a service."

Nazario and Wilson got up from the table.

"Didn't hear anyone talking? Didn't get any clues that he was in danger? Caught up in anything bad?" Nazario asked.

Millie broke into a sob.

"No," Stan answered for her. "He was real quiet, came every week, worked at Isabelle Jimenez's restaurant, kept to himself. We haven't heard anything." Stan's hands started to clench and then unclench. Detective Nazario cocked a brow at Millie's husband.

"Something wrong with your hands, Pastor Goodwin?" she asked casually.

"I think I'm getting carpal tunnel," Stan said conversationally. News he hadn't shared before. Stan avoided Millie's eyes. "Don't worry, I've made a doctor's appointment to have it checked out."

"Good idea," Wilson said.

"You said Yago never missed a Sunday. He come alone then? Have any family you know of? Next of kin?" Nazario inquired.

"Always came alone. Come to think of it...we've never seen him with family." Stan turned to his wife. "Am I right, honey?"

Millie dabbed her face. "Never seen him with anyone. Don't think he had family."

Stan sat next to her and clasped her hand for support.

"We'll come back if we have any more questions." Wilson took out a card and handed it to Stan. "Let us know if you can remember anything else."

"You sure you don't have any further questions for me?" Stan asked. "I'm more than willing to answer anything you need. Especially when it comes to one of my members."

"Appreciate the cooperation, Mr. Goodwin." Nazario nodded. "We may ask you to come down to the station if we find out anything more."

When the detectives left, Stan put his arms around Millie.

"You all right?" he asked, but she didn't respond. She sobbed in her hands.

No, I'm not. A man's dead, and all I've been thinking of are lustful thoughts.

"Don't you have that Bible study?"

"I shouldn't go," she said. *I really, really shouldn't.*

"It might make you feel better," Stan said.

If you only knew.

Millie got up from the table, went to the bathroom, and cleaned off any mascara that had run down her face.

"If you're going, better hurry before traffic gets bad," Stan called out. Millie took a deep breath and knew that she couldn't stay away from Eric Myers, no matter what tragedy faced the congregation. If it was the end of the world, she'd go.

I'm being selfish, and you know what? I don't care.

Millie laughed quietly to herself even as her eyes grew wet. She dabbed with a tissue again, and then the reality struck her. That she'd never thought of herself. Millie had been a good wife. A caring mother despite feeling like she'd failed Gideon. She'd thought of the church. It'd been a life of serving other people. Never once had she been selfish. Not once, until now.

"Drive safe," Stan said, handing Millie her Bible. "Don't forget to pray for Yago. That's what I'll be doing."

"Don't bother waiting up." Millie kissed his cheek. "Think I might be a little late."

FIFTEEN
THE WITNESS

ISABELLE ASKED Esperanza to stop by Jimenez Mexican Grill. It was mid-Saturday, and already a swell of hungry locals was gathering at the popular restaurant, making Esperanza wonder if Isabella and her staff were prepared for the Saturday-night rush. Since Alex was at the library with a friend from school and his mother was supervising, Esperanza had time.

The smell of authentic Mexican food hung in the air: refried beans, enchiladas, fajitas, tamales, and more. Esperanza closed her eyes, and for a moment, she was in her small kitchen in Mexico before Alex was born. Hector was making chicken enchiladas with mole poblano sauce. The dark, rich, bittersweet chocolate was subtly blended with pepitas, cinnamon, peanuts, peppers, and other spices. Hector's mole poblano, made the hard way with over thirty-two ingredients, revealed his soul.

The chocolaty coating over the chicken stuffed corn tortillas meant everything.

It was more than a taste of culture; it was reliving the best moments of her life.

Her mouth watered.

Not even she knew Hector's special mole poblano recipe.

If she had, Mrs. Goodwin would surely be in heaven. The thought of her employer scattered memories of the past.

That Mrs. Goodwin was acting unusual. Esperanza had never seen her behave this way. The pastor's wife had never tried anything new. Esperanza wondered for a minute what had caused the change but then shoved the thought out of her head. She had made it a habit to mind her own business.

The cacophonous lunch crowd packed the quaint restaurant with full booths and even fuller bills. It was an eclectic sea of ethnic origins and skin palettes of all shades. The core of Los Angeles was diverse—unlike anywhere Esperanza had been. It made her feel embraced in a way she hadn't expected. She knew of many undocumented immigrants that didn't fear deportation. It wasn't that they were oblivious, but a simple fact of having lived under the radar in the country for so long. They'd found a livable routine.

But Esperanza never could get comfortable or put her guard down. She'd witnessed first-hand how many families were torn apart, how many naturalized kids like Alex would live without their fathers or mothers. Hector had been deported, and his radiation treatments were terminated. He'd died in Mexico while she was left a single mother, scrambling to pick up the pieces in California, one of the most expensive states to live in. Moving out of the state was also costly, so she stayed and fought to keep up with Alex's constantly developing intelligence.

When he got into one of the best-ranking private schools in the country via a transfer and scholarships, she knew that she'd have to make every sacrifice to ensure his continued enrollment at that Palos Verdes school.

On her way to Jimenez Mexican Restaurant, she faced the yellow smog hanging over the city. She faced the grunge that stuck on street corners where drug dealers lounged, drive-by shootings occurred, and the homeless lay in makeshift tents within the Garment District. Grunge defaced the buildings tagged with spray paint, eroded the dilapidated businesses, which were once so alive. Now, the filth of Los Angeles had strangled an undocumented man with its poisonous hands and left him to die under *El Puente de la Serpiente*—that cursed bridge.

As she struggled to survive in Los Angeles, one question continued to surface. It swirled in her head at night, tangled in the wail of distant sirens, whispering through the grime-streaked windows of the LA Metro bus during the long, weary commute to Isabelle's restaurant.

She knew Alex would go on to become much more than a poor Mexican kid from South Central, but was this all there was for her?

She couldn't let that matter. Esperanza had to remain inconspicuous, obey the law, keep her witness of Yago Rios' murder a secret.

No matter what Isabelle Jimenez needed to speak to her about, Esperanza had to keep what she'd seen from even her dearest friend. As she made her way through the restaurant, she was overwhelmed by the perpetually busy joint. She minced and wove through the hungry, laughing crowd as they crunched chips and salsa, clinked afternoon margaritas, and devoured Mexican dishes whose scent was thick in the air.

"Can we get more chips here and double the salsa?" a pale, red-faced man in an expensive navy business suit hollered at her. And another margarita with Patron?"

The man sucked down his classic margarita and thrust the glass at Esperanza, his brows furrowing, deepening the vertical lines in his forehead. He glared at her like she couldn't speak English, that same condescending look she received from the Palos Verdes moms.

One had wrinkled her nose and asked, "So you're Alex's mother. District transfer student, I assume?"

She'd assumed correctly.

Maybe those arrogant Palos Verdes mothers were jealous that a poor Mexican kid could outperform their privileged, tutored children? Maybe Esperanza was jealous that she couldn't afford Palos Verdes, one of the most expensive areas in South Bay, where the average home was around a million dollars. Of course, most hard-working Angelenos couldn't afford Palos Verdes, no matter where they came from, regardless of their skin color or ethnic origin.

The red-faced man waved his empty margarita glass at her face.

"I don't work here, sir." Esperanza straightened her back and strode toward the bar, ignoring the man's apology. The bustling restaurant suddenly closed in on her. Isabelle surfaced from behind the counter just in time to fill Esperanza with relief.

"More chips and salsa, middle table, and another margarita with Patron." Esperanza folded her arms and looked down at her watch.

Isabelle apologized and waved for Esperanza to follow her behind the bar. She flagged a college-aged waiter.

"Table nine needs refills all around," Isabelle told the flushed young server. As the boy turned and rushed off, Isabelle explained, "Just started."

They walked into her office in the back, passing a kitchen that looked slammed with orders. Isabelle's family restaurant had always been popular, regardless of the time of day.

"I've gotta catch the bus and pick Alex up at the library."

"I know, I'm sorry. It's been so busy. We hired that new kid; he's still learning the tables. Needs to pick up his pace."

"There was something you wanted to talk to me about?"

"Oh...I know you work for Mrs. Goodwin. Go to the church much?"

"We attend when we can, but I mostly work for the Goodwins. Why?"

"So, you know Yago Rios? He works for us. He does so much. Buses tables, knows all the drinks, bartends when we're short a hand, and he's our fastest waiter," Isabelle sighed, wringing her hands. "I haven't seen him. Mrs. Goodwin hasn't seen him. He's never late for work. I don't know where he lives. He doesn't have a phone."

"You couldn't call me to ask me this?" Esperanza said.

Isabelle whispered unnecessarily, *"Caminas cerca del puente Serpiente, ¿no?"*

You always walk near The Serpent's Bridge, don't you?

Esperanza answered her friend in English. "What does it matter?"

The air dried up. Moisture clung to her—palms, forehead, neck.

"Did you *see* anything?" Isabelle said, prodding her.

"No vi nada," Esperanza lied.

Esperanza retrieved a napkin from her purse and wiped her forehead and neck with a trembling hand. Isabelle looked at her —concern etched across the soft curves of her oval face. Isabelle was a sweet and generous woman, this much Esperanza knew. Isabelle opened the pint-sized refrigerator next to her desk and pulled out a cold bottle of water, reading her mind the way a woman with years of hospitality experience knew how to do.

"Thank you." Esperanza's hands were trembling so badly her fingers couldn't navigate the bottle cap. Isabelle reached for the water bottle and helped take the lid off. Esperanza gulped down the water, breathing heavily. Her pulse thumped in her ears. For a moment, she could feel hands around her throat, that familiar nightmare taunting her even during waking hours.

"Are you feeling good?"

"I'm fine. Tired. That's all." Esperanza took another gulp of water. She looked down at her watch. She'd have to leave soon to beat LA traffic, especially with the bus stops and pick-ups.

"Yago—"

"I said I haven't seen him." Esperanza heard her own voice squeak. She looked away. Blood rushed to her ears, and her pulse beat harder. Just then, the new young waiter knocked on the door. Esperanza nearly jumped out of her skin.

"There's a couple of detectives—" He looked down at his napkin. "Nazario and Wilson, here to see you. They say they have a few questions they wanna ask."

Isabelle's face blanched. "Tell them...tell them I'll be there in a minute."

Esperanza didn't wait for her busy friend to see her off.

It was the perfect moment to make her exit.

"I'm late getting Alex." Esperanza knocked the water to the ground, spilling it. "The library closes early on Saturdays."

Just as she was making her escape, hoping to leave unseen, to be buried in the crowd, her eyes made contact with that female detective. It was like the detective saw right through her.

Esperanza scrambled out the door. As she was charging down the street, she heard footsteps following behind her. She turned around and didn't look up at the face, only glimpsing legs and worn running shoes. She bumped into a man who angrily screamed, "Hey, eyes ahead, lady. Watch where the hell you're going!"

"*Perdoname,*" she apologized, head swiveling around again. She glanced up. It was a man wearing a jacket, dark pants, and running shoes. He was young, but panic made her mind go blank. Was he the man following her around? She'd heard somewhere that you were supposed to memorize victimizers, but she had been too frightened to commit his features to memory.

She tried to recall the last bit of conversation she had with Isabelle, something about a *Quinceañera*. Still, Esperanza's legs had a mind of their own, propelling her swiftly out of the packed restaurant and down the street.

Her brisk walk turned into a jog.

The stranger started jogging, too.

Terrified, her legs picked up speed.

She ran and didn't look back.

SIXTEEN

THE DETECTIVE

TUCKED AWAY in a dilapidated strip mall in East Los Angeles, the rundown shopping center was tagged with more graffiti than working store signs, most of which were faded or falling off. The neglected mustard stucco exterior now looked more like corroding rust.

Bullet holes pitted the thick storefront glass. The overhead sign was splintered, missing the "k" and "o." It now read: "Tae_-wond." The dojang ran lukewarm without working AC, carrying the stale aroma of mildew and sweat. The strip mall's owner let them use the abandoned space every Saturday at no cost. Regardless of its ghetto cosmetic appearance, it was a neutral location that worked for everyone.

"Ki, in Chinese, is like the word 'Qi' or 'Chi,' both are basically considered your spiritual energy." Leaning against her crutch, Nazario hobbled down the line of girls, looking each of them in the eyes. "And 'hap' is 'focus.' In Taekwondo, the common shout means more than simply yelling nonsense."

The girls giggled.

"It's about spiritual energy and channeling that force inside of you."

Gus stood a couple of feet behind the ladies: All the girls wore generic spandex shorts and bras except for Avery, who sported designer gear.

Nazario had been doing this for more than twenty years, having earned her fourth-degree black belt in taekwondo before she was the legal age to drink and become an all-star track athlete. Because it was a self-defense class with a mixture of Taekwondo and MMA techniques, Gus and Nazario didn't require the girls to wear a *dobok*, the traditional Taekwondo uniform and belt. Nazario brought her taekwondo style, while Gus brought her MMA, street-style grappling techniques. Both styles worked beautifully to teach self-defense in a common-sense way.

Before each of the students stood a portable, freestanding punching bag.

"Let's warm up, ladies," Gus's voice boomed. "We wanna hear you from your diaphragm. Let's start with a basic sidekick. Ready..."

Nazario and Gus executed the shout in unison: *"Kihap!"*

The girls tried the shout timidly, each kicking the bag.

"From your gut, c'mon," Nazario coached.

Nazario and Gus repeated: *"Kihap!"*

Voices grew more confident: *"Kihap!"*

They continued the kick and shout a few more times, each Kihap growing in volume, each kick growing in force until the girls were all sweating.

Nazario clapped. "Good job, ladies. Now, let's clear the bags. Let's practice what we learned last week. Gus is attacking you from behind. Let's see your over-the-shoulder throw."

The girls moved the portable punching bags to the side and gathered around. Gus rushed Sammy from behind, the student who inspired them to start the classes in the first place. Despite being lean and muscular, Sammy hesitated as she tended to do, causing her to be knocked on her back with Gus on top.

"C'mon, Sammy, get your hips into it. You hesitated," Nazario commanded, "you'd be choked out by now."

"I suck at this, Detective," Sammy admitted, as her shoulders slumped.

The girl could use reassurance—after all the hell Sammy'd gone through.

"No, ya don't," Nazario encouraged, "it's gonna take some practice. Try that again. Wrist-grab. Pivot. Throw the attacker over."

By the second time, the move was executed without hesitation. Sammy grabbed the wrist, pivoted her hips correctly, and hurled Gus over her shoulder.

"Thatta girl," Gus wheezed from the ground. Concerned, Nazario made eye contact, but Gus gave her an *I'm good* dismissal with a wave of her hand.

"Did I hurt you?" Sammy gasped, cupping a hand over her mouth.

Gus shrugged it off. "No. I'm happy you got it down."

Nazario knew better; she could see the pain in the captain's eyes. But they quickly moved on to the next girl in line to stay on time. Each girl made the rotation—some needed to perform the move a few times before perfecting it. Nazario smiled at Sammy, who had come the farthest in terms of coordination and form. A quick learner, Avery had been a pleasant surprise, having executed all the moves with expert precision.

That Avery's a natural, Nazario thought.

"Let's break up in pairs and practice that aikido move. One of you will punch, and your partner will swipe the wrist and move away," Gus said, breathing heavily. "Couple up."

The girls broke up into pairs. Each took a turn, being the attacker and the victim. The attacker threw a front punch while the victim dodged her head to the right or left and swiped aside the wrist of the assailant in an effort to misdirect the blow.

Nazario leaned into Gus. "Maybe we should get a sub in here."

"I'm fine," she said, labored.

Nazario recognized the same stubborn streak in her best friend as she saw in herself. Knee surgery was one thing. Chemo and recovering from breast cancer was an entirely different level of stubborn.

Nazario hissed, "I mean it, Gus. If we've gotta cancel class, then so be it." She looked at her watch. "Shit. Wilson'll be here any minute. I hate not being able to drive or walk without help."

"I'll trade you," Gus said with a laugh.

Nazario grew somber.

Gus caught herself and said, "Sorry, bad joke."

"Wished I'd been there," Nazario said. "Wished you'd let me."

"Last time we're discussing this. You were on the Morris case. We needed you mobilized. Un-assed. AOTFC. That's ass-off-the-fucking-couch. Not sitting around in a damn waiting room. And if it makes you feel better, I didn't want anyone around. This is the one thing in my life—my tits getting chopped off—that I had to do solo." She put a hand on Nazario's shoulder. "Don't take it personally, Nazario."

Wilson honked the horn from the parking lot.

It is personal, she thought, but decided it best to keep her mouth shut.

"That's my cue. We're following up on a lead on that DB under The Serpent's Bridge," Nazario exhaled. "Thanks for coming over."

"Don't ever have to thank me." Gus smiled wide. "I've got a hot date tonight with a Badge Bunny, smoking fem-type. And I think she's the one."

"Who lit a fire under you?" Nazario glared at Gus like she'd grown a second head. "Never said that about any of the long-timers you've dated."

"I'm alive when I could be dead—that's what changed, Detective. And I'm living my life from here out. Life is way too short. My advice for you is to do the same, and I'm not talking about getting drunk or one of your pump-and-dumps—talking about making a commitment for once in your life."

Nazario wondered if this was Gus-code for Blake Huxley. He'd always been like a brother to Gus. Had they run into each other at the hospital? Did they talk about her?

Nazario pushed away imaginary conspiracies.

"Since when do we talk about relationships?" Nazario huffed, limping away. "Getting soft on me, Captain?"

The girls rushed up to say goodbye. They ambushed her with a sweaty group hug. Each planted salty kisses on Nazario's cheek, and she surprised herself by laughing. In this moment, Nazario wasn't jaded by the job, struggling to stay sober, or affected by a father she couldn't seem to leave dead.

"Can we grab coffee sometime, Detective Nazario?" Avery asked. This was the third time she'd asked in the past two months.

"Sorry, honey," Nazario smiled regretfully, "but I've got a case I'm eyeballs deep in. Raincheck?"

Avery's blue eyes darkened with a disappointment that transformed her entire face.

Gus hollered at Nazario. "Hey, about relationships, I've always been a softy. I'm the lover. You're the fighter." Gus burst into chuckles. "Always been that way, girl."

Nazario chewed on Gus's words, unable to deny the truth in them. She looked back at Avery, and a pang of guilt hit her. Maybe she would say yes to that coffee just as soon as things slowed down.

———

Jimenez Mexican Grill was bloated with authentic Mexican food-loving people of different cultures: Middle Eastern, Asian, Latino, black, white. There wasn't a seat available—except for two stools at the bar. Lucky her. Wilson was already busy crunching away at the chips and salsa.

"You're a bottomless pit, you know that?" Nazario said.

"I need to go on a diet. I'm just always hungry," Wilson admitted.

"Esperanza, don't forget about the *quinceañera*. I'll be catering," a petite Mexican woman called out to another as the two hustled out from the back. Nazario thought she recognized one of the women.

"I dunno, Isabelle. I'll try," Esperanza said, face flushed, eyes darting away.

Esperanza Flores. She was that cleaning lady at Sanctuary Baptist. She had been there the night the boy had died. Her son had been screaming Nicky's name. Esperanza looked at Nazario for a moment with something that appeared to be a mixture of fear and recognition before waving goodbye to her friend and rushing out the front door. Nazario watched Esperanza leave, unable to dismiss the memory they'd both shared.

Wilson leaned in to ask what was wrong. Nazario shrugged it off, turning her attention to the person of interest they came to question.

Isabelle Jimenez had her hair pulled back in a bun, a burgundy Jimenez Mexican Grill shirt, and black pants. Nazario was in the habit of remembering what people wore. The restaurant owner was sporting black nursing shoes made for someone on their feet all day. She had kind eyes and olive skin that had aged well. She wore a thin wedding band and a Fitbit watch, though she wasn't out of shape.

"Sorry for making you wait." Isabelle bowed her head at them as if to apologize with her whole body. It reminded Nazario of some Asian cultures. It was a respect thing, but Nazario wasn't into over-apologies. It just wasn't necessary.

She waved at Isabelle. "It's totally fine. Our visits are often unexpected."

Nazario couldn't tell whether or not their presence was causing anxiety or if the restaurant owner was distracted by her lively clientele. Isabelle's eyes were unsteady nonetheless, darting around the room that was now at full capacity. The air shimmered—body heat and steam from the kitchen tangled in the room.

"Would you like to talk in private?"

"This is informal," Nazario said, noting that it was too damn crowded and noisy to hear her easily, "it won't be necessary."

"Can I get you a drink?" Isabelle asked. "Margarita, beer, wine?"

"NO!" Wilson barked loud enough to startle Isabelle. A tortilla chip fell out of his mouth, breaking apart as it landed on the bar counter. Nazario let out a breath and slid a sideways glare at her partner. Isabelle looked puzzled, perhaps because most people would never reject free booze. But they were cops, after all.

"Stupid me, you're on duty," Isabelle replied. "Would you like anything to eat? It's on me." Her gaze ping-ponged between them. Wilson's mouth opened—soggy bits of tortilla chips sprinkled his tongue. The last time Wilson wore this look was when he landed a gift certificate to Hometown Buffet at a white elephant Christmas bash their unit had a couple of years back. He'd stolen it from Chief Johnson, who was not too pleased.

"Nope," Nazario answered. Wilson frowned. "I can't. But you can?"

"That's different," Wilson objected.

"Thanks, but no thanks. We won't take up too much of your time. Yago Rios worked here, right? Know if he has family? Friends?"

Isabelle's fingers intertwined and then untangled themselves.

"He's worked here for eight years." She gulped. "Wait—did something happen to him?"

Wilson coughed, taking a sip of his water. Isabelle searched their faces.

"Yes," Nazario answered, not saying the words.

"You mean he's—" Isabelle's voice was a tiny whisper, audible enough for them to hear. She flopped down on the stool, her head in her hands. "How? What happened?"

"We can discuss those details at a later date. What's his real name, Mrs. Jimenez?"

"I don't want any trouble." Her hands flew up. "My family has worked hard. This restaurant has been in our family for three generations."

"It's okay." Nazario gave her a solid look—more like a personal oath. "Know what I mean?"

Isabelle's shoulders slumped. She took a paper. Wrote. Slid it across the bar.

Pablo Jimenez.

Nazario handed the paper to Wilson.

Isabelle wept into a tissue.

"Brother?" Nazario prodded.

"Cousin." Isabelle sobbed.

Wilson slipped a card into Isabelle's hand. Nazario leaned in as if to give her a hug and whispered in her ear. "Gonna need you to come in. Identify the body. We'll need to ask you some more questions. Don't worry, we're cool. Got it?"

Isabelle nodded, wiping her face. Then Wilson's special phone rang, the one designated for homicides and the same one that informed them about the first murder under The Serpent's Bridge. Nazario studied Wilson and knew what that look on his face meant.

"Yeah, uh huh." He let out a loud exhale. "Okey-dokey, we're on our way." Wilson ended the call and returned the phone to his inside coat pocket.

"Thanks for your time, Mrs. Jimenez. We'll see you soon." Nazario smiled at her.

Isabelle walked around the bar, helped Nazario with the crutch, and then unexpectedly threw her arms around her.

"Thank you," Isabelle whispered, but Nazario wasn't so sure what she was thankful for. Was it that she finally knew her cousin's whereabouts, even if the result was her worst fear? Was she thankful Jimenez Mexican Grill wouldn't be hit with penalties and fines for hiring undocumented workers? Most of the force had more important matters on its collective plate than to hunt down every single business that hired new employees without running an I-9. Unless a situation involved a violent crime, they let ICE take care of it. Though from the looks of it, Pablo Jimenez, aka Yago Rios, had been the victim. Now, they had yet another cold one.

"I wish I'd let you have a sip," Wilson admitted.

"I wish I'd let you have a plate," Nazario said. "What're we looking at?"

"DB, 'nother Mexican. Looks like a knife wound. Might be gangs this time," Wilson said, opening the door for her. "Don't you give me lip. You've been on that leg too long. Keep it up, and you'll never do that Karate Kid shit you do."

Nazario didn't fight him. She allowed Wilson to help her in the vehicle. He set the crutch in the back seat. She rubbed her knee. The healing process was taking longer than she anticipated. But what could she do? Sit home? Crimes came and went in waves. Sometimes, nothing but gang violence and drive-bys.

Other times, massive drug rings, like in Connor Morris' case. Lately, there had been dead Mexicans: two murders and three deaths, counting Nicky, in three weeks. She'd dealt with suicides and murders, though usually one-offs, often crimes of passion and rage.

Multiple murders in such a short span wasn't something typical.

It was a record in her career that she'd been hoping to avoid.

SEVENTEEN

THE PASTOR'S WIFE

MILLIE SAT QUIVERING in her idling car, her right hand on the stick shift. All she had to do was put it in reverse and drive away. She prayed again for the millionth time that the Lord would force her to turn around before it was too late. But the car remained parked and unmoved.

Millie squeezed her eyes shut, letting her forehead fall against the steering wheel. Her blood pressure was rising, bringing on that familiar lightheadedness that followed. After a beat, she finally gripped the keys, turned off the ignition, and knocked on room 326.

The door creaked open. "Well, well...I thought you chickened out."

Millie gulped, looking behind her. It wasn't too late. She could still jump back into the car.

"I've..." her voice cracked. "I've never done something like this before."

"Oh, I couldn't've guessed." Eric's smile widened. He leaned his lumberjack frame against the door. "And I've never seen a therapist—your choice. I'm not holding you hostage. You gonna run back to the car, Millie, and do more praying, or you coming inside?"

Millie stalled, rubbing her throat, suddenly too warm despite the brisk night.

"So be it," Eric said, closing the door.

"Wait..." Millie stuck a high-heeled foot between the door. She lifted her chin. "I'm not running anywhere, Eric Myers."

———

Millie could hardly believe she was actually in a hotel room—alone—and not just with any man, but the most hated man at Sanctuary Baptist. Eric plopped on the bed and put his arms behind his head, making his biceps bulge. Millie fanned her face with a hand and crossed her legs, sitting a little too stiffly on the hotel chair.

"Guess this is the good ol' Freudian Sleeper," Eric said, getting comfortable. "My own personal shrink sofa."

"Looks more comfortable than this brick I'm sitting on."

"Plenty of space for the both of us. I don't bite unless it's on your menu." Eric winked at her, causing blood to flood her cheeks. "All kidding aside, don't really know where to start."

Millie cleared her throat and smoothed a palm down the hem of her dress.

"Why doncha start from the beginning? What made you decide to be Nicky's guardian? Wasn't that a conflict of interest?"

Eric sighed, then admitted, "Always hated kids. Made it easy to be a perpetual bachelor. Was gonna go into law enforcement or the military—this job opened up, and I got right in."

"I know whatcha doing, Mr. Myers, skipping all around the issue. Lemme repeat the question: Why Nicky if you...dislike kids so much?"

"I'm getting there, I'm getting there. Hold your horses." He laughed, showing off that distracting dimple. The low light from the nightstand's lamp illuminated his face just enough to cast shadows across his face, exposing teenage acne scars that reminded Millie of the late Ray Liotta's infamous uneven skin texture. God bless his soul. It was a shame the actor had died of heart failure. As fat as Stan was, she couldn't understand why he hadn't had a heart attack yet.

Wishful thinking. You can't have it all, Millie Ann.

Eric's laughter suddenly transitioned into a different sound, like a cough. He put the crook of his elbow and forearm over his eyes, and the ICE agent's entire body shook.

His voice, rough with emotion. "He was only supposed to stay with me for about a week. Was like a lost puppy, didn't have a home to go to." A sob crept out. "I knew I couldn't just toss him to the state to be stuck in some group home. Never forget how he begged me if he could stay with me. Said he'd be a g-g-good boy."

"You gave him a home. That was the most selfless thing you could've done."

"God fucking damn it." He pounded the bed with a fist in fury, a tortured cry tangled with rage ripped the tough guy wide open. "Why him? Why Nicky? Why, my boy?"

Her heart trembled, and her eyes welled. The last time she had a relationship with her son was just after the near drowning. In her mind, he was perpetually that child in little Superman swim trunks, cold and blue. Despite knowing what it was like to almost lose Gideon, she was unaccustomed to a man expressing such emotion in this way. Stan hardly even shed tears over their son.

Millie didn't have the answers but hurried to Eric's side. The counselor didn't know what to say. In all her years of working with the grieving, the lost, and the downtrodden, she truly had nothing to say. She lay there next to Eric, driven by an instinct she couldn't name, as he covered his face with his hands.

"I didn't want kids 'til Nicky, and now I can't imagine life without him," he said, and as all the sorrow came out, it was all Millie could do but to lay next to him. Finding fear leave her, she scooted her body close to him until the space between them had vanished. She tried soothing him with a hand on his shoulder.

"I have a son of my own, one I also feel I've lost for good."

"Did he get hit by a car? Is he dead?" Eric dried his eyes with the back of his shirtsleeve, bitterness in his tone.

"No, he's alive. But it feels like a death nonetheless."

"It's not too late for you. Trust me on this one." Eric turned to look at her now with a stern expression. "You don't wanna wait until you can't talk to them no more. You're the therapist— you oughta know that."

Millie blinked back tears of her own and nodded her head. He glanced down at her hand that had wandered across his large chest. A part of her wanted to pull away, but the other side won—the side that couldn't care less about her marital duties or whether or not her husband joined Ray Liotta in a round of golf in the afterlife.

"You're absolutely right," she said, and they shared companionable silence before her lingering hands found their way down to his abdomen. The mood shifted with new energy, charging the tension between them.

"You're a good listener," he admitted. "I've...never really talked so much with anyone."

"I really appreciate your trust," she said. "As for talking *with* me...well, I don't think I said much."

"Didn't have to. Sometimes, all people really need is to be heard—uninterrupted."

"That's what I do," she said, turning to meet his wet eyes.

"Now it's my turn to give you what you need." His mouth abruptly took hers hostage, tongue darting hungrily. It was a forceful kiss, lips pressing hard, bruising hers, a hot blend of Eric's personal pain and sexual desires. His hands roamed over her breasts, kneading their tender flesh with his fingers. Her nails dug into his back as he explored all the right places, breaking their kiss and sinking southbound.

"What...what're you doing?" she gasped.

"Looking for my lost contact lens. What do you think I'm doing?" Eric's sarcasm was swallowed up by panic as he lifted her skirt, snatched her panties off, and buried his face between her thighs. She'd been a pastor's wife for so long. She'd only ever made love to Stan. It dawned on Millie that this was the first time a man had ever pleasured her down there, and it was more glorious than God Herself.

New sensations exploded through her as she arched her back and groaned from an unholy pleasure. One moment, they were talking, and the next moment, she was drowning in a kind of ecstasy she had never experienced.

Time slowed to a stop. How long had it been since he'd begun to pleasure her: thirty, forty-five minutes? Stan was as selfish as they came, never even caring whether or not she orgasmed. In fact, Millie wasn't sure if she'd ever had one before. Eric was a complex man and a generous lover. His tongue flicked her sweet spot, fingers moving deeper inside of her, opening her up. She wanted to scream, but a gasp was all that she could manage. She stopped looking at her watch when it was fifteen minutes past because, for once, her mind was Jell-O. There was nothing she could do. She couldn't stop him. She wouldn't stop him.

"Please." She heard her voice quiver, begging.

"Tell me," he ordered from down below, "what you want."

But her voice caught in her throat.

Tell him what she wanted?

Oh Lord, she couldn't do that.

She shook her head, even though he couldn't see it, buried under her bright yellow dress, flipped over her face. Her thighs ached, unaccustomed to opening any longer than five minutes, which was how long her husband lasted. Eric had been down there for too long, like some ungodly machine that teased her just as she was about to shudder and then stopped.

The climactic wave that was meant to sweep over her dissipated.

She balled her fists and punched the bed, throwing a tantrum. Her black heels were still on; it was not too late to gouge him. He let out a laugh, enjoying her ache in places she'd never ached before. Made her beg. What was she begging for? What did she want? He leaned in and flicked her with his tongue again. She gasped, biting her lower lip.

She was glad he couldn't see the silly faces she was making. Her eyes rolling back, hands clutching the pillow, mouth open with nothing coming out. Then he stopped. He completely stopped. Why was he stopping? Oh, she wanted to scream now, really scream. Then, the layer protecting her face, her shame, was being pulled away, uncovering her sweaty, flushed face.

Eric, still fully dressed, smiled at her. An amused smile. Like he'd won something. She cleared her throat, lifting her chin at him.

"Why'd you stop?"

"Think we'll call it a day." He wiped his mouth and gave her another sensual smile.

"Excuse me?" Millie sat up on the bed and folded her arms.

"I'm not sure you're up for this," he said. Was he trying to call her bluff? Was this some trick, some poker game? He turned and headed for the door. He was leaving his own motel room?!

"Eric Myers, you come right back here and finish what you started!" Millie demanded in a booming voice—one that was all hers. He turned around, eyes wide, a giant grin spreading across his handsome face.

"I asked you to tell me what you wanted," he said, leisurely swaggering back to her, unbuckling his belt—slowly. Way too slow. "You stayed quiet as a mouse. Which isn't any fun because, Sunshine, I wanna hear you."

A flutter escaped her belly as she began to breathe shallow and quick. He was on the bed, hands crawling under her dress, fingers between her thighs. His lips ravaged hers, a hard and scathing kiss with tongue. Raw. Hot. Passion. Eros. Eros was lustful. Not Agape, on the other hand. Agape was selfless love, even though her husband might smell like prunes and Mylanta and had never once used his tongue with her, not in her mouth, not on her neck where Eric performed this suckle-bite that left her arching against him.

No, Stan had never used his tongue.

Dear God, she was married! She was married. Her mind was racing. His fingers teased her ever so slightly, moving in and then pulling out. He would not give her what she wanted. He only gave her enough, and then nothing and not Stan or God could stop the blazing need, this awakened yearning that had been left neglected for too many years.

"I want you to take off our clothes and finish what you started." Millie's lips quivered, every cell shaking and hungry with desire. Her body was demanding him. Eric stripped naked, and while she hastily tossed off her blouse, he yanked off her yellow dress.

In one swift movement, one very deep thrust, he was inside her.

A wave of pleasure erupted through her as her body welcomed him in. Her red, manicured nails clung to his back.

She heard a scream, and the voice was her own. Her fight for self-control was lost in a world of sensual sin. It was everything she was taught to run from—the Serpent in the Garden of Eden —that had tempted Eve, had snuck its slithering body between her thighs. Millie no longer cared if she was the pastor's wife. She'd come to realize her own pleasure, her own happiness.

For once, she flaunted her thick, luscious curves as Eric ran his hands along her full-figured hips, whispering, "I hate thin women. You're absolutely beautiful, Millie."

Millie realized that she was far more sacred than the vows of her marriage.

Yes, the Serpent had tempted her to sin, and she was prepared to sin again.

EIGHTEEN

THE WITNESS

SLEEP NEVER CAME FOR ESPERANZA, and it showed as dark circles rimmed her eyes. Night after night, she'd been too terrified to leave her home and had even called off work. Mrs. Goodwin kept asking if she was well, like the pastor's wife knew Esperanza wasn't really sick. Alex needed to go to school, and she was late on her rent. They not only needed the money, but she had a duty as a mother.

Lumbering alongside Alex, she wished she could reschedule her responsibilities, but as a single mother, she couldn't lay all day in bed.

Estamos a salvo. Estoy a salvo. We are safe. I am safe.

But the chant couldn't dissolve her deepest fears.

Someone was watching them. Following her.

Someone knew her secret and could deport her.

Someone could tear her away from her only child.

"You need to sleep, Mama," Alex said as they walked toward the private Palos Verdes school. "You look like a Walking Dead extra."

Mr. Ortiz, Alex's physics teacher and "absolute fave," as her son liked to say, walked ahead of them. The man was engrossed in a conversation with Mrs. Zimmerman, the school principal, whom Esperanza was supposed to meet within fifteen minutes. The subject of their banter might as well have been Russian to her ears.

"Geeze, I'm getting old," Mr. Ortiz said. "I can't believe I'm unable to remember how many specific neurons make up the brain. Ugh...well...it's in the billions. Somewhere in Europe, they're doing some sort of test regarding the brain and A.I. Oh darn...this is gonna bug me all day. Where did I read it?" The teacher frowned, tapping his chin with a finger.

"Oh, c'mon, this one's easy," Esperanza's twelve-year-old said with a laugh as they walked past. "Are you kidding me? 100 billion neurons make up the human brain. You know that." He turned around and continued. "Netherlands, Radboud University developed what's likely gonna be used in artificial intelligence. Check it out—they've created this awesome network. The idea is that it interconnects atoms that basically act like a 'quantum brain.' Can you believe it? It mimics how a real brain responds. How friggin' cool is that?!"

Stunned, the physics teacher pushed up his glasses.

"This your one-sixty?" Principal Zimmerman asked him—as if Esperanza and Alex weren't standing there.

"He's the one." Mr. Ortiz's face brightened as if eyeing prize money. "Still working on that top-secret software?"

Esperanza's son wasn't some show-and-tell toy. He was still a boy who should be treated no differently than any kid his age. But with every passing day, she felt that simple dream slipping from her fingers. Alex had been spending a lot of time on his new laptop, not watching stupid videos on YouTube like every other kid but doing some sort of "software coding." She hadn't a clue how he even picked up on developing software in the first place.

"Yep," Alex answered his preferred educator. "Almost finished."

"Alejandro, Santa didn't buy you that laptop for this," Esperanza hissed, "and what *special* reason? You don't wanna do something, *no lo sé*, normal?"

"C'mon, Mama," he said, "would you prefer that I be addicted to video games? You should be glad I'm putting my early Christmas present to use."

¡Ay Dios mío! What am I gonna do with this kid?

"Watch this," the physics instructor told the principal, and then to Alex, "7,485 multiplied by 4,557."

"Alex, don't—" Esperanza put up a hand to stop her son from participating in this all too familiar "quiz the child-prodigy game."

"34,109,145," Alex spat out coolly, as though the number challenge bored him.

"I said don't answer," Esperanza scolded.

"Why? It's so easy," Alex said.

"That's not the point," Esperanza chided Alex and then turned to his teacher. "He's more than one-sixty. More than a number, than his IQ. *¿Entiende?* He's still a child with a name, by the way. It's *ALEX*."

"Honestly, we meant nothing by it." Mr. Ortiz assured, then apologized in her native tongue. "*Perdóname*—I just wanted to know if Alex, well, if he could help me with one of my classes. We've arranged a generous incentive. Principal Zimmerman will tell you all about it."

"You want him to do your job now?" Esperanza folded her arms. "So, this is what my meeting's about?"

"Mama...*please*. Don't say no until you've heard Mrs. Zimmerman out."

"Fine," she sighed, unable to say no to her son's big brown

eyes. She kissed him on the cheek. "Have a good day at school, *mijo*."

The physics teacher thanked her profusely and left with Alex chatting next to him.

When Esperanza was in Principal Zimmerman's office, she eagerly explained, "Mrs. Flores, we asked Alex to help be a teacher's assistant to the advanced AP physics class. It'll actually be more of a co-teaching/TA hybrid role. It's our tenth-grade honors course, and it'll just be one class. If he does well, we were thinking of letting him continue for the rest of the year. Once a week."

The principal wrung her hands with anticipation.

"Alex...co-teach the tenth grade? He's...twelve," Esperanza's eyes grew large.

"According to the head of our science department, he's already completed the advanced physics courses. I don't think we need to remind you that your son's a genius. As you already know, he's been in Mensa since he was eight. Look, he should take the tests to see if he can pass on to the—"

"He's not skipping another grade," Esperanza insisted with motherly protection. "If I left it up to you, my Alex would be graduating!" Esperanza exhaled, realizing that she was getting defensive. "I just want my son to have some sort of normal childhood."

Mrs. Zimmerman placed a soothing hand on her shoulder.

"Mrs. Flores," Mrs. Zimmerman gently began, "he's already very bored with all the advanced classes."

The principal held up her hands. "He did it on his own, Mrs. Flores. He was given all the ninth-grade subject matter tests and passed them all with perfect scores. We can't keep him in lower grade levels. As head of the curriculum department, it's my duty to see that we place Alex in a grade level that matches where he's at. Your son is highly, *highly* advanced. I mean, advanced isn't even the word for what Alex's capable of."

Esperanza groaned. She knew there wasn't a word that could describe her son's capabilities.

"Here's the thing...the teachers all thought it would be more of a challenge for him—*less boring*—if he were to actually help our physics teachers. He'll be the youngest TA, but the students will get to learn a difficult subject matter from one of their peers. If he does as well as we expect, his tuition will be paid for," she pled, putting both palms together in prayer. "You won't have to constantly hustle for scholarships."

Esperanza was too physically exhausted to say no. After all, wasn't her goal to put her son in the best possible position to thrive? This was his opportunity, and he earned it on his own. She nodded her permission, and Mrs. Zimmerman threw her arms around her. Esperanza didn't fight the affection.

All throughout the bus drive home, she searched around, scrutinizing every passenger, worried that someone had climbed onto the bus with her. When nothing of the sort took place, she laughed aloud to herself, catching wayward glances from fellow passengers who thought she was *loca*.

When her phone rang, she put it on speaker. She pulled up to her apartment complex and parked. It was Isabelle, no doubt checking up on her since Esperanza had confided she thought someone had tried to scare her when she left the restaurant the other day.

"Everything okay, Esperanza?" she asked, concerned. "Did you get that new lock installed?"

"No," Esperanza said, chuckling incredulously, "*estoy bien, estoy bien.*"

"*Bueno,*" Isabelle resigned, then pled, "but I still think it can't hurt to call my guy. I told you; I'll pay for the new lock—*Lo pagaré.*"

"I rent, remember? I can't just change their locks. Besides, I said I'm fine," Esperanza insisted. "I'm climbing into my bed and taking a nap. I'm so tired. Call you later—*estoy bien*."

Esperanza hung up before Isabelle could keep her any longer from the rest her body had been desperately yearning for. She hadn't even seen the man's face. No one stopped her while she boarded the bus. No one followed her home. Lack of sleep had likely led to her paranoia.

She didn't make it halfway down the hall, before noticing her door. Her heart slammed against her chest as she crept slowly forward, her body trembling. The door was cracked open just enough. She had no weapon to defend herself. Should she call the cops? What would they do? Protect her or deport her? She couldn't call the cops. Esperanza pushed the door open, trepidation filling her body.

Inside, everything looked untouched.

Not one thing was out of place.

Fatigued, had she forgotten to lock up?

Relief swept through her. Her heart fell back into normal rhythm as she closed the door. She went into the bedroom, pulled back the covers, and then froze. With trembling hands, she picked up what looked like a stack of photos: she was leaving her building with Alex, dropping him off at school, shopping for groceries, walking up to the Goodwin's home. But worse were the pictures of Alex at the library with his friends during times she'd dropped him off to check out books. Pictures of Alex by himself walking into his school. A single line in Spanish was typed at the center of a blank sheet of paper:

Habla y te mueres.

Speak and you die.

NINETEEN

THE DETECTIVE

RED CRIME TAPE bordered twelve feet around the perimeter of the body. On the wider outside edge, yellow tape cordoned off a larger outer circumference, beginning with the Redondo Beach Pier and extending toward the surrounding restaurants.

There were dozens of Redondo Beach police officers positioned on the outer tape to ward off curious onlookers. Esplanade, the street that faced the ocean and led to the populous pier, had been shut down for several miles. The city, with more than sixty-seven thousand people and an average annual income of over one hundred thousand dollars, didn't see murders often.

Today, nearly every nosy cop on duty and fellow adrenalin junkie was at the crime scene. Which was no surprise given the homicide rate at this particular beach city was about one per year. It wasn't like they saw any action other than traffic stops and the occasional rich-man-loses-money suicides. No wonder every bored South Bay cop showed up acting like they were doing something other than standing around.

Already, Nazario spotted scientific investigators Chuck Whittier and Ellen Yang. They normally came unarmed. Their job was not to question witnesses or even be involved in solving anything. They gathered, processed, and analyzed evidence. SID did go to the crime scene but was mostly stuck in the lab. This was partly why Nazario declined to join SID. She wanted to solve the crime, be more hands-on and in the action.

"Nothing around the body," Yang said, "checked several feet around the perimeter."

Nazario walked toward the body with Wilson trailing behind. It was tucked under the pier, near a large gap just beneath the Redondo Landing and El Torito Grill. It was a perfect dark little cave, hidden away from the thousands of tourists who routinely visited the beach on a daily basis. Because Redondo Beach had such a low homicide rate, the local police department didn't have a homicide division and leaned on the LAPD to take the lead. This was especially true if it was not an open-and-shut case like in a suicide or a murder-suicide.

The man's brown skin was now mute ash—arms spread wide on either side, his face an image of frozen fear. Nazario wasn't stupid and chose to lean on her crutch this time rather than attempt a squat and potentially strain her bad knee on uneven beach sand. She couldn't wait to be rid of the contraption for good and retain full leg function.

The body was damp but not a "floater," as they called drowning victims.

"We collected residue under his fingernails. We'll test it," Whittier said. Wilson squatted to take a closer look, knees cracking under the burden of his weight. He breathed heavy and hard as he did after walking longer distances.

"Looks like he fought." Wilson inhaled a ragged breath. "Bruises on his hands. Hopefully, you'll find something under those nails. DNA or something."

Nazario took a gloved hand and tilted the arm, careful not to move it too much. She saw the slash marks on his forearm where he tried to cover his face.

Yang closed the small evidence bag that contained a sample of the dirt or potential skin scrapings from under the victim's nails, taken by the blunt end of a toothpick.

Nazario scanned the body from head to arms and then to the belly, where an incision had been made just below the sternum, right where the thoracic diaphragm began. The laceration continued past his lower abdomen, ending just above his pubic hairline. The victim had been sliced open like a gutted fish. The wound near his pelvic region looked a bit larger. Nazario lifted the bottom of the sliced flannel shirt. Judging by the size of the puncture wound, the first stabbing took place near the victim's lower abdomen and moved up to the chest, stopping at the sternum.

Nazario studied the eight-inch incision. "Wilson, you fish, doncha?"

"I certainly do," Wilson admitted, too jolly. "A huge family activity."

"How do you gut a fish?"

"Well, usually you start at the tail and move on up..." Wilson made a face. "...toward the belly." His explanation hung there as his eyes scanned the body.

Based on victim one, Nazario knowingly queried, "Find an ID?"

Yang answered, "Confiscated his ID, Mexico license, looks like an undocumented."

"Luis Vargas," Whittier filled in, avoiding eye contact with Nazario. "Forty-one, resides in South Central. Oh, Yago Rios—and now this Vargas fellow—were both called in. Tipped off to the DA for prosecution and deportation just days before their murders."

"No papers?" Wilson asked, meeting Nazario's eyes. "And the caller was anonymous?"

"That's correct," Whittier said, straightening his shoulders.

"Okay, let us know what you find. If there's DNA under the nails and we get a database match," Nazario said. "I get the feeling there won't be."

As they walked to the car in contemplative silence, the pre-dawn light melted into the swollen grey atmosphere. Thunder rumbled, and the smell of rain permeated the air. She looked up at the sky, threatening to break open. It was a good thing the body was under the pier, where potential DNA could be preserved. Unless there were bloody fingerprints on the t-shirt matching the killer, there would be none found on the skin. Human skin made getting prints a challenge because sweat was ninety-nine percent water.

So, trying to recover quality latent (invisible) fingerprints from the skin of a corpse was extremely difficult. They'd likely not find any prints on the body; they usually didn't. There might be DNA under the nails, but it'd be unlikely that the murderer was in their crime database. It'd be too easy, and something in the pit of her stomach told her that this latest murder would be anything but simple.

Wilson put an arm behind Nazario's back and under her left arm to help her into his car.

"Don't give me lip. I've let you struggle through the sand. But I put my foot down when it comes to a potential re-injury— if you haven't already done that." He tossed her crutch in the back seat and helped her into the car. "When do you go back to see the doc?"

"Got the stitches out of my face yesterday," Nazario muttered. "I dunno about the leg. Maybe sometime next week. He's gotta take out more stitches."

"You gonna tell him you haven't been doing PT?"

"Yes, honey." Nazario rolled her eyes. "Why do I feel like we're married?"

Wilson coughed out a laugh, his belly jiggling under the steering wheel. "Practically."

As Nazario looked out the window, a bolt of lightning burst across the sooty sky, reawakening it, turning the vault of heaven electric-white. As if God was playing with a light switch, darkness reappeared, and the swollen storm clouds let loose. It wasn't the kind of rain that started with light, flirtatious sprinkles. There was no foreplay. Punishing drops came hammering down, and the dry Los Angeles atmosphere was instantly transformed.

Nazario sighed, spotting the blue body bag in the back of the coroner's van.

"Another dead Mexican immigrant," Nazario finally said, pivoting the conversation back to grim reality. "Our immigration donations—I think we should go public with it. Put the word out to the Los Angeles Times. Your buddy still work there? We need to do more—help in some way."

"You mean try to raise more money? Bring some awareness?"

"Absolutely. These murders don't always hit the news. More has to be done. We haven't caught the killer, but the very least we can do is show the public we care about their lives and the families they're leaving behind."

"Done. I'll give my contact a call. He mostly does PR now, but I'm sure he would love to publish a donations piece on undocumented and separated families. Most folks won't expect that the LAPD has been raising donations already. Might even be a morale booster."

Despite the torrential rain pour that didn't occur in LA, except for the occasional tantrum, Wilson was relaxed behind the wheel. While Nazario hated to drive in the rain, Wilson grew up near the Laurel Mountains just west of Salem, Oregon, where the average rainfall clocked in at one hundred and twenty-two inches.

"I can hear you thinking," Wilson said. "What's your theory? I mean, why would someone tip off the DA and then kill said victims that were gonna get prosecuted under the law?"

"Someone with access to rap sheets," she guessed, "like an immigration and customs contact? It's been bugging me, too. Back-to-back ain't nothing for Los Angeles, but two illegals killed within weeks of each other? Now, that's something."

Wilson put out a palm, as if to say, "Give it here."

Nazario grumbled, took out a five-dollar bill, and handed it to him. Wilson leaned over and reached for a bulging red vinyl zippered money pouch in the glove compartment labeled "Immigration Separated Families Donations."

He tucked the five in with the rest.

There were stacks of fives, tens, and twenties that must already equal at least two grand. While it started as an inside joke after the sensitivity trainer schooled the unit on proper verbiage and ethnic sensitivity, it'd now become a hefty contribution to the cause. The Chief's leather moneybag in his office alone once contained around ten grand collected from all departments before it was finally deposited into an account for the cause.

"Better deposit that soon," Nazario said.

"Dropping it off today." Wilson put the money away, then asked, "Why kill Vic-One and Two differently?"

"I dunno. Strangled Jimenez. Filleted Vargas. Like a damn fish. We need to look at the pictures again," Nazario said. "Wanna see if there are other similarities we're not catching. If I recall, both bodies were positioned almost exactly the same."

"That's right. Arms stretched out on either side. You thinking a hate crime?"

"Hate crimes tend to be more violent, fueled by passion. The strangulation was clean. The knife wound was also pretty clean. This was premeditated."

"They might be linked somehow," Wilson said, "but this could be gang-related, too."

"We'll need to talk to toxicology—see if we can get results back sooner rather than later. They're backed up, got over a hundred bodies. They'll move ours up. Just gotta make a call."

"So, that's how Pablo Jimenez's tox reports came back so quick," Wilson mused.

Gazing at the darkening night, she said, "Pray another don't pop up under some bridge."

In the car, the rain pelted her window with the same ferocity as it had about half an hour ago. The cold window felt good against her palm. As it stood, both cases could be closed due to insufficient leads plus very little evidence at the crime scene. They were scheduled to talk to Isabelle Jimenez again in the morning. Nazario didn't wish for a third murder, but if it occurred, it'd be easier to identify. Her gut told her these DBs were different than her other cases.

In fact, these murders weren't your run-of-the-mill homicides.

They were not gang-affiliated, drug-related, or an act of revenge.

This might be a career changer and her very first serial killer.

TWENTY

THE PASTOR'S WIFE

MILLIE FELT sore in all the right places. She decided against the body-shaping Spanx mid-thigh tights and threw them on the top shelf of the closet, where unused clothes went to die.

"You better take that contraption off the next time I see you," Eric Myers had said. "You don't need it." It had been the single nicest compliment she'd ever heard. She had to bite her lip to hold back her emotions. The night with Eric, she had been liberated. But now, she returned to the pious prison of Stan.

She expected to be stricken with guilt over succumbing to Eric. She primed herself for a flood of remorse to overwhelm and eat away at her conscience. She figured she'd hear the Holy Spirit admonishing her to repent. But the verses she used to recite again and again—how to be a good wife, how to submit and be perfect—dissolved entirely from her memory. All she'd been able to think about was Eric, and then Millie realized an appalling, thrilling truth.

She was not guilty. She wasn't sorry for any of it.

The door hurled open, slamming against the wall. It was Stan. She could smell the prunes he ate. Instead of jumping, her nose wrinkled in disgust. Stan's circular face ripened; his hanging loose jowls turned the color of a fresh sunburn. It reminded her of a turkey's wattle. Funny, that was what they actually called that red, wrinkly flesh that resembled old shriveled-up ball skin after removing the nuts. And Stan, well, he looked like someone had removed his testicles.

Square glasses framed his beady eyes. The sockets appeared cartoonishly spread apart, as they always had. It wasn't like she didn't notice these things before. Yet, suddenly, she saw all of Stan's flaws under a magnifying glass. All of his weird smells and idiosyncratic imperfections were bursting forth. She felt as if a small earthquake was forming inside Stan, like the tectonic plates of his life had started to shift. His hands began to clench and unclench, a behavior he'd been doing lately.

Oh no, was Stan mad? Too bad.

Her husband's "gobbler," as Millie pet named it, was flapping back and forth in protest. He was shaking so badly—it looked like he was suffering from early-onset Parkinson's disease.

"We need to have a family meeting. My office." Stan directed with a quivering finger.

His eyes were wide as his nostrils flared, sweat collecting on Stan's upper lip. Unsteady hands fidgeted with his glasses, unsure of where to place them. He folded his arms across his chest and then planted them on his hips like a bungling gunslinger. She bit her lower lip to force herself not to laugh, and at this moment, she didn't care if Stan knew.

"We're doing no such thing. If you wanna talk, we talk right here. I'm not an employee or a member of our congregation."

"We *will* have a family meeting in my office."

"Want your family meeting?" Millie inched close to his face. She screamed with all the force her lungs could bear. *"Why don't you call our son, and we'll have a family meeting!"*

"He's not well, Millie Ann," Stan snarled. "He. Is. Not. Well!"

"How would you know? How would I even know? Gideon doesn't wanna see either of us, and my head keeps going over and over why. I'm still trying to figure it out."

"You know why. He's got that borderline personality disorder, and he's violent. Since he's twenty-one now, he can make his own decisions. You know, and I know—he wants no communication. Frankly, I'm fine with that. He's dangerous."

"Gideon is not dangerous. Our son, who you refuse to talk about, is not a danger to society. I didn't raise him that way. He's a sweet boy, and now he won't even speak to me, and I can't help but wonder if it has something to do with you."

Millie strode past Stan, shoving his shoulder with hers. His hand gripped her upper arm, yanking her around.

"Where were you last night, and who were you having Bible study with that late?" Stan's eyes narrowed, as his fingers curled around her upper arm. Thick digits dug into her shoulder.

"Esperanza," Millie lied, trying to pull her arm free. "I was having Bible study with Esperanza and Alex. They were teaching me how to make her homemade tamales."

"Why don't I believe you?"

Millie swelled with rage. "Maybe I was spreading my legs wide open! Maybe I was having sex with another man!"

Before she could move, Stan's thick hand flew through the air, his palm striking hard upon her cheek whipping her head back. She reeled in shock. Her face burned, but not as much as the rage building inside.

"I want a *divorce*!"

"Not in God's holy house! There'll be no such thing!" He seized her shoulders, shaking her violently, his voice rising like Jesus after the third day. "What in God's holy name is going on with you?" His face turned a blood-clot red. Spittle flew from his mouth. "Ephesians 5:22, you've gone against God's order!"

"Get your hands off me!" Millie struggled with everything in her and finally swung, her fist connecting with Stan's nose, knocking his glasses off. He tumbled, losing his footing, his chubby frame crashing to the floor. His arms flailed, trying to lift himself off the ground.

Fury held her spellbound momentarily. Then, without thinking, she lunged forward. Both hands found his throat. Stan let out a gurgled hack, and with a thud, his stubby legs faltered, sending him careening back to the floor.

Millie straddled him. Her elbows locked. Hands squeezed around his neck with everything she had, her weight thrown, every muscle straining.

Loose, droopy neck-fat oozed between her fingers. Bile rose in her throat.

It was disgusting.

In a flash, the past began to rise from where she'd buried it— hot lava rumbling to the surface. She could feel Gideon in her arms the moment she first held him. Too small a body for a scream that loud—vociferous, defiant, announcing him to the world. From the moment he was born, she knew that Gideon wanted to be heard–needed everyone to hear him. And she had failed.

She had failed to hear his cries.

The day Gideon nearly drowned had become one great, mysterious cloud. Each year, a legion of Millie's unanswered questions remained suspended, unspoken, unheard. She would have defied God's holy order, broken one of her sacred rules— no, their sacred rules—to demand answers.

If only she had been there for her son.

If only she hadn't gone grocery shopping.

If only. If only. If only. If only. If only.

Guilt, for a mother, was endless.

The elephant in the room had been ignored for so long that it had eaten the entire house. It was as though she and Stan didn't have a son at all. As if Gideon hadn't immediately attached his angry, scrunched face to her swollen breast, that perfect moment where he drank from her, and they immediately bonded.

That moment was pure.

He was simply faultless.

Her boy. Her sweet boy was never the same after the day he'd almost met death.

That was when his mood changed. When the rounds of medications and the awful subject matter of "mental health" first reared its ugly head. She remembered how his big blue eyes looked into hers with questions and fear.

He was asking her without speaking, "Mama, you want me to swallow this pill?"

He held the medication in his hand, watching and waiting for her to make a decision, to say something, to tell him to stop, to tell him that he was fine, that he didn't need antipsychotic medication. He wasn't crazy. After all, the world that scared him and had made him scream as a newborn had disappeared when he could sense Mama there to protect him. It was as if, by instinct, her son knew he was safe with her. So why did she let him take those pills?

A voice returned her to her present actions.

"Mrs. Goodwin? Hello...we're early..." Esperanza yelped. "¡Ay, Dios mío!"

Millie ignored Esperanza. Her focus narrowed on Stan, now a pretty shade of pastel blue. Millie released her grip, and blood rushed to Stan's round cheeks.

"We'll have tamales for dinner," Millie snarled at Stan, "wanna hear you say it."

Stan made a hacking and wheezing sound. "T-a-m-a-l-e-s."

Millie stood. Brushed wrinkles from her skirt. Wiped her brow.

She beamed down at Stan. "Tamales for dinner is a *wonderful* idea, hon."

Stan gasped, hacking and sucking in a large lungful of air.

"Let this be a reminder," Millie cooed soft and sweet. "I've opened up lots of stubborn jars. So, don't ever hit me or put your *almighty* hands on my arm like that again. I really don't like it," Millie warned, forcing a smile.

His eyes grew large.

She spun around to face Esperanza. "Sorry about the little... tussle. It was so nice having Bible study with you last night. And I'm glad you taught me how to make tamales."

"Yes...the...uh..." Esperanza fumbled for a response. "Bible study was nice?" The lift to her voice made it a question.

"Stan and I were just discussing dinner, weren't we, dear?" She tapped his face twice with a palm, though it was hard enough to be more of a slap. Her palm print glowed on his pale, plump cheeks.

Stan stumbled to his feet and nodded obediently.

"Now, don't be so dramatic, Stan. What was it that you wanted for dinner again?"

"Tamales," he said, over-enunciating each letter as he did the first time.

"I stay. I cook," Esperanza offered. "I got the text. Alex is putting the food in the fridge."

"Oh, that would be lovely," Millie fetched her purse. "How much do I owe you?"

"I can't remember." Esperanza waved a hand, her eyes not quite meeting hers. Sweat beaded on her forehead. She wiped it away and cleared her throat, backing out of the room. "It's okay, really, Mrs. Goodwin. I am fine."

"Don't be silly." Millie dug into her purse and took out forty dollars. "Keep the change."

"*¡Ay, Dios mío!*" Esperanza clutched the money in her hand and stumbled back against the door. It knocked and bounced against the wall hard enough to leave a mark. "I know you just painted the walls, Mr. Goodwin. I'm sorry." Esperanza's eyes darted to Millie's husband. "I'll stay longer tonight if you need me to."

Millie turned to Stan, who expected this from Esperanza.

Stan's annoying monologue about striving for perfection echoed in Millie's brain word for word. He repeated it to her and Esperanza anytime he saw an unclean spot, an error Millie made with the calendar, a name she'd not memorized from their congregation, a member who hadn't been accounted for, tithing that she'd forgotten to reinforce.

They didn't always happen...mistakes, but when they did occur, she'd be forced to listen to Stan's rebuke.

"Mistakes are avoidable, Millie Ann. Perfection isn't about pride," Stan had lectured repeatedly. "It's about paying attention, and when you don't pay attention, mistakes happen, and God does not like the foolish. Errors should be caught like sin ought to be caught. Perfection is possible."

Her husband's words no longer sounded sane to Millie—and so, they no longer held power over her. A light chortle escaped Millie, and she bristled now with new freedom, a sense of power, and control she hadn't felt in a long while.

"Don't you worry, Esperanza, there'll be no more lectures from now on."

Esperanza nodded, bouncing hard against the door. It racketed against the wall for a second time. *No biggie.* Millie would repaint the wall if there were marks. She thought she heard another apology but couldn't be sure, just before her housekeeper turned and bolted down the stairs.

TWENTY-ONE
THE WITNESS

THE AIR WAS heavy with the rich, intoxicating aroma of masa —its sweetness mingling with savory notes of tender pork, all wrapped in corn husks. She took extra care to perfect her mother's special spices this time: three tablespoons of cumin, a tablespoon of black pepper. But it was the garlic—three tablespoons —and six of cayenne, mixed into the shredded pork, that was savory enough to carry through the Goodwins' kitchen and across time.

The flavors of her old Mexican home, of her mama's kitchen, bloomed in her mind. A ray of sunlight broke through the dim, small kitchen. Her mother's tender voice hummed "México Lindo y Querido" by the iconic actor and singer of her time, Jorge Negrete. Esperanza didn't keep up with old classics. But she remembered one song, heard her mother's melodic croon. On occasion, she'd slip a word or two from the lyrics between finger dabs into the spice mixture to taste and approve it before placing the pork in the center and rolling the tamale in the corn husk.

Unlike what had routinely occurred, Mrs. Goodwin insisted

that she carry the rectangular deep-dish glass of tamales to the dinner table herself.

"You're not our servant. We can serve ourselves. Stan can serve himself," Mrs. Goodwin said and ordered her husband to take a side chair.

Esperanza now assumed the head of the table, per Mrs. Goodwin's direction, ones she'd rather not disobey. Her shirt stuck to her back, and pools of sweat collected between her breasts. The cooking had heated things up, but something else had, too.

Things were getting very strange.

Alex sat at the other end of the table, another superior spot they weren't used to. To someone else, a chair was a chair. A spot was a spot. To someone else, a meal was a meal. You ate what you felt like eating, leftovers or whatever was in the fridge.

But to the Goodwins, a chair wasn't just a chair—a spot at the table, not just any spot. To the Goodwins, you didn't simply eat what you felt like eating. You didn't eat leftovers because, you see, everything had to be pre-planned.

All the changes began with Mrs. Goodwin—her fire engine red lipstick, her frosted new haircut, and bolder shades of color like electric purple and hot pink, which, according to her son, were a "retro-eighties thing."

"She has been behaving, I don't know, *extraño?*" Esperanza mused while on the bus ride there. "They call this in English, *como lo dices, mid-life?*"

"Nope. It's not a mid-life crisis. She's sick of her weirdo husband's schedule. I bet all that schedule stuff is all his idea. Who can blame her? It's neurotic," Alex had said.

She didn't expect to see what she saw, but her eyes didn't deceive her.

Mrs. Goodwin was on top of her husband, hands around his

throat, his face as blue as the sky. And that smile she gave her, that smile after she released him...

*Gracias a Dios—thank God—*Alex wasn't there to see it all.

Should she have done something? She just stood there.

She stood there for at least five, maybe eight seconds—watching her.

Should she have tried to save Mr. Goodwin?

Mr. Goodwin sneezed, making her jump in her chair and return to the present. Esperanza blessed him in Spanish, too, which the pastor enunciated in a very Anglo, painfully non-accented way.

"Gra-ci-as." Mr. Goodwin's ruddy face appeared to be shifting like waves between anger, fear, and utter humiliation and with such transparency.

Alex was staring at him, amused. She wanted to kick her son under the table, to wipe away that smirk he had across his lips, to order him, as she always did, to obey and respect his elders. But she couldn't, not with Alex at the other end of the table. Each leaden breath sank to the pit of her stomach. Everything about the evening sent a cold chill up her spine, one that flooded every cell with trepidation.

Mr. Goodwin shifted in his seat. The old floors groaned under his load. His waistline, an Earth-like equator, was captured against the table. The pastor wasn't morbidly obese, but he was not fit by any stretch of the imagination. One hand lifted to his neck where his wife's dainty fingers left their red autograph. His eyes swept to the side under his thick glasses, catching Esperanza's watchful gaze.

Pastor Goodwin's eyes narrowed at her, and she looked away.

"Mrs. Goodwin, Alex has to wake early. We catch at least two buses to get to his school," Esperanza reasoned, hoping to escape this strange dinner. She couldn't focus on food. Pastor

Goodwin grimaced, staring at the pile of tamales stacked into a neat pyramid. Red fingerprints grew darker across his neck with each passing moment. Maybe it was her eyes playing tricks on her. Her eyes were drawn to them like a magnet. All she could think of was Yago Rios lying under The Serpent's Bridge and those cold hands that clenched her throat in her dream. The voice familiar, the face shadowy, becoming a blur.

The face was a haze of smoke, like the thickening clouds of vapor that night, unusually heavy fog for a fall Los Angeles evening. The shape of the lips reformed: thin, plump, wide, tight, narrow. The color of the eyes became a kaleidoscope, rapidly shifting between brown, green, blue, yellow, grey, and black. Like a short circuit, her brain seemed to be misfiring, or God was playing tailor, making alterations. Man. Woman. Short. Tall. Thin. Fat. Muscular. Gaunt. The face long as a horse. The face, round as an apple. Jaws square. High cheekbones. No cheekbones. Chin pointy. A rounded chin that connected to the neck. Nose crooked. Nose arrow straight. Nose bulbous. Nose pinched tight.

Man. Woman. They. Them.

The killer contorted in her mind.

Shapeshifting.

Out of the millions of people that crossed The Serpent's Bridge, how was it that she was the one to witness a murder, to hear a dead man's last call for help? Out of all the little boys riding around on bikes, how was it that Nicky, Alex's Nicky, would be the one that would get hit by a car and die?

She needed to pray more.

She needed to attend church, not the Goodwin's church, but a church that made her feel like the Spirit of God was present.

"We really need to get going." Esperanza shot up, jostling the ancient, splintered chair back, its legs hiccupping against the ground. Millie put a hand on Esperanza's shoulder, light and delicate as if touching a babe. Esperanza eyed those hands wearily. They were strong, strong enough to nearly kill her husband just a couple of hours ago.

Esperanza sat back down, obedient. Nervous adrenaline made her shiver.

"Oh, you can stay for one tamale, can't you, dear?" Millie grabbed one and plopped it on her plate, encouraging Alex to do the same with a wave of her red-manicured fingers. Across from her, Alex waited for his mom to give the go-ahead. After a nod in his direction, her son tore into his tamale while she peeled open her own with nervous hands.

The pastor was the last one. He plucked up one of the tamales like he was picking up cow shit, placed it on his dinner plate with two fingers, and jabbed his pointer finger at it to determine if it was alive or dead. Millie unwrapped her tamale and took a fork to it. Esperanza waited and watched. Millie took a bite, and her eyes rolled back. A guttural moan escaped her throat. Pastor Goodwin clenched his fork, and his jowls constricted.

Alex snickered at the end of the table.

The landline rang, which made Alex laugh even more. His eyes widened as he bellowed, "You guys really have a landline?"

The pastor ordered his wife like he had already forgotten that the sweet pastoral counselor almost strangled him to death this very same night, exclaiming, "You answering it, or are you gonna just sit there?" He wrinkled his nose as he unwrapped his tamale.

Unexpectedly, time no longer moved at all.

The room and everyone present evaporated.

A tall man, young, no older than twenty-one, stood on the other side of the large open window facing the living room. He was motionless, wearing a simple white t-shirt and a grey jacket with pockets on either breast. Hair sprouted out from under a red baseball cap, and a burgeoning shadow of a beard tapered close to the jawline.

He was handsome.

In the dark, the light from the living room hit at just the right angle. She could see his eyes, brilliant azure orbs glowing in the dark. A fresh set of goosebumps prickled her spine, spreading up her body and reaching across her forearms where the hairs rose. There was something familiar about him, something too familiar.

She had seen him before. *Where? Where? Where?* Think, where had she seen him before? She knew his face. Even his clothes looked familiar. Was he the man from outside Isabelle's restaurant? She shivered.

Might he be the killer?

Was he the killer?

Did he write that note? Leave those pictures in her bed? Was he the one chasing her?

The phone rang, but neither Mr. nor Mrs. Goodwin made any effort to answer it.

"Someone's standing out there," Esperanza choked out, pointing to the window. "He's right there."

Alex glanced up to where she'd pointed, and Stan did the same. But the young man was gone. Mrs. Goodwin turned around and looked behind her, the pastoral counselor staring at the empty window. No one was there anymore.

Seeing nothing, Mrs. Goodwin asked, "Something wrong, Esperanza?"

"Someone was standing there," Esperanza insisted, her voice shaking. "Looking in the window."

Millie got up, walked out to the back porch, glanced around, and then sat back down just as the phone rang.

"Sorry, Esperanza," the pastor's wife said with an empathetic smile, "but I didn't see anything out there."

The phone rang again.

"Are you not gonna answer the phone, Millie Ann?" Stan barked.

"We're having dinner. Whoever it is can wait. You wanna answer the phone so bad? Get up off your lazy butt and get it yourself!" She slammed a fist down on the table, rattling the silverware.

Alex's eyes grew large, and he nearly coughed out his food.

The phone rang again. Millie ignored it. Red hot flames shot across the pastor's pale cheeks. Esperanza needed to leave this crazy house before the strange man came back. She had to protect her son. Whoever that man outside was, he'd found her. Clutching her purse, Esperanza jolted up and motioned for Alex. He shoved another bite in his mouth before getting up.

Esperanza grappled with an explanation, one they'd understand.

Anything she said, no matter the words chosen, would sound *loca*.

"Lock your doors," Esperanza said, "someone's been following me, and I fear—"

Concerned, Alex blurted, "Who's been following you, Mama."

"C'mon Alex, we have to go. Now!"

Millie put her hands over her mouth. "Esperanza, calm down. Have a seat now. If you're in danger—"

"Just please...lock your doors." Esperanza grabbed her son's hand, turned her head one last time, and looked into the pastor's wife's wet eyes.

"Esperanza, honey, I looked, and there was no one outside," Millie insisted, "but we'll call the cops right now if that'll put your mind at ease."

"We're not calling the cops for a non-emergency, Millie Ann," Stan grumbled. "Unless we tell them what happened to my neck."

Stan pointed at the hand marks around his throat. "You call, and only one person in this house is going straight to jail."

"I don't know what you're talking about," Millie denied.

"Uh-huh." Stan folded his arms across his chest.

Alex eyed the confrontation with concern. "You might wanna give whoever's calling your cell phone," he suggested with caution.

"She said she saw a man out there, Stan, some man standing outside our home. Looking in on us like some, some, creep," Millie said. "Shouldn't we at least consider—"

"Consider what?" Stan shot up. He stalked outside and called out. "Hello...anyone out there? This is private property. Come out, come out, whoever you are." But the strange young man Esperanza saw was no longer in sight. Would he follow them home again? She wondered.

Stan stalked back in and slammed the door. He threw his hands in the air.

"Well, you should consider it...consider it a warning from God," Esperanza said, ignoring Millie's offer to drive them. She grabbed Alex's hand and ran out the door.

TWENTY-TWO

THE DETECTIVE

RETURNING FROM HER ORTHOPEDIC SURGEON, Nazario hobbled out of her vehicle, defeated after the doctor reported that her knee had somewhat deteriorated rather than improved.

"You have *not* been using the ice machine, Detective Nazario." he'd stated as fact.

"I've turned it on when I can," she admitted.

"Gonna take out the stitches now," he'd said, using tweezers to gently remove the black threads that knitted her knee together. "I'm warning you. If you don't take it easy, you might end up permanently disabled. You get what that means?"

"Been busy dealing with a homicide case that's turning into a serial killer situation," she said frankly, "so, I strap up to that stupid ice machine when I can."

"Your body isn't gonna wait around for you to figure out a case you're trying to solve," the doc lectured. "You can delay the healing process and cause further complications. Your knee looks a little swollen; I'm prescribing antibiotics to prevent infection, which may cause nausea. I'm not blowing smoke here; take my advice or leave it. As your doctor, and I've been working in orthopedics for thirty-five-plus years and have seen this happen countless times, I'm telling you: you will not have a strong enough knee to run down your next perp if you continue disobeying post-surgery instructions and neglecting your health. Ignore this warning, and in a few years, you'll need a total knee replacement."

Hobbling to her next meeting would be akin to crossing a football field. "Okay, Doc," Nazario grumbled to herself, "heard you loud and clear."

Despite arriving at the station on time, she arrived late to the interrogation room. As it turned out, Isabelle Jimenez was anxious and early for her appointment. Wilson opened the door for her, and Nazario limped in, then slumped onto the chair next to him. Isabelle's knee bobbed manically. Her once-bleached hair showed dark roots and unkempt grey strands that sprouted like weeds in a neglected garden.

"Let's talk about your cousin," Wilson began. "We ran his background."

Isabelle shifted uneasily in her chair. She wiped her face as tears began making marks through her foundation. Wilson pushed the box of tissues at the center of the table toward her.

"Thank you," she sniffed, grabbing a couple and dabbing her face.

"We stand by our deal, you get that?" Nazario tilted her head until Isabelle lifted her eyes. "Not losing your business, okay? We wanna find who killed Pablo just as much as you do."

Isabelle sniffled and nodded, dabbing her face again with crumpled tissue.

Wilson looked down at his notes. "Your cousin was caught with a fake ID under the name Roman Garcia. Tried to get a passport, was flagged by Passport Services within the Bureau of Consular Affairs. Went to court. Slapped with a misdemeanor and deported. Got back in a year later," Wilson paused, and Nazario jumped in.

"Got himself another fake ID under the name Yago Rios. Did you know the DA had his case, and it went to a grand jury at the Los Angeles County Superior Court? They indicted Pablo just two days before he was killed. He was looking at a felony charge, fines, and prison," Nazario explained.

Isabelle's eyes grew wide. Her hands covered her mouth. "I didn't know this."

"Grand juries are a private matter, Miss Jimenez," Wilson told her in his usual, more formal style, a contrast from Nazario's direct approach. "Suspects aren't aware they're being investigated, and a case is pending against them until a grand jury finds them guilty."

"You help him cross the border?" Nazario threw it out there —no reason to delay.

Not answering, Isabelle wept again.

"Here's our theory." Wilson folded his hands in front of him. "He called. You got him back in. Offered employment. Are we right?" Wiping her face, Isabelle nodded her answer.

Wilson extracted a tissue from the box and handed it to her.

She plucked the tissue with her index finger and thumb, careful not to touch Wilson—as if doing so might contaminate her. She sobbed harder into the tissue now, mascara and foundation commingling into a muddy mess streaking her face.

"We're close. Not like the gringos. I hear them complain. They come to our restaurant with their money and their mouths. I hear them talking loudly like they do. Bragging. Like it's a good thing to turn their backs on their own flesh and blood. They cut off family, afraid to loan them money, rather have them homeless and out on the streets than to help." Isabelle's chin rose, conviction weighing on her words. "Our culture works hard, but what matters more is that we're always there for one another—*always*."

"We respect your perspective," Nazario said.

"Oh, do you? What's your real color, Detective Nazario—brown, or is it really blue?"

"Think you're looking for some black-and-white answer." Nazario exhaled, steepling her fingers, "But I think it's quite possible to be both, represent both. Look, just 'cause I wear a badge, don't mean I'm whitewashing the color of my skin. We're sensitive to the climate of diversification. My own father busted his ass to rise the ranks and was the highest Puerto Rican detective, head of Vice and Narcotics before he was murdered while working undercover. Your cousin was murdered, too. I know what it's like to have family killed. We're not your enemy, *comprendes?*"

"Well, we Jimenez are a proud Mexican family," the restaurant owner continued defensively. "It's always been a family promise to take care of one another. Even if family breaks the law. Even if this means I must break the law, too. I am willing to go to jail for *mi familia.*"

She raised her chin, gaze shifting between Wilson and Nazario, daring them to arrest her.

"You're absolutely right, Miss Jimenez. I truly and sincerely admire the Mexican culture. I really do." Wilson put a hand over his heart. "I've been divorced twice, and I'll admit, I'm one of them white folk that don't talk to family. I have an older brother I hate, okay? And I got cousins on my mom's side of the family that I refuse to speak to. It's all stupid and petty shit, too. I wish I could adopt the Mexican culture—that healthy attitude toward family. Look, I'm just another one of them cultureless, Anglo assholes that don't give a monkey's ass about them rules on blood."

Isabelle's tense body loosened in the same way that others had under Wilson's smooth monologue. He gave Nazario a sideways glance, and now it was her turn to take over. Nazario leaned in, keeping sober eyes fused on the businesswoman.

"Someone out there might not care too much about your culture," Nazario said, understating the gravity of the situation. "This case, well, it's prompted us to raise awareness about our donation efforts—"

"I saw the paper. I read the article. It's kind of you to raise money for undocumented families. Didn't think you people cared. What I care about right now is who killed Pablo." She searched Nazario's face for answers.

"That's what we're trying to figure out. Someone else came up dead yesterday—another immigrant. No papers. We can't say for sure if the murders are linked, but we have our suspicions."

"Someone is killing..." Isabelle stalled, "...undocumented?"

Nazario and Wilson waited for a beat, but Isabelle Jimenez seemed lost for words.

"It's partly why we're raising the money," Wilson continued gingerly, "just hoping to bring more attention and urgency to the matter."

"Let me ask you again, and please, we need your complete honesty here." Nazario narrowed her eyes at Isabelle, who tucked her hair behind her ear with a nervous hand. "Did you know that someone tipped off the authorities and that your cousin was likely to do jail time?"

A visible clamping of the jaw and aura of discomfort washed over the restaurant owner at the two words: jail time. Like many others under interrogation, this was the moment they withdrew. They could blow the interrogation and had to be careful. Nazario eyed Wilson, who took her clue to soften things.

"He said something about a full-time job," Isabelle said, "but wouldn't tell me what it was. He said it wouldn't conflict with the part-time hours at the restaurant. That's all."

Wilson added in that same easy tone, "Well, someone made

an anonymous call to the police, and the DA's office was subsequently made aware to prosecute. He'd been on ICE's radar, too."

They waited a minute or two—still nothing. Isabelle stared down at her fingers.

"Do you know who could've made those calls, Isabelle?" Nazario asked, this time using her first name. The businesswoman adjusted in her seat at Nazario's directness, or maybe she had been used to Wilson's formality. "Think and think very hard. Did Pablo have any enemies? He worked for you, but did he come into contact with anyone who knew him and had reason to turn him in? You know anything else about this job?"

"I said I know *nothing* about his new job," Isabelle replied definitely, "Didn't even know where it was. Pablo said it paid well, but that's it. I know nothing. *Nada.*"

"We're not sure if the caller has anything to do with the killer, but we find the call and the timing of his death...peculiar," Wilson maintained.

Her eyes darted back and forth as if thinking, and then a hand covered her mouth.

"Wait a minute," she paused, then her words bit out angrily, "there's this guy—*Eric Myers.* The Devil."

Wilson jostled in his pocket and retrieved a caramel Werther's Original hard candy. "The Devil, huh?"

"He attends our church," Isabelle clarified, "and he is the Devil."

Nazario raised a brow at her partner as he plopped the candy in his mouth. It clunked and rattled against his teeth. "You mean Sanctuary Baptist?" Wilson mumbled around his mouthful of hard candy.

Isabelle nodded.

Wilson jotted the name in his notepad.

Nazario leaned back in her chair. "Why him? What makes you suspect this, Eric Myers?"

"He's ICE!" Isabelle Jimenez shouted louder than Nazario expected.

Nazario leaned in and plunked an arm inches away from Isabelle.

The restaurant owner scooted back and braced herself protectively.

"Devil in the flesh or not, Eric Myers is nothing more than an immigration and customs enforcement agent," Nazario replied evenly, "who has every religious right to attend the church of his choice. Now, what makes you think he's connected to your cousin's murder?"

"He's no Christian. Almost all the members are Mexican, except for the Goodwins, who have made it their mission to help Mexican immigrants. This is no secret; Eric Myers just comes to church looking for people to put in jail. Everyone knows it. We've lost members because of his attendance. Everyone's afraid they'll be next. Several members have been deported because of that horrible man."

Nazario clarified, "I'm pretty damn certain the only thing this Myers guy is guilty of is doing his job."

"And the only thing Pablo was guilty of was wanting a better life. A felony and jail time for a dream? *Maldito estúpido!*" she cursed in Spanish. "Child molestation is a felony. Kidnapping, burglary, rape, these are felonies. *Those* people should be in jail. But trying to have a better life? To have dreams? This they call a felony with the rapists and perverts?"

"We don't make the law," Nazario conceded, adjusting her leg uncomfortably.

Wilson put a hand on Isabelle's shoulder. She stiffened. Isabelle glared at Wilson's hand. As cops, regardless of their rank or ethnicity, there was a visible adverse reaction to their presence, and it never got easy.

The fight against the bad-cop stigma was one Nazario was determined to win.

"We'll interview Mr. Myers, ask him a few questions," Wilson reassured. "If there's anything else that comes to mind, or anyone suspicious, please let us know."

"May I go now? Are we done, then?"

"We're all set, Isabelle. Thank you for your time," Nazario said.

Wilson got up. "Do you need me to walk you to your car, Miss Jimenez? It's dark out."

"No." Isabelle hugged her purse to her chest. "Just find out who killed my cousin."

———

In the conference room, Chief Johnson sat at the head of the rectangular oakwood table. Nazario and Wilson were the last to arrive. After the long interview with Isabelle Jimenez, they were entitled to be a few minutes late to an impromptu meeting with the Chief.

Chief mentioned something about the Feds.

Of course, the FBI would get involved; they usually did.

They sometimes cooperated with the cops, but usually, they took over the case entirely. It was demoralizing, implying the cops couldn't do their jobs, like they were too stupid to do investigative work. It became a pissing contest between the Homicide Department and whichever federal special agents were assigned to the case. She couldn't help but think that the FBI was passive-aggressively retaliating because she'd turned down a lucrative job with the Bureau.

"Anaya, hija, the world isn't always out to get you," she could hear her dad say. If he were still alive, he'd set her straight, tell her she was being paranoid, tell her to knock it off.

Investigators Chuck Whittier and Ellen Yang were seated next to Chief Johnson. SID occasionally sat through meetings, but if the Feds were already involved, anyone associated with the case was called to be present. The low babble of the room faded away. Rolling her eyes, she didn't bother to look at the two FBI agents.

"So, we've got babysitters taking a squat already? Maybe you guys should come back after a third pops up cold." Nazario diverted her eyes, slicing the tension with vinegar, ignoring SID, looking at her like she was crazy for talking this way in front of their boss.

They didn't know that Chief, who'd worked with Daddy, had begged her to stay on—begged her not to quit almost two decades ago, after she'd worked with a few shady beat cops— ones who lacked any moral compass. Nazario was astonished that she'd known Chief Johnson all forty-three years and had never once censored herself around him. In fact, he'd been there at the hospital the day she was born.

"Watch it, Nazario," Johnson barked.

Wilson's laughter rang out, dissolving the tension with the same effortless grace he exhibited during a hostage negotiation or making people like Isabelle Jimenez open up. Nazario welcomed Wilson's open-door chivalry, too tired to let her pride tell him she could do it herself. She shuffled in, ready to set her crutch against the wall, but stopped cold at a familiar voice from the past.

"Anaya," he said.

"Blake," she jabbed back, "didn't tell me you were gonna take this case."

"Had you returned my text messages, you might've been informed."

Bodies shifted in the room. No one had ever heard Detective Nazario addressed on a first-name basis. There was an intimacy in the use that made her uneasy. The discomfort was thick in the air—like "We Used to Sleep Together" was a song blaring on a loudspeaker.

He'd texted her three times since their collision outside the men's restroom: first to ask if she wanted to grab lunch, a second time for coffee, then a third time to see how her knee was doing and ask if they could "chat."

Hopping on her left leg, she clumsily attempted to lean her crutch against the wall. She swayed, lightheaded. It occurred to her that she hadn't eaten anything...again. She'd rather have a drink than a meal, she thought as the room began to spin.

Wilson went for her, but of course, he was too slow.

With swiftness that stirred the room, Huxley was right there.

One large hand steadied her. "Gotcha," he whispered close to her ear, breath tickling her lobe, sending a shiver down her spine. He steadied the crutch against the wall. A warm sensation filled every cell. She couldn't prevent her cheeks from burning or stop Huxley from coming to her side.

"I'm fine." She waved a hand in the air. "You know toxic masculinity is a thing."

"And falling on your ass and re-injuring your knee is a thing, too," Huxley said, leading her to the chair anyway like some medieval gallant knight. His fingers lingered on hers a second longer than they should.

"You good, Nazario?" Chief Johnson gave her the same look he did when he'd visited her at the hospital. "Need to reschedule?"

Huxley took his seat, though she still felt his eyes on her.

"Let's do this," Nazario powered on. "We don't have much to go on yet. Had a couple of interviews, which is more than we thought we'd get. We're running on nothing unless SID's found something, which I doubt. I just need to know if the Feds are here to take over. This hasn't crossed state lines, so I don't know why they're here."

"May I?" Huxley directed at Johnson.

"You may—since y'all apparently know one another." Chief eyed the two of them, sending Wilson into a fit of jolly laughter. Huxley flushed ripe peach, color showing dramatically on the man's pale face.

"No one's taking anything over. Look, I'll cut to the chase. We've found information that could be vital. Both Pablo Jimenez and Luis Vargas were working for the same company. We tracked their checking accounts and bank statements. Both were paid decent wages—60k a year, which isn't a bad living for someone without papers."

Huxley's partner piped up in a thick Russian accent, "They sent money home to Mexico, to family." The Russian turned to Chief Johnson. "I specialize in...research."

Huxley's partner was a very serious and intimidating guy who reminded Nazario of Ivan Drago from *Rocky IV*. She sized him up. He was either Russian or Ukrainian. Probably spoke three, maybe four languages. Huxley himself spoke fluent French and, from the last she'd heard, Spanish. She'd worked with enough multilingual agents.

"So, Pablo Jimenez was working part-time at his cousin's restaurant and also had a full-time gig." Nazario shrugged, playing devil's advocate. "Vargas and Jimenez knew each other, went to the same church, and one referred the other to this job. What, you don't think Mexican immigrants can get paid more than minimum wage?"

"Course they can, but statistically, they're paid much less

than native workers. We all know that," Huxley pointed out. "And secondly, it was an anonymous shell company."

The agent's reveal caused a stir of suspicion and unspoken theories.

"So far, we haven't found whose shell company it is," Huxley said, "but we're digging."

"Anonymous shell companies ended as of January 1, 2021," Wilson reminded.

"Well, other than someone having to pay ten grand in fines if caught, I'd imagine shell companies are alive and well. I'm not sure this one has anything to do with the murders. But it's suspicious," Nazario said, then nodded to Huxley and admitted under her breath. "Good find, Huxley. Keep us in the know when something pops up...a name, something?"

"Absolutely, Detective Nazario." Huxley's smile widened a little too much. "That's why we're here—just a part of the team, here to help."

Chief Johnson nodded to Huxley. "Special Agent Huxley, give us the 4-1-1 when you have some names. Anything that might help us know the owner of that company." Johnson turned to Nazario and Wilson and glanced between them. "We cool now, kids? Y'all got interviews? Catch us all up. Whittier, Yang, let's include y'all SID folk so no one feels left out. Whatcha got on Vic-Two? We've got nothing on the first...am I correct?"

"That's correct, Chief," Yang chimed in, though Nazario recalled the torn piece of paper from a physics book. It came back with no prints. They did have the book's title, but that didn't help unless they could track down who it belonged to.

"Found DNA under Vic-Two's nails, but no hits in the database," Whittier interjected.

"So, the killer has no sheet, huh? Straight normie?" Wilson loudly opened a bag of Hershey's Kisses from his inside coat pocket, unwrapped one, and tossed it in his mouth. Heads turned as he slid the bag toward Nazario. She waved it off. "Think you need it," he said. "Sugar levels are probably low. You don't eat something, you're likely to faint. I'm hypoglycemic. I've gotta eat. Anyone want a Kiss?"

Nazario met Huxley's eyes, and a flood of primal heat washed over her.

Johnson narrowed his eyes at Wilson. Everyone knew the chief had one weakness—chocolate. "Hand them over. That's an order."

Wilson slid the bag of chocolate toward the chief as he casually ate one.

Rubbing her temple, Nazario glanced down at her watch as she inhaled long through her nose and exhaled through her mouth, adrenaline making her hands jittery. Huxley did this, the bastard. He could still do this to her all these years later.

"Let's get this going. I've skipped lunch and am running on twelve hours now. Need to ice my knee and eat something other than *chocolate*," Nazario bit out.

"You *better* ice that knee," Johnson warned in that fatherly way. "What's your theory? I know you've got one. Wait, let's back up and start with the interviews."

"Millie Ann Goodwin, the pastor's wife. Spoke to her first. Yago Rios, Vic-One, went to her church. Got a tip from Millie to talk to an—*Isabelle Jimenez*," Nazario began.

Wilson jumped in. "That Jimenez Mexican restaurant is as authentic as it comes."

"Anyway, Yago Rios," Nazario said, redirecting the conversation, "is Pablo Jimenez, her cousin. Deported once before. Came back. Got called into the DA. Case went to a grand jury —indicted him. He was supposed to get arrested but came up dead instead."

Johnson tapped his pen on the table. "What did Jimenez have to say?"

"Isabelle's pinning Eric Myers, ICE agent," Nazario sighed, "goes to Sanctuary Baptist. She thinks he has something to do with it. Says we should have a chat with the guy."

"Vic-Two? No papers? Got a rap?" Chief Johnson asked.

"Yes, and yes," Wilson answered. "Luis Vargas, illegal, felony DUI after he swerved into a couple on the sidewalk. They survived, but they were banged up pretty good. He was supposed to be deported just before he got filleted."

"Cough it up," Chief said, putting out a hand.

"We're still doing that?" Yang asked.

"We sure are," Chief said, "as the sensitivity trainer said, *illegal* as it relates to *undocumented* has become a racial slur. We're trying to change our image. Build trust back between law enforcement and the community."

"I was doing so good. I was on a streak." Wilson dug out his wallet and handed the chief a five-dollar bill. "Oh, and I just got a message on my phone from the clerk at the DA. It looks like an ICE agent tipped them off on both men—knew about Pablo Jimenez and Luis Vargas. She didn't get the name."

"We need to shake Myers down," Nazario said, "but I think you know my theory, Chief."

"Let's hear it," Huxley said. She *was* doing a great job ignoring him. She swiveled and finally made eye contact.

"Same killer, targeting undocumented immigrants, motive's unclear. Maybe a hate crime? Maybe a moral or political conviction? Jimenez and Vargas—killed two different ways, positioned in the same way, under some bridge-like structure, arms stretched out vertically." Nazario sat back and slid her eyes away from Huxley.

Chief Johnson rubbed his chin again. "And if you're wrong, we're putting up a hell of a lot of resources for a couple of random killings. Who knows why the men were killed? I still think it could be gang-affiliated. We've got so little to go by. We can close this out—put the kibosh on this pointless investigation. Know you don't like to hear this, but there are insufficient leads. I mean, we don't even have next of kin. Okay, so y'all found out Yago Rios is a Jimenez. But the new guy?" Chief threw his pen down on the table. "Only thing the Homicide Department has managed to do's run that article for immigration donations in the LA Times—*that is it.*"

"Both victims were tipped off to the DA by an unnamed ICE agent, from what Wilson just found today, before they were killed. Something isn't right here," Nazario said, "it's not a coincidence."

"If an immigration officer tipped off the DA, it sounds like they were doing their job." Chief Johnson shrugged. "What? You think an ICE agent's our killer? This Eric Myers?"

"It's not an impossibility," Nazario said, and Johnson shook his head, running a hand down his face. "Regardless, we're not just looking at a couple of random dead undocumented Mexicans—we're looking at a goddamn serial killer who will likely strike again." Nazario pounded a fist on the table. "The donations to undocumented immigrants are better than keeping the old narrative running, that we're a bunch of racist cops that don't give two shits. But if we close these cases out, that narrative will be reinforced. I guarantee you. Don't matter if we're both brown, sir. You said it yourself; they don't trust us. Our community. The media. The only color they'll see is the racist color of blue. The headline for months will read: *The prejudicial LAPD stops investigating serial murders of immigrants. Would they've stopped if these murders were white people?*"

The room shifted. Bodies moved, legs crossed, arms shuffled.

"You know what, that's all I've got for today," Nazario

continued, getting up from her seat. "There's not a lot of evidence except that something's just not right, and I think that our perp is going to kill again. And next time, the hit will be harder."

"All right," Chief said, pushing back against the table, adjusting himself in his seat. "Let me know when you have that chat with Eric Myers."

Nazario got up and hobbled toward her crutch, making a beeline for the door.

"Get that knee iced, and wouldya please eat something?" Wilson warned. "You can't go all day without eating. Keep it up, and I'll strap you down and force-feed you if I gotta."

She couldn't focus on anything other than putting space between herself and her past.

"Oh, for Christ's sakes, Detective, wouldya slow down," Huxley called out. "You'll wind up making that knee of yours a whole lot worse."

Holding steel focus on her mission to get to her vehicle, Nazario refused to look back. She needed to leave history behind her. She had to. Blood abruptly began to drain from her brain. Another swell of nausea hit her hard, the kind that told her that it had been too long since she'd eaten.

She reached her car, but a wave of vertigo flooded her. The ground slid from beneath, temporarily suspending her in mid-air. Her arms swam, trying to catch her fall, trying to grab for the car, but there was only one place she was going, and that was down.

"*Anaya...*" Huxley's voice boomed into the frigid night. She collapsed, sucked in by a void, her body falling through black matter, eyes caught a rhapsody of stars as she fought the pull of oblivion. His large arms wrapped around her, lifting her to him. She was floating, her body pressed against his chest. She could hear his heart beating at an illegal speed as a dizzying wave lulled her eyes closed.

The scent of his familiar musk soothed her.

"Gotcha," he whispered in her ear. She floated in the air against his warmth. Despite the darkness swallowing her whole, in Huxley's arms, she was safe.

TWENTY-THREE

THE PASTOR'S WIFE

Subject: *On the Loose*
Dear Mrs. Goodwin,

I've been attempting to call, but you have no voicemail for your landline, so I can't leave a message. There isn't a cell number on file because your husband took it off and only approved the landline as a main contact number. I need to make you aware that Gideon asked to be released, but since he had a breakdown just a week prior, we advised against it.

After a thorough evaluation, we felt it in his best interest that he remain under suicide watch and under psychiatric care at our facility. During a shift change between swing staff and graveyard, he managed to escape. We believe your son is highly unstable and potentially dangerous. If he contacts you, we advise you to please call the police immediately and contact us so that he can be reinstated under our care.

Please call me as soon as possible.

Dr. Marcel Bennett, M.D.

MILLIE QUICKLY SENT Dr. Bennett her cell number and asked him to call her straight away, ordering him to put her cell number on the approved contact sheet. Once the email was sent, she erased her sent messages because Stan checked their shared emails daily.

She could've sent Dr. Bennett her cell number long ago but didn't, partly out of loyalty to her husband and partly out of sheer stupidity. After the message was sent and evidence deleted, she quickly tapped in a Google search:

How to get a divorce?

It was 8:38 p.m., and her husband was still up. Stan had been fasting all week to get right with God, perhaps to ask the Almighty to return his former, obedient wife to him. That wasn't going to happen, though. Not even God Herself, if She rode down from the heavens on a lightning bolt, would make Millie go back to what she used to be, that syrupy, devoted pastor's wife.

There was a faint noise that caught Millie's attention. It must be the wind, Millie dismissed, but she found herself staring at the door for at least ten seconds—enough time to turn her stomach sour. Without wasting a second more, she sprinted toward the door and opened it. Her breath caught in her throat, and she covered her mouth.

Gideon stood there, soaked in the rain, hair matted over his eyes.

Could he have been the stranger that Esperanza saw?

"Honey!" Millie put out an unsteady hand the way one would to a snarling dog, abused by humans, unable to trust yet another potentially dangerous stranger. He didn't move, didn't speak—hadn't spoken to her, or to anyone, in almost twelve years. Mute. Millie took another small step forward, then another, her hand still outstretched.

"Gideon, you know I love you, right? Gideon, honey,

Mommy's been trying to talk to Dr. Bennett. I've wanted to see you, sweetie." She took another step forward. "Mommy has missed you so, so much."

The thudding sound of Stan's feet rushing down the creaky steps caused the hallway pictures to rattle. Millie stepped closer to her son. His mouth opened as if he was ready to say something. Rain pelted his sunken, ashen face.

"What are you trying to say? Sweetie, what are you trying to tell Mommy?"

His lips trembled. Mouth opening wider, eyes searching hers.

Words so close to escaping from his closed spirit.

Gideon took a step back as Stan stepped forward.

"Millie Ann, close that door." He grabbed her upper arm. *"I said, close the damn door!"*

"Let go of me." Millie grappled for her freedom. Stan's stout fingers closed around her upper arm, squeezing, maybe to repay her for earlier. Gideon took another step back.

"No, baby, don't you leave, please," she begged him.

Bible in hand, Stan thrust it out, jabbing his son in mid-air with the word of God.

"We're calling the cops. Gideon, we love you. But we can't help you, son." Stan began altering his seething righteous anger into a hushed tone. "That's what doctors are for. We're calling Dr. Bennett. You're safer in his hands." Gideon narrowed his eyes at his father. Like flames burning, he torched Stan with an ugly hatred that made Millie shudder. Gideon bared his clenched teeth like a snarling dog.

"He's our son! We're not calling anyone." Millie yanked her arm free from Stan's grip. She pushed him, sending him tumbling back. Before she could stop him, Gideon was running. Ever since he was young, her boy could run like the wind. She ran into the rain, ran after her son. Her shoes sloshed and sank into the muddy earth.

"Gideon, Gideon…please come back!" Her voice was muted under the sound of clattering thunder that dared her to continue into the night's electric madness. In the dark, there was no trace of him anywhere. She looked to the right and left, spun around, screaming his name.

Gideon was gone.

Millie ran back into the house and grabbed her purse and car keys.

"Where do you think you're going?" Stan's face was blotchy with anger, his turkey chin hanging there to mock her. Oh, how she wanted to choke him again, only this time—she'd wait until the "Holy Spirit" in him stopped breathing.

"Away from you, that's where I'm going."

Stan trapped her at the door, blocking the entrance. "I could call the cops for what you did to me, nearly killing me." He put a hand around his throat, eyes bulging again. "You've gone and lost your mind, like Gideon."

"Go ahead. Call the cops. Think I care?" Millie balled up her fist. "Get outta my way. I wanna speak to him. My son!"

"You know our rule about keeping our son's mental health a private matter. You went and told Esperanza. She said she saw somebody out here. What'd you tell her? You told her about Gideon, didn't you? You know Gideon is not right in the head, and it's no one's business."

"*You're* not right in your head. I said nothing to Esperanza. Have you ever thought that maybe he was out here? That she really did see him? That maybe Gideon was trying to reach me. I'm his mother. He needs me. All you did was donate your sperm. Now get out of my way." Millie shoved Stan with all her strength. He stumbled back, but unlike before, he managed to keep on his feet.

"The Devil's inside you!" Stan shouted with hysteric conviction, wide-eyed.

"The Devil's inside us all," Millie gritted between clenched teeth as she rushed out into the rain, slamming the door behind her. In the car, she put her head on the steering wheel and wept the way only a mother could. A terrible, horrible mother. Her phone buzzed, as it'd been buzzing all night. She hadn't had a chance to look.

She picked up her phone.

Study Group: *Think we're due for another Bible study.*

Eric was relegated to a pseudonym in her phone, partly to throw off an ever-nosey Stan and an attempt to hide her dirty deeds. But after blurting it out, she no longer cared. She didn't answer the phone. She turned on her high beams and slowly drove around the neighborhood, hoping to see a glimpse of her son. Nothing but the heavy downpour and empty sidewalks remained.

Her phone vibrated again.

Study Group: *Come on over, Millie.*

For a second, she ignored the text and thought about her son. She'd finally seen Gideon. He was trying to tell her something. What? What was he trying to say? She exhaled nervously and looked again at her vibrating phone.

She finally replied: *You at that hotel?*

Study Group: *Back home. Hang on...will txt the address.*

Her phone buzzed with his address in Ojai. It was a bit far, but she could use the drive.

She typed it into her navigation, which gave her an ETA, and then texted Eric back.

Be there in 1.5 hours.

———

When she arrived, she didn't expect a small farm in Ojai with horses and chickens. The rain pelted relentlessly, making it hard to see as she pulled up. The house was isolated—lonely at night, but probably beautiful during the day. She didn't bother with an umbrella or with a jacket.

"You're gonna get sick," Eric said, greeting her with a knife in hand.

"I don't care," Millie said, and she didn't. "I didn't know you had a farm."

Millie walked inside, brushing the rain out of her hair. Eric set the blade on the counter, adding it to a collection of seemingly high-end knives. He handed her a towel and she dried herself with it.

"I'm not in the mood for sex," Millie snapped.

"Oh, really?" Eric's taunts were irresistible in a problematic way.

"Yes, really."

"You hungry?" Eric asked. "Got freshly caught bass."

"Y-yeah...maybe a little," she admitted, noticing that instead of a cabinet, fishing poles of various sizes and types leaned in a neat row against his empty kitchen wall.

The smell of fresh baked bass wafted through the air. It wasn't a fishy smell, rather a freshly caught aroma, and something in the pit of her stomach turned. Eric whistled a tune she didn't recognize while sliding the plate of herb and lemon-drizzled bass with asparagus onto the table.

She cut into the fish and forked it into her mouth, where it promptly melted. She closed her eyes and moaned. Eric laughed approvingly. "Not to turn your stomach, but uh...you hear about the body found at the Redondo Beach Pier?"

"Body?" Millie took a few bites of her food before her eyes began darting around the room. Something about the way he said it made her uneasy. She thought of the trench coat and black gloves she'd seen in his motel room that first night and couldn't quell the prickle of unease that went through her. Was there something more she'd missed? She glanced at his work desk just a few feet away between the living room and dining table. When Eric turned his back, she wandered the room, pretending to look around. All the while, she was edging closer to his desk.

"A dead body is certainly not a very good dinner conversation," she said over her shoulder, grateful he remained facing away from her and in the kitchen, making himself a plate. Heart hammering, she shuffled through random stacks of hunting and fishing magazines on his desk. Buried beneath was a small black notebook.

She flipped it open, and her jaw dropped at what was written there: the names of two of her church members with lines crossed through them and a small "note-to-self" regarding their criminal records.

~~Yago Rios (Pablo Jimenez) felony, multiple offender~~
~~Luis Vargas felony reckless driving~~

Eric's voice boomed out from the kitchen. She looked up in fright, worried she'd been caught, but all she could see was his back.

"The dead guy was Luis Vargas," Eric said, sharpening his knife on a granite stone—the man on his list and someone familiar to her. Millie gulped, watching the steel slice against the granite. "They say he was gutted like a fish."

Millie's hand trembled as she noticed another note scribbled below the two names.

Called DA's secretary - only available after 11 am.

"How...how do you know that?" Millie closed the small notebook and swiftly stuffed it into her purse—which, thankfully, she hadn't hung up—and quickly sat back down at the dinner table. Detective Nazario would need to see this notebook. The question: Could she turn Eric in—and for what? What was she admitting to herself? That he might be involved in the murders? *No. No. It couldn't be true.*

She watched the man she'd been sleeping with mosey toward her, knife still in hand. Bile rose up in her throat.

"Got my sources." Eric gestured toward the row of hooks on the wall where jackets were hung. "Why doncha put your purse away?"

"It's fine right here." Millie hung her purse over the chair behind her, shoved away her half-eaten plate of fish, and rose to her feet. "Why'd you call me here anyway?"

How could she finish eating it now?

"Why do you think?" He stabbed a piece of bass with the point of his knife. Millie now noticed not only the collection of fishing poles Eric had on display, but also knives, guns, and more fishing poles lining the wall—along with various dead animal heads mounted like prized trophies.

She wondered if she was a trophy. If this was some hunting game that turned him on.

He could be with anyone he wanted, and yet he chose her.

Millie was the one who started this entire relationship off by trying to counsel him and play savior in the first place. She'd never been able to shake the truth: they'd always been on opposite sides of "good and evil." Was this some game—catch and mount the prey? How did he know about the new dead man?

Luis Vargas always sat in the same spot every Sunday, third row to the left. Vargas was yet another member of the church targeted in such a brutal manner. The reality slicked sweat across her brows and sent a shiver down her spine.

Eric fed her a bite of fish, lemon juice, and butter cascading off her lips. She kept her eyes on him. All the while, the knife tickled her shoulders as Eric slid the tip gently down her arm close enough to touch her skin, close enough to put fear in her, close enough to cut her open.

Cut her open like Luis Vargas?

The knife's tip tickled down her forearm, toward her palm, across her hips, and now between her thighs. It brushed up between her legs. She was shaking, throat hoarse and arid, stomach-turning as each breath quickened. Her chest rose and fell in panicky pants.

"Luis...Luis Vargas," she gasped, letting out a shaky breath. "He goes to the church."

He leaned into her and whispered, "He did, as in past-tense. Looks like he won't be coming back now, will he?"

The nice guy who cried over Nicky had been replaced by this *other* man.

He lifted her skirt and, with one swift move, sliced off her panties with his knife. She gasped part in fear and yet pleasure, a dangerous thrill. She couldn't speak. Did Eric Myers kill Yago Rios? Did he kill Luis Vargas? He unzipped his pants, pulled down his underwear, and proudly held his hard dick in his hand. For once, she was desired. For once, someone thought she was sexy with her thick, curvaceous hips, naturally large breasts, wider frame.

"Where does he belong?" he teased, fingers caressing his shaft, stroking. "Wanna hear you say it."

Despite being flooded with unanswered questions, she didn't move. Millie couldn't will herself away even if she tried. He began stroking himself with more vigor. Her mouth watered. Jealous, she watched his hand caress what should be hers.

She reached out. Fingers that had stolen a notebook with dead men's names grazed his hard shaft. This was what Eric Myers did to her—he forced her to face herself—one hypocrisy at a time. He'd shown her that God was a woman and that She

was an almighty, majestic Queen, one that allowed for the celebration of carnal urges that were both natural and human.

"Inside me," she moaned, unable to be persuaded away by
the warning signs and danger.

He lifted her dress, spun her around, and made one hard
lunge, entering her from behind. There was nothing soft or
tender about the moment. It was animalistic. It was raw.

She was angry.

Angry at Stan.

Angry with herself for letting him scare Gideon away.

Angry at herself for not being there for her son.

Angry about having to be so good, so perfect all the time.

And, of course, she was angry with God.

Guilt?

She felt none.

Her face was shoved against the wall. She felt Eric's teeth
bite hard against her neck. His voice let out a growl-like groan,
like a starved wild beast. She screamed—a howl not of pain, not
fear, but pleasure.

Yago Rios. Luis Vargas. They flashed for a moment in her
head, but a wave of hypnotic heat cascaded through her. The
fact that she might be sleeping with a killer disappeared into the
wet space between her throbbing thighs.

Stan was right about one thing: The Devil was deep
inside her.

TWENTY-FOUR
THE WITNESS

FATIGUE SWAYED ESPERANZA'S BODY, but she willed herself to stay awake. The raucous chatter and laughter from the quinceañera celebration held at a local community center auditorium were plenty loud, but not enough to keep her from nodding off.

Armed with Starbucks, she took a large sip.

"This is stupid. Can we go yet?" Alex whined, rolling his eyes at a fifteen-year-old, adorned in a pale pink traditional full-length gown. A photographer took pictures of the honoree as she was handed *El Primer Ramo de Flores*: the first flower bouquet to symbolize the arrival of her womanhood.

"*¡Cállate!*" Esperanza scolded.

"Ugh...she got her flowers," Alex complained, "I wanna check another book out before the library closes."

"You don't wanna stay for cake?" a clean-cut man interrupted. He looked Hispanic, maybe Puerto Rican, if Esperanza had to guess. But she didn't recognize him and was unsure of his relation to her friend.

"I have to return my book," Alex responded, nudging the volume with his fingers.

"Fundamentals of Physics: Mechanics, Relativity, and Thermodynamics?" The man read. "Impressive. May I?"

Esperanza didn't like the way he was ogling the book, as if he recognized it. This was her fault. She should have been firmer about making Alex leave it at home.

"I'm sorry, do we know you?" Esperanza folded her arms across her chest.

"Officer Gomez," the man said, showing her his badge. "Friend of the family. Can I see that book?"

A wave of dread filled Esperanza, but what could she say? Nervous she nodded to her son, who was waiting for her to give permission. Alex handed it to him. Officer Gomez leafed through the book and paused at a page with a torn corner.

"There's an ongoing investigation," Gomez began. Alex and Esperanza exchanged knowing looks. "Can I keep the book? We'll make sure to return it for you. Got a name and a number?"

Esperanza's stomach turned, making her feel queasy. For two days without sleep, she'd relied on coffee to keep her awake. She'd been too afraid to allow herself eight hours of sleep. But her worries about someone breaking in again as they slept didn't hold water to this new fear that Alex's stupid science book would place them at the scene of the crime.

Dread soured her belly. Would they deport her?

The cop took out his cell phone and waited for her.

"Esperanza Flores," her voice shook as she gave him her phone number.

He pulled out a card. "You'll wanna call Detective Nazario and...*no te preocupes*," he said. *"No seras deportado."*

Esperanza nodded hesitantly.

"Ugh, I hate that. I don't understand what you just said. Thanks to my paranoid mom, I don't speak Spanish," Alex sighed in exasperation. "Translation?"

Esperanza had never hit her son, but right now, she wanted

to smack him. But the last thing she needed was to, *Dios no lo quiera*—God forbid—have child protective services called on her. Americans took hitting your child seriously, no matter how much they deserved it.

"Detective Nazario is gonna be contacting your mom. She'll need to come by the station and answer some questions."

"They're gonna question my mom?" Alex threw his arms around her as if he could keep the authorities from prying her away.

"Like I told your mom, you won't have to worry. Cooperate with us, answer some questions and nothing's gonna happen. Okay? Your mom isn't getting deported. There's a dangerous person out there we're trying to catch." Gomez tucked the book under his arm and then told Esperanza. "*No te preocupes.*"

But she did worry as she bit out in English, "How do I know I can even trust you?"

"You don't have a choice," Gomez said for her ears only.

Esperanza's friend spotted them and made her way toward them, breaking the tension.

"Esperanza, Alejandro, so glad you made it," her friend said. "You met Joey Gomez?"

"Your daughter looks beautiful," Esperanza said. "I'm sorry, but we have to go."

"Oh, no. Please stay. Isabelle is coming with food from the restaurant."

"Thank you, but we can't stay," Esperanza said, gripping Alex's hand. She turned to the LAPD officer, who had confiscated her son's library book, leaving her to be grilled by detectives. "It was nice meeting you, *Joey.*"

TWENTY-FIVE

THE DETECTIVE

THE LAST THING Nazario remembered was trying to put distance between her and her past only to collapse in Huxley's arms before she could reach her car's door. Now that she was back in her own apartment, the familiar surroundings revived her in bleary flickers. The aroma from the chicken noodle soup on the TV tray wafted in the air. Groggy, her eyes scanned her leg. It was propped up and attached to the ice machine that was sending a frosty chill up her thigh.

"You passed out." Huxley got up from her lounger and handed her a napkin. He took the opportunity to sit an arm length closer to her on the couch. "Wilson left about ten minutes ago. Dropped me off. Car's back at the station."

She looked down at her leg, hating nothing more than being helpless.

Stomach grumbling, she reached for the soup and ate half the bowl in several large swallows, ignoring her table manners or what Huxley had to think about it.

"Why'd you pick this assignment? They're all siting insufficient evidence. Maybe it's because they're undocumented that they wanna shut it down. Heck, who cares about a few no-named Mexicans? Right?" She gave him dispassionate eyes. "You gonna sit here and tell me you've suddenly picked up immigration policies as a passion project? I don't think so. Why this one? Why mine, Special Agent Huxley?"

He reached out and his fingers grazed her cheek as they swiped a wayward strand of hair from her eyes. For a moment, her eyelids closed, and he was holding her in the bathtub, blood pooling in the water. He'd clutched her to his chest and had encouraged her with typical things often said like, "We'll try again, okay? We'll keep trying."

The miscarriage had devastated her more than she'd been equipped to handle.

"She'd have turned twelve this year." He returned her to the present and to the reality that their baby hadn't survived her body. She had failed. "I try to picture what she'd look like," he scanned her face with slow deliberation, his fingers lingering on her cheek.

"*Stop!*" The uncomfortable moment held them both hostage, forcing them to rewind time. "You signed up for this leadless case, to come here and go down memory lane?"

"You're right. I'm sorry...I think I'll be on my way," he said gently. She absorbed his unmistakably impressive profile, noting the contrast between his intimidating exterior to his gentle inner world. A hand curled around the doorknob, his knuckles popping white.

Could she let him leave?

The answer was simple. "Blake..."

Slow and steady, he turned around.

For a long beat, their eyes held, frozen. Breaths strained for oxygen that seemed to be siphoning from lungs. Nazario shut her eyes, willing back tears, biting her lower lip. She could hear him bridge the gap between them in two long-legged strides.

The couch dipped from his weight, and she slowly opened

her eyes. Beside her, the tough exterior of the federal agent melted away, revealing a man touched by the bittersweet memories of love. A love that had deeply etched itself in his being. She could see a profound strength, that he was ready to leave the shadows of their past behind. But the real question loomed: Was she ready to offer him the one thing he'd longed for—her heart—in return?

Hunched forward and elbows on knees, Huxley stared down at his dress shoes.

"Remember how we met?" he asked without looking up. "You were drop-kicking my roommate."

"He pinched my ass." Nazario adjusted her bum knee. "You almost hit the floor. I didn't expect you to duck."

A smile softened his lips. "Shit, I thought you were gonna go Jackie Chan on my ass."

They remained in silence for a five-count before allowing themselves a laugh.

She unstrapped her leg from the ice machine. "I should lay down."

"I'd like to help."

"Of course you would," she sighed. Then reminded him, "That's always been our problem."

They exchanged a look, knowing their past codependent relationship was never healthy then...was still not healthy now. Huxley was good at playing the savior. It made him great at his job but bad at relationships. Maybe his ex-wife wasn't damaged enough, wasn't an alcoholic with daddy issues?

Huxley moved the ice machine to the side, carried Nazario to the bedroom, then deposited her on the bed before she could protest.

"Get some rest," he said, slipping out her door.

"Stay." Her request betrayed the rational part of her mind.

Nazario unstrapped her S&W 5906 from her left ankle, put

it on the nightstand, removed her wallet and badge from her back pocket, and plunked it next to her gun. Huxley took off his blazer, kicked off his shoes, removed his Glock 22 from his waist, and put it next to hers.

She laid down, curling on her side, facing away from him. The bed sank beneath his weight, his body emanating feverish heat and warming her clammy frame. He wrapped a heavy arm around her, and the weight of his muscular frame felt good. His fingers wove through hers. She could feel the roped muscles in his legs and chest. His nose and mouth a breath away against her neck.

His chest rose as he breathed her in, hardness growing against her.

"Sorry," he whispered, adjusting himself. "Jesus...I don't know if I can do this."

"Do what? Nothing's happened."

"Yet. Nothing has happened—*yet*. You think we're gonna just lay here and cuddle?"

"Asked you to stay," Nazario said. "Didn't ask for an erection or a wedding ring."

"You're unbelievable," Huxley hissed, moving away.

An age-old void reminded her of the years that had gone by, yet it almost felt like they were back in college all over again.

They were the same two people back then and now.

"It took me years to try and move on with my life." He inhaled sharply. "It ended every single relationship after you, including my marriage, because I'd compare what I had to what I shared with the one woman who was always beyond my reach. And you know what? I swore to myself I wouldn't see you again."

She turned around to face him and held her breath.

Looking down, he pulled further away from her.

The space dividing them ached and expanded.

She gulped. "We got pregnant. Then the miscarriage happened. Then you pull the whole Superman move, claiming you were gonna find who killed my father?"

"She was my baby, too. I was...devastated." He quietly gazed out the window. "Not a year went by that I didn't think of her or you—"

He turned from the window and faced her.

"—and I meant what I said about finding your father's killer."

She looked down at her hands. "It was too much for me."

"Of course it was. I was always too much for you. I'm still too much for you. You can go and have cold, one-and-dones with random dudes...I can't be one of them. I won't be your goddamn fuck buddy."

"Didn't assign you that position." She cleared her throat.

Huxley raked his hands through his thick hair.

"Oh c'mon...you didn't have to." He scoffed, releasing an incredulous laugh. "Thought I could do this, I really did. See you again like this."

"You know I'm an asshole. Never been relationship material. Stop acting surprised."

"I can't just leave, walk away like you can without so much as a call to ask me how I was...I mean completely disappearing like that? After everything we went through?"

"I thought it would be...easier that way. Cold turkey."

"E-easier? You kidding me? All these years later, and that's your answer, Detective?"

He jolted up out of bed and paced the room.

"Quitting someone cold turkey, like, quitting smoking or some bad habit?" He crossed the room and confronted her.

Nazario wanted to avoid his scornful admonishment. Daddy and decades of martial arts training always taught her that, good or bad, you always looked someone in the eyes.

"You wanna know what it was like for me, or do you not give a shit?" His face was so close she could feel his hot breath against hers.

"Should I answer that? Sounded to me like a rhetorical question." Sarcasm fell out before Nazario could censor herself. "Did just fine after your divorce, locking lips with Chatty-Cathy six months freshly single. Looks to me like you bounced back."

Huxley narrowed his eyes and exhaled loudly.

"Leave it to you to be a smartass when things get serious," he snapped. "It killed me when you left. Nothing, not the divorce or anything in my life since has hurt worse than the day you decided it was 'easier' to ghost me."

Fearless, he continued his tirade, eyes still arresting hers.

"I can't sleep with you and walk away the way you want me to. I can't, Anaya, I just can't. I'd want more. I've always wanted more."

She touched his hand and urged him to sit. "Sorry."

"Sorry?" Huxley sat back down next to her on the bed. "What do you want from me? You want me to stay? Then what? What happens after that? You leave again? What happens when it *all* becomes too much for you?"

"I honestly don't know," she said, resigned. "I'm asking—"

She closed the chasm between them, leaned in, her lips touched lightly against his. His breath was warm and sprinting, matching the rise and dip of his chest.

A need grew inside of her, a carnal yearning.

"Asking for what?" he uttered against her lips. "You're hard on everything: yourself, people. You'll be more than hurting that leg of yours rolling around in bed. Do you even care if you hurt me?"

She hesitated.

Huxley slowly rose to his feet as if this cyclical argument was a weight about his neck.

"Exactly," he said, fatigued. "You don't know. You never do. That's the problem. What're you asking? For me to let you play Russian roulette with my heart?"

Nazario shook her head.

"I wanted—"

Her phone rang.

"A fuck?" Huxley spat out, unflinching. "Like the good ol' times? Have the balls to admit it, Detective."

"Fine!" She hurled a pillow across the room, sending her crutch crashing.

Widening her arms, she lifted them in surrender.

"Maybe I wanna fuck you, okay? From what I recall, it was the one thing we were pretty damn good at!"

Her phone continued to ring. They stared at it. Facedown, the caller ID was hidden from view, but she knew it was Wilson. By the fifth ring, she answered.

"Yeah...no, it's fine. Damn it. Really?"

Huxley studied her.

"Yeah, he's still here," she continued, looking at her watch, "see you in fifteen."

She turned off her phone and shoved it roughly in her back pocket.

Huxley met her eyes, anger, and resentment smoldering.

"Two DBs, nice and cold. We're gonna need you there."

———

Wilson parked in front of what appeared to be a random, barren location and finally broke the tense silence that had made for a strained drive. "Pacific Electric Railroad Bridge."

Nazario was first out of the car. She hobbled toward the Irvine Gill-inspired, modern architectural-style bridge built in 1913, which now appeared phantasmal at night. The historic double-tracked arched bridge was now desolate, with ruddy Boston Ivy wrapping around the pillars and creeping up the arches like protective fingers.

There were no streetlamps where they trod. Darkness swallowed everything up. Wilson's flashlight showed the way as they met two patrol officers waiting on either side of the bridge. Unlike the nearby and very public Redondo Beach Pier, which was so busy it required more officers, the abandoned bridge was a prime location for a murder with minimal foot traffic. It was no surprise that there were only two patrol cops at the scene.

They ducked under the yellow crime tape and introduced themselves to the two officers on duty. Both looked young enough to be mistaken for high school kids, making Nazario feel her age.

Nazario inspected the victims: first, a Hispanic male, shot three times in the chest.

"Undocumented?" Nazario called over her shoulder. The vic was a handsome man—potentially mid-twenties—dark hair, green eyes, and a well-built frame. His arms were spread vertically on either side, feet close together like the others.

"Yes, ma'am." An officer handed her a bag with his wallet. "Angel Hernández, twenty-five, Mexico license, no fake ID."

Nazario handed the bag to Wilson. "SID been called?"

The officer explained, "They're running a little behind. Said they'll be here in about ten...fifteen? The coroner is also stuck in traffic."

Nazario and Huxley moved to the second victim.

"Avery Elizabeth Vanwell," Huxley said, "Madison Vanwell's daughter."

Nazario's breath caught in her throat. "No," she whispered. "Jesus—"

Avery's blonde hair was matted with blood against her face. A knife-like jab of panic stabbed Nazario in the chest, the brief moment of a panic attack rose with a flood of grief. She seemed to hear Huxley and Wilson from a distance asking if she was okay, but she was unable to answer.

"Can we grab coffee sometime, Detective Nazario?"

"Sorry, Honey, got a case I'm eyeballs deep in. Raincheck?"

"She was my...she was my student."

Huxley furrowed his brows. "Saturday self-defense you and Gus teach—"

"Yes, Huxley!" Nazario squeezed her eyes shut.

Huxley muttered an apology.

Daddy's advice repeated: *Focus on solving the case. Worry about emotions later.*

Wilson put an arm around Nazario, she opened her eyes as they pooled.

"If you need to step aside," Wilson said, concerned, "just say the word, 'kay?"

Nazario turned her back to Avery, a hand covering her mouth in disbelief. Wilson's words reached her, and she collected herself, wiping her eyes with the back of her hands.

You can do this, Nazario. Think about Avery.

"Wilson and I can take it from here," Huxley offered gently.

"No," she said eventually, her tone so low the word was barely audible.

Gulping down a shaky breath, Nazario turned back around and followed an urge inside to kneel down this time as if paying homage to her former student's lifeless body. No matter how uncomfortable, Nazario weathered the strain of her right leg, erect at an awkward side angle thanks to the full leg brace. She made a closer inspection of Avery; her dark blue eyes now had a milky sheen. Death eyes, as they called it.

"Burn marks," Nazario choked out inspecting the entry wound. "Close range. Perp pressed the barrel against her forehead."

Leaning against her crutch, Nazario grunted as she rose slowly to her feet.

"This was personal." Nazario looked down at Avery, rubbing her forehead. "I should've been there for her."

"This is going viral come morning, hittin' all the news stations," Wilson said. "Affluent Caucasians hit the news faster than dead minorities, unfortunately."

Huxley turned to her. "You couldn't have predicted this."

Nazario ignored his concerns, not in the mood for coddling. "Huxley, we need you to do some digging on Madison Vanwell, find out if she has any enemies, extended family members, that sort of thing."

"Will do, Detective," he returned in the same professional tone she used.

Nazario hobbled away from the bridge and began piecing together the events.

"She was dragged," she said, pointing at the marks on the ground and blood spatter, "the killer took her out. Then moved the body under the Pacific Electric Bridge. This is our guy. The Bridge Killer. Same person, but why Avery?"

"Did a preliminary search," one of the officer's added, "didn't find the shell casings yet."

"Hand what you bagged to SID, should be Whittier and Yang," Wilson said, passing the bag with Angel and Avery's wallets back to the officer.

Huxley gave each of the two officers on duty his card. "Have the coroner contact me directly when the bullet is extracted. I'm on an old cold case that's a little familiar."

Wilson and Nazario frowned at each other.

"My student's dead, Huxley. So are other victims, immigrants whose lives are unimportant enough that they never even hit the five o'clock news. But Avery, a Vanwell, her face will be plastered on every goddamn news outlet in the country," she said, venting. "Mind telling us about this cold case that might aid in solving these murders?"

Nazario threw her hands in the air.

"Can't," Huxley pled, "it's ATS. We can't release it to *anyone*."

"That is horseshit," Nazario fumed, "so that's why you're here?"

"Anaya—"

"It's Detective Nazario. Get it right. We're done." Furious, she turned to SID. "Just send *Special Agent Asshole* over here the intel since the FBI seems to know something about this case that we don't."

She turned back to Huxley and let him have it.

"You got shit you know, might actually help, and it's *above top secret*? When were you gonna tell me? What's so goddamn special it's SCI?!"

Info deemed "sensitive compartmented information" was rare and above top secret; not even homicide or personnel with top-secret clearance could go near the intel. Only individuals with additional SCI clearance were granted access, which neither Nazario nor Wilson had.

The two patrol officers at the scene shifted uncomfortably.

"When SID gets here," Wilson began, handing one of the young officers his card, "have 'em call me too once the bullet's retrieved."

Furious, Nazario limped back toward the car, ignoring her old flame.

"Wouldya hang on—" Huxley called after her, but she strode off.

"Hey, can I have a minute with my partner?" Wilson asked. Huxley silently obeyed and Wilson unlocked the car. Huxley sat in the back seat. A few feet away, Wilson managed to block Nazario from moving forward.

"It's terrible that this Vanwell girl was your student. Some of us have had the misfortune of being on scene when the victim is someone we know. Remember when we were called out for Chief's baby brother? Heck, you were there when my college roommate got shot up." Wilson sighed.

How could Nazario forget the murder of Chief's drug-dealing only sibling, a polar opposite of the direction Johnson had taken his career. How could she forget when Wilson's college friend of many years was murdered over gambling debts? First time she'd ever seen two grown men break down and cry so hard. The only other time was most recently when Eric Myers lost Nicky Sanchez.

"Nazario, you know it's big, especially if it's an ATS. They'll let us know when they can share intel. Another thing—" Nazario met Wilson's warning glare. "He's not like the others you've chewed up and spit out. When was the divorce? He's got that divorced look. Tellin' you, don't do this one like the others. Take him out to dinner, a proper date."

"Why we having this conversation?" she asked. "Pardon me if I'm not thinking romantic thoughts after one of my students winds up popped in the head. We've got FBI lurking around with some ATS that's gotta be connected. Four unsolved murders, Wilson. *Four*."

She looked up at the starless night, the fog dissipating. Avery *Vanwell*. No wonder she didn't want to give her last name at the Saturday class. But why? What was she wanting to tell her when she'd wanted to meet for coffee?

"All I'm saying," Wilson interrupted her thoughts, "is a few hours off the clock will do ya some good."

As they headed back to the car, Mrs. Goodwin called but Nazario let it go to voicemail.

"You drove me to Nazario's earlier," Huxley reminded him. "My car's back at the station."

"Oh, I remember. She really shouldn't be driving with that brace. One slip up at that bar you drove to the night of Nicky's terrible accident is all I'm giving you." Wilson wagged an admonishing finger at her. "A little easier to drop you both off. You can call Uber from her place, can'tcha, Huxley?"

"If it's okay with—" Huxley hesitated.

"It's fine," Nazario said, then answered her phone not letting the pastoral counselor speak first. "I hope this call is more urgent than to tell me you're rescheduling our counseling session Mrs. Goodwin because if that's the case, you could've simply—"

Nazario looked up at Wilson and Huxley, stunned.

"What is it?" Wilson mouthed above a whisper.

Nazario put up a hand for her partner to bite his tongue and turned her attention to her caller. "We'll try to ensure your anonymity, but I need to know what sort of intel you're offering up." Nazario waited a beat, gathering herself. "If what you're saying is true, we need him home tomorrow. You making a date with him to make sure he is? Millie, that might not be a wise choice. But we can't force you not to. Appreciate your willingness to do this for us." Nazario shook her head, listening. "We can't guarantee he won't be arrested at some point, but no, not tomorrow."

"Please tell us it's good news," Wilson said once she hung up.

"We've got 'im," Nazario said. "Tomorrow at Eric Myers' house. It looks like he's our ICE snitch, and he might be our killer."

"Dunno if it'll be enough probable cause," Huxley admitted.

"As I told Mrs. Goodwin," Nazario started, clenching her jaw, "not enough for an arrest tomorrow. But you bet your ass if he's our leading suspect—I'm working overtime to make sure the bastard goes down for this."

———

By the time they arrived at Nazario's apartment, the recent better news about Eric Myers being their guy, had almost made her forget that Huxley was being dropped off at her place and was without his vehicle.

"Get along, kids. Make love, not war," hollered Wilson as he drove off, reminding Nazario that she wasn't alone with her thoughts on the case after all. Once Wilson turned the corner, she grabbed her keys and opened her apartment.

Huxley had been silent for the entire car ride and remained so, standing outside.

"You got your lead," Huxley said to her back finally breaking his silence. "I'll help you get an arrest warrant in any way I can, once we get enough on him."

"Don't you go changing the subject," she said, roughly manhandling the door. "I'm still really fucking pissed off and you know why—*you know why*."

"Look, you have to trust me," he insisted, "if I could tell you, I would, but I can't. I've been working on an open cold case for years. It's big, but I'm under strict ATS order to keep things under wraps until we've mounted solid evidence."

When she didn't answer, he puffed out air, making his cheeks swell.

"And I'm sorry about Avery Vanwell. If you can recall anything she said to you—"

"I know how investigations work, Special Agent, don't need a reminder. Truth is, Gus and I didn't know her all that well. Avery was extremely private. Wouldn't give her last name. Said she was wealthy, that's it. Had I taken up three coffee invitations—*three*—all of which I turned down, of course, I might've gotten to know her better."

"Don't do it," he urged. "It is *not* your fault."

"What if she was trying to tell me something important? Now she's dead. *Dead*."

"No one wins playing the what-if game, Detective," Huxley said. "You need time to process this, and clearly, I'm not helping matters. At least we got this Eric Myers lead. It's something and something is better than what we had before which was—*nada, zip*. I'll catch an Uber back to the station."

"Is that really what you want?" Immediately regretting the suggestive question, she began closing the door. "Forget it. Do yourself a favor and get outta here."

He took a step forward. "It never mattered what I want. But since you asked, I'll tell you what I want. I want *you*. I want you now. I want you tomorrow. I want you the day after that."

He took another step closer. She took a step back, heart speeding.

"I wanted you twelve years ago...I wanted our daughter." His eyes moistened. "Thing is, I want all of you and not just pieces of you."

Huxley closed the space between them, capturing her with firm conviction.

"See, I know what I want," he held her face firmly in his hands. "Do you?"

Breath shallow, she warned, "You...you know where I stand."

"And it changes nothing. You're all about control. I got news. You can't control how I feel. I'm still in love with you, Detective—with or without your consent."

She slapped him across the cheek, hard enough to leave a print. "*Stop it!*"

Huxley breathed harder as if the assault did nothing but stoke the fire.

"I'm not a robot. I'm not made out of wires and metal." The words gritted out between clenched teeth, voice volumed in frustration. "Go on, slap me again. Knock some sense into me, please. Hell, I loved you then, and I love you now. And there's not a damn thing you can say or do to stop me."

He cursed under his breath, taking in rapid breaths that matched her own.

"You asshole." She grabbed his face, bruising her lips against his in a hungry kiss.

He lifted her into his arms and carried her away—into a night of passion that continued long enough to provide an anesthetized feeling without red wine. It was a night where her swollen knee got a long dose of the ice machine, where she allowed herself laughter, and conversation, and Huxley's warm body wrapped tight against hers—for the best eight hours of "sober" sleep she'd had in years.

TWENTY-SIX

THE PASTOR'S WIFE

"WE'VE LEFT you a few messages, Mr. Myers," Wilson explained from the public side of the porch screen doors. "Since you didn't come by the station like we requested, we figure to save you gas money. Given you live out in the sticks and got that big ol' truck. With gas prices so high now—fillin' up ain't cheap. Seeing as it's your day off, it might be a good time to have us a little chat. May we come in? Smells mighty nice. Cooking up some fish?"

Wilson shot a knowing look at Millie. Caught red-handed—she didn't care.

"Nice to see you again," Wilson emphasized, "*Mrs.* Goodwin.*"

"Don't believe you've got a warrant?" Eric cocked a brow.

Oh dear, this is going to get ugly. Millie thought, wishing she could run and hide.

"Don't need one to ask a few questions," Nazario replied, "but, funny you ask, the judge'll be granting our search warrant this week. Whatever else is going on here—none of our business."

"Be my guest." Eric delivered a smug smile. "C'mon in, *mi casa es su casa*, the brotherhood of blue, ya know?"

"Our apologies if we've interrupted dinner," Nazario said.

"So, you're here about that 187 at the Redondo Beach Pier, huh? Or that rich white girl and her alien boyfriend?" Eric launched right in, waving the detectives into his kitchen. "Care for a beer? One won't hurt. I won't tell if you don't."

"I'm sure glad you're healing after Nicky's untimely," Wilson paused for a three count, then continued, "death, as I'm sure you're still mourning his loss."

"People grieve in different ways," Millie jumped in to provide her expertise.

Eric gave her a reprimanding look. *Don't fight my battles*, he said with his eyes.

"We know you were the one that tipped off the DA," Nazario said, "for both Pablo Jimenez and Luis Vargas."

Eric pivoted slightly toward Millie once again. He knew she was the one that said something. Millie's client—that Nazario—didn't have to take out the little black notebook Millie had stolen from Eric to know it was her. She wiped sweaty palms on her dress and clamped them together to prevent them from shaking.

"I sure did call them in," Eric admitted, "cause...*er*...last I checked that's kinda my job."

"And they kinda both ended up being killed, so um...you called in Luis Vargas, then how'd you find out about his murder in Redondo," the always-hungry detective asked, "when it wasn't released publicly yet?"

"I was surprised as anyone. But I was just doing what they pay me to do, turning him in. Don't mean I wanted to see Vargas dead. Nearly every RB shield was down there. A few of them are my friends. They talk. After all, it's not every day that a body ends up filleted like a halibut. I'm sort of a pescatarian myself."

Wilson smiled at Millie. She flushed.

Millie's heart banged with a swell of panic. "Stan doesn't need to know I'm here," she blurted out to Nazario. "I'm planning on filing for divorce."

Nazario shrugged. "Like I said, none of our business. Seriously. Your relationship with Eric is between the two of you. We're trying to figure out who's targeting immigrants. Our aim is to catch the son of a bitch and put an end to these murders."

Wilson meandered around the open floor plan, starting with the living room, dining area, then lastly, the kitchen. He scanned the knife set, fishing poles, and guns, calculating the odds in his head the same way Millie forced herself not to. She could almost hear him speaking the accusations aloud.

Wilson paused at the *Proud Republican* sticker she wanted to peel off of Eric's fridge.

"So, you're patriotic, huh? Looks like you do a lot of hunting...and fishing. Got yourself a nice knife set, too...Yoshihiro, right?"

"I'm impressed, Detective, you know your knives and you can read." Eric's smile tightened. "Why don't we cut the shit and get to your questions?"

"Hey now, Mr. Myers, that's not very nice," Wilson admonished. "But I am pleased to hear you sound like your old self. Mrs. Goodwin help you get over Nicky's death? That is your job, isn't it, Mrs. Goodwin? Pastoral counselor?"

Millie straightened her spine, and replied, "Yes, it is and yes I have been helping Eric through that horrendous tragedy."

Taking a fork from the dish rack, Wilson helped himself to a piece of salmon.

"Delicious." His eyes rolled back. "A man of many talents. You've got culinary skill."

"You missed the bass I caught last week. Millie can tell you just how much she loved it. Salmon though, it's my specialty.

Go on and help yourself." Eric's grin widened. A tense vein protruded from the middle of his forehead. Millie twirled a strand of damp hair around her jittery finger, tousled and humid from the sex they'd had earlier.

"Where were you last night?" Nazario asked.

"Hmmm, last night? Lemme think, oh, that's right...I was having sexual relations with the pastor's wife."

Millie's face turned crimson.

"Do you concur, Mrs. Goodwin?" Wilson didn't wait for an answer. He turned his full attention to the salmon. "Mmm, this is *real* good. You need to tell me your recipe."

"Yes," Millie cleared her throat.

"Of all churches, why attend Sanctuary Baptist?" Wilson asked. "Predominantly Mexican immigrants?"

"Makes my job a little easier," he admitted without remorse.

"And two weeks ago," Nazario interjected, "that Tuesday when Luis Vargas was killed?"

"Like I said, I had me a little chat with my DA friend," he said, "and then went to work. If you insist on the juicy details, I was detaining an alien at his home, or should I say immigrant? I wouldn't wanna offend anyone." He looked directly at Nazario, who shook her head and emitted a stiff laugh.

"Very PC of you," Nazario said, "such a thoughtful gesture."

"Look, I get the political climate. Nevertheless, it's my job to follow the law. I'm not gonna apologize for doing my job. So, there's a bunch of dead illegals. Don't mean I'm the killer. I tipped off the DA—don't mean my knife cut open that man or my gun killed that rich white chick and her fiancé. Heard they were going to elope. Looks like someone was mad that she was marrying outside of her social circle. If you wanna search my home, forget the search warrant. Go right ahead. You want me at the station, I'll be there bright and early in the morning with a dozen donuts," he eyed Wilson, "and some coffee to wash it down. Got nothing to hide. Get a search warrant and let me know in advance, so we can have dinner on me."

Millie tried breathing through her nose, hating the way they'd behaved toward Eric.

"We may just do that," Nazario said. "Millie, does Luis Vargas go to your church?"

"*Did,*" Millie repeated, recalling Eric correcting her earlier, "he did attend."

"Angel Hernandez?"

"No," Millie answered. Nazario looked at Wilson, who raised an eyebrow.

Wilson handed Millie and Eric his card. "Call us if you remember anything else. And Mr. Myers, we'll definitely take you up on your dinner offer. That's some good-ass fish."

"But first," Nazario said, "coming down to the station tomorrow and cooperating is a smart move."

"And while y'all are digging, why not get acquainted with my boss—verify my whereabouts on said dates to ensure I was arresting an illegal and not killing one."

Eric took out his wallet and handed Wilson a twenty.

"For your little..." Eric smiled, "kangaroo court donations."

Millie frowned, looking at the money. It must be some insider cop thing.

"Generous of you," Wilson said, taking the twenty, "and thanks again for the salmon. It was mighty delicious."

"You're more than welcome."

Eric saw the two of them out. He watched them peel out of the driveway before pivoting to Millie with a strange smile.

"What was that look I saw on your face?"

"What...what look?" Millie cleared her throat. Eric took a step toward her. She took a step back. "I was providing my professional opinion. Everyone's allowed to grieve in their own—"

Eric let out an incredulous laugh. "Not Nicky," he said, tone clipped. "You think I'm guilty, don't you? You think I'm a killer?"

"I...I didn't say anything," Millie protested.

"Didn't have to. I can see it on your face," he said, clucking his tongue. "Shame on you. I'm gonna have to punish you for being a bad girl."

The doorbell rang again.

"I don't think they've returned with a warrant in under five minutes." He sauntered toward the door and began to open it. "If you're back for more salmon, I'm sorry I didn't..." Eric paused leaning against the door. Puzzled, he asked, "Can I help y—"

Bang!

He staggered backward and collapsed; blood pulsed out of the wound in his forehead. Millie screamed, running to Eric. His body spasmed and jerked. Holding Eric's head in her hands, she glanced up at the open door. A hummingbird drank from the wild buckwheat that grew adjacent to Eric's porch. Its wings were moving as fast as her heart.

The gunman was gone, fled into the mid-August afternoon.

"Eric!" she wailed at the top of her lungs, hands quaking, covering her mouth. She rested his head on her blood-stained lap, her hands a sticky crimson. His bewildered eyes stared back at her.

"Who was it? Who did this Eric?"

"Care-ah-ful..." he exhaled, and his eyes fluttered closed. Screaming, her shaky hands grabbed her phone, drenched in his blood. She couldn't think. Instead of calling 9-1-1, she clutched the detective's card and dialed.

On the second ring. "Wilson here..."

"Turn around!" she screamed. *"He's been shot! Eric's been shot! Oh my God, turn around and come back here! Oh my God!"*

"We're not far," Wilson began calmly. "Flipping-a-bitch now and heading your way as we speak. Where was he shot, Mrs. Goodwin?"

"*Eric!*" There was so much blood everywhere, all sense of control fled, leaving her in utter hysterics. "*Oh God...he got...shot in the head!*"

"If he's shot in the head, we don't got much time. Put pressure on the wound. Need you to calm down, we're calling 9-1-1 now and will be there in under a minute, m'kay," Wilson's voice was smooth and controlled. She felt her body relax. "Is he still breathing?"

"*Y-yes.*"

"He's still breathing," Wilson repeated.

She heard Detective Nazario in the background. "This is Detective Nazario, we've got a gunshot victim. Need an ambulance stat—victim's still alive." Nazario rattled off Eric's address.

"I'm hanging up now. We're pulling up."

"*O-okay.*"

She turned the phone off. Eric's eyes drifted to the ceiling. A gurgle emanated from his throat. His chest rose and dipped to a shallow breath. He was alive, but barely.

"Eric..." She sobbed, holding his head against her. His limp, bloodied hand collapsed on her lap. She grabbed his crimson fingers.

In less than a minute after their phone call, Nazario moved as swiftly as she could, handing her crutch to Wilson. The detectives hadn't gotten very far at all, and for that, Millie was relieved. Nazario knelt with control, ensuring her bum leg wasn't bent. She checked for a pulse. Millie braced herself as she stood moving back and out of the way to give them room.

"Got a pulse," Nazario said. "He's still alive." Nazario applied pressure to his head. "This is good, it looks like the bullet entered at the right angle. Had it been point blank, he'd be dead by now."

"Did he say anything? Did Mr. Myers say anything? Anything at all that you can remember?" Wilson asked, moving her to the side.

All at once, sounds began to crank and crowd.

The faucet dripped with tedious repetition, where Eric had been cleaning the dishes. Ambulance sirens screamed at her, causing her windpipe to tighten. The room blurred and swayed in a way that made her knees buckle.

Wilson's heavy hand grabbed her upper arm and maneuvered her to the kitchen, her legs wobbling beneath. Millie heard the faint cry of Eric's name from her lips, the name she once was desperate to hate, she was now desperate to save.

She said his name again and again.

"Take your time, Mrs. Goodwin," Wilson said gently.

"Don't you call me that." Her bottom lip jittered, her teeth chattering. "Call me Millie," she said, lifting her chin. "Don't you call me a Mrs. anything."

She closed her eyes, trying to shut it all out.

"I'm sorry," she heard him whisper. His slow and steady voice soothed the chaos enclosing her. "Millie, you can take your time. Didn't mean to press you. But while it's all fresh in your head...we just need to know what happened, m'kay?"

"He...he thought it was the two of you." Her voice cracked. "He seemed confused by the monster who did this. I dunno if he knew the person or not."

"Did he say anything? Did he manage to tell you anything at all?" Wilson asked.

"He said...he said..." Millie cried into her hands covered in Eric's blood.

"What did he say, Millie?" Wilson prodded warily. The

sound of the ambulance shrieked through the barren outskirts of Los Angeles.

"He just said one word," she sobbed.

"And what word would that be?"

"C-c-careful." She sobbed into her hands.

"He said...*careful?*" Wilson asked.

Millie nodded.

"Where's Stan?" Nazario threw over her shoulder, grunting as she applied pressure to the hole in Eric's skull.

"Not here. He left two days ago for Texas. He's headed to a correctional facility where he does Bible study on a yearly basis. Livingston."

"Polunsky Correctional Facility?" Wilson asked.

"Yes, that's it," Millie answered. "He goes and visits inmates once a year."

"Don't matter," Nazario said as the emergency unit arrived. "We need us a little chat."

When the EMTs arrived, Wilson filled them in, and they extracted Eric Myers from the scene, hauling ass in a desperate attempt to save the ICE agent's life.

All was left was Eric's blood staining the hardwood floor and the pastoral counselor who'd been so gifted at assuaging Nazario's pain. Now, Millie Ann Goodwin could use comfort herself.

Sniffling, Millie grabbed paper towels and Clorox spray.

"Don't worry about that. This is a crime scene. We've got more investigators that need to come on the scene and check it out," Wilson said.

Millie slumped.

"Is there anything that sticks out, Millie, a conversation, someone that might wanna hurt Eric?" Nazario asked.

She hesitated, cupping her hands over her mouth. Millie squeezed her eyes shut.

"What is it? Is there something we need to know? You can tell us, Mrs. Goodwin...I mean Millie, you can trust us, m'kay?" Wilson put a gentle hand on her shoulder. "If you know something, we need anything that can help Eric out right now."

"He...he was going to help me locate my son," Millie whimpered, voice breaking.

"Son?" Nazario gave her a look of bewilderment as she used her crutch to hoist herself back up on her feet, covered in Eric's blood.

"Wasn't aware of a kid. Is there a reason why he's not around?" Wilson asked.

"He...had a near-death drowning when he was about twelve," she said, wrapping her bloody arms around herself. A piece of Eric soiling her blouse.

"And then?" Nazario said.

"He just wasn't the same after that. He doesn't talk anymore. Been mute for years. He'd go on these angry rages. We couldn't help him. I couldn't help him. Hates Stan now. I dunno why. Gideon escaped from the mental hospital, and the doctor said he's dangerous. *My b-b-baby's dangerous.*"

"M'kay, this is good intel. When did he escape?" Wilson asked.

"Don't know. Dr. Bennett kept giving me the run around. He finally e-mailed me and told me that Gideon left without their consent."

"Does Eric know what your son looks like, Millie?" Nazario asked. Millie began to weep harder. She nodded yes.

"We were just talking about Gideon earlier; I showed Eric a picture of him. Got it off Facebook. Gideon's got an account, but he doesn't post much. He came to see me...my son...he came to my door. He was trying to tell me something!"

"Slow down. What do you mean he came to see you?"

"He just showed up out of nowhere," Millie said at last.

"Right in front of our door. In the rain, he just...he just stood there. He opened his mouth this time. He looked like he wanted to say something."

"We're going to be frank here," Nazario said, "when we find him, we're bringing him in for questioning. If there's anyone else that is involved, we need to know right now."

Millie thought about Alex, such a smart boy, and Esperanza. They'd deport Esperanza and take her son away from her. She couldn't let that happen. No, they'd know nothing about Esperanza's initial sighting of her son at the house.

"No one else," Millie said, shaking her head.

"We need his doctor's info," Nazario said, "and text us your hus—Stan's number."

"I'll send you what I have, but Gideon hasn't been talking to me and especially Stan. So, I honestly don't know if what I have is enough."

"Then you go on and send us whatcha got, m'kay? What's his full name?" Wilson asked.

"Gideon...Elijah...Goodwin," Millie felt sick. Saying her son's name aloud took hold of her. Had he been at the door? Did he shoot Eric? If he had, what more was he capable of? Had Eric tried to warn her the same way Stan had? Eric had said, "careful." Careful of her son?

Suddenly the room began to sway.

"You don't look too good. Let's have us a seat on the couch," Nazario said.

Detective Nazario caught her before she hit the ground.

TWENTY-SEVEN

THE WITNESS

"MRS. FLORES, can you tell us where you were...say...three weeks ago?" Wilson began with a disarming smile. "To be specific, Thursday, August 1st at around 7:30 p.m.?"

The room felt tropical and torrid. Sweat trickled across her brow, steeping her shirt.

The *Fundamentals of Physics: Mechanics, Relativity, and Thermodynamics* book sat at the center of the table.

That damn book.

"Look, Esperanza, tell us what you know and don't worry about ICE, alright? We're serious, you're fine. You're safe. We need to catch this sick bastard," Detective Nazario looked her straight in the eyes.

Esperanza clutched her purse close to her, still unsure if she should hand them over what her intruder had left on her bed. Still, she brought it all with her including that terrible note. She shivered as dread filled her body and tightened around her throat, making the thought of speaking of the traumatic events difficult.

"Are we good, Miss Flores?" Esperanza jumped at Wilson's

touch. "You wanna reschedule? We can talk to you another time."

"I was..." Esperanza's eyes teared up. "My son and I were walking home toward Serpent's Bridge when we heard someone calling out for help."

"So, you recognize this book?" Nazario said, sliding Alex's physics book before her.

Esperanza looked away. "Yes, Alex borrowed it from the library."

"You were both there at the scene of the murder?" Nazario asked.

Esperanza nodded.

"We need to hear your answer for the record."

"Yes...yes, we were there." Esperanza coughed, wiping the sweat from her head.

A deathly chill crawled over her skin as she recalled that dreadful night. How Yago Rios/Pablo Jimenez lay gasping for breath. How she had her cell phone. She could've called the cops but didn't. Esperanza was lightheaded. The room spun. She gripped the table with such force her nails screeched against the wood.

Tears blurred her vision as her teeth chattered.

"Esperanza—*Esperanza*—you okay?" she heard Nazario ask.

It didn't matter that her freedom was at stake. What mattered more than her own life was telling the truth about what happened the night she witnessed a murder. She told her son she wouldn't tell the cops but what kind of example would she set for him if she was caught lying? Wouldn't it be far worse if she went to jail over her lack of cooperation or was deported?

Nazario took the box of tissue and gave Esperanza a handful. Esperanza seized this moment, clutching the detective's hand in hers.

"Did someone come to visit Mrs. Goodwin?" Esperanza

asked, holding Nazario's hand, despite the detective trying to pull away. "He did, didn't he? A young man...he was standing outside her home." She dug into her purse and pulled out the photos along with the warning note left in her bedroom. "I've been...I've been followed since The Serpent's Bridge. I'm scared. I can't sleep. He said he was going to kill me if I said anything."

The detectives reviewed the pictures first and then paused for a long beat as they read the threat. She took the time to explain what had happened. They listened quietly, taking it all in with indecipherable expressions.

"So, your door was ajar as you walked up, and you said nothing at all was out of place anywhere," Nazario summarized, rubbing her chin, "nothing at all?"

"That's correct. I was tired...I haven't been sleeping very good since all this happened," she said, glancing down at her fingers. "I was going to take a nap. I pulled back the covers, and the note and the photos were in the bed."

"And you said you saw someone outside the Goodwins' home?" Wilson asked.

Esperanza nodded. "But he ran off before they could see. They thought I was crazy. They didn't believe me."

The detectives exchanged a look and Nazario slid a picture toward her.

"Can you take a look at this picture?"

The sandy blond hair.

The blue lost eyes.

The familiar facial structure.

"It's him. That's...that's him," Esperanza said, pointing at the photo. "He was standing outside the window. They didn't believe me. I'm not going crazy. I know what I saw."

"Gideon Goodwin," Wilson said. "He's mute, or so we've been told, anyway. Here's the thing. The timeline in which you claimed someone was chasing you...don't add up to Gideon's escape."

"But he was standing there. He had a jacket..."

"You take a look at the man who was following you carefully?" Nazario asked. "Did you really have a good look at his face? You're certain Gideon was standing outside his parents' home, which does fit the timeline of events. According to his doctor, he'd escaped around that time. But before that, he was accounted for in the mental hospital."

"What're you saying?" Esperanza couldn't breathe.

"He's not your stalker, Mrs. Flores," Wilson clarified.

"Gideon most likely stopped by to see his mother. Why? We don't know yet. He doesn't have a good relationship with his father. So, we highly doubt he was stopping by for a little father-son bonding," Nazario said dryly.

Esperanza recalled the physical altercation the Goodwins had.

Nazario arched a brow. "Is there...something you wish to share, Esperanza? You'd be really helping us out. You'd be helping the undocumented victims that don't have a voice."

"All I ask is for my son's safety," Esperanza said with more confidence than when she'd entered the interrogation room, "and for my citizenship."

"You help us out, we'll do what we can to...expedite your citizenship." Wilson slid the digital recorder toward Esperanza. "Now, tell us what you know."

"I saw Mrs. Goodwin," Esperanza stalled, touching her throat.

"Go on," Nazario urged, "you saw Mrs. Goodwin...?"

"I saw her trying to strangle her husband."

Nazario and Wilson looked confused.

"Um...Mrs. Flores, are you sure they weren't horsing around?"

"You asked for my help. Just before this Gideon...before I spotted the Goodwins' son outside their house, I came by to cook, and they were in the bedroom. Mrs. Goodwin was on top of her husband. Her hands were around his throat. I think she was...I think if I hadn't come up those stairs she would've killed him. And I know, I saw with my own eyes that Pablo Jimenez was strangled." Esperanza inhaled a shaky breath. "If you want to catch this killer, you must look at everybody."

TWENTY-EIGHT

THE DETECTIVE

NAZARIO HAD LOTS OF QUESTIONS. Questions that had surfaced since the strange interrogation with Esperanza Flores. Did Mrs. Goodwin really have something to do with these murders? Esperanza was right, they had to look at everyone. Though a hands-on violent dispute between a couple didn't mean that the pastor's wife had motive to kill a string of undocumented immigrants and a wealthy winery heiress.

One way to find out was to ask Stan Goodwin himself via Zoom meeting. Her phone chimed just minutes before, prompting Wilson to nosily glance over her shoulder.

Nazario read Huxley's message: *Just seeing how ur doing... disappearing on me already?*

"You ghosting him, aren't you?" Wilson accused his partner knowingly. "Why doncha just answer his dang question?"

"Why doncha mind your beeswax. Let's get to Stan before our meeting with Chief Johnson, shall we?"

"Nice dodge." Wilson logged them into Zoom. Pastor Stan was patiently waiting.

"How's Texas?" Wilson began.

"Alright. Quite busy. Sorry, been out of reach. What's so urgent?" Stan asked, concerned.

"We only got about ten minutes before we gotta hop into another meeting, Pastor Goodwin, so we won't take up too much of your time," Wilson began.

Nazario decided to leave the pastor's wife out of it. "Luis Vargas and Eric Myers...they're members of your church?"

"Yes, why? Is there a problem?"

"We think so, Pastor Goodwin," Nazario leaned in, "for starters, one's dead—"

"And another's almost dead," Wilson finished, "like as in Eric Myers. How's your relationship with the ICE agent?"

"E-Eric Myers...why, he's an upstanding member." Pastor Goodwin pushed up his glasses, then admitted, "My wife and I have argued about his staying or leaving. She and a few other members take issue with him being at the church and—"

"So, you're saying your relationship with Mr. Myers is fine," Wilson began, "but what about the wifey? We kinda heard there was a scuffle?"

"I have nothing against Eric Myers, and regarding my wife, it was just a...just a disagreement."

"Getting choked by your wife is a little more than a disagreement," Nazario added, then asked, "you know our first victim was choked out, too?"

"Wait a sec...you think that - that I had something to do with all this," Stan grew defensive, "or that my wife...I'm no killer and my wife...Millie Ann's only problem is that she's always trying to help people. She's the last person—"

"Hey, it's not personal, we can't afford to leave any stone unturned." Nazario folded her hands behind her head. "Your church, it wouldn't happen to be under an anonymous shell company, would it?"

Perplexed at the question, the pastor repeated, "Anonymous? The church is a nonprofit and so is the food pantry we run. I don't...I don't understand. You told us about Yago Rios, but—"

"His real name is Pablo Jimenez," Nazario corrected, "or did you already know that?"

"No, I didn't already know that." He shook his head, denying it. "He went by Yago Rios. We didn't know that wasn't his real name. We had nothing to do with this."

The pastor looked to be distraught. They refrained from giving him too many details on Luis Vargas' murder and asked him questions, all of which led to a dead end. The pastor flashed his airline tickets and rattled off his hotel info. They took down everything they needed and thanked him for his time.

"I'm sorry that I couldn't be of more help." Stan Goodwin took off his glasses and wiped his eyes. "I don't know why someone's targeting my members. I spoke to a reporter not long ago about our mission to help the undocumented, and maybe... maybe someone doesn't agree with what we're trying to do at Sanctuary Baptist."

"Would that someone include Gideon, Pastor Goodwin?" Nazario queried directly.

Stan looked shaken at the sound of his son's name. He bit his lower lip, and a flood of tears came rushing out. "He's not well," Stan pleaded. "He's a good boy, but he's not well, and he's...he's violent."

"If you can come by the station upon your return, that'd be great," Nazario said.

"Of course," he said, "and in the meantime, Millie Ann will be able to help, answer any more questions you got. I believe... she's got Gideon's doctor...Dr. Bennett's information."

Wilson nodded. "We best get to our other meeting. Appreciate you answering all our questions. We'll be in touch."

After they ended the call, Nazario looked to her partner. "Well, that was a waste of time."

"Don't seem like he even knows of his wife's affair." Wilson scratched his chin, then added, "I dunno, but my gut's telling me that he's not involved."

"Same here," Nazario admitted, "but we just never know."

When they entered the chief's office, Huxley tracked her with laser focus as she hobbled across the stuffy room. Nazario avoided direct eye contact. She'd been ignoring his texts and calls since Eric Myers was shot.

"It's a goddamn zoo out there," Chief barked. "This better not be a waste of time."

The noise from the turbulent sea of reporters and paparazzi penetrated the concrete walls.

Nazario limped toward her seat and adjusted her crutch, so it slid beneath the chair. She faced Chief Johnson. Feeling Huxley's burning gaze, she didn't look his way.

"The press conference is in twenty. They've asked me to do it. But Homicide's lead on this," Huxley said. "I'll be on standby for Fed questions."

"Well, don't got much time to do this *powwow*," Chief Johnson eyed his watch. "Nazario, you ready to speak with the press?"

"I'm down," Nazario said, then filled the chief in. "We just got done confirming Stan Goodwin's whereabouts. He's got an alibi during the time Eric Myers was shot. The airline's system's still down, but he showed us his airplane tickets over Zoom video conference."

"That goofy pastor at Sanctuary Baptist?" Chief Johnson let out a hoot. "You for real?"

Wilson added, "Millie Goodwin and Eric Myers have, you know, been getting busy."

"Did his wife corroborate Goodwin's whereabouts?" Chief

Johnson sounded fed up. Like he was ready to dismiss the theory entirely. Nazario could tell and didn't blame him. They had next to nothing. No leads.

The person who could identify the shooter—Eric Myers— was in a coma.

"Wife says the same." Wilson leaned back in his chair, making it squeak. "Says he's in Livingston, sir. We just talked with the guy from his hotel in Texas."

"Y'all can check on that goofy-ass pastor and if he's remotely connected to Eric Myers. But I was with y'all on Myers. Shit, I thought he was our prime suspect, too, before he got shot upside the head." Johnson webbed his fingers behind his neck. "This is unbelievable. We got hotel receipts and confirmation from the hotel desk clerk that he was there? Ordinarily, I'd suspect the husband in a lover's shooting. Does that pastor even know what his wife's been up to? He don't have a clue, do he?"

Nazario and Wilson shrugged.

"We've no idea, sir," Nazario admitted. "Millie called me confessing she's been with Myers. Said she found a suspicious notebook of his. That's how we found out he'd been the ICE agent to snitch out Pablo Jimenez and Luis Vargas."

"The Goodwins had a—" Wilson stalled, then continued, "—little fight. Apparently, their house cleaner, Esperanza Flores, walked in and Mrs. Goodwin was on top of Pastor Goodwin." Hands demonstrated a strangling motion. "Choking him out."

Chief rose a brow. Nazario clarified, speaking slowly, "When we asked the pastor, he brushed it off and got defensive. Acted like it was a typical argument."

"Well, that's a helluva a lot more than a domestic dispute," Chief chuckled, eyes bulging incredulously as a brown hand raked across his freshly cut fade.

"Yeah," Wilson added dryly, "it's called attempted murder."

"And Mrs. Flores didn't say anything until now?" Chief queried, glancing out the window at the cacophony of reporters, camera crew, news stations, picketers with various signs that read "stop illegal immigration."

"Damn, it's crazy as hell out there. They didn't care this much when immigrants were being killed," Chief said, shutting his blinds. "Anything about an anonymous shell corporation paying decent wages to undocumented workers?"

"Nothing yet, sir," Nazario said, then eyed Huxley. "But maybe the FBI knew something about it, since they're keeping things from us in this ATS bullshit." Nazario forcefully grabbed her crutch from under the seat. "I'm not special enough to be given clearance. Huxley on the other hand, he's *real* special. Aren'tcha, Boy Scout?"

"We'll be releasing the ballistics report soon," Huxley said. "We went over this."

"And that was two weeks ago." She looked at her watch. "We got ten minutes. I'm getting air. Wilson, when you're ready."

In the lobby, a sharply dressed man strode forward and introduced himself.

"As PR rep for Madison Vanwell, I'll step in after you," he said. "It looks like we're ready. Now I know you know this, just a friendly reminder it's undocumented immigrants. Not illegal immigrants. Not illegal aliens. Dodge the race questions and the Angel-cartel queries. It's a fabrication. Got it? And you'll be fine."

"I'm fully aware, but it sure don't hurt to be reminded." Nazario nodded soberly and headed toward the podium in front of headquarters. Huxley was already standing next to the lectern.

A bunch of reporters and camera operators collected in a

clamoring cluster. A collage of lights flickered at them in hot white flashes that agitated Nazario's eyes.

Wilson nodded to her, and she stepped up, adjusting the microphone.

"Regarding the deaths of Avery Elizabeth Vanwell and..."

An image of Avery's lifeless body flashed before her eyes, replacing the crowd with details her brain couldn't seem to leave: the burn mark residue surrounding the bullet hole, the scatter of skull fragmentation, the milky eyes of death, and the blood pooling around Avery's head, pasting crimson hair against her cheek. Avery's smile and sunshine returned to mind. She'd shown so much promise in martial arts. Her bright future was gone, but so were the immigrants who'd come here hoping for a better life.

Nazario gripped the podium, taking a long breath until the tightening in her chest eased.

"...and Angel Hernandez are ruled homicides. The LAPD Homicide Division, along with the FBI, will make public what we know as we discover our findings. At the moment, we know that Avery Vanwell and Angel Hernandez were engaged and that they were shot by the same individual. We have no other information or details involving this case."

A reporter jumped in as she paused. "Is it true Angel Hernandez was here illegally?"

"Yes, Angel Hernandez was an undocumented immigrant."

"Are you able to identify whether or not this was a drug-related crime involving Angel Hernandez and his potential ties with the Mexican drug lords?" another member of the media shouted out.

"We're looking into his past along with all other possibilities. With regards to his citizenship status, it's doubtful it has any bearing as to why they were murdered," Nazario said into the microphone. "One other thing: let's be clear that there have been two other undocumented immigrants killed that may be connected, and not just Angel Hernandez and Avery Vanwell. The LAPD is taking donations for Madison Vanwell's nonprofit that helps undocumented immigrants and their families."

"What's the FBI's role in the investigation?" A reporter pivoted back to Avery and Angel's case. Of course, they would. Nazario wasn't surprised. The donations and other immigrant murders were glossed over.

Nazario exhaled loudly into the microphone, gritting her teeth.

Huxley stepped up to the podium, placing his body in front of hers like a barrier.

"As Detective Nazario has indicated, the Federal Bureau of Investigation is working closely with the Los Angeles Police Department. We will release pertinent information to the public as it's available."

The mob erupted with rowdy questions that braided together until there was nothing left but shouts. Nazario stepped off the stage, followed by Wilson and Huxley. The PR rep took over the microphone and emphatically stated that they were working together to do everything they could to stop the killer.

Yes, they were working to stop *Avery's* killer.

But what about all of them dead Mexicans?

After the press conference, Huxley avoided her altogether and charged straight to his vehicle without a glance in her direction. Her weeks of ghosting him had resurrected old memories and recycled her usual self-destructive patterns. She leaned against her crutch and hobbled toward him. An anxious flutter turned her stomach.

He unlocked his car and opened the driver's door.

Nazario cleared her throat. "Huxley?"

He turned half around, not looking at her but past her.

"Yes, Detective Nazario?" He exhaled through his nostrils. "Can I help you?"

His formality left an unexpected sting.

"I, um, I just wanted—I wanted to apologize for—"

"Having a busy life? No need for an apology."

"Eric Myers got shot, and then the interview with Esperanza...it uh...didn't turn out the way we expected." Nazario wished he'd look at her, but he kept his distant stare. "It was just a lot."

"You wanna go at it all alone? Do your thing." He ducked into his car.

Damn it, she was no good at this sort of thing.

"Can I make it up to you?"

"By disappearing for another two weeks? If it weren't for the fact that we're working the same case, you'd have ghosted me for a month or longer, like back in grad school, then show up when you wanna get laid and disappear when I get too soft for your taste."

Nazario reached for his face, but Huxley shoved away her hand. "I'm busy, Detective."

"You have a right to be pissed. Work's been—"

Huxley got out of the car and faced her, nostrils flaring, his jaw clenching.

"This is *not* about Eric Myers or Esperanza. I guess I shared too much. We spend a night together, and poof, you're gone. Hell, I'm not asking you to marry me or anything. You could've taken ten seconds to respectfully respond. An 'I'm fine, thanks.' But not hard-ass Nazario. So, no, Detective, this isn't about work. It's your thing. Leaving. Disappearing. Well, guess what? I'm not gonna keep doing this. I'm not playing your game. I got your message loud and clear. I played your games twelve years ago...I refuse to play them now."

"I don't know why I shut people out," she admitted, "didn't mean to shut you out."

"Well, that's what you do best."

Nazario stepped closer, her chest against his, her heart accelerating.

"Let me make it up to you."

Their breaths mingled. His eyes still told her he was holding back, arms pinned against his sides. She grabbed his hand and put it on her face, brought him to her lips, and tried to apologize with her kiss. His body softened. He moaned and then kissed her back.

She brushed a finger across his mouth. "Are you...busy tonight?"

"Might be..." he replied, smiling at her. "...might not."

"Can I take you out to dinner?" She blurted the words out without calculation.

"To discuss the case?"

She exhaled. "No."

"I really don't believe this." Huxley put his hands on his hips. "You asking me on a date, Detective Nazario?"

She steadied herself. "Yes."

"Hmm, let me see," he waited a beat.

"If you're busy—"

"Guess I can pick you up around—" he looked at his watch.

"No!" Nazario blushed at her forceful tone. "I'll...*um*...pick you up. Dinner's on me."

Huxley laughed, eyes wide with disbelief. "Really? You okay to drive on that leg?"

"Long as I ice it and don't bend the damn thing. Pick you up after the self-defense class." She limped back to her car, her heart thudding in her chest. "Don't forget to text your address."

Huxley still stood there with his mouth open. "What's the dress code?"

"Wear something nice." She put her shades on, stepped on the gas, and peeled away.

TWENTY-NINE

THE DETECTIVE

SAMMY'D CALLED Nazario after hearing the bad news and had arrived a few hours earlier at Nazario's apartment to process Avery's death. All the girls in the self-defense class had been in disbelief over their friend's murder. However, Gus had made efforts to steer the conversation back to the present. Now, Nazario waited as Sammy finished adding the final touch of red lipstick.

It had taken effort not to stew about Avery and the unsolved homicides.

Nazario never wore makeup or did her hair, but thanks to Sammy, who was in school for cosmetology, she probably looked like an entirely different person. She'd yet to see herself in the mirror.

The last time she was in a dress had to be when she was a toddler. Even as a kid, she'd scream at Mama every time she put her in a dress. Daddy would stick up for her, tell his wife to let their daughter be a tomboy, and wear what she wanted. Awkward butterflies danced in the pit of her stomach, and she couldn't help but feel like she was in some Halloween costume.

"Girl, you look amazing," Gus said, fluffing the loose curls that accentuated Nazario's already wavy hair. "Oughta get dolled up more often."

"You look FAB." Sammy clapped.

"I'm afraid to look." Nazario wiped her clammy hands on her dress.

"Don't be." Gus turned her around to face the mirror. "Homicide's taking a break from them DBs tonight."

The contemporary, asymmetric neckline left her right shoulder bare. On her left shoulder, a strap wrapped around the top and bottom of her shoulder, leaving a hole at the center where skin poked through. The red dress was elegant and form-fitting, ending at her knee. A slit ran up her right thigh.

She gulped, taking in her own reflection.

"Wow, Sammy," her voice wobbled, "you've got some talent. I know you don't think your parents respect what you do, but I bet they do. At least your older sister should."

"You really think so?" Sammy bit her lower lip. "I dunno. My sister Wilder is a veterinarian. Mom's a psychologist. Dad's one of the best brain surgeons in the world. Can you believe it? I dunno if they care much about hair and makeup. It's not medical school." Sammy paused, her voice now distant. "I stopped talking to them after you guys found me. It's been hard...since I clammed up at trial, they've been...I dunno. Disappointed in me."

Sammy's self-esteem issues had always hurt Nazario's heart in a maternal way.

"You're amazing, Sammy." Nazario put her hands on Sammy's well-defined shoulders, earned by pounding the weights since her student was rescued. "You survived what many young girls couldn't. Kidnapping, sexual assault, trafficking? You being here today. Clean and sober. Doing something with your life despite what happened, that tops any stupid medical degree. You hear me? As for those bastards that hurt you—if you ever feel like your life is threatened, if you sense someone's following you, or anything at all, and I mean *anything* —you let one of us know. You call one of us at any time. Don't matter if it's three in the morning. We'll get a unit over to guard your apartment. Hell, I'll come down myself and beat some ass. We clear?"

Sammy's eyes glistened as a tear plopped down her ruddy cheeks. She wiped it away.

"That's right," Gus chimed in, giving the girl a Gus-bear-hug, "all that other shit is monetary. And it's okay if you're not talking to your family. Nazario and I are your family. Hear me? Besides, sometimes we need space from those we love in order to make room to love ourselves."

Nazario gave herself another look in the mirror and hardly recognized herself.

Sammy hugged her. Then she said as she always did, "Love ya, Detective Nazario."

"Ditto," Nazario returned, unable to say the words to anyone other than Daddy.

"I'm fixing to get you to say the L-word if it's the last thing I do," Sammy said.

"No shop-talk when you're out tonight. Y'all keep the case file closed for a few hours. That's an order," Gus gave her a firm kiss on the cheek, "and *no* wine."

————

The balmy evening required no jacket. If she was going to do this, she wasn't covering up or hiding herself. The red heels were a perfect match for the dress. Luckily, the crutch made it easier to shuffle in the heels she was unaccustomed to wearing. She wobbled in them and finally found her balance. It took her fifteen minutes to get to Huxley's Brentwood home.

If Mama could see her now, she'd totally flip; she might even cry. Her hands were shaking. She tried to steady them, but her nerves were shot. She got ready to knock, inhaling a shivery breath and exhaling.

C'mon, Nazario, you can do this. It's just a stupid dress. It's just makeup. It's just a date. You can handle looking at dead bodies. You can handle one stupid date with Blake Huxley.

She worked up the courage and knocked on the door.

A long, awkward minute passed.

Nazario faced the street. Her stomach turned as a wave of nausea hit her.

She thought she was going to be sick. The nausea had gotten worse since her stitches were out. Maybe it was the antibiotics? She should call the doctor. Maybe it'd calm her nerves.

The door opened and she turned around. Huxley scanned her from head to toe. There was nowhere to hide. She stood before him, letting him see her, really see her. He closed the door behind him and, without taking his eyes off her, stepped toward her, leaving only half an inch between them. She tucked a hair behind her ear, noticing her hands were still shaking.

"I...uh...got here a little early. I was thinking of sushi. Katsuya? If you're not feeling sushi, that's totally fine. I'm open for whatever, really."

His fingers brushed down her cheek. "Sushi's just fine," he whispered.

"I'm not wearing my brace. My doctor...he'd kill me if he knew. But I figure as long as I don't bend it, I should be fine. Hopefully I don't fall on my ass with these heels; I don't really wear them. Obviously. They're actually the only pair I own. This is the...only dress I own," she rambled, wringing her fingers together. "Sorry. I'm a...I'm a little nervous."

His gaze softened into tenderness. She looked down at her heels.

"You did all this for me?" He lifted her chin so that she met his eyes.

"Is it too much?" she gulped. He took her hands in his.

"Too much?" he leaned in and kissed her cheek then whispered in her ear. "Detective Nazario...you look absolutely beautiful."

―――――

The cacophonous evening sushi crowd packed the restaurant that evening. A collection of distilled spirits were everywhere. Beers, wine, sake, and mixed drinks on almost every table accompanying raw dishes. It was temptation of the worst kind for someone barely sober. Her hands became damp and sweaty, and her mouth watered. Dinner guests sat there talking, and all the while, Nazario was staring at their drinks. Why would anyone neglect their beverages and just let them sit half full?

Because they can have just one and be done, Nazario's conscience whispered. It surprised her that she could hear it at all. *They can have a normal conversation instead of being obsessed over the next cocktail. That's what makes them different than you. That's what distinguishes normies from someone like you, Nazario. That's what makes you an alcoholic.*

Despite the strongest urge for a bottle, she and Huxley settled for sparkling water.

Two remaining delicious slivers of yellowtail sashimi with thin slices of jalapeño on top and drizzled in ponzu sauce sat on an empty white rectangle plate. They'd just finished the salmon sashimi with caviar, masago aioli, and onion chutney. But the sashimi chef's combination plate with more of an assortment of the chef's pick hit the spot. The red sea bream, which was a firm, fleshy white fish much sweeter than sea bass, made dinner a pleasant surprise.

Nazario glanced at a one-hundred-dollar bottle of Williams Selyem Fanucchi-Wood Road Zinfandel. Huxley noticed, but she managed to deflect by taking the yellowtail sashimi between her chopsticks, swirling it in the ponzu sauce, and slipping it into his mouth.

He chewed in silence, but she could hear him thinking, wanting to ask.

"Started on and off after Grad school." *After I left*, she thought. "Got worse a few years ago." *After you got married*, her heart said. "That's why I was there at Sanctuary Baptist. I attend the AA meeting there. A regular young kid backed up into Nicky Sanchez."

"I don't drink," Huxley admitted, "alcoholism runs in my family."

"Was that club soda with Blondie, then?"

He inhaled deeply. "Affirmative."

"I got no excuse. No one in my family drinks," Nazario said, "except for me."

"Appreciate your candor." Huxley wove his fingers through hers and then changed the subject. "Tell me more about the self-defense class. Avery—what was she like?"

She offered an appreciative smile. "Gus and I started it three years ago. Not in the best location, but we love the girls. Avery didn't share much about herself. She was a natural in the dojang." Nazario took in a shaky breath, and Huxley apologized for bringing Avery up. "Your peeps at the Feds got the 4-1-1 on Avery and Angel's job status, didn't they? Care to fill me in on it now rather than later?"

Huxley cocked a brow at her and smiled, shaking his head.

"You're real quick and perceptive, Detective. It just came in as you were picking me up," he said, capturing the final piece of yellowtail sashimi topped with jalapeño. "Both got paid wages from the same shell corporation, 60k for Angel and 100k for

Avery." She leaned in. Ponzu sauce dripped on her lips as the delicate morsel slipped into her mouth. As much as she enjoyed the crunch of the jalapeño accenting the sweet taste of lemony ponzu, the explosion of flavors did little to distract her mind from the haunting reality of Avery's death.

"And you were planning on telling me *when* exactly?"

"*When* the time was right." Huxley chuckled lightly. "But I gotta admit, you got me feeling like a boy in high school on his first date right about now, and I thought we were supposed to lay off the subject of work for at least an hour or two."

"All paid from the same shell company, huh?" Nazario couldn't hide her puzzlement. She pulled out her phone and sent a quick text to Wilson, who replied that the Feds just filled him in and promptly scolded her to get back to her date.

"We can't seem to trace the owner," Huxley admitted, leaning back in his chair. "Could belong to anyone that runs a small business, a nonprofit, or a corporation."

Nazario flushed, muffling as she chewed. "Promised Gus no work-talk."

He chuckled, suggesting, "So, let's talk about that self-defense class."

"It started with Sammy. Narcotics and Gang Unit. Actually, Gus found her. Sammy'd been used—fill in the blank—by a group of..." she mouthed the words, so they were not audible, "*white supremacist assholes.*"

Huxley shook his head. "Scumbags are the worst. Our human trafficking division busted another ring just outside of Boston." In their profession, they'd seen too many young girls become victims of sex trafficking, sexual slavery, manipulation, and abused by various types of gangs or cults.

"Aryan?"

Huxley nodded.

"TAG busted a ring. Doing all sorts of shit. Dog fighting,

prostitution, human trafficking, you name it," Nazario recalled, shaking her head, "I do *not* miss being on Narco and Gangs. It got to me. It really did. That's why I made the switch to Homicide. One thing seeing a DB, another thing to see someone so young, life ahead of them, and dead on the inside."

"Trauma does that. I couldn't work our trafficking division... no way," he said, shaking his head vigorously. "Our guys were on that one, too, by the way. Worked with the Texas Anti-Gang Center. TAG's a sharp group. On top of things."

The mood shifted. They shared a collective sigh.

Breaking the moment with levity, he said with a chuckle, "Gus would have both our asses right about now for talking shop on our—dare I label it because I know you hate labels—*date*."

Nazario laughed. "She would." She paused to take a sip of sparkling water. "On a positive note, and back to that self-defense class—Sammy inspired us. Gus and I wanted to help young women like her learn to defend themselves, to never be a victim, some man's tool."

"That's fantastic," he said and leaned in. "You're amazing. What both of you provide for those girls—"

"Nah. They're amazing. Especially Gus. She's a survivor," she said with sincerity, putting a hand over her heart. "Love those girls like they're my own. We both do."

"I'm sure you do," he said softly. "How's Gus? I tried to be there for her during her recovery."

"She shut me out, too." Nazario looked down at her water and then back up again. "Said she needed to do it solo. But she's good. A little winded during class the other day. Had me worried, not gonna lie."

"Need a stand-in, someone they can practice on, let me know. Give Gus a break."

"Really?" she said, surprised by his offer.

He rubbed her palm with his thumb. "Absolutely."

Nazario exhaled, feeling the tug of his fingers tighten against hers.

A warm sensation crept from between their hands and up her arms.

The waitress brought the check, and Nazario paid before Huxley could interfere.

After dinner, Los Angeles traffic had eased up. In less than ten minutes, they were at Huxley's doorstep.

"Thank you for dinner." His warm smile arrested her.

"Thank you for listening," she said, and meant it. "I'm sure you have a busy day tomorrow."

"Crazy as always," Huxley admitted. "But I'm gonna wager your schedule tomorrow is worse than mine."

She chuckled. "You wagered correctly."

"Would you like to come in anyway, Detective?"

Nazario stood outside his home, considering her options. He extended a hand, and she took it. Once inside, Huxley started up his fireplace, and it blazed with natural warm brilliance.

"This home's old, got a fireplace. Like we need one in SoCal?" He stoked the flames.

"Love fireplaces," she admitted, kicking off her heels, wiggling her numb and achy toes.

They warmed before the fireplace. Orange flames flickered, mirroring the smoldering embers that had ignited between them long ago. At the exact moment, they turned toward one another. He leaned her crutch against the sofa and brought her against him, cradling her lower back with his left arm as he held her right hand in his.

"Your leg okay?" he asked.

"I'm not bending it," she said, "a couple of hours without the brace won't kill me."

She rested her head on his chest, and they swayed to the crackle of flames, their shadows flickering against the walls.

They slow danced to the sound of familiar police car sirens screaming in the distance and to the music of their hearts drumming against their chests.

She lifted her head. Their faces were close, sharing the same breath.

His cell phone rang twice. She ran a thumb against his lower lip as he swore under his breath. "I've waited more than a decade for this moment," he whispered in her ear, frustrated.

"And I'll be right here after the call," she whispered back, "you should answer it."

By the fourth ring, he dug into his blazer pocket and stalked into the kitchen. He muttered something in Russian. The language sounded almost violent and harsh to her American ears. But what did she know? She'd never bothered to learn anything but English, some French, and conversational Spanish. Enough to have understood, Daddy, anyway.

She took the crutch, leaning against the couch, and limped closer to the fireplace.

He turned off his phone, and they stared at each other from across the living room.

"French, Spanish, and now Russian?" She arched a brow. "I'm impressed with your linguistic aptitude, Special Agent. But given that I don't understand a single Russian word, you could've finished your conversation."

He took a few steps toward her. "I asked him if it could wait until tomorrow."

"Let me guess," she mused, "it can't?" Nazario adjusted herself on the crutch.

"No, it can't." He took her crutch and tossed it to the side. She fell forward, gripping his shoulders for support. "And neither can this," he whispered and then kissed her.

It was a slow kiss, one that began feathery, lips first, parting hesitantly, until tongues met and moved with hunger, desire building with each stroke, swimming and swirling, inhaling each other. She wrapped her arms around his neck, gripping handfuls of his thick hair as she let him lower her to the floor.

Hands removed barriers: his pants and briefs, her red panties, forgetting his shirt, skipping her dress, sliding inside her with slow deliberation, savoring long strokes, feeling him fully, causing her to arch and throb.

Her moan.

His ecstasy.

Time dissolved.

Work on pause.

Rhythmic passion moving.

Joined, at least for this hour.

———

She laid her head on his chest, listening to his heart race. He was still collecting long, ragged breaths. A lone finger ran lightly across her cheek, down her neck and back.

She shivered.

Huxley's phone rang again.

"That call sounded important. Better take it," Nazario said. Huxley let out a sigh, wrapping her tighter against him. He kissed the top of her head, and then it was Nazario's phone that chimed, alerting her to a text message.

His phone.

Now hers.

They shared a look and then a laugh.

"I'd love just one night with you without any interruptions," Huxley said. She brushed her fingers through the back of his hair. He closed his eyes. She used to do this when he had longer hair and it always made him relax. Sometimes he'd fall asleep.

"Will you stay tonight?"

"Do you want me to?"

"I've got this killer Jacuzzi tub, had it installed two weeks ago, and I've got bubbles..."

They'd do bubble baths in college. Nazario's smile widened.

"Two weeks ago?" she leaned on her crutch, limping behind him into the bathroom. "Well, had you left a message about the Jacuzzi tub, I might've answered the phone."

"I haven't used it yet, so it hasn't been devirginized," he flashed her a wicked grin.

"Help me out of my dress."

The large round tub started to fill, brimming with lavender scented bubbles, her favorite. A calculated purchase on Huxley's part. He brushed her hair around her shoulder and took his time unzipping her dress. She could feel his hot breath against her shoulder, his nearness, and the slow deliberate pull of the zipper was sensual.

The dress fell to the floor. Still standing behind her, his warm hand followed the curve of her hip. She held onto one of his strong and steady arms as he helped her in the tub. She rested her right leg on the brim. The bubbles tickled her skin and the heat of the water felt good on her achy joints.

His phone rang again, he answered stepping out.

She heard him pacing outside of the bathroom as he said something in Russian before returning to English. "Okay," he sighed, "thanks."

Nazario dried her hands on a towel, reached for her phone as it chimed again and read Wilson's text.

Sorry if I'm interrupting. Did Huxley tell you about the ballistics report yet?

No. Why? It came in? Nazario replied.

Wilson texted back. *I'll let him tell you.*

She turned off the phone and sat it back on the bathroom ledge. Huxley returned with a sober look on his face she couldn't place. Gus was right, they should've kept work out of their date tonight. They should've turned off their phones, let whatever intel involving the case or "emergency" go to voicemail.

Trying to lift his spirits, she teased, "C'mon, Special Agent Huxley," she laughed, "got too many clothes on."

He sat at the edge of the tub, looking at her with a seriousness that shifted the mood.

"About the ballistics report...that phone call I received."

"Yeah, Wilson texted me about it. Didn't give details. Whatever it is, you can get naked and talk about work." Nazario smiled. "We got through grad school that way."

"The shell casing from Eric Myers and the bullet that was found, well, they're a match with the Vanwell and Hernandez case, but there's more. It's a .45," Huxley said.

Nazario furrowed her brow. "What're you getting at?"

"The cold case that's linked, the one I've been working on for several years, it's Lucas..." He exhaled loudly. "Lucas Rafael Nazario, your father. We think it might be the same killer."

Nazario blanched, her hands cupped her mouth, and an anguished cry escaped.

"Please...please don't hate me," he begged, hands folded before him. "I can take anger, justifiably, but not hate. I'll leave you alone if you need space, and for as long as you need it. If I was able to tell you sooner, I promise you, I would've. We needed more evidence. We needed a ballistics match."

Huxley raked his hands over his face, then slowly got up from the edge of the tub and headed for the door.

"Wait," Nazario whispered, feeling the avalanche of pain ready to fall. "Please don't go."

He had told her twelve years ago that he would find who killed her father. The promise was too much for her to believe. She'd thought he'd say anything, that he was making false promises he couldn't keep, and that it was wrong of him to make such a grandiose vow.

"Are you...are you sure?" he hesitated at the door, knowing her dad had always been a source of pain.

That night so long ago, she'd lashed out at the mention of her father and had completely walked away. It was their final argument, his promise to her.

First, they'd lost the baby at seventeen weeks. She'd begun experiencing contractions, then she was bleeding, and it wouldn't stop. There was so much blood. They were in a tub like this one, only it was filled with crimson water, their baby dying inside her.

They hadn't been trying for a baby, but after Huxley playfully ate half her birth control pills one evening, she never bothered to get more. The pregnancy was part-planned, part-surprise. After the miscarriage, she hadn't expected to feel such despair. During dinner a month later, Huxley brought up her father, brought up the case and that he'd like to look it over.

"I'd like to re-open the case," Huxley had said. "I've got an interview with the FBI, and I'd like to work on cold cases. Your father's case really inspired me—"

"What're you implying?"

He had clutched her hand and claimed, "I'm gonna find who killed your father."

"You have no right saying that. You don't know what the hell you're saying. You can't possibly promise that and deliver."

Nazario stormed out. Left cold turkey. Changed her number. Moved apartments.

She'd admittedly been too immature to handle it all and did the easiest thing—ran.

Now, Huxley's eyes told a tale of genuine fear that history was repeating itself. When she asked him to stay again, he walked in and slowly closed the door.

In the dim ambiance, he unbuttoned and slipped out of his dress shirt. The light cast soft shadows against his hard, muscular silhouette. He stepped into the tub and slid behind her. She turned to face him, and he ran a wet hand against her face.

"I've never stopped looking," Huxley whispered in her ear. Nazario let out another sob, curled on her side, careful not to bend her right leg, and put her head against his. He wrapped his massive arms around her in a protective embrace, and for a long moment, they sat in silence. She didn't care that she was weeping uncontrollably against him, that she was letting herself be vulnerable before him.

He kissed her forehead, planted a kiss on either cheek, the tip of her nose, her chin, and then lips. Nazario clasped on to him, her body, mind, and soul unraveling. Each tender touch, each soft caress, each parting of his lips against hers, each stroke of his hand stole away the pain, replacing a history of loss and sadness with an unwavering love that had never changed.

THIRTY

THE DETECTIVE

THE CLICK, click, click of the crutch against the tile floor ricocheted across the small auditorium, sending murmurs across the room until curious gossip hushed into silence.

Heads turned.

Nazario surveyed the attendees she did recognize.

SID's lead investigators, Chuck Whittier and Ellen Yang, sat with their trainees Redhead and Gomez, the latter whom Nazario recalled from the first murder of Yago Rios, aka Pablo Jimenez. As expected, there were some unknown faces from the Redondo Beach Police unit on scene for Vic-Two—Luis Vargas —along with the two young patrol officers from the recent homicides of Angel Hernandez and Avery Vanwell.

Huxley stood at the podium, though what made her heart sink into her sour stomach was that there was another podium next to him. Huxley's Russian partner sat in the front row next to Chief Johnson and Wilson. There were about a dozen federal agents and others she didn't recognize—likely undercover— flanking each side of the room.

Nazario was the last to arrive. She made her way down the center aisle with Huxley's gaze steady on her. Circumstances revolving around Daddy's case, most of which Huxley could not divulge, kept them apart for a week. In addition, he'd had to deal with the mountain of paperwork the FBI had to document and keep track of tedious work that was seventy percent of their job.

She noticed the room shifting as she approached.

Everyone from beat cops to the Feds gave her their eyes as if each one was paying homage to the famed Lucas Rafael Nazario. She limped along, feeling a swell of something unidentifiable in her chest, returning stares with a quick glance, returning nods with her curt one.

Shooting up from his chair, Gomez said, "Detective Nazario, you can take my seat."

"I think I'm gonna stand, Gomez," Nazario gave an unwilling smile.

"You sure? It's no problem."

"Sit down, Gomez," Nazario ordered with stiff resolution.

Gomez took a seat but looked pleased with himself that he'd had some type of dialogue with her. Nazario made it close to the stage and stood next to two federal agents. They made space as she approached, not speaking a word, giving her respect she'd somehow earned.

Why? Because she was a damn good detective, or because of her last name?

Nazario leaned against her crutch and met Huxley's gaze. This time it was not one of his coy maneuvers; it was one of a serious nature.

"Most of you here know of Detective Lucas Rafael Nazario's case. That is why we're really here. He was considered the best of the best. At the bureau...I fought like hell to reopen this cold case ten years ago." Huxley looked down at Nazario. She swallowed. "It was granted, but it had been red-taped as ATS. My partner and I were the only two with access until we were given the green light to hold this briefing because it connects directly with the Bridge Killer. Now, I'm gonna need Homicide that's been on the Bridge Killer murders to come up and lead. This is primarily your case, not the FBI's."

Nazario swore under her breath. She gripped the bottle of Gabapentin shoved in her coat jacket. Her psychiatrist increased the dosage earlier in the week when she'd complained of worsening heart palpitations and nausea.

Wilson looked her way, then gave a nod to the stage. He got up and handed her a small water bottle. "It should be you," he whispered to her. "Take your meds?"

"Six hours ago," she said quietly enough for his ears only, feeling the panic rise.

"Take another. Looks like an episode might be coming on. I can see it on your face. If you can't finish, signal, and I'll jump up there. You can do this. I know you can," he said, squeezing her shoulder.

Nazario took the water and clopped toward the stage.

Huxley stepped aside, and Nazario hobbled toward the podium on the far end of the stage. For a moment, it was as if no one took a breath. They watched her with collective anticipation. She clicked on an image on the laptop that displayed on a projector, an image she'd been avoiding her whole career.

Her mind went back to one of the last conversations she'd had with her father. Daddy sat her down after she insisted on wanting to follow in his footsteps. His dreams for her to do anything except become a cop went out the window.

Daddy whispered to her, "If you wanna do what I do, no matter how hard and how much it rips at your heart, you keep your emotions separate from the case you're trying to solve. It doesn't matter if it's a family member or even if it's me. You stay strong. Focus on solving the case. Worry about emotions later."

*Even if it's me...*The words tugged at her.

Nazario adjusted the microphone and turned to the image;

her hands were shaking. She could hardly breathe. Her chest began a familiar tightening.

"Excuse...excuse me," she squeezed the words out into the mic. Quaking fingers unscrewed the rattling bottle of Gabapentin hidden behind the podium. She popped one, chasing it down with water.

Huxley covered the microphone. Brows furrowed as his intense eyes searched hers.

"Are you fine?" he seemed to ask.

She nodded and allowed the image to hold their audience's attention.

"Sorry. According to the federal investigations..." A heat-wave passed through her, one that made her nauseous. "Special Agent Huxley will fill you in on the specifics of the ballistics."

She zoomed out on the picture of her father's body. Sweat trickled across her brow, her chest constricted, followed by a sharp jab causing her breathing to go shallow. Daddy's opened eyes had that death stare. He lay in a puddle of blood that oozed from the hole in his chest.

Focus on solving the case. Worry about emotions later.

She repeated the line in her head and then lifted her chin. Nazario scanned the room, clenching her teeth as she inhaled through her nose. Nazario attempted a quick breath as another dizzying wave swept over her.

"The positioning alone of...Lucas..." Gripping the podium. "...of his body matched."

Nazario clicked through each of the victims in order of death beginning with Daddy. Avery's picture was last. She blinked away from the picture of her former student's ashen face, blood pooling, burn marks at the center of her forehead. The image had caused her to lose sleep and increase her anxiety medication dosage. Avery's apparitional voice clawed at her insides, duplicating.

"Can we grab coffee sometime, Detective Nazario?"

"Can we grab coffee sometime, Detective Nazario?"

"Can we grab coffee sometime, Detective Nazario?"

Nazario clutched the podium, her shaky knuckles knocked against the wood.

"All bodies that were found under some sort of bridge-like structure were undocumented Mexican immigrants, except for...Avery Vanwell and Lucas Nazario."

Nazario pulled at the shirt sticking to her chest, then fingered the collar choking her. Her heart was sprinting too quickly. The tightening in her lungs continued. The medication hadn't kicked in yet. She white-knuckled the podium to keep herself from falling over.

Huxley spoke, and temporary relief washed over her. "No one took notice of Detective Lucas Nazario's body in his old pictures, because the case had been sealed and forgotten. It even took me a while before I actually noticed the similarities in the positioning of the body and placement under a bridge structure. He was working undercover with the Narcotics and Gang Unit at the time of death. If we're looking for ethnic similarities, it's possible that the killer assumed he was Mexican."

She wiped her brow as Huxley nodded at her from his podium to continue.

"Yago Rios, rather Pablo Jimenez, and Luis Vargas are the only two that weren't shot. They were members of Sanctuary Baptist, a church out in Compton that services a Hispanic population. Most are undocumented. Every victim was paid wages through an anonymous shell company—with the exception of Eric and my...my father. We don't know diddly-shit about the owner's identity. We've interviewed Pastor Stan Goodwin twice now and also questioned his wife, Millie Ann Goodwin." Nazario paused, thinking carefully about her choice of words. She decided to keep the pastor's wife's extramarital affairs out of the presentation. "We've verified that the pastor was in Texas at the time of Eric's shooting."

Nazario switched to a photo collage of the victims, including Daddy.

Still breathing from her nose, she continued, "As you can see, all the bodies were positioned in the exact same way. Arms out vertically. Feet together. Jesus Christ pose."

Wilson chimed in from the front row, "We can't say for sure if this is a hate crime." He pivoted in his chair, so everyone could hear. "We think it's a different motive. Haven't put our finger on it yet, but it's especially true now that Avery Vanwell's been killed," Wilson added, "and that Myers, some of y'all are not gonna like hearing this, but he came off suspicious as hell."

Wilson turned back around to face Nazario and swiped a hand for her to continue.

"Eric Myers was our number one suspect at one point," Nazario explained. "He had motive. He had what appeared to be all the tools to have been the killer. He tipped off the DA on the first two vics. Like Wilson said, we're aware some of you—Redondo Beach Police—are his friends. This isn't personal. Let's look at the facts. We had an ICE agent that the Mexican community knew. They were scared of the guy, frankly, hated his ass. And honestly, it appeared as if the feelings on his part were mutual. So, yeah, he came across suspicious. Then recently, he was shot in the head at point-blank range. He got real lucky. He's in a coma but alive."

"He had an impressive knife collection that would've linked him to Luis Vargas, who was sliced open," Wilson chimed in again. "He was a fisherman, had a massive gun collection, too. Could've linked him with the shootings—he's a pretty damn good cook, I might add—but not our guy."

"So, he was shot with the same gun?" one of the assembled

cops asked. He looked to Nazario like one of the officers at the Luis Vargas scene at the Redondo Beach Pier.

"That's correct. An eyewitness testified that Eric Myers saw the shooter. At this point, he is the only one that could identify our killer." Nazario switched pictures to Eric Myers' bloodied head, flesh ripped away at the entry wound to expose his skull.

A few officers gasped, likely Eric's friends. A couple got up and strode for the exit.

"Patrol, when you're working your beat, BOLO for anyone suspicious near a bridge. We believe the killer is likely a male. We don't have the age or ethnicity. Statistically speaking, most serial killers are Caucasian men. Still, even that is a myth, and it would be inaccurate for us to say we are one hundred percent certain of age and ethnicity."

"Ms. Vanwell," another officer began, "and Eric Myers... hard to see the connection. The string of dead Mexicans, sure, but...it don't make much sense."

"Yeah, well, welcome to the world of Homicide," Nazario retorted, and a few officers chuckled. "You're right. It doesn't make sense. We'll be interviewing Madison Vanwell next. That's all I have at this time."

Huxley stepped up to his podium.

"In terms of the ballistics reports, the striations on the bullet casing in the Eric Myers, Avery Vanwell, and Angel Hernández shootings all matched. When I dug up the casing from Lucas Nazario's murder, it was a solid match, too. He's the only victim that wasn't paid through the shell corporation, as the shell company was erected just after his death. This is a complicated case. We don't know who we're dealing with here. I suspect a smart individual; someone we wouldn't expect. As Nazario said, please be on the lookout. All of you have had some hand in investigating these recent murders. I'm going to repeat myself, do *not* talk to the media about this. Do not discuss this case with anyone, not your girlfriend, not your husband or your wife. No one. Especially since it deals with a highly sensitive and well-known cold case involving one of our own." Huxley paused, scanning the room. "Any questions?"

Baby-faced officer Joey Gomez rose a hand. "I got a take on it, may I?"

Of course, Gomez had something to say. Huxley pointed. "What's your angle, Officer—"

"Gomez, sir. Have you ever been to Germany?" Gomez queried.

Despite the meeting's intensity, Nazario leaned into the mic, not giving Huxley time to answer. Distraction was one way to take the focus off the pain, the Gabapentin easing the anxiety.

"Special Agent Huxley has been all over the world—just ask his wife."

The line earned her a few chuckles, especially from federal agents.

An agent called out. "She got you good, *dawg*."

For a moment, she could breathe. It was not about Daddy, and all eyes were not watching her, waiting for her to reveal her pain and break down.

Even Huxley's straight-faced, intimidatingly serious partner, cracked into a stiff and agreeable chortle. Huxley's face turned bright cherry. He threw Nazario a look from the corner of his eyes, raising a brow.

Nazario shrugged at him, playing it cool to buy time to collect herself.

A moment of temporary relief. The ache cramping her stomach abated.

Huxley coughed into his mic. "To correct the record, I have been to Germany, and actually, it's one of many countries I did not visit with my *ex*-wife."

A swirl of light laughter floated around her swaying body. Chief Johnson and Wilson, however, weren't laughing. They stared at her with knowing concern, instead. Blinking in hopes of banishing the vertigo, Nazario continued to clutch her podium for support. She swiped the sweat from her brow with a visibly trembling hand then took a sip of water. Grabbing the napkin wrapped around the bottled water, she dried her sweaty palms. It was as though she dunked them under a faucet.

Forcing a nervous laugh, she said, "What a shocker. You mean to tell me, Special Agent Huxley, that checking out the Berlin Wall wasn't on your list of romantic places?"

As always, the laughter settled quickly, and the mood returned to stoic.

Huxley raised a brow at her, then turned to Gomez. "Gomez, as you were saying?"

Officer Gomez continued. "Have you ever heard of a Devil's Bridge? There are several in Europe, actually. Some are man-made bridges, and others are natural wonders, like in Sedona and one in Coconino National Forest. But the name comes from folklore that a man wagers a bet with the Devil. The Devil helps to build the bridge on the condition that a human sacrifice be made. It kind of reminds me of The Serpent Bridge here locally and the rumors of superstition, dead bodies popping up around it. Maybe there's a reason that bridge was chosen for the first murder?"

Nazario and Huxley exchanged a look.

Wilson rubbed his chin and returned a similar intrigued glance.

Was Gomez onto something?

"Okay, so, bear with me 'cause this is gonna sound kinda 'out-there,' but I dunno, maybe the killings are tied into this folklore in some way? Like the killer has personalized it, made it his own, like it's some type of metaphor?"

"Very interesting, Gomez. Please continue," Huxley urged.

"So, like, that's why the way he kills each person, it's different. Like the law, right? There are degrees of law. Punishment is given based on the degree of the crime. What if he's doing the same? What if he's killing them based on what he believes they deserve?"

"Come see us after we're done." Nazario winked at the eager student.

"Anything else?" Huxley asked.

"Germany *is* romantic, sir!" a young officer called out, spreading scattered guffaws.

"Maybe I'll take my girl there," Huxley said, passing Nazario a secret grin. "If there's no further ball-busting, I believe that's a wrap."

The room wound down, leaving behind straggling chuckles mixed with conversation and the sounds of chairs scraping against the carpet. Chief Johnson, Wilson, Officer Gomez, and Huxley's partner remained.

Chief leaned into her, "All jokes aside, that could *not* have been easy. Need the afternoon off? Say the word."

Nazario coughed, adjusting the crutch under her arm, wiping her damp, shaky palms on her jeans. She tightened her grip around the crutch's handle, trying to steady her hands.

"You know what they say." She pressed her lips into a thin smile, looking down at her legs, avoiding the concern so transparent on everyone's face. "We all have defense mechanisms, sir." Nazario blinked away moisture before anyone noticed.

Huxley watched her but she dodged his gaze, not capable of eye contact.

"Gomez, thanks for sticking around," she said, shifting the awkward spotlight that suddenly loomed over her. "Your input was invaluable. Do you have an interest in Homicide apart from working with SID?"

Gomez gushed, "Oh, yes, like I said, as a Puerto Rican, I've followed your father's career. I followed your career. I know that you took down Morris and hundreds of others like him. You've been practicing Taekwondo since you were five years old, you've got a fourth-degree black belt, and you're one of the most lethal detectives we have."

"Well," she nodded at her bum leg, "it's gonna be a while before I can do any sort of kicking. Would you like to help us out with something? If it's okay, Chief?"

"If you're serious, Gomez, we can start you out helping us on a few things. It'll be small stuff at first," Chief Johnson said. "You still have your SID trainee duty. Can you juggle it?"

"Absolutely," Gomez said.

"Millie and Stan, they got a son that is mentally unstable, considered violent. Gideon Goodwin escaped from the mental hospital. Hated his father. He was mute, so he may not even open up to us. But I think we need to try and bring him in," Nazario explained.

"He's obviously too young to have killed Lucas Nazario. He's like twenty-one or something; he would've been in diapers at the time. But something about the way Mrs. Goodwin talked about him...I don't know," Wilson mused.

"Can't there be two killers, one that killed Lucas Nazario and maybe recruited Mrs. Goodwin's son?" Gomez pointed out. "The kid's mute, but that doesn't mean he's not a psychopath."

Nazario and Wilson eyes met as they considered the possibility.

"I'll track Gideon down," Gomez assured, face lighting up like a child on Christmas morning. There was something refreshing about the young officer's countenance. He wasn't jaded, and in their profession, that was becoming rarer and rarer. "One more thing. You know, Mexican immigrants, they cross the border to have a better life, right? That in and of itself is a metaphorical bridge, doncha think?"

Nazario noted the expression on everyone's face as they chewed over this kid's theory. She was going to talk to Chief, see if she could take this one under her wing. He had good instincts and would be of better use on Homicide Division rather than SID.

"It definitely is Gomez." Nazario smiled at him. "You have a mind for this stuff."

"I'm gonna get on this right now," Gomez said. "Thank you for the opportunity, Detective Nazario. It's an honor."

He strode out of the room with an extra pep in his step.

"Gonna make a call," she said. "Need the pastor's wife there when we question her son."

"I can get Gomez on that, too," Chief said.

"I'm heading out. I can call Mrs. Goodwin on my way," Wilson offered.

Chief and Wilson shared a look of concern.

Nazario bit the inside of her cheek, then said, "Nah...forget it, I'm good." She coughed unnecessarily. "I got this."

Huxley turned to Wilson and Chief. "I'll drive her home."

"Well, lemme know how the Vanwell meeting goes tonight," Chief said resignedly, looking down at his watch. "Y'all take a break, and I mean you specifically, Nazario. Ice that knee. That's a direct order."

"Yes, sir."

Chief turned and walked out of the room with Wilson in tow.

When the room was empty, the silence was all-encompassing and unbearable.

Huxley gave her a look, one that saw right through her. "You've never seen any of the pictures, have you?"

Trembling hands took out the rattling bottle of Gabapentin.

"These ain't doing a goddamn thing," she told herself, popping another pill, vowing to get the doctor to give her something stronger.

Huxley whispered her name, but she shook her head as if fending off demons.

She shoved the bottle of anxiety meds back in her pocket and limped ahead.

"Gotta call Millie." She hobbled, trying to move faster than her body was willing.

"No, you don't, not right now." His fingers grabbed for hers.

Pausing for a moment, she slid her hand away.

"I've got a job to do," the words teetered out.

He put a hand on her shoulder. "Do you wanna talk about it?"

Biting her lower lip, she stared down at the worn carpet noticing the coffee blotches and track marks from soiled shoes, decades of wear and tear needing to be replaced, made brand new, without all the stains, the scars from all the years. Her vision blurred, and she bit her lower lip until she tasted the familiar metallic tang of blood.

He called her name again, and she shook her head with vigor, gulping back words, afraid to speak, afraid of what she'd say. Nazario inhaled deeply through her nose, fighting off sorrow, knowing she couldn't keep it caged for much longer.

Restless energy pushed her forward, and she limped ahead until his hand slipped away.

"Hang on, Detective, the call can wait," she heard him say from behind her. But she was hobbling faster now, as if trying to escape the one thing she couldn't.

Herself.

THIRTY-ONE

THE PASTOR'S WIFE

MILLIE HELD Eric's hand in hers. It was limp and cold. His head was wrapped up and the swelling on his face had gone down considerably. When he was first admitted, Millie could hardly recognize him. If not for the bullet he took to the head, he actually looked to be peacefully sleeping.

She leaned in and whispered in his ear, "I don't wanna be the pastor's wife anymore."

Oh, how she wanted to stay all night, curl up next to him and hear his heartbeat against her ear. Millie kissed Eric's cold hand. What were they trying to do? Give him pneumonia? They'd kill him with the AC alone! That stupid nurse with that stupid nasally voice reminded for the millionth time, "Visiting time is up, ma'am. If you don't leave now, you won't be allowed to return."

"Oh, all right, *all right*," Millie huffed, "for crying out loud, I heard you the first time."

She brushed her fingers delicately over his stubbly face and across the bandages that covered up most of his head. She kissed his cheek once more. "I'll be back tomorrow."

The sound of her phone startled her. She fished for it.

Maybe it was the doctor? Maybe it was Gideon? She exited Eric's hospital room, whispering goodbye, giving him a peck on the cheek.

It was a number she didn't recognize.

Her heart skipped, "Hello, Gideon? Is it you, honey?"

"Mrs. Goodwin...I mean, Millie." Detective Nazario breathed heavy into the receiver.

"Detective Nazario? Is this a new number or something? I didn't recognize it. Is everything okay?" Millie asked, stopping in the hallway and clutching her purse.

"It's, uh, the landline. At my office." Voice breaking, the detective inhaled. "Sorry. Been one of them days."

"Are you sure you don't need to come in to talk?" Millie asked her client of two years.

There was a pause on the phone and then, "I saw...saw Daddy's crime scene photos."

"Oh my," Millie clutched the phone to her ear. Nazario had mentioned multiple times that she refused to see them. It must've been a big step for her. "I'll clear my schedule for you, Detective. You're vulnerable right now and—"

"Appreciate it, but a counseling session isn't why I called. Gonna need you to come by the station as soon as possible." The detective's voice cracked. "I'm sorry. Just trying to catch my breath."

"I want you to know that I'm here for you," Millie whispered. "Those panic attacks can sometimes feel like a heart attack. You gotta do those breathing exercises."

"I'll be...I'll be just fine," she said, but Millie didn't believe her. "Since your husband is away, we'll need you to be there when we interview your son."

Her heart came out of her chest. "You found Gideon?"

"Not yet, but we will. Got one of our guys tracking him down," she said. "We spoke with Stan the other day via Zoom. I know he's flying back from Texas, but we think it's best that you're present at the station instead of him. Given he doesn't have a good relationship with Gideon and might set him off."

"I think you're right. Stan could be a trigger for Gideon. Frankly, I don't care when that fool comes home." She paused and whispered, "This about them murders?"

"Just giving you a heads-up that you may need to come down to the station," the detective said in that sad tone she knew too well.

"Well, I hope you..." The detective hung up. "...feel better." Millie finished staring down at her phone, her lower lip trembling as she thought of her son.

The question returned: Could her baby...Gideon be the killer?

Dear God.

Please, no.

THIRTY-TWO

THE DETECTIVE

THE MUSCULAR HISPANIC man who opened the door was in a fitted, moisture wicking workout shirt and shorts she'd often seen on runners and gym rats. Nazario reasoned he was in his late thirties, early forties and not quite Huxley's height, though he must've been at least six-feet and easily two-hundred pounds of muscle.

"You expecting someone?" he threw over his shoulder to a stunning, slender, tall woman Nazario had only seen on the bar's television during her relapse. Madison Vanwell looked even better in person. She had aged gracefully, with hardly a fine line or wrinkle, making turning grey look glamorous. Her sapphire eyes looked right at Nazario, and her mouth fell open.

Madison put a hand on the man's shoulder in a way that told Nazario that he was more than her personal trainer. Given how beautiful, successful, and youthful Madison looked, a young lover didn't surprise the detective.

"Thank you, Antonio, I'll take it from here." She put a hand on his broad chest as he stepped aside. "Mr. Martinez and I were just doing a little...exercise. You must be Detective N-

Nazario?" Madison sputtered her name as if afraid to say it aloud.

"Yeah, that'd be me." Nazario furrowed her brows, felt a stir in the pit of her stomach, unsure why she was suddenly uncomfortable.

Avery Vanwell was Madison's only child. She'd had her when she just turned forty, from what Nazario read. Avery was their "miracle baby." Nazario could only imagine the loss. She couldn't imagine raising a baby, seeing him or her go through all the stages of life. Then, one day, receiving the call that was every parent's worst nightmare: their baby wasn't only dead but had been murdered.

A familiar knot formed in Nazario's throat.

"I was hoping it would just be you." Madison Vanwell's eyes darted wearily to both Wilson and Huxley.

"Sorry, Ms. Vanwell. This is my partner, Detective Wilson, and Special Agent Blake Huxley. We're all working on this case. It's a team effort."

"FBI?" Madison gulped as a long, slender hand played with the pearls around her neck. She gave Huxley a once over. "Very well, then. Please come in."

They entered the decadent estate. Marble floors, cathedral ceilings, expensive paintings, and ornate chandeliers decorated the lavish mansion. As beautiful as it was, the ostentatious abode looked more like a museum than a place where actual people lived. They took a seat in one of the living rooms. Nazario was sure there were more.

Madison grabbed a tissue and held it to her face. "I'm sorry," she said, weeping.

"Take your time," Nazario began. "I can only imagine what you must be going through—to lose a child."

"I miss her so much," Madison's lips trembled, and her wet

eyes met Nazario's. It was a vivid heartbreak that turned Nazario's stomach.

"We understand that Angel Hernandez was her fiancé?" Nazario said. "Did you have reason to believe that Angel was involved in—"

"He wasn't involved with drugs or gangs. All the stuff the media is saying about him, it's a lie. He was a sweet, sweet boy. They met on spring break when she was in Cancun. My lawyer was in the process of getting Angel's work visa approved just before...before they were killed."

She stood up and glided toward her cocktail bar to pour herself a whiskey.

"Would any of you care for a drink? It's a 1964 Glenlivet. Winchester Collection? It's quite delicious. It's a twenty-five-thousand-dollar bottle of whiskey, but worth every drop, I guarantee you."

"We'll pass," Wilson said. "Thanks for the offer."

Madison returned with her expensive whiskey in hand. It was definitely a long pour.

She took a large sip.

"Twenty-eight years ago, when I was forty, I had a longish affair with a married man. One that lasted three glorious years. We were both married but very much in love."

"Was this before or after your husband's sudden death?" Nazario asked.

Madison began pacing like a caged animal. She took yet another sip.

"The affair took place while William was in the hospital." Madison sighed. "They said it was some sort of autoimmune thing. Organs started shutting down and I got lonely. But it was lonelier for William. Imagine, three years is a very long time to be in the hospital waiting to die."

"How's this connected to the death of your daughter and Angel Hernandez?" Nazario redirected.

"Quite simple, really." Madison took a long sip of the single malt. "Vengeance."

"Who in this story of yours wanted vengeance, Ms. Vanwell?" Wilson asked. "Did your husband know you were having an affair?"

"Story? Are you implying that this is all a fabrication, Detective Wilson?"

"Fabrication? No, that's not what I meant, Ms. Vanwell. Bad choice of words."

"To continue with my partner's questioning," Nazario pivoted the conversation, "who wanted vengeance?"

"James Vanwell." Madison took another sip. She got up, went to the bar, and poured herself more of her expensive distilled spirit. For a moment, Nazario's mouth watered. *That has to be some great whiskey.*

"We're not familiar with James Vanwell," Huxley admitted. "There's no record of him—whoever he is—in relation to you."

"He was my son, from my marriage. He was the true heir to the Vanwell—my legacy." Madison took another long gulp from her Glenlivet. "Had him when we were young, while I was still going to school, before I started the winery, and while I was still working for my old boss at his winery for minimum wage. The winery was the one thing William wanted no part of. It was all mine. So, we agreed, if I started making money and we got ourselves a divorce—he'd take what was his and I'd take what was mine." Madison fingered the rim of her whiskey glass. "While William couldn't care less for the winery or for the finer things in life and always wanted to give more of my money away than to keep it...he was a great father. James was the apple of his eye. He loved that boy no matter what he did."

The explanation earned the entrepreneur quizzical looks from all three members of law enforcement.

"Then why'd you hide James from the public?" Nazario countered.

"He was—how should I say this—*different*. James found out I was in love with someone else while his father lay dying in the hospital. Things got real bad after that. Especially after James found out about Avery."

Nazario nudged. "Can you elaborate on what 'real bad' means to you?"

"I wanted to share this with Detective Nazario alone, but..."

"Whatever it is, you can say it in front of all of us," Nazario said.

"Avery was..." Madison paused swearing to God. She lifted her head to the ceiling collecting herself. "She was your half-sister." Madison met Nazario's eyes. Wide and transparent. "It was your father. I was in love with Lucas. I'd told him I was pregnant, and he was happy. I never pressed him to get a divorce, but he said that's what he wanted right before he was killed."

Nazario was blindsided, a punch to the gut that knocked the wind from her lungs.

The antique clock ticked away seconds that felt more like hours.

The scent of costly Glenlivet whiskey lingered as Ms. Vanwell gave another choking sob.

After an eternal moment, Nazario limped to the window.

Wilson blew out a noisy breath breaking the silence. "Umm, Ms. Vanwell, we can assure you we were *not* expecting this news."

Bile rose in Nazario's throat. She could hardly hear a thing.

Was Avery going to tell her that she was Daddy's love-child? Her half-sister?

Her grip on the windowsill tightened, and she was unaware that she'd been holding her breath until it escaped her lungs in uncontrolled, inaudible stutters. Her chest squeezed tight again. Sweat collected between her breasts, down her chest, at the back of her neck, causing her hair to stick. Her last conversation with Avery repeated in her mind, night after night.

"Can we grab coffee sometime, Detective Nazario?"

"Sorry, Honey, got a case I'm eyeballs deep in. Raincheck?"

Six hundred milligrams of Gabapentin was *not* strong enough.

The clench in her chest became a stabbing pain.

"Please don't be angry with your father," Madison Vanwell said. "Please don't hate him. He loved you. We fell in love. I couldn't stop it; he couldn't control it either. I cannot apologize for loving Lucas. I will not apologize. He will always be the love of my life." Madison's voice quivered. "And now the piece that I had left of him is gone. My baby..."

That familiar guttural anguish came roaring out of Madison, the type that was unbearable to witness despite Nazario's years of working Homicide: that of a mother losing her child. Her agony sent a cold chill through Nazario. After a few seconds of physically being unable to breathe, a gush of oxygen finally flooded her lungs. She panted as though she'd been held underwater.

The pain eased, and the tightening in her chest relaxed.

Nazario wiped the sweat from her forehead, breathing deeply.

Antonio asked Madison if she was okay and if his boss needed anything before walking over to Nazario and handing her a bottled water. Nazario drank deeply before turning around to confront watchful faces. Madison wore an expression of agony Nazario had felt once before. She caught a glimpse of Huxley's concern and appreciated his restraint. Nazario didn't want him to help or come to her. Maybe he knew she needed to walk through the pain and come out the other end alone, despite his desire to save her from it. No, this pain she must feel. This pain she would not run from. It coursed through her veins; it dripped out of her pores, twisting her gut.

"How'd you and...my father meet, Ms. Vanwell?" Nazario asked, her voice quieter.

She intended to say the words in a formal, snarky tone—to scream them out. Something had already begun to shift inside, and for a moment, she met Huxley's eyes again. It was a tender moment they quietly shared. He gave her a supportive nod.

Nazario understood the job and the high divorce rate among cops. Looking back, maybe Mama became resentful despite once deeply loving Daddy. Their love changed with the stress of Daddy's work.

She hadn't seen this before, but it hit her now like a freight train.

Nazario's gentle tone betrayed her internal turbulence. Everything she'd once known and believed was now undone. She could feel Daddy's gold ring dangling against her chest, and in this moment of truth, she understood that the reason no longer mattered.

People changed, and what she was left with was a choice.

And the choice was hers alone.

She chose forgiveness.

It washed over her, soothing her soul.

Madison answered her question. "At one of those fundraisers, a charity for the LAPD memorial fund. We donated our wine for the event and helped cater the food. He was standing at the entrance of the door, and he gave me this look..."

Her shoulders sagged as she absently played with the pink pearls around her neck.

"Let me make sure I got our timelines correct, Ms. Vanwell.

Your husband was in the hospital for three years, you met Lucas Nazario at the start of that, then I'm guessing, three and a half years in, William's condition worsens, he's transferred to hospice," Wilson looked down at his notes, "then passes on right about the time you got pregnant. You're now a widow and that put you at forty years young. Am I correct?"

Madison nodded absently at a picture on the wall of William kneeling next to a shot deer.

"As much as he was a hunter, William was a gentle soul." She smiled wistfully. "He would've accepted a divorce without a fight but died before I had the need to file for one. He even left this earth without a fight. He just didn't have it in him anymore. I think he knew I was seeing someone. The estate was in my name. The winery, mine." She pointed her glass to a framed article mounted on the wall and then looked back down at her glass. Guilt washed over her face.

A True Rags to Riches Story the newspaper headline read.

"I'm impressed with your hard work," Huxley said, "not an easy task. You earned scholarships to get through college, then earned your MBA working as a manager of a vineyard. Your boss appreciated your tenacity and gave you a personal business loan to open your own winery. Not only did you create a true dynasty for yourself—you paid the business loan back with interest. Then you continued William's charity organization for the undocumented and separated families. The LAPD contributes to your 501c3, by the way."

"And I'm impressed, Special Agent, that you actually did your research," Madison replied evenly. "I support the nonprofit that William had begun. He...he had a big heart for immigrants wanting a better life."

"It's a great organization," Nazario praised the winery owner.

"Thought I'd keep William's spirit alive." Madison pivoted the conversation, turning to Nazario. "You were all Lucas ever talked about."

Nazario fidgeted with her father's wedding ring dangling on the gold chain around her neck. Then she tightened her fingers around it until it embedded itself into her palm.

"Earlier, you said your son was different. Different how?" Nazario asked.

"Oh my." She sighed, lifting her glass to her lips. "Like his father, he loved to hunt. It was like...it was like he enjoyed seeing animals suffer. He begged William to let him cut open the deer," she whimpered. "I should've never let him go hunting with us. It wasn't...it wasn't normal. I told William it wasn't normal. I don't even have any pictures of him. I've got a tiny wallet one from when he was five in my purse, but that's it. James burned all of them before he ran away."

Wilson's mouth fell open. "You only have one picture of your son?"

"He literally took all of our family albums and torched them," Madison lamented, her shoulders slumped in defeat. "He even got rid of any digital images I had on the family computer. It was sheer madness, I tell you—*insanity*. Search the premises, I'm telling the truth."

"We believe you," Nazario assured.

"We're gonna need to confiscate that image you have of James. Our cyber team may need it to do a progressive scan." Huxley held out his hand and Madison handed it over. "Did you get an eval?"

"Yes. It was quite baffling because he was smart. In fact, he passed the general psych evaluation with flying colors." She gulped. "Except when they studied him more, spent more time with him, they saw what we saw. He was apathetic and a little antisocial. But then things got rocky when..." She anxiously poured herself more whiskey.

"Please continue, Ms. Vanwell," Huxley urged gently. "When did things get dicey?"

"James always wanted to be a big brother. Well, it was quite obvious when William was sick in the hospital, and I got pregnant...he put two and two together. He knew the baby was from another man, not his father...dying." Madison closed her eyes tightly then whispered, "He told me in the calmest voice that he wanted to kill the sin inside of me and the man responsible."

"Kill the man responsible?" Huxley repeated.

"James was sixteen. I tried calling up a treatment facility to have him admitted. I told them what he said. I was frightened. Their advice was to give him time to adjust to the stress of his father dying and to the pregnancy. I laughed at them. It was ludicrous. My son threatened murder, and I needed to give him time to adjust? They gave me some generic suggestion that if he truly got 'unsafe,' I should call the police or place him in an institution. I told them he was still a kid. They kept telling me to call 9-1-1 if I was that afraid. A week later, Lucas was dead, and James was gone."

"And why *didn't* you call the police," Wilson prodded, "or tell them about his threat?"

"I was afraid. Everything would crumble. It'd hit the news, damage the business I built. My whole life would unravel. So I said nothing—and I'll never forgive myself for that."

Nazario braced herself, but the tightening in her chest was not present this time. Relief flooded her as she welcomed a large gulp of air. Her body was more relaxed than she expected.

"What're you implying?" Nazario asked pointedly.

"I'm saying that my son had met Lucas at a fundraiser once and knew what he looked like. After I threatened to put him in an institution, he bolted out the door. Ran away at sixteen. I've never heard from him since. I didn't report it to the cops. There's no law against running away, but it's the parents that get into trouble. I admit, I was thinking about myself and all that I stood to lose. So, I tried to track him down myself, but it's as if he'd disappeared. Even hired the best private investigators. Nothing. He's fifty this year. I haven't seen him in thirty-two years. No mother wants to admit their child is capable of murder. I think James killed your father and maybe even Avery. I can't prove it, but it's a mother's gut instinct." She paused for a reflective moment and lifted her eyes to Nazario. "You...look so much like her."

Nazario felt sick.

She hadn't realized Avery Vanwell, her half-sister, looked like her until now. Her mind rewound, revisiting the dojang and self-defense classes and the crime scene. She remembered Avery had long legs like she did. Although their hair and eyes color were different, they shared the same straight nose, angular jaw, and full lips.

"So, you didn't tell the police and not one PI was able to track down a runaway?" Wilson repeated, perplexed.

"No. Trust me, I hired the best investigators money can buy," Madison said. "In my gut, I know he is out there, and I'm terrified of him. Terrified of my own son!"

"Thank you for your candidness and your time," Huxley said. "The FBI will be looking into this. I've been personally on the Lucas Nazario case for ten years. I'm not giving up on finding who killed him."

"We'll have a unit closely patrolling your estate and the neighborhood just in case your son decides to...pop up." Wilson handed Ms. Vanwell his card and thanked her for her time.

"Do you like wine? Have a couple of bottles," Madison

strode toward Nazario with two bottles of red. "And when you can, please come back...so we can talk alone?"

Wilson stepped in. "No thank you Ms. Vanwell, we'll pass on the wine."

"Ah, shit." Huxley raked a hand over his face, as if he knew this wasn't going to go well.

"I'll have my wine with or without your permission," Nazario bit out. "You're not stopping me from getting drunk tonight. Move outta my fucking way, Wilson."

"I'm sorry...did I do something wrong?" Madison said, looking confused.

"Nah." Nazario snatched the bottles from the woman's grip. "Appreciate the gift. We normally don't accept them. But I'm making an exception."

Thank you, from one alcoholic to another, Nazario wanted to say but stormed off instead.

Disavowing the twelve steps, she strode to Huxley's car without so much as a look back.

———

Huxley walked Nazario to her door. They'd been virtually silent the entire car ride. She unlocked her door and turned around. He stared at her without words.

"I'm sure your day is pretty full tomorrow, Special Agent Huxley."

"You've got a lot to process." Huxley blinked at her formality. "Call me if you need anything."

Nazario looked down at her shaky hands and tried to stop the sharp stabbing at the center of her chest, but it continued. It felt like she was having a heart attack. The clenching at the center wrenched tighter with a grip that made her breath judder in her throat.

She was choking for air again.

Nazario clutched the bottle of Gabapentin in her pocket.

Huxley glanced at the wine bottles in her hand and then back up at her with that helpless look most non-drinkers gave her. Like they wanted to help, instigate one of them stupid interventions. But they knew they'd have to forcibly tie her down to rip the bottles away. As the saying went, no one could help someone who wasn't ready or willing.

Nazario could only help herself. She was the only one that could stop drinking.

"The night Daddy died, he told me in Spanish, *'No matter what happens, I love you. Remember that.'* I told him I loved him, too, and then that very night he was murdered, and a part of me died with him. I swore that I'd never let myself love someone because they'd...they'd..."

Die.

The thought sent a sharp pain through her.

"I...I..." She inhaled a ragged breath.

He put a hand on her face. His eyes glittered with raw emotion. He seemed to be waiting, waiting for her to finish, to tell him.

She took in a large gulp of air, catching her breath. Then the warmth of forgiveness cascaded over her, filling her with new clarity.

This reality ignited every cell in her body.

She loved Blake Huxley.

She loved him with every fiber of her being.

Tell him now. Tell him how you feel.

But the words locked up in her throat.

Instead, she said, "I...I gotta go. Goodnight."

When the door closed, she threw the anxiety medication across the room and leaned against the door. She should call Gus, but then again, maybe she wouldn't this time. No, she wasn't calling anyone for help. Not tonight. For the next two hours or more, she'd turn to an old friend instead, one that had always been able to help her forget, help her numb it all away.

She'd open up both bottles of wine.

She'd allow herself a long hard cry.

She'd then drink until she blacked out.

THIRTY-THREE
THE WITNESS

ESPERANZA SHOULD'VE CALLED the cops but after the interrogation, what was the point? They did nothing to the crazy Goodwins. Maybe they asked them a few questions but that was it. Hell, she felt like they gave her a harder time than they did those two gringos who were liable to kill each other if she didn't step in.

Mrs. Goodwin even joked, "Oh, they just asked me if I tried to kill my husband, and I said he struck me first. You damn right I wanted to, but I just put a little...fear into him."

The glint in her eyes chilled Esperanza.

Mrs. Goodwin went on to tell her that they warned her to work things out with her husband in a civil way. "Use your therapeutic training," they told her. The pastor's wife got to leave and carry on like nothing happened. If Esperanza had been caught nearly strangling someone to death, would she be treated the same way by law enforcement? She'd be in jail. She'd be separated from her son. She'd have her freedom and life stripped from her. She'd have the book thrown at her.

One of the Goodwins was the killer. She was almost sure of it. And if they knew she was on to them...Esperanza shivered.

She wasn't waiting to see if they'd tail her. She was going to follow *them* this time. She was sick and tired of being a victim, too afraid to stand up for herself in a country that still marginalized people like her, denying them the respect and rights afforded to others. She was not putting up with it anymore. Whoever her stalker was, they weren't going to make her hide away in her apartment all day, afraid to run errands, terrified of living her life.

They were not going to threaten her anymore.

She was going to uncover the truth, learn why someone had broken into her apartment, why someone was sending her threatening messages. She and Alex wouldn't be safe until she brought the truth to light—before whoever was after them could silence her permanently. One more dead Mexican under a bridge. She'd lived her whole life trying to hide from the law and from society.

She wasn't hiding anymore.

The past few days she'd noticed a strange car parked down the street from the Goodwins. Were they some undercover cops spying on the Goodwins or someone dangerous following her? She had to find out. All of this had started after she witnessed the murder under The Serpent's Bridge.

She made plans for Alex to stay at a friend's house for the evening. Once Alex was safely at his buddy's house, Esperanza borrowed Isabelle's car, making sure no one had seen her. It was dangerous, driving without a license, but her stalker wouldn't look for her behind the wheel. She parked on a side street and watched the suspicious car until it pulled away from the curb. Her heart hammered as she followed two cars behind, keeping them in sight, praying they wouldn't notice her. Staying invisible was all the harder as they headed out to the sticks. She hung back further, fearing she'd lost them when she glimpsed the stalker's car parked in front of a dilapidated house and barn.

Parking her own car out of sight, Esperanza crept up to the house's window. She could see nothing, but she heard voices. She hesitated, knowing it would be safer to turn back, but she couldn't. She had come this far. She had to find a way to end this.

Quietly, she crept through the open door. A thick veil of dust on the furniture indicated that it had been uninhabited. The wood beneath her creaked with age.

As she got closer to the dining room, dread filled her to the bone.

"Hello...anyone here?" someone called out.

The voice was familiar. Where had she heard it before? She peeked around a wall. It was that young cop. What was his name...Joey Gomez? That was right, Officer Gomez. He'd confiscated the physics book Alex borrowed from the library. Now he was dressed in civilian clothes and seemed to be searching for someone. Joey Gomez must've been staking out the Goodwin's home, knowing what she knew that one of them was a killer or was someone else in the house, someone else who was her stalker?

"Hey, come out wherever you are. You said you'd meet me here, though why you had me drive all the way out here to sign the papers, I'll never know," he griped. "I read the dead peasant insurance papers, okay. I don't give a shit. I've already signed them. Got them right here. Look, I could use the job. I don't care what type of insurance policy you got on me. I'm good with it."

She didn't hear anyone answer.

"You can trust me," Gomez continued. "I'm no 5.0. I'm just some dude that really needs his bills paid. I told no one about this, like you said. I could use the cash, bro. Papers are right here. Leaving them on the table. You got my number when you're ready to start me on the payroll."

Dead peasant insurance? What job? Why was he saying he wasn't a cop? Was he undercover? A dirty cop?

Gomez casually looked around. He fingered the dust on the table. The windows were bare, revealing an empty night that exposed a deep feeling of isolation. No one had lived here for at least a decade, this she knew.

She could hardly breathe as she hid watching Officer Gomez walk around the dining area. What was this all about? What did it have to do with the Goodwins? With her? Possibly with the murders? Whoever was behind this was taking great pains to keep it secret. If they found her here...*Talk and you die...*

Fear took over her body. Her hands quaked with adrenalin. Trying to stay quiet, she reversed her steps. She eyed the back-door. Almost there. She needed to run back to the car and leave. She needed to stay out of this. Whatever it was.

The ancient wooden floors creaked.

"That you?" Officer Gomez approached and the next thing she knew he was standing in front of her, his hands on her shoulders. Hissing, he whispered, "What're you doing here?"

She shook her head. "I...I saw nothing. I heard nothing."

She didn't trust Officer Gomez. She didn't trust the Good-wins. She didn't trust law enforcement, including those detectives that put on a show like they were on her side. The only person she trusted was Isabelle Jimenez and she needed to get out of this house and return the car to her friend.

Another sound came from the front door—closer this time. Someone stood in the shadows, the night and the lightless home silhouetted the figure, cloaking their face. Esperanza muffled a yelp with her hand. Officer Gomez turned to her and in Spanish ordered, *"Vete ahora!"*

Esperanza escaped quietly out the backdoor and ran. She

stifled a scream as she heard it. A single gunshot pierced the night.

—————

Esperanza huddled in the bathroom and peeked out the door. She was glad that Alex had stayed the night with a friend. He'd come home early this morning and was getting dressed, but he was taking his time since it was a Saturday.

"Want oatmeal? We're out of eggs and chorizo," he called out.

"That's fine," Esperanza returned. She needed to make sure Alex was out of the apartment. She didn't want her son to hear a word of the conversation she was having with Isabelle. "Can you go check the mail?"

"Now?" Her son whined. "Why?"

"Because I said so. Just check the mail, Alejandro. For your mother, please."

"Fine," Alex grumbled. When the door closed, Esperanza dialed. The phone was answered in one ring.

"Isabelle?" Esperanza whispered. *"Necesito un arma."*

"A gun?" Isabelle's voice rose in concern. "Esperanza, *que pasa?* Why?"

"And I need your car again."

"But you still don't have your license. What's going on? You're scaring me."

"Just do as I ask and please watch Alex for me," Esperanza pled.

"When? ¡*Dios mío!* I'm gonna need a couple of days—"

"Whatever you can do."

"We took a chance last night. But what if you get pulled over? And why do you need a gun, Esperanza? What're you gonna do with a gun?"

"Don't you understand, it'll not stop," Esperanza said, "someone has to do something."

"What's not stopping?" Isabelle cried, exasperated. "If you're in trouble, call the police—*please*."

Esperanza thought of Officer Gomez. No uniform. The furtive signing of papers...likely breaking the law. Who had been the stranger Gomez had been waiting for? Which man had died?

"No," Esperanza refused forcefully, "and no more questions. *No le digas a nadie!*"

Esperanza warned Isabelle not to tell anyone about the call and turned off the phone. Sitting on the floor, she leaned her back against the bathtub and covered her head with shaky hands. Never in her life had she felt stronger than at this moment. She knew precisely what she had to do.

She'd stop the killer from killing again.

"Mama! Mail for you. An envelope." Alex called.

"*Gracias.* Just slide it under the door."

Alex did so, the manila envelope framed against the scuffed linoleum. The hairs on the back of her neck prickled. "Gimme a minute, *mijo*," she said, taking the envelope with shaky fingers.

Feeling the envelope's contents with her fingers, she guessed it was about the size and thickness of a passport. But when she tore the manila flap open, it was a black wallet.

Her fingers shook as she folded it. A badge. An LAPD ID. *Officer Joey Gomez.* It read like a punch to the chest.

A folded note was impaled on the badge's pin. She read the single typed line: *I know you were there.*

THIRTY-FOUR

THE DETECTIVE

HUXLEY STOOD next to a slideshow presentation, accompanied by a man in a dark blazer and glasses. He looked to be the analytical type and was probably a part of cybersecurity or cyber-crimes in charge of facial recognition.

Nazario and Wilson were in the front row next to Chief Johnson. Meanwhile, Huxley's partner sat a couple of chairs away. It was a small audience of those close to the case.

"I'd like to introduce you to our cyber-crimes division lead and expert in terms of facial recognition," Huxley began, pointing to the cyber expert.

The cyber division supervisor adjusted the mic and explained, "There seems to be no trace of James Vanwell. Madison Vanwell gave us his social security number and the only picture of her son—a little wallet two-by-three when he was five. She confirmed with our cyber team what she'd told Homicide during interviews, that James had burned all of their family pictures before he disappeared. We ran a future scan of what he'd look like today."

The man clicked on an image.

Typical white boy—blond, blue-eyed, cute in that catalog-kid way. The gold chain around his neck looked borrowed, too big, the crucifix heavy at the end. The cyber lead zoomed in on the pendant. Script on the back, faint but legible: *James Vanwell*.

"The bodies were all positioned in the Jesus Christ pose," Nazario said.

The cyber supervisor nodded at her and explained, "Interestingly enough, James wore this crucifix everywhere he went. A Mexican family that worked for them gave it to him when he was young."

Next to James Vanwell's five-year-old picture was a digital futurized image that hardly looked like the little boy. The man was thin, sported an oval face but no other discernible features: no glasses or anything else out of the ordinary. The before-and-after pictures didn't link to anyone they knew off hand.

Nazario rubbed her pounding temples, results of a significant hangover thanks to yet another bout of relapse. "Do you have a scan, a comparison, or a match?"

"Despite our software's 99.4% facial recognition accuracy, James Vanwell's scan doesn't match anyone we know to this date," the cyber specialist explained.

"Can we have a copy of these progressive scans?" Nazario asked.

"I'll make sure to deliver the biometric facial scans directly," Huxley assured her. "Both digital and print."

"We think James Vanwell might have changed his name. We're currently in the process of tracking that down," the specialist said. "Special Agent Huxley will let you know when we have a definitive identity. At this point, the sketches can resemble anyone. It's not enough proof."

Wilson and Nazario exchanged a glance.

Wilson piped up. "How long will it take, if you don't mind me asking? I mean, with a Social Security number and all, it oughta be easy to track down someone with an alternate identity."

The cyber expert chuckled. "It would appear that way, but it isn't so easy. It's not like a Google search and wham—the new name and identity pops up. There are ways to digitally bury the information, recoding, potentially encrypting information so that it's not searchable. Let's look at the facts. Social media wasn't around thirty plus years ago, so it wasn't too hard for Ms. Vanwell to keep her son out of public knowledge. Especially if the kid was showing signs of psychopathy. I mean, no one even knew James existed, am I correct?"

The cyber lead looked to Nazario for the answer. "That's correct. The only child made known to anyone was her daughter, Avery Vanwell."

"Image is of utmost importance to Madison Vanwell. She seemed," Wilson paused, rubbing his chin, "almost embarrassed by her son."

"Heard Gomez located Gideon Goodwin," Huxley said, "and he's in custody?"

"Yes, that's correct. Delivered him to us a few days ago but couldn't stick around. Had another assignment. You're more than welcome to join us. Interview's in half an hour," Nazario said, looking at her watch, "but I'm not so sure we'll get anything out of him. He's non-verbal."

Huxley nodded, "We should get going, then. Any other questions about James Vanwell? Sorry, this meeting is a bit anticlimactic. All we know is that he's switched his identity."

"Keep us in the loop," Chief Johnson said, standing up.

Huxley turned to Wilson, "Did you drive together?"

"Yeah, but I'm thinking of going for a walk around the block real quick," Wilson said, pointing to his new running shoes.

Huxley hesitated, then asked her, "Drive you over?"

She nodded, noticing Wilson's cautious smile. "Sure."

Wilson winked at them in passing. "See ya in thirty."

Alone, Nazario and Huxley walked side-by-side in companionable silence.

Then, breaking the quiet, he asked, "How've you been? Well, you're limping a whole lot less," Huxley noticed. "Pain gone? Doctor give you any specific instructions?"

She smiled, relieved they were at small talk. "When the doctor took out my stitches, he ordered me to take it easy."

Huxley laughed. "Like that's ever gonna happen."

———

Nazario peered through the pane of one-way glass that gave onlookers a window into the interview room, watching Gideon Goodwin as he sat across from Huxley and Wilson. Millie Ann Goodwin stood next to Nazario, gazing upon her son, her eyes wet with tears. This standoff had been going on for an hour now, and Gideon still was not talking or writing anything. But if anyone could get information out of Gideon, it would be Wilson and Huxley. They were the two best negotiators she had ever known, but could they get Gideon to talk?

"We understand that there is something you wanted to say to your mother. You know she loves you, right? She loves you, and she's watching you right now, on the other side of that mirror," Huxley began softly.

Gideon looked at them with lost eyes before peering back down at his hands.

"We've got paper and a pen," Wilson said. "You can write down whatever it is that you need to tell us. Why did you run away from the mental hospital? What was it that you were coming back around home for?"

They waited. Wilson leaned back, stretching his legs. Huxley exhaled, leaned in, and tried again.

"We've got several dead bodies. We're trying to find a killer. Someone angry. Maybe someone violent? Someone who's trying to punish their victims."

Huxley took out the sketch of James Vanwell and put it in front of Gideon. Gideon stood up, fists balled against his sides, and then rushed for the mirrored window, pounding his fist. Screaming. Face snarling. Spittle spraying out of his mouth. He banged his head against the mirror.

Huxley and Wilson hurried to apprehend him, but Gideon spun around, erratic and fast, clocking Wilson in the face. Wilson stumbled back, falling on his ass. Huxley threw an elbow to Gideon's face. Gideon lunged for Huxley, who did a quick Muay Thai sweep, using one foot to sweep at Gideon's feet while his right hand cradled the back of Gideon's head. In one fluid motion, Gideon was taken to the ground. Before Gideon could kick or throw any more blows, Huxley pinned his left arm with his knee and hooked Gideon's right arm behind his back.

Gideon cried out in pain.

"Settle down, tough guy," Huxley said. Wilson, nursing his jaw, struggled to his feet. He pulled out double-flex cuffs and bound Gideon's hands behind his back.

Millie Ann wailed.

"I don't understand why he's so angry."

"Would you like to talk with him? Think he'd open up to you?" Nazario asked. "Given your experience as a counselor."

Millie shook her head with more vigor than Nazario antici-pated. "We haven't had an honest relationship in years. If I go in there, he'd flip. I'd trigger him. Make it a whole lot worse. Do you think he'll open up if you go in there? Can you try?" Millie begged, looking at Nazario.

"Me?"

"Please...*please.*"

"Okay, Millie, I'll do my best."

Nazario entered the room. "May I?" she asked Wilson.

Wilson looked at her wearily, handed her a small black flex cuff cutter. They were used specifically to clip off flex cuffs to avoid injuring the detainee and then exited the interrogation room. Nazario pulled up a chair next to Huxley.

Gideon, for once, looked at her with boyish curiosity. Good. She could use this.

Nazario took off her blazer, exposing her snug blouse. She tossed her long hair behind her shoulder, exposing her neck and the opening of her blouse. She leaned into him, and heat rose in Gideon's cheeks.

He was watching her intently.

"I was five years old when Daddy put me in Taekwondo classes. Something clicked with me, and Daddy realized I was good at it. So, I stayed in. Year after year, I got better and better. Entered tournaments, won them all. Trained five days a week, earned a fourth-degree by the time I was eighteen, which was when my father died. And I remember being so angry that all I wanted to do was fight."

Nazario paused.

Neither Wilson nor Huxley knew this story. She was not proud of her old behavior, but her gut told her that with Gideon, she needed to get personal for him to open up.

"Found reasons to start fights. Daddy and I...we were close. Closer than I've ever been with Mama, and honestly, that's still the case today. I'm closer to my dead father than I am to my living mother. Kids at school, they'd see us at the mall. They'd see us everywhere together."

Nazario paused and absently toyed with Daddy's wedding band around her neck. Gideon raked his eyes from her fingers to her breasts.

"There was this girl I didn't like in high school. Ran into her the day of my father's funeral. Cheerleader type. She didn't know why I was alone, why I was dressed all in black. She said the words I'll never forget, 'Aw, Daddy's girl finally venturing out on her own.' I should've walked away. I didn't."

Nazario exhaled loudly and leaned closer, folding her hands in front of her. Gideon, mesmerized, was listening.

"She was in the hospital for a month." Shame and remorse swept over her. She peered at the mirrored glass, at her own reflection staring back at her. She imagined Wilson and Millie Ann Goodwin watching on the other side.

"If it wasn't for my father's then-partner, Detective Johnson...it's Chief now—" Nazario paused and swallowed a breath. "I wouldn't be sitting here right now. Wouldn't have my job. If he hadn't arrived on scene to pull me off of her, I'd have...I'd have killed her."

Her own words sunk in, and she stared down at her capable hands.

"Had I not been my father's child, had I not had that close affiliation with the PD, I'd have spent time behind bars instead of picking up trash on the side of the road."

Nazario looked Gideon dead in the eyes.

"I know that I'm capable of taking out another human. So, Gideon, when I tell you I understand anger, I mean it. I've lived most of my life angry."

It was a cathartic moment, releasing what had been weighing her down all these years. Nazario paused, and for once, she briefly turned her eyes to notice Huxley looking at her with a soft, watchful stare. She saw wonder, surprise, and compassion in his blue, crystalline eyes. She redirected her attention to Gideon, who nudged his head toward the paper.

"Do you wanna write something down, Gideon?" Nazario asked. He nodded, and she got up and knelt next to him. She inched closer to his face. His breath was heavy.

She whispered. "Do something stupid; I'll put you right on your ass. Got it?"

Gideon nodded, and Nazario cut the flex cuffs off. As she returned to her chair, Huxley gave her a very subtle and approving smile. Scooting her chair forward, she leaned in again, awaiting Gideon. He grabbed the pen and paper and then began to write.

He didn't write much—only one sentence: *Why didn't you protect me?*

Nazario read, then looked up. "You wanted your mom to protect you? Protect you from who?"

She slid the paper back to Gideon.

James Vanwell.

Nazario texted Wilson: *Pull Chief Johnson in.*

"What did James do to you? How do you know James Vanwell?" Just as the questions came out, Nazario could see Gideon shut down. He wrapped his arms around his chest and cast his eyes down.

Nazario handed the paper to Huxley, and he met her eyes.

"If you know anything, where he is and who he is, we can work with you. You can take a plea deal, and we won't even charge you for assaulting an officer."

Gideon regressed to his original non-engaged disposition. He studied his hands. Chief Johnson entered the room. Nazario handed him the paper.

"We can't keep him based on this. We can't even hold him on assaulting an officer, given he's considered mentally unfit. This isn't evidence he's linked to the crime," Chief responded in a hushed tone. "Y'all have been at it for a couple of hours now. Looks like he's shut down for the day. A couple of guys from the psychiatric facility are coming to get him. Should be here any minute."

Chief confirmed what she'd known, returning the paper to her.

"Have a call to make," Chief said as he walked away. "Keep me posted."

Ten minutes later, they collectively watched as two men from the psychiatric hospital entered at the far end of the hall to collect Gideon. Gideon turned to Nazario and clasped her hand. Huxley erected a thick, muscle-bound arm to ward off the two men from interrupting what could be a break in the case. If Gideon was going to talk, they need to hear what he had to say.

Gideon looked her in the eyes, "John 8:44," he said, still holding Nazario's hand. She heard Millie Ann gasp at Gideon's first words in years. Nazario's eyes widened at his deep baritone voice. "Come to the hospital—*alone.*"

Gideon's eyes went wide, breath heaving manically, teeth clenched in time with his fists.

The two men from the psychiatric facility broke free from Huxley's barricade and grabbed Gideon, manhandling him. Gideon yelped in pain, his eyes darting to Nazario's as if he were pleading for her to intervene. She lunged forward. A maternal protectiveness rushed through her. Millie Ann whimpered louder.

"Is it necessary for you to be so rough? You're hurting him!" Nazario bellowed. Huxley roped his massive arms around her. She struggled against his grip.

"Nothing you can do. They're treating him the way they treat someone who's violent and has escaped. They're doing their job," Huxley said in her ear. She disagreed emphatically but was too depleted to argue.

"Got that Bible verse written down. You did great, Nazario, and it looks like he's gonna talk to you," Wilson said, "which is what we need."

"Thank you, Detective," Millie whimpered.

"Gotta ask, Millie," Nazario began, "what's your son's connection with James Vanwell?"

The pastoral counselor looked up and met Nazario's eyes. "I dunno. I've never heard of him. Don't know who he is. I swear. I just can't take much more of this. The questioning, seeing Gideon that way. All of it. I don't know who the hell James Vanwell is! I don't even know my own son anymore!"

Nazario placed an arm around Millie, who turned and buried her head.

"I'm sorry, Millie. I'm sorry you had to see your son like that."

Nazario gave the pastor's wife the only thing she had to offer.

What Gus had given her: a shoulder to cry on.

THIRTY-FIVE

THE PASTOR'S WIFE

MILLIE GRIPPED THE SINK. It had been a few days now since she'd seen her son, and each day living in the home she shared with Stan no longer felt like hers. Her shoulders sagged, and as much as she begged for the tears to stop, they defied her. She sobbed an ugly, uncontrollable sob. The kind that turned her makeup into mud. The kind that weakened her knees, forcing her to collapse to the bathroom floor.

"My baby," she cried, seeing Gideon in her mind. The way he was banging his head violently against the interrogation room window. She squeezed her eyes shut, flooded with the angry image of that sweet little boy she no longer recognized. But what was worse, what she couldn't get out of her head, was what he wrote down for Nazario. The detective had made her a copy of it. Millie inwardly thanked her and fished it out of her purse. She ran her fingers across Gideon's unmistakable left-handed slanted cursive.

Why didn't you protect me?

Millie hugged the paper against her chest.

"You bastard, it's your fault you kept him from me!" Millie

screamed at Stan despite him not being there. It gave her more reason to do what she needed to do. The doorbell rang. He was here. She got up from the floor and stole out of the bathroom, not bothering to adjust the makeup wrecked all over her face. *Screw it all to hell.*

Millie should've spoken to the police about her suspicions. But what would she have said? That she thought Stan did something to their son? Hurt him in some way? She'd chosen her husband over her child, and for that, she would always live with regret.

She folded the paper with Gideon's question in her purse. While she appreciated Nazario allowing her to keep a copy of the paper, the question had plagued her the last few nights. Though the decision to finalize the divorce had been as clear as a cloudless California day. God didn't speak to her. No, she didn't pray about it. Millie made the choice all on her own. She made the decision without anyone's consent. She opened the door to her lawyer, a sixty-something-year-old, pint-sized bald man in a wrinkled casual dress suit that looked as old and tired as he did.

Abraham Berman, a Jimenez Mexican Grill regular, came recommended by Isabelle.

Mr. Berman furrowed his brows and gave her a paternally concerned smile.

"Hi...*er...uh*...Mrs. Goodwin?" he scanned her makeup-smudged face.

"It's just Millie," she clarified firmly, "please don't call me by my married name."

"I'm sorry, Millie, um, is this still a good time? I can reschedule. Tonight was the best time for me, but I can come back in the morning. It won't take too long."

"Now's just fine." She opened the door wide. "Come on in, Mr. Berman."

Abraham Berman did, grunting as he flopped on the couch. Millie didn't ask, just brought him a cup of warm tea. He sure looked like he could use one right about now. But she was not the one to talk. Berman thanked Millie and took a gingerly sip of his Earl Grey before getting started.

"You don't want the food pantry or the church, but are you certain that you don't want the house?"

"I want none of it," Millie began defiantly.

"Well then, this'll be quite easy. I've calculated alimony. All you need to do is sign the papers, and your hus—*Stan*—will be served. Is he still in Texas? Where can we find him?"

"He just got back from Texas a few days ago. He spends a lot of time at the church; you'll probably find him there. These days, I haven't been keeping track of his comings and goings. We've been...avoiding one other." She folded her arms against her chest, then added defensively, "About that alimony, I've got my own clients, you know. It'll take me longer to open up my own counseling practice, but it's not impossible."

Berman sat the tea down and leaned in, clutching his knees. "Millie, I'm not trying to burst your new...*er...uh...vision* for your future, but you're fifty." He blew out a breath. "I highly suggest you take the alimony. You just never know how long it'll take for you to get on your feet. Opening up a business is expensive. You've only ever worked for the church?"

"Yes. I've technically worked in the non-profit sector for fifteen years." She absently looked down at her nails. "I was thirty-five the last time I was a counselor for the public sector. But I'm still young."

Berman sipped his tea then gave her a sympathetic smile, like he felt sorry for her.

"Agism and lack of work experience are two factors going against you. Having your counseling credentials and opening up your own practice may be the best way to go. Otherwise, the market is competitive now. They're looking to hire experienced young folk several years out of college."

Mr. Berman handed her the divorce papers. He pointed out where to sign, and she did.

"That it?" Millie almost wanted to laugh at the simplicity of it all.

"That's all, folks." Mr. Berman gave her a weary smile. "I know this is a hard time. I've been doing this for forty-five years and I've never dealt with a *happy* divorce. Not a one. No matter what people try to post on social media." Berman stretched his back, the popping sound appearing to give him some relief. "Anyhow, I'll advise you just as soon as Stan is served. And like I said, based on experience, the easiest and best way is to be gone by the time he gets home."

"Got my bags packed." Millie smiled despite the tears at the corners of her eyes. "Thank you for coming by so late at night."

"I'm used to working long hours," Mr. Berman said, drinking down the tea and handing her the empty cup. "Been working sixteen hours most my life. Lemme know if you need anything at all. Goodnight, Millie. There are better days ahead. You're a praying woman. It's gonna take a little faith and trust in the Big Man."

"If I learned one thing, Mr. Berman," Millie said, hands on her hips, "it's that God's pronoun is *she*."

"I stand corrected, Millie," Mr. Berman chuckled, filing the papers in his briefcase. "My wife would agree with you."

She watched him leave and waited until he'd driven off before she closed the door and locked it. Millie took the empty teacup to the sink. She climbed up the stairs to get her bags. The doctors said that Eric might actually recover.

Regardless, she'd wait the rest of her life for Eric to heal from his injuries.

Millie clutched her suitcases when suddenly the power in her home shut off.

It was pitch black in her room, especially with black-out curtains over all the windows.

"Mr. Berman?" Millie swallowed, sitting her suitcase down on the floor. "Mr. Berman, did you forget something?"

She fumbled for her cell phone and turned it on, realizing now she had it shut off. Millie had turned off the phone since Stan had been back, avoiding unwanted text messages and inter-actions, breaking their "never leave your phone off" family rule.

I'm breaking all your rules, she thought, *beginning with our vow "'til death do us part."*

She pushed the flashlight icon, heart slamming rudely against her rib cage.

Her phone buzzed. She looked down, realizing she'd missed a message.

Oh dear, why she'd actually missed several...four messages from the mental hospital. She spent so much time at the hospital with Eric, she often turned it off and kept forgetting to turn it back on.

Creak...Thump
Creak...Thump
Creak...Thump

Millie inhaled, feeling her ribs expand. She held her breath, hearing the sound come closer. Her hands were damp with sweat. She panicked, trying the lights, but they didn't work. Without making a sound, she inched out her breath in micro-doses.

"Stan, you lumbering fool," Millie chided. "Your big feet make more noise than that. If you need to come up here and talk to me, then go on and do it. Stop playing these childish games, and yes, that was a lawyer at our house!"

Creak...Thump

The footsteps drew closer. No, Stan's big old feet were way harder on the steps. He'd never tip-toed in his life. He didn't know how. Stan was at church. She knew he must be there and if he was then whose footsteps were walking up?

The mental hospital. Of course, her son escaped the hospital for the second time.

Millie's heart pounded, her feet frozen in place. She was not afraid of her son. Who else would it be, if not Gideon, who'd most likely left the hospital again? Yet her entire body quivered as she fumbled with her phone, clumsily dropping it in a noisy clatter to the floor. The light on her phone cut out, sending her into an inky abyss. The footsteps stopped. Millie bent down. It was so dark, she couldn't even see her hands in front of her.

Millie found her voice. "G-Gideon?" His name scraped out. "Honey, that you?"

Fingers shivered, raking the wooden floor, sweeping from left to right.

Suddenly, her phone slid toward her. She hesitated and then felt the tips of boots camouflaged in the darkness. "Gideon...Gideon...I'm...Mommy is..."

She rose slowly extending her arms, fishing her way in the dark. Abruptly, something came over her face. The intruder was behind her, body far enough away from her touch. She tried to claw at their arms, but the pressure of the bag began to squeeze around her throat.

Breathing in...Breathing out...Breathing in... Breathing out...

The plastic bag sucked inward, hugging her face, sealing her nose shut.

Her voice wheezed out in gasps. Every inhale dragged the bag tighter—cleaving to her skin, taking more of her. Vertigo spun the inky room. For a moment, she was floating in space. No air. Just panic. Just pressure. Delirium licked at her edges, suffocating the life from her. She raised her arms to claw free—but large arms pinned them down.

Breathing in...Breathing out...Breathing in...Breathing out...

She found the strength to finish her apology a decade too late.

The word weakly eased out of her parched throat. "...sorry."

Breathing in...Breathing out...Breathing in...Breathing...

THIRTY-SIX

THE DETECTIVE

THEY OBTAINED a warrant to search Stan Goodwin's home with Huxley's help, as the FBI could expedite matters that no one on Homicide could. The contingency was that the Feds would help do the search, and so they let Huxley, and a small team of his colleagues do the honors.

Nazario would ordinarily get a little territorial and want to be there, but she'd been feeling like shit all morning. Her body had been reacting terribly to the new anti-anxiety medication dosage her doctor had put her on. She'd rather suffer through nausea any day than to experience almost debilitating heart palpitations that often resembled a heart attack. Wilson sat outside Eric Myer's hospital room, as Nazario raced to the bathroom, hunched over the sink. She splashed cold running water on her face and, after a beat, dried off with a paper towel.

It'd been brought to their attention that Eric Myers came out of his coma but was asleep.

If the ICE agent could simply identify his shooter, the case would be practically over.

Suddenly her phone chimed, and it was a picture from Huxley. It looked to be business documents that might as well have been in Greek. On closer inspection, it appeared to be a list of banking activity where checks were made out to individuals. She squinted, expanding the image so she could fully read the small print. It hit her that this could be more information on that anonymous shell company.

Huxley confirmed, texting: *Stan Goodwin in possession of anonymous shell company info. The shell company cashed out millions in dead peasant insurance. BOLO for your boy Gomez. He followed a lead to an address connected to these accounts – think it's an abandoned house with a barn out in the sticks. Haven't heard from him. MIA for 2 days. Worried.*

Nazario's gut did flips. Gomez MIA? It wasn't like the rookie to be late on anything. She made a mental note to call him. But Nazario wasn't too concerned. Her number one fan was more reliable than many seasoned officers she knew. She thought about the DP insurance again and then she remembered something that hit the news in 1992. Corporations used to be able to place dead peasant insurance on their workers and collect when they died. There was an AIDS case where a Hispanic male had died of the disease. The man's family lived below poverty but didn't get a dime because he never bought life insurance. However, the man's work put out a dead peasant insurance on him and collected over three hundred thousand dollars at the time of his death.

Nazario responded quickly back: *Gomez didn't call us back either. He'll surface soon. The kid's on top of things. Wilson or I will call him later today. About that DP insurance – thought companies can't do that shit no more? Will call Goodwin now. The man of God will meet us at the station or we're arresting the SOB.*

Huxley clarified the laws, texting back: *They still can put out dead peasant insurance on workers as long as they get consent. These undocumented workers might not have known what they were signing. Myers awake yet?*

Still asleep, she sent the reply and thought about this new DP insurance intel.

It made sense. The undocumented workers could've easily been swayed by the promise of new employment. Was that what persuaded Avery Vanwell and Angel Hernandez to work for the pastor? Nazario had subpoenaed bank statements and found their names on it from the same shell company that had employed the others. If they had signed employment papers, most likely they had no idea they were signing an agreement to dead peasant insurance, like the others. Did Stan promise he'd sponsor Angel's work visa? How did her half-sister and her fiancé know Stan Goodwin? Was this how Stan was able to keep his church in a run-down neighborhood of Compton afloat?

Nazario quickly dialed Stan Goodwin, not wasting a second longer, and was surprised that he answered on the second ring.

"You back from Texas, Pastor?" Nazario asked, and there was a ten-second stall. There was no way in hell they were allowing the pastor to fly anywhere else as he was a flight risk and their prime suspect. She explained what they found, and the pastor sounded befuddled, denying any knowledge. "If you're here, then you haven't come by the station like we asked you to. You're in violation and impeding a criminal investigation. Now, let me ask you again. Where are you, Mr. Goodwin?"

"I...I've been back from Texas," he admitted, noisily breathing hard in the receiver, "but I don't know what those papers are—"

"There *will* be a warrant out for your arrest if you're not at the station by—" She looked at her watch, factoring in a busy day. First, she had to try to talk with Eric, and then she had a meeting with Gideon. "—by five this evening," she finished.

When she hung up, she sent another text message to Officer Gomez but got no reply.

———

Wilson was sitting in a chair next to Eric Myers. Nazario didn't sit down, too filled with adrenaline. She thought about Officer Gomez and a sense of dread hit her gut like a twenty-pound medicine ball. Struggling to push aside her concerns, she shifted in place.

"You wanna sit down, Nazario?" Wilson asked, furrowing his brows at her. He obviously knew she was rattled about something.

"Nah, I'm good; it's nice to have my leg outta that brace. Has he said anything?"

Wilson shook his head, "I don't think he remembers anything."

"Shit," Nazario groaned, leaning against the wall. She looked down at Eric Myers, his head wrapped in white gauze. Eric's eyes blinked open.

"Eric?" Nazario tried, waving a hand before his zombie gaze.

"Mr. Myers?" Wilson prodded, as well. "Hey buddy, can you hear us?"

Eric finally glanced at Nazario, to Wilson and then back at the wall zoning out entirely.

"I don't think we're gonna get anything from him," Nazario said but angled back towards Eric. "Eric, do you know who shot you? Can you blink twice to let us know if you recognized who shot you?"

Eric Myers stared into space. Nazario retrieved a sketch of

James Vanwell from the inside of her blazer pocket and placed it in front of Eric Myers.

Eric didn't move, didn't blink—nothing.

"I think he needs more time," Wilson said.

Nazario dialed their boss and relayed that it was a no-go with Myers and then texted Huxley the news: *Unresponsive.*

"I've gotta head to the Gideon Goodwin interview," she said plopping her phone in her blazer pocket. "Gotta run solo on this one—Gideon's request, remember?"

"I remember," Wilson nodded, getting up. They exited the ICE agent's room.

Nazario slipped from the scene and drove with her head in a fog. Soon, she was sitting in the parking lot ready to meet Gideon. She looked at her watch and realized that she only had five minutes until the interview.

Nazario stared down at her phone. Huxley hadn't texted her back regarding Eric Myers. He was probably busy. An urge hit her again. Fingers hovered over the keys and her gut flipped.

Just do it.

It's now or never.

It was an urgency she couldn't explain. It was a hunch.

Shaky fingers texted Huxley.

No matter what happens, I love you. Remember that.

It was code, and Huxley would get the meaning. Though part of her knew that the words meant more than a warning to the special agent. Her father said it before he died. So why did she do this now? Did it have something to do with Officer Gomez suddenly going MIA when the up-and-coming cop would ordinarily respond within minutes after a text?

Nazario gulped. If something should happen, at least Huxley would be the first to know.

Huxley called her immediately, but she let it go to voice-mail. She was out of time. Making her way into the locked mental health facility, she was still unsure if she should've sent the warning text, but something in her gut told her she had to.

———

The room was brightly lit with large windows that faced a yard where patients were taking a walk, tossing a football, talking to staff or to themselves, reading a book, and other various activities. Gideon gave her that same boyish, lustful look as she sat down before him.

"John 8:44...Talks about the father being a murderer, a liar... the 'Devil' in a nutshell," Nazario read from her phone, noticing Huxley had called three times. "Can you tell me what the verse means to you?"

Nazario didn't expect him to answer. In fact, she assumed he'd clamp shut and that this was all a waste of time.

"How do you know James Vanwell?"

Gideon rubbed his eyes and shook his head grappling with something only he could see.

Nazario folded her hands in front of her. "I'm willing to wait as long as you need."

The babble of the hospital started to amplify, yet they sat in shared silence for more than ten minutes before Gideon opened his mouth.

"Yes, Gideon? Please...please tell me why you gave me this verse?"

"At first, I couldn't remember until Dr. Bennett kept pushing hypnotherapy," Gideon began at last. "I just remember we got into an argument. He tripped over some toys and yelled at me to put them away, but I wasn't done playing with them. The next thing I knew, I was under water and couldn't breathe" He choked out a loud sob, his shoulders shuddering. "I was ten years old, and my father, a holy man of

God, tried to drown me. I was clinically dead for two minutes."

Nazario recalled saying those exact words to Millie after Connor Morris choked her. She knew all too well what it was like to beg for air and the fear that overtook you.

"Is that when you stopped talking?" Nazario asked, leaning closer. Gideon nodded.

He met her eyes, and the torment she saw there sickened her. "I don't know who this James Vanwell is, but I do know that if this man in that picture is James Vanwell, then I belong to the..."

Nazario frowned. She re-read the first line of the verse. "Your father, the..."

Devil.

And then it hit her.

She took out the sketch.

Holy shit, why didn't they see it before?

Stan's face was rounder. The advanced facial scan had James Vanwell much thinner, lacking Stan's double-chinned neck and the glasses. That was why they weren't able to recognize him. The sketch was by far not an exact match, but it was close. Due to department budget cuts and lack of bandwidth, Homicide was only granted one progressive scan instead of multiple age progression possibilities of what James Vanwell could look like as an adult. Add weight, glasses, and Stan's loose jowls and...

Nazario looked up, her mouth fell open.

"Listen," he clutched her hand. "That is Stan Goodwin. That picture, it's my father. I tried to call my mom four days ago and couldn't get ahold of her. I called again yesterday, and she's not at home or answering her cell phone. You have to find my mom. I think he's going to kill her if he hasn't already."

"Is that why you escaped?" Nazario could barely breathe.

"Well, yeah...I had to warn my mom. I had a feeling. I heard a couple of guards here talk about the killings, how the body was positioned, and that's what got me. I couldn't find information on it. It wasn't on the news. I finally found a report on the Internet from a small news station, and it confirmed how the bodies were positioned. See, when he drowned me, and I'd stop breathing, the EMTs found me with my arms stretched out on either side of me, like Jesus on the cross."

Nazario whipped out her phone and texted Wilson: *Stan Goodwin is James Vanwell.*

"You have to be careful," he warned. "You don't understand. He's a psychopath, and he's extremely dangerous."

It suddenly dawned on her that Stan hid the knowledge of his son from the public in the same way Madison had done to him. Nazario got up with not a second more to lose and in a rushed tone, quickly told Gideon, "Thanks for your time. I'd stay longer, but this is urgent. We need to find your mom and track Sta...James down."

Gideon clutched her hand and squeezed so tightly her fingers grew numb.

"If you find my father, kill him."

Nazario slid her hand from his grasp and rushed out the exit.

Gideon stood up and screamed again: *"You have to kill him!"*

Two burly male nurses seized Gideon, one on either side.

Once outside, her stomach clenched with residual anxiety.

Nazario opened her car door and glanced down at her phone noticing a text from Huxley. She suddenly felt foolish for sending the message that she was sure would stir concern, which wasn't hard to do, especially if it involved her wellbeing.

Huxley: *Please pick up the phone. Called 5 times need to know you're safe!*

Nazario: *I'm...*

Her fingers fumbled and sent the unfinished text just as a sharp prick of a needle stung her arm. Before she had time to throw an elbow to the rib cage, a hand covered her mouth with strength she didn't expect. The familiar smell of chloroform choked her immediately. She tried for an arm hook pivot to throw the attacker over her shoulder, but her body started to drift into a deep, dark, dizzying tunnel.

Whatever it was she'd been injected with was working swiftly. Outside, the hospital parking lot was a ghost town. No one was around to help her. Even if they were, she couldn't scream. Her body absorbed the substance as quickly as alcohol on an empty stomach. The world swam. Her phone dropped to the hard parking lot asphalt. Unable to retain control of her limbs, her body collapsed in a boneless heap.

THIRTY-SEVEN

THE DETECTIVE

THE UNMISTAKABLE SCENT of death accosted her senses, even before her new world came to focus through strobe-light winks. Though she couldn't locate the body, the odor must've come from a corpse that had been in the barn at some point.

Fresh death permeated her new surroundings.

She shifted, her neck bruised from the hefty chain wrapped twice around it, so taut that the steel had broken skin. She could feel her flesh rubbed raw from the short chain connecting to the top rafters. Twice, she'd almost strangled in her own struggle to free herself.

James Vanwell must have positioned her like this on purpose. If she moved slightly at the wrong angle, she'd choke to death. It was not so much the rusty fetters around her throat but the combination of death, decaying wood, and mildewy hay that caused waves of nausea to splutter through her.

Ordinarily, the stink of a corpse wouldn't turn her stomach, though it had made her throw up once or twice. Having not eaten, her stomach growled and tightened into a spell of dry heaves. Her head pounded with a relentless throb. Her mouth and throat sandpaper dry, lips parched and cracked.

How many days had she been here? She didn't know. Time had passed in a haze drifting in and out of consciousness. She struggled to keep herself from panicking, getting through each hour by recalling her girls at the self-defense class. Her mind revisited Vivi from the AA meeting and being reunited with her little girl. How great it felt seeing Caylee running into her mother's arms. Then Huxley returned to her heart and mind. Nazario loved him and might die before she got to tell him face to face.

In the days that she'd been sitting there, the detective in her had tried to piece things together in order to keep her mental faculties from failing altogether. But her human side had been impacted by dehydration, hunger, and the pain of being chained up by the neck, making cognition dull. Head in a fog, she loosely understood that James must've made the connection that Avery Vanwell was her father's daughter. But she was unable to focus beyond this generalized knowledge. Though the answer was almost within reach, if only she could catch her second wind.

Vaguely lucid, there were times when she'd nearly passed out but didn't.

Her neck burned, caused by the chain lacerations that sliced into her flesh.

Nazario guessed it'd been at least three days and wondered why she was still alive. After counting the sun going down twice, by the third day, hunger pains had vanished. But her thirst intensified. She'd give anything for water. She hadn't seen or heard James Vanwell this entire time until suddenly the barn doors behind her swung open. From where she was sitting, she couldn't turn to see who was approaching. If she did, she'd slip from the elevated mound on the ground and could choke on the chain.

A blindfold was placed over her eyes to cover her vision. Unable to see, something cold touched her lips. It was water she had been thirsting for. She greedily drank, but the killer gave her just enough, pulling the glass away after two swallows.

She felt gloved hands around her upper arm.

"You don't have to do this, James," Nazario pled just as a needle punctured her skin.

The drug worked as swiftly as it had before, making the world fade out once more.

———

When she stirred awake, the stink of rotting sewage was much more pungent. The unique odor had a peculiar juxtaposition to the classical music playing in the background, along with a fancy dish at the center of the table with an assortment of expensive cheeses, crackers, caviar, and bottles of red wine.

Nazario tried to look around, her neck scraped raw from the chains.

The room swam, and she squinted, trying to force blurred surroundings into focus. Her arms were bound before her, giving her leeway as she reached and touched her raw neck. The chain was gone. That sent a temporary relief through her exhausted body, though it quickly dispersed. Her eyes tried to gain focus, and as they did, she saw that young officer with so much promise. Her skin broke out into gooseflesh as Officer Gomez's brown eyes, now grey and milky, stared blankly. Gomez wore plain civilian clothes and had taken one to the head. He must've known something, and like Daddy, went undercover.

Residual burn marks framed the bullet hole at the center of his forehead.

Execution style just like Avery Vanwell. Same killer.

"*Detective Lucas Nazario was my idol.*" The young ambitious officer's voice returned to her, haunted her as Avery's had. *"As a Puerto Rican, you know he's the reason why I joined."*

"No, no, no...Gomez," Nazario cried out weakly, as tears pooled in her eyes. "Goddamn it, not you...not you, Gomez."

A stir at the corner of her eye caused Nazario to snap out of her tunnel vision, out of the beginning of what would be a long process of grieving over the young Puerto Rican cop that wanted to represent the good, that as a minority, wanted to transform society's negative opinions of police officers. Yes, if she lived, she'd never forget Officer Gomez. Regret bit deep and she knew it would never let go completely. If she could take back all of the times, she was short with the eager officer, all the times she was rude in that veteran, jaded detective sort of way, she would've.

Gomez had been a breath of fresh air.

He wasn't jaded. He believed in doing good, in being a good cop. He was the type that hadn't lost hope in turning morale around. He was the type that felt like he could represent people of color and his brothers and sisters in blue without having to choose between the two. She should've insisted the rookie stick to his SID duties and should've never involved him in Homicide.

Nazario knew she and a deceased Officer Gomez weren't alone.

As her vision faded in and out of focus, Nazario gently attempted to get a better scope of the table, nudging her sore neck to the left and right. All the while, fatigue gripped her, threatening to pull her under the darkening abyss. Millie Ann Goodwin sat shuddering at one corner of the table. Her black mascara ran down her face, pink lipstick smeared haphazardly across her lips and cheek. Her hair was in disarray, but she was alive and so was Pastor Stan Goodwin, aka James Vanwell, who sat at the other end of the table.

She observed him more closely, comparing the face to the

police sketch that made James look much thinner, more
calloused, less human. His gaze all but scuttled her way, as if
direct eye contact for too long would burn his soul. His prom-
inent turkey neck jowl hung loosely, a significant feature not in
the FBI sketch. Sweat dripped down his forehead, weaving a
path along his flushed cheeks.

They were each seated around a long dining room table
meant to fit at least ten people.

"What're we," Millie began, trying to wrench free from the
ropes that bound her arms to the chair, "what're we all doing
here? What is this? Did you see who did this Detective
Nazario? I didn't catch the face. What's happening? Why're we
sitting at a table with a...with a d-dead man?"

"Dead cop," the words scratched out of Nazario's parched
throat. "I'd like to ask the pastor the same thing or shall we call
you James?"

"What is she talking about, Stan? Who's James?" Millie
questioned and when James didn't answer, her voice rose in
hysterics. "What's going on? Say something! Do something and
don't just sit there. Why are we tied up and you're sitting there
like a damn lump—"

His first words came out as an even, low staccato tone.
"Shut. Up."

"You shut up," she screamed back, "should've killed you
when I had my hands around your turkey neck. Wait a second...
my lawyer served you, is that it? You can't handle the fact that I
filed for divorce. But involving Detective Nazario and killing a
cop, Stan? They had nothing to do with our marriage or lack
thereof. You are crazy if you think I'm gonna stay married to
you. You're gonna have to kill me first."

"Millie, please—" Nazario tried to warn but James cut in.

"And you're an adulterous whore," he snarled. "Go on and
have Eric Myers. I bet you'll be spending your time wiping his

ass and cleaning the drool off his face. You deserve each other."

"You bastard!" Millie struggled against her ropes. "Let us go."

"I don't think that's gonna happen," Nazario replied evenly, "am I right, James?"

James didn't respond. He sat there staring at them with angry eyes.

"Madison Vanwell identified you as her son. You were jealous of the fact that she was having a baby with my father, and you killed him and then positioned his body under the 405 freeway," she began gathering renewed strength and energy to see things clearly. "You took a sabbatical after changing your name and created a whole new reality, a new life that involved a church in rundown Compton. Since your church wasn't making ends meet, as most nonprofits aren't cash machines, you created a shell company, employed undocumented workers, placed dead peasant insurance on them. You needed them dead in order to collect the insurance money. You positioned the bodies like you did my father in an effort to recreate some sort of sick play. You couldn't stand that he loved your mother and found happiness just as your father was dying." Nazario took a breath.

"What I can't figure out is how you managed to employ Avery Vanwell," Nazario continued. "Did you lure her undocumented fiancé with the promise that he'd get his green card? Is that how you roped your half-sister, *our* half-sister to sign papers as if she was an employee of your shell company? How many millions have you stashed away in some offshore account, James?"

James broke through Nazario's monologue with a snicker.

"You think this is funny? Gomez found out this was the house that once belonged to a family of Mexican immigrants your father employed. He'd discovered you and was gonna tell us and that's why you eliminated him. It'll make sense to kill your wife. After all, she's leaving you. Then, I'll be last. Your prized possession. The reason you placed all the bodies in my jurisdiction was so that I could uncover them. They'd be assigned to LAPD's homicide team. You couldn't handle the fact that I was the last Nazario spawn. The man who ruined your family."

"Dear God...who in the hell did I marry?" Millie shook her head. "You sick bastard!"

"Is that your hypothesis, Detective?" James flushed, his mannered tone belied rage that visibly swept across his tempered face. "How 'bout you explain why my ankles are hog-tied under the table?"

Nazario then noticed that the long tablecloth touched the ground. She didn't understand. First, they were wrong about Eric Myers, but how could they be so wrong about James Vanwell? Hadn't he been cloaked in pastoral clothing, luring the needy into his web?

A large male figure came out of the shadows accompanying a tall slender woman. Her perfume mingled with the stench of Gomez's decaying body. Madison Vanwell clip-clopped in her red stilettos. She wore a matching red pencil skirt, an ivory blouse, and a black blazer. Her professional business attire made her look every bit like the CEO of the impressive empire she built.

Antonio, Madison's personal trainer and lover, pointed a gun at them. Madison smiled brightly. "Bravo," she said, clapping, "you were brilliant. You see, Antonio, I told you. Your theory, Detective Nazario, is precisely what everyone will believe."

THIRTY-EIGHT

THE WITNESS

WHEN ESPERANZA HEARD that Detective Nazario was missing, she'd stopped by the station and asked for Special Agent Huxley and Detective Wilson, but they'd been out of the office. She could've flagged any officer down but was no longer waiting around for someone to hurt her, Alex, or kill more immigrants. She'd even left a message on their cellphones, but they never called her back.

Though her conscience nudged her to do the right thing, so she gave it one last chance. Esperanza had tried calling them—a last-ditch effort when she'd arrived at the abandoned home.

No signal.

She'd tried again.

And then again.

Still no signal.

Her cheap pay-as-you-go phone cut out even in the city, so it was no surprise it failed her in the middle of nowhere. If Wilson or Huxley were trying to call her now, bad reception would shoot it straight to voicemail.

Pulling up in front of a vacant home on a large plot of land, it seemed even more deserted than when she'd followed Officer

Gomez the other night. A barn sat behind the property. Recognizing the landscape, she was grateful she remembered how to get there.

She shivered, realizing right then and there that she was risking her life and that if something happened to her, no one would save her. Esperanza clutched the gun lent by Isabelle and edged toward the main house with careful trepidation. It had stood unlived in for years on a desolate plot of land, neglected and abandoned, just outside Los Angeles County. She held her purse against her, afraid to jostle the gun. Esperanza had never fired a weapon before and didn't know much about guns.

She had an irrational fear: bounce it wrong, and it would boom like a tripwire.

She knew this wasn't true but hugged her purse against her side anyway. The padding of the handbag was thin enough that the grip of the gun nestled around her fingers. If not for the weapon, she'd feel more vulnerable, more terrified. Today, courage and will were on her side. It was as though everything in her life had culminated to bring her to this moment. She was risking deportation, being separated from Alex, and even her own life, but she couldn't simply sit back and do nothing. Despite her apprehension and mistrust toward Nazario and other law enforcement like Officer Gomez, she didn't want to see them dead.

Esperanza covered her nose with the crook of her elbow as she entered the home, and the stomach-churning stench of death engulfed her. It seemed to penetrate her pores and was enough for her to change her mind. Self-doubt swept through her, trying to convince her that she could flee once and for all. This was the moment—to turn around right now, be rid of these Americans, *loco en la cabeza*. Maybe it wouldn't be so bad to take Alex back to Mexico with her. They could live in Mexico City. It would be more affordable. But she knew her son. He was a born and raised American. His culture was Mexican-American.

Alex would be miserable—she knew this as a mother.

Could she flee to her homeland with blood on her hands?

No, Esperanza's mind and heart fought against her former frightened self. Before she got any closer, Esperanza took her phone and pressed the voice memo button. While she didn't have cell reception, the digital voice recorder still worked. Instinctively, she knew that the conversations in the dining room would be essential for the authorities. Following voices, she heard a woman she'd never met.

"We're all here," began the woman, "my son, James. His wife. And the woman who was almost my stepdaughter. One big happy family."

Esperanza peeked around the wall before her and glanced at the familiar voice. That's where she knew her from. She gasped and put a hand over her mouth to stop herself from yelping out. It was that wealthy winery owner who'd held all of those fundraisers for Mexican immigrants and their separated families. She remembered now— seeing the local news conference. But her son? James? Esperanza stared, stunned. It was Pastor Goodwin...and Mrs. Goodwin?

"Mrs. Vanwell...Madison? I don't...I don't understand," the detective appeared stupefied, glancing between the wealthy winery owner and a muscular Hispanic man holding the gun to Nazario's head. Nazario muffled weakly, "So, Antonio's more than your personal trainer?"

Suddenly, Esperanza was under The Serpent's Bridge, recalling the hitman's face—*him*.

"So clever, aren't you? You were always Lucas's favorite," Madison said softly as Antonio pressed the barrel against Nazario's temple. "All your father ever talked about was you. At first, it was cute until he said that he couldn't break up his little family. He wasn't even talking about his wife. It was always you."

Pastor Goodwin—no, *James Vanwell*—glared at Madison with such disdain that it made Esperanza's skin crawl. Esperanza crept closer and placed her back to the wall. Her hand sunk slowly into her purse until she found the grip of the gun and curled her fingers securely around it.

"It was you who made Dad sick, wasn't it?" James accused. "I always knew it was you."

Esperanza's mind wanted to default to the old Goodwin name, the name he'd used to try to outrun the shadows of his wealthy past. Like him or not, she began to see why he might've wanted to leave it all behind. The woman in the red heels was someone you wouldn't want to mess with.

Madison took deliberate, leisurely strides in her red high heels, clipping down the length of the long dining room table. Stopping midway at the wines in the center, she poured herself a glass. The millionaire, self-made or otherwise, twirled the maroon liquid until it swished in a circular motion and tsked, "Now, James, that's no way to speak to your mother."

"This your mother?" Millie shrieked.

But James wasn't listening. He looked up at Madison Vanwell, eyes glittering behind his glasses. "Tell me the truth," his voice trembled. "You owe me that."

Mrs. Goodwin stared in horror as Madison paused between Millie and her soon-to-be ex-husband.

Madison sat her drink down, and the next thing Esperanza knew, the woman's hand cracked across James's face—the sound reverberating across the room, penetrating the wall Esperanza was hiding behind. She peeked around the corner again, knowing she was in a good blind spot. Still undetected.

James's face was as bright as a ripe tomato.

Millie gaped at her husband. "I thought your father was sick from some illness."

Face still marked where his mother had slapped him, James glanced up at Madison as if asking for permission to speak. Smiling widely, Madison walked over to the expensive cheeses, cut herself a slice, and plopped the piece in her mouth with the tip of a knife. "Go on," she muffled as she chewed, "tell them."

James licked his lips and began. "The vineyard was going under until he got sick. Next thing I know, he's dead, and they're suddenly back up and operating. I was a wreck, but she didn't look like she was grieving, wasn't behaving like a widow. That's when I knew, I knew she'd done something to him. I was too young. I was only sixteen at the time...couldn't prove a thing. They didn't check for poisoning back then."

Madison rolled her eyes but didn't interrupt James while he told his story.

James looked up at Nazario in a pitiful, pleading way as he continued, "She killed Lucas right in front of me and made me help her get rid of the body. I didn't know what to do with him... so I put him under the overpass, near gang territory since your father was working undercover with them gangs." His voice rose in defense of his actions. "She had a gun pointed at my head. I swear she threatened to kill me if I didn't do what she said. She threatened she'd take away my inheritance."

"What about that Mexican family?" Millie asked. "Did you really stay with them, or was that a lie, too?"

"Let him finish," Nazario said weakly to Millie before shifting her eyes between Antonio and Madison.

"It was a family of undocumented workers we'd employed for a very long time. They gave me this gold crucifix as a birthday present when I was five years old. The one time I took it off, she grabbed it from my dresser and kept it. After we dumped Lucas's body, she went over and moved his arms in the position of Jesus Christ—spread out, legs together—like he was pinned to the cross. Since she had my crucifix, she said she could convince the cops I put the body like that. I was so scared."

James heaved in a long breath and collected himself for a beat.

"I knew I should've gone to the police, but my fingerprints were on the gun. She'd tricked me into holding the gun afterward —when I had no gloves on. She threatened that if I said anything, the cops would think I killed him. Between the position of the body and the fingerprints—I was screwed. I was young. I was scared. I was afraid she'd kill me. So, I ran. That's when I went to stay with that Mexican family and grew to love the culture. I wanted to help the way Dad did. He had a heart for displaced migrant workers. I had plans for medical school before he got sick, but after he died, I changed my name, changed what I was gonna do with my life, and I...I never looked back."

James looked to Nazario again, but she gave the pastor neutral eyes.

"God knows every day I pray for His forgiveness, and what I did never seems to leave me. I'm sorry, Detective, I'm really sorry," James begged. "If I had told authorities I suspected my mother poisoned my father, maybe yours would still be here."

Madison took something out of her blazer pocket and dangled it before her son.

It was a gold chain with a crucifix. She flipped it over and showed the detective.

"It's the original?" Nazario mumbled, recognition creeping in.

"Sure is. And they'll still think you killed Lucas Nazario." Madison swayed the necklace side to side in front of him like a wicked hypnotist. James froze. Horror swept in. His eyes widened at the sight of his old jewelry. "You could've been the Vanwell heir, inherited the empire I'd worked so hard to build. You could've helped me run my business. Mother and son. Side by side. But, no...you couldn't do that, could you? You're just like your stupid father. He loved giving away my money to a bunch of people that don't belong here." Madison glanced at a dead Officer Gomez and then smiled at Nazario. "People that should go back to their country."

"You evil, sick woman," Millie cried out.

Madison gave a nod. Antonio shoved the gun in Millie's mouth. Her gag was instant. Sharp. Tears filled her eyes. Her former boss looked like she was struggling to breathe. Esperanza shifted from foot to foot. Her body jolted an inch as she steeled herself to brave forward. Madison snapped her head in Esperanza's direction. She jumped back, heart sprinting in her chest just as Antonio retracted the gun.

"All it took was a little antifreeze in his green smoothies he'd love to drink. Every morning for three months. Considered arsenic and rat poisoning, but that combo would've been too suspicious. Would've killed him too quickly. I had to be smart, not stupid. So, I planned the portions just right, and he got sick gradually. It looked so much more natural that way. Whenever I go under the knife, I always tell my plastic surgeon—*natural*. Please don't make me look like Joan Rivers. Bless her spirit wherever it may be," she said, pouring a separate glass of zinfandel and taking it to Nazario's lips. "It's delicious. Zinfandel, your favorite and my award-winning batch."

Nazario moved her head from side to side, but Antonio persuaded her with the gun. The detective swallowed a sip, but it was quickly rejected by her body as the red liquid spewed out and onto the floor.

"I knew you did it. I knew you killed him." James's head

slumped, and his shoulders bobbed. Wet-faced, the man mumbled incoherent prayers—for God's ears only.

Once the vomiting stopped, Nazario wearily glared up at Madison. Worry filled Esperanza, that if she didn't act soon, there would be more bloodshed. Maybe they'd all be murdered, Esperanza included. This winery owner, this crazy old woman with brains, power, and wealth, would get away with it all.

"You're seventy years old, and while you look fantastic, you're in no physical condition to snuff out the victims on my caseload," Nazario said, glancing at the woman's personal trainer. "So, you paid Antonio over here for more than weight training. You enticed Antonio to do your dirty work by giving him a generous cut of the insurance, didn't you? It worked the first time with your husband, so why not continue? Yago Rios and Luis Vargas were both paid by the same shell company that took dead peasant insurance out on them. Same with Angel Hernandez. What I can't understand is why kill your own daughter? Why Avery? Even if she knew Lucas Nazario was her father, it wouldn't justify—"

"She was too smart for her own good," Antonio spoke for the first time, "and nosy."

"She found our shell company, claimed that I tricked her and her fiancé into signing the insurance and that she was," Madison paused to pour another glass, sipped long, then continued, "gonna tell her big sister, the detective, all about it. I loved my daughter, but the little brat got everything she ever asked for her whole spoiled life. She wanted for nothing, and I wasn't about to let her take me down."

The detective looked confused, glancing suspiciously at James and then back to the gunman and his wealthy boss, asking, "Why did Gideon tell me that James, or should I say Pastor Stan Goodwin tried to drown him when he was a child?"

"W-what? That's why—*that is why*—of course." Millie

snarled at her soon-to-be ex-husband. "I hope they kill you 'cause if they don't, I swear if I get outta this—I'm fixin' to kill you myself!"

James coughed and cried at once. "I never hurt that boy."

"You're no better than Mommy Dearest over here," Detective Nazario challenged.

"I've been very patient. Letting you all talk this all out. But this isn't a therapy session, now is it, Millie? I can't tell you how nice it is to finally meet my daughter-in-law. I love this dress. The color suits you." Madison smiled at the pastor's wife, brushing fingers along the shoulder seams of Millie's sundress. "None of this'll matter soon because they'll believe exactly what I planned—exactly what Detective Nazario hypothesized. No one will suspect a sweet old lady like me had any involvement in these murders. Especially since I have a 501c3 dedicated to the undocumented and their separated families—one the LAPD donates to. Why'd someone with my kind of money, thanks to a few *dead peasants*, have to murder people?"

Nazario blinked, voice hoarse, "You're not a stupid woman, give you that, Madison."

"Why thank you, Detective." Madison smiled brightly and then turned to her son and daughter-in-law, continuing, "The truth is, Gideon had no memory of the accident at the pool. But I've been privately visiting my only grandchild since he was admitted to the hospital, and I've been paying Dr. Bennett very well for the past twelve years to make sure Gideon remembered the events...*as he should*. According to Gideon, his father's a monster, a serial murderer, and someone he's so terrified of that he'd rather be in a mental hospital than go anywhere near him."

"You planted false memories!" Millie shouted.

Madison turned to her lover and assistant, then instructed, "Antonio, it's time for James to kill his estranged wife for cheating on him with that stupid ICE agent. He was the easiest to fool. I bought out one of his ICE buddies to whisper in Eric's ear and convince him to tip off certain members of Sanctuary Baptist. Then, my psychotic, vengeful son will kill the last remaining Nazario and then turn the gun on himself. All the guilt. All the sins that God could never forgive."

James squeezed his eyes shut again and muttered more prayers.

Antonio pointed the gun at Millie, and Esperanza moved even closer. Her heart hammered against her chest with enough force to knock her to her knees, but she stiffened her spine, inhaled a generous gulp of oxygen, and checked her phone.

Good. It's still recording.

The detective seemed to have found the strength to negotiate quickly. She turned to Antonio and said, "If you tell us what you know—if you tell us everything, she made you do...we can work something out, some plea deal. You don't have to do this, Antonio. The Feds and the LAPD, they're already on their way. They know Officer Gomez was en route to come to this location. He's been missing for two days. You prepared to go down for her? It doesn't matter how much money she promised you, Antonio. You won't be able to touch it inside a prison cell. The Feds will seize all of the funds and her assets along with anything she gave you, and you'll go away for a very long time. Life in prison for these murders, that's how long. Are there other dead bodies just waiting to be found?"

Antonio shifted from foot to foot, and then his eyes darted anxiously to his boss.

"There're others," said the detective with a level of confidence that made the gunman visibly nervous, "aren't there? Other dead peasants? Undocumented Mexicans. They were easier to target. You scouted them out, didn't you? Picked ones without a family, someone no one would miss. Tell us the location where you dumped them. Work with me, Antonio, and I promise—we'll cut you a deal. It won't be immunity, but it will spare you a life behind bars."

Rivulets of sweat beaded across Antonio's brow, glistening down his neck. "You...you told me this was gonna be simple."

"Ignore her. She's trying to scare you," Madison replied evenly. "Everyone here will be dead. Not one single witness left."

"That's your end game, isn't it, Madison? Antonio, you're just another brown person she's using. She had her own daughter killed. Think about it. Her own flesh and blood. You really believe she's gonna let *you* live?" Nazario reasoned. The man raked his free hand down his face. "C'mon, man, put the gun down. Think about what you're doing. She's not on your side. I'm the only one in this room that you can rely on right now, the only one who can help you outta this."

Antonio pivoted and turned the gun on Madison. "I'm not going down for this shit."

THIRTY-NINE

THE DETECTIVE

SOMETHING SHIFTED IN HER PERIPHERY, but Nazario did her best not to call attention to it. It could be the cops, the Feds, it could be—no—*Esperanza Flores?* Nazario was astounded by the little, brave woman hiding behind the closest wall. As she poked her head out, their eyes locked.

By the time Antonio swiveled the gun and pointed it at Madison, Esperanza sprung out from her cover and shot the gun twice. Antonio and Madison were both hit. Nazario briefly caught Antonio's gun arm jerking away as the weapon dropped to the ground. He was thrown back and knocked to the ground by the force, as was Madison. Both appeared to have been shot in a non-lethal area, probably the arm or shoulder region.

Dazed by Esperanza's actions, Nazario watched as she dropped the gun as if shocked by what she had done. Before it could clatter to the ground, the doors burst open. Sirens and voices seemed close yet still out of reach, as though at the end of a long, distant tunnel.

Huxley and Wilson charged in. *"FBI! LAPD!"*

Cops fanned out, some racing toward Madison and Antonio

while Huxley checked Esperanza, who was pale-faced and stunned.

Two other uniformed police officers hurried in to help Millie and James.

"The Goodwins are secure. Get to Nazario," Wilson said, "and I'll stay with Esperanza."

Huxley hastened to her. Tears flowed down her face.

Huxley knelt before her, uttering words, but she was unable to register them. They floated into nothingness, her mind freefalling.

The sound of police vehicles and ambulances finally drew closer. She heard the words "in shock" as her bound wrists and ankles were cut free. Familiar hands wiped her face with a damp cloth. She couldn't meet his eyes. Her own stared blankly. Tight, searing pain knifed the center of her chest as she struggled to breathe.

Tears crawled out the corners of her eyes as a burst of oxygen finally filled her lungs.

"That's it," Huxley said, "you're okay. C'mon, keep breathing. You're okay."

Nazario's vision cleared, and she looked around the room for the unlikely hero.

"Es-Esperanza?" She blinked, breathing heavy and long. "Is she okay...?"

"She's fine," Wilson said, draping a blanket around Esperanza's shoulders.

Nazario's eyes pooled. Her mouth fell open. Thank you wasn't enough, and the words caught in her throat. Esperanza's gaze held hers for a long moment before Wilson escorted her out the door.

The world resumed in slow motion.

She saw a gloved EMT shine a small flashlight in her eyes.

"Pupils are dilated," the EMT said, "Detective Nazario, can you hear me?"

Nazario saw faces looming over her, Chief Johnson, Wilson, and Huxley, wearing the same expression, looking like hell. The EMTs hovered in front of her. The room was caving in on her, suddenly stifling and claustrophobic.

"She's dehydrated and in shock and suffered severe lacerations on her neck, wrists, and ankles. We need to take her to the hospital," one of them said. "You can follow us."

"I'm riding in the back with her," Huxley demanded.

As the voices faded, darkness beckoned her again.

Her body went slack, and she sank into the void.

FORTY

THE FORMER PASTOR'S WIFE

MILLIE WATCHED Eric and Gideon at a distance, as Eric showed her son how to feed one of the horses on Eric's Ojai farm. Eric talked to Gideon in soft tones. Even from here, Millie could hear Eric's slurred speech. The horse therapy had not only been effective for Gideon's PTSD after being manipulated by Dr. Marcel Bennett but for Eric's trauma, too.

Millie adjusted the volume on her Bluetooth earbuds, her gaze glued to the screen on her iPhone as the two perps that had held her hostage walked through a crowd of reporters. Antonio Martinez had his head down. Meanwhile, Madison Vanwell, in an expensive business dress suit, photo-ready makeup and hair, smiled for the cameras. The screen cut to Millie's ex-husband, James Vanwell, being escorted by his attorney to the courtroom as the news broadcaster began his commentary.

"Madison Vanwell collected millions of dollars in dead peasant insurance, which funded her winery business. The savvy businesswoman admitted to poisoning her husband with antifreeze more than two decades ago. Investigators claimed that the first murder and the big insurance payout that followed gave

Vanwell the idea to continue to find more victims and attempt to frame her own son for the serial murders."

The screen cut to Madison's winery, and the news broadcaster continued. "In addition to the murders of Pablo Jimenez, Luis Vargas, LAPD's newest recruit, Officer Gomez, Angel Hernandez, and Madison Vanwell's daughter Avery Vanwell—the FBI uncovered human remains from seven other bodies buried in her vineyard. All of which are said to belong to undocumented immigrants."

A picture of Stan—no James Vanwell—Antonio Martinez and Dr. Marcel Bennett showed up on the screen.

"Antonio Martinez wasn't the only one duped by Madison Vanwell," continued the broadcast journalist. "Psychiatrist Dr. Marcel Bennett had his license revoked and is being charged with planting false memories into an anonymous patient connected to the case. Like Antonio Martinez and James Vanwell, Dr. Bennett has reached a settlement and a plea agreement in exchange for his testimony against the winery owner. Madison Vanwell is being compared to Dorothea Puente, the 'Sweet Granny' serial killer who poisoned her roommates through the 1980s to collect social security checks and then buried the bodies in her backyard."

"I fed Ruby a carrot," Gideon called out to Millie. "Come see!"

"Great job, honey," Millie said.

"Mom," Gideon said impatiently, "you should ride Ruby. It'll be fun!"

"About time you try something new," Eric slurred as he spoke, but the sound was beautiful, nonetheless. Distracted by the news, Millie turned off her phone, loving how "Mom" came out of her son's lips and the sound of Eric's voice. The man she loved smiled at her from afar and waved for her to come over.

The sun warmed her skin, and a light breeze kissed her cheeks. Many saw aging as doomsday. But, at fifty, her life was only beginning, and freedom had never tasted sweeter.

Every day, she aimed to try something new. After all, Millie Ann had been reborn.

FORTY-ONE

THE DETECTIVE

NAZARIO FOUND her breath and pulse slowly returning to a steady rhythm, her nostrils flaring with each inhale, mouth expelling every breath. Eyes darted to her surroundings. Sizing up her emaciated arms, she lifted them as if manipulating a marionette. They appeared lifeless and detached from her body. Her wrists were wrapped in thick bandages, her neck stiff and achy.

She groaned in pain as she reached to massage it. A thick wrap covered the place where the chains had been. The same bandages were on her ankles, but the one on her neck was the thickest.

Her gaze raked the stark surroundings and skimmed down the scratchy white bed sheet. The sanitized room smelled of rubbing alcohol and disinfectant. A hospital. She turned her head, squinted from the sharp sting in her neck, and finally saw him.

Surreal, somehow. Dream-like.

The television, mounted high on the wall, showed the FBI and several personnel from the coroner's office removing several body bags from Madison Vanwell's vineyard.

"There were seven bodies found, there could potentially be more—"

Huxley reached for the remote, turned off the television, and heaved out a deep sigh. His chair was as close as it could be to the bed. She could reach him and was grateful.

"You've got a beard," she finally said, voice hoarse.

"Anaya?" He turned to look down at her, the flesh around his eyes red and swollen.

Her cold fingers shook as they touched his beard. The hairs prickled under her palm. A thin layer of dark gold told of more than two weeks of growth.

"How's Esperanza? She...she saved our lives."

Huxley reached into the nightstand, pulled out a 5 x 7 card tucked amongst a bouquet of wildflowers, and handed it to her. On the front, it simply read "Get Well" in silver script letters on a banana-colored background. Nazario opened it.

I know you're worried about me, but I'm more than fine. For once, I feel like I helped serve a greater purpose. The LAPD and Chief at the homicide unit offered me a part-time job at the station office. Flexible hours so that I can spend time with Alex. Thanks to Special Agent Huxley, I'm in the process of receiving my citizenship.
Esperanza

Nazario set the card down on the nightstand and slumped against the pillow.

"Thank you for getting Esperanza in the clear, pulling strings to expedite her citizenship."

Huxley cleared his throat and gave her another nod. He handed her water. She sipped with a quaking hand and attempted to set it down, but her arm was uncoordinated.

He took the cup of water before it could spill, and she thanked him.

"I've had a lot of time to think about what I'd say if I lived because when you think you're gonna die, it makes you see everything you want and everything you wished you'd done differently," Nazario paused, adjusting herself against the bed.

Huxley, still silent, stared down at his hands and listened.

"All those years ago—the way that I left, the way I just disappeared. It was wrong. It was more than wrong. I was a coward. It was cruel. And I know I can't erase our past with a fucking apology."

Huxley shook his head with vigor, as if the words were beyond his reach.

"And don't you dare apologize." His voice was ragged and hushed. "I don't give a damn about the past. I mean...when we got to the barn, and that stench hit us. We saw that chain hanging from the rafters—God, I thought you were dead!"

Huxley clasped her hand and squeezed. The muscle in his jaw worked, and she could sense a myriad of feelings raging through him, as though he'd wept in private and was now being strong for her.

"About the text message—"

"Code." He looked away. "Got whatcha meant. You were trying to warn me."

He got up from the chair and gazed out at the window.

Her heart pounded against her chest.

She stared at his back, wishing she could see his face.

"Huxley, I...I..." the words stayed stuck in her throat.

He turned around and faced her, waiting for her to tell him.

"That's what I thought," he said with exhaustion.

The doctor walked into the room, breaking through the moment. "Hope I didn't interrupt anything?" he said.

"You didn't," Huxley said in a low, terse tone.

"Fuck," Nazario bit out, raking her hands over her face.

Damn it, Nazario.

"I can give the two of you another minute..." the doctor offered awkwardly.

"I was just leaving." Huxley reached into the inside coat pocket of his blazer and retrieved what looked like airplane tickets.

He handed them to her.

"What's this?" she asked.

"Get some rest," he avoided her eyes. "Open it later."

She didn't wait. There were two tickets to Amsterdam in the Netherlands.

"Thought you'd like to visit Amsterdam."

Nazario raised a confused brow. "And what's in Amsterdam?"

"Python's Bridge. Thought it would be special since, you know, everything started with The Serpent's Bridge," Huxley uttered, his voice now laced with disappointment. "Think I'll bow out. But you should still go. Got insurance on the tickets. You can change the name out and take Gus."

Nazario sighed, "Huxley—"

The doctor gave them an anemic smile. "I don't believe Detective Nazario should fly anywhere. Not anytime soon."

"Take me where? And why the hell can't she fly?" Gus's voice boomed from the door. She stalked into the room and threw her arms around Nazario.

Nazario moaned in pain. "Ow—"

"Damn girl, sorry. Glad you're not dead, bitch." She kissed Nazario's cheek.

"Where do you think you're going?" Gus chided, grabbing Huxley's arm as he moved toward the exit. "She could've been killed, and y'all in a fight already?"

"Going to bed." Huxley paused wearily. Dark circles framed his tired eyes. "Now, stay the hell out of it, Gus."

The doctor tapped his pen anxiously on his clipboard and turned to Nazario. "Due to severe dehydration and shock, which caused you to pass out, you were placed in a medical coma for a week."

A shock wave rippled through her. "A medical coma?"

"It's been a very long week," Huxley's baritone voice grated out, raspy and exhausted.

"But she's not in a coma," Gus said, "trust me Doc, I've been in one, too, and I've been able to travel just fine."

"I'd like to talk to my patient in private," the doctor ordered.

"Look, whatever it is, you can share it with us. My best friend, someone we both love—" she said, shoving Huxley with her hip, "almost died, and to hell if we're leaving."

Huxley exhaled, an arm wedged tightly under Gus's biceps. He met Nazario's eyes. Too many unsaid things passed between them.

Adjusting herself against the pillow, she said, "It's fine." She winced as pain surged.

"Your blood tests—" He glanced down at the chart and then back up again. "This really is a private matter, Detective Nazario."

"What about my blood tests? I know, I know—I'm iron deficient, that ain't news."

"We ran a full panel. Your HCG levels were high."

"Her what?" Gus frowned.

"You're pregnant," he finished, matter-of-factly.

Gus gasped and looked between the two of them.

Huxley's eyes glinted at her like pale blue stars on a dark night, a storm of emotion, vivid and open on display. His eyes scanned her abdomen before lifting to meet her shocked expression.

"Given your history and your age and what you just went through, this is a high-risk pregnancy. I would strongly advise no travel and minimal stress. That means taking some time off work. I cannot emphasize this strongly enough."

For a long moment, no one took a breath.

"I'm gonna be an Auntie!" Gus cried, breaking the silence. She hugged Huxley, who stood there stunned.

A moment ago, Nazario wasn't sure if she'd ever see him again. Now, life grew inside of her. Part his. Part hers. A life that lived through her capture.

A fighter. A survivor.

"How far along?" Gus asked, grabbing Huxley's hand. "C'mon, Daddy, it's gonna be fine. Y'all will figure this shit out." She nudged him, and he slumped in the chair next to the hospital bed.

"We're not outta the woods. A high HCG can still be present during a miscarriage. I'll need to do an ultrasound. We'll need to confirm a heartbeat," he said. "Detective Nazario?"

Nazario choked out a cry, unable to resist. She grabbed a pillow and put it over her face. She let out a sob.

"It's just shock, Doc." Gus removed the pillow from her face. "Wanna see how far along you are, sweetie?"

Gus wiped her face. Nazario blinked back tears. She turned to Huxley, "Well?"

Wordless, he scooted the chair closer and nodded.

After summoning a nurse to bring in the ultrasound machine, the doctor pulled back the blanket and lifted her hospital gown. Gus and Huxley leaned in—her hand clasped between theirs. In this moment, they were a family of blue. That's what working on the force had always been to her. And for once in her life, since Daddy died, she didn't feel alone. She didn't have to do this alone.

She didn't want to.

The gel felt wet, slimy, and cold. Nazario wanted to close her eyes to avoid hearing no heartbeat. Suddenly, it occurred to her what she wanted.

More than anything, she wanted the baby to have survived.

Please be alive. Please.

She braved the screen, and within seconds, a tiny, rapid sound escaped the machine.

"Thwat, thwat, thwat, thwat, thwat..."

ALSO BY S.Z. ESTAVILLO

The Serpent Series

The Serpent's Bridge

The Serpent Woman

Twilight of the Serpent

ABOUT THE AUTHOR

SZ Estavillo has been passionate about writing since childhood, with a defining moment in second grade when her teacher predicted, "You're going to be a writer someday." Her biracial heritage, being half-Korean and half-Puerto Rican, deeply influences her book themes. As a staunch advocate for diversity and inclusion, SZ works tirelessly to amplify the voices of underrepresented and marginalized communities within the publishing industry.

SZ is not only a feminist whose principles echo throughout her works, but also a true crime aficionado, having devoured every episode of true crime on networks like Discovery ID and Oxygen. Her interest in justice is deeply rooted in her family history. Her uncle, Nicolas Estavillo, retired as the highest-ranking Puerto Rican cop in New York's history, and her father, Jose Estavillo, has served in both the Air Force and U.S. Customs and Border Patrol. These familial connections to law enforcement enrich her storytelling and understanding of justice.

Balancing her roles as a devoted mother and an enthusiastic digital marketer, SZ brings her professional expertise into her personal passion, amassing over 85,000 followers on social media. She uses her platform to inspire and uplift the writing community with motivational and positive content. Along with her two children and two senior dogs, she enjoys the simple pleasures of family sushi outings in their Los Angeles home.

If you enjoyed this book, consider following her on social media or posting a review. Your support helps extend the reach of voices that matter. Thank you for reading and being part of this journey Stay tuned for her upcoming books, "The Serpent Woman" and "Twilight of the Serpent."

Please follow SZ Estavillo:

Goodreads: https://www.goodreads.com/author/show/49349032.S_Z_Estavillo
X: @szestavillo
Instagram: @szestavillo.author
TikTok: @szestavillo.author
Facebook Page: https://www.facebook.com/sonyozofiaestavillo

www.ingramcontent.com/pod-product-compliance
Lightning Source LLC
Chambersburg PA
CBHW020527110726
47899CB00004B/1274